The Witch Within Her

By Nick Iuppa

THE WITCH WITHIN HER

Cover photo: forewer © 123RF.com

Published by Dos Milagros Press

Visit the author website: http://www.nickiuppawrites.com

ISBN 10: 0-9989806-0-9
ISBN 13: 978-0-9989806-0-7

10 9 8 7 6 5 4 3 2 1

Novels by Nick Iuppa

Taken By Witches
Bloody Bess and the Doomsday Games

Novels by Nick Iuppa
& John P. Mendoza

THE CARLOS MANN TRILOGY
Alicia's Ghost
Alicia's Sin
Alicia Bewitched

Avenging Adelita

Esteban's Quest

Dedication

For Natalia Manelska for her friendship, faith,
support, good will, and her Polish.
Hope all is well

Acknowledgments

I'd like to thank all the friends who offered valuable advice and support during the creation of this book, especially: Gershon Weltman, Debbie Thrush, Bill Habeeb, Bill Idelson, Larry Touch, Judy Singer, Seemah Idelson, Kimberly Behl, Bob Gibbons, Bram Druckman, Alex Singer, and Marc Wade. I'm grateful every day for my beautiful wife who put up with all those terrible hours when I was behind closed doors creating this story, and as always was very positive, supportive, and hopeful about it all. I appreciate the excellent graphic services of Laurie Douglas. Thanks to Janet Grady for her creative suggestions and editorial support, and a special thanks to Clare McGlinchey who gave such sterling story direction.

Madness... it all begins in dreams

— Babcia Michalina

Contents

Introduction

THE WITCH WITHIN HER is the second book in the long and complex story of Babcia Michalina Sapalski, a witch born in 11th century Poland who suddenly finds herself living in mid-twentieth century America. If you've read the first book, *Taken By Witches*, feel free to dive right into this story. If not, you can still jump ahead. The story tries to fill you in on previous events as it goes along. Or you can go through the summary of the previous work at the back of the book before you read this one.

The Witch
Within Her

Prologue I
Zakopane Poland

Walter Sapalski began riding in the nighttime. The year was 1177, certainly not a safe era to be night riding, and yet he did. And, if ever his friends would ask him why he had undertaken such a dangerous practice, with all the brigands that were on the roads and all the wild beasts in the forest and the witches too, he would answer with one of three reasons.

The first was his horse, Arra. Won in a lottery at the village fair, she was surely one of the finest horses in the countryside, finer in fact then her owners knew when they had offered her up as a prize. Surely, Arra would let him outrun any evil creature who set out to do him harm.

The second reason was his daughter, little Michalina, taken by witches in only her sixth year of life. Much of it was his own fault, and he knew it. He had not watched closely enough, had not seen as she had slipped out the door of their cottage to gather firewood so that her father could be warm on that blustery night, a night when witches were surely about.

The third reason for the night rides, which Walter might admit to no one but himself, was the absolute despair of it all. For, in those dark moments, he was certain that he had forever lost his little girl, the one person he had lived for after her mother had died in childbirth.

Everyone he loved had been taken from him, it seemed. So, why not be caught by brigands, destroyed at their hands, suffer the punishment that he knew he deserved for his carelessness in losing his daughter. Better to pay the price in this world than face eternal punishment in the next.

"A rough night," Walter grumbled to his horse as he pushed the bit into her mouth and pulled the reigns around her head. Arra didn't seem to care. She was eager for the run.

"Will you find her for me tonight?" he asked his horse, "Or will it be evil and destruction in her place?"

Arra whinnied, shook her mane, and pawed the ground.

"It'll be somethin', I wager," he added. "Now let's be off." And he flung himself up onto his steed, and together they charged from the stable.

"Michalina!" he cried as they burst into the open air. "Find me, sweetheart!"

But Michalina had already found him. She stood only yards from the entrance to the stable. She watched her father astride Arra bolt from the door and charge off into the night. And almost as quickly as he, she ran through the forest alongside him. A girl who was somehow more than that, a girl with the power of the animals she lived with; strong, young, twelve years old now, drawing nearer to womanhood, and as beautiful as the moonlight that spun through the swirling mists.

Michalina was with her father, but he could not know it. For she was a witch, converted to the ways of the coven and hated for it by everyone, especially by the Polish church. The institution sought to exterminate her kind and anyone who cared for them. Walter was in mortal danger, should he ever be known to come in contact with his beautiful daughter. And so she chose not to allow it.

But oh, how she yearned for that reunion.

Prologue II
The Forests outside of Zakopane
Poland - 1970

Twenty young witches made their way around a huge marble circle that had been set into the base of a quarry many centuries before. Above the circle, narrow rows of stone seats looked down, turning the place into what must have been an ancient amphitheater. To the right of the circle, a freshly pressed velvet cloth covered a low, flat surface, perhaps some hidden altar. To the left, a great, unlit bonfire stood dark awaiting only a torch to set it aflame.

Starlight, the only illumination at that midnight hour, offered a magical glow to the setting. The stars seemed huge, brilliant... so close that it felt as though they were pressing down upon the circle and its attendants. And all around, giant trees hunched like ogres standing guard on all those present and the evils they had come to commit.

In the background, the sharp, snow-covered ridge of the Carpathian Mountains sliced up into the night, rising higher it seemed than the stars. Much closer, an enormous tower jutted equally tall into the blackness.

The witches wore coarse, black robes that reached their ankles but were unbound at the waist so that every step exposed a glimpse of thigh, a peeking breast, a hip, or a delicate ankle.

Most of the girls were Polish, and their white-blond hair and pale blue eyes glistened in the starlight. Only one of them was over the age of nineteen, an ebony girl from the inner city of Los Angeles who was long-fingered, bright-eyed, skinny, and almost invisible in the dark except, that is, for the bright whites of her enormous eyes and ivory teeth that bit her lower lip while she tried to navigate the trail up from the circle and into the seats.

Twin highborn sisters had come from England to join the preparations. Their chatter made them sound like royalty, and their turned-up noses and haughty gaze seemed to offer a harsh judgment on all that was happening around them. Still, they were as stunning as the other young witches, as though beauty itself was one of the principle requirements for becoming a member of this coven.

Some of the witches rushed in excitedly, seemingly anxious to have a hand in whatever great evil was about to begin. Others giggled and chatted, appearing unaware of why they had been asked to attend. But there were also those who seated themselves slowly, fearing this night and all it would bring.

Eventually, all found places on the cold stone and fell silent as a keen sense of anticipation filled every young woman at the gathering.

"He's here," one of the girls whispered, and it was true. Wicktor the Warlock had arrived.

He made a dramatic entrance, leaping high into the air, spinning around three times, and coming down in the middle of the circle.

The warlock stood then and surveyed his helpers. They were all so youthful, so childlike. All he could really see were wisps of the blondest hair, eager eyes, and smiles of anticipation.

He flashed his left hand, and an enormous fire exploded in the great pyre that had been built at the very back of the clearing. The flames illuminated his muscular body and the thick black hair that covered it. He strutted out into the crowd, up the stairs, and into the first row. The young women instinctively pulled back from his animal presence.

"There is no time to waste, my young witches," he said. "SHE is coming very soon, and we must be ready."

"Babcia is coming?" gasped one of the highborn, young witches who expressed the hope of every member of the youthful coven... that they would soon meet Michalina Czarownica: Babcia, the greatest of all witches.

"And what is your name?" the warlock asked.

"Megan Cummings," she answered.

"And I'm Morgan," said the twin who sat beside her.

"Come all the way from England, then?"

The girls nodded.

"Well, if you've come to meet the great witch, then too bad for you, because Babcia has other business. She has left a very delicate task to us, and we must complete it successfully. Still, don't worry, ladies, there will be plenty of evil doings to satisfy you, believe me."

The twins looked at each other and giggled at the news. And then the warlock turned and looked across the crowd to a sweet, round-faced, Polish girl who had just made her way to the very edge of the gathering.

"Can you guess who is coming, Matryoshka?"

The shopkeeper's daughter stood and smiled flirtatiously at the warlock. She had been dreaming of joining his coven for years and had just now managed to escape a possessive father who had warned her incessantly about the dangers of Wicktor and his brood.

"Is it Holly Madonie?" she asked.

"Ah," answered the warlock. "Mistress Matryoshka knows much of this story. Holly Madonie is the wife of Niko, beloved grandson of the great witch."

Matryoshka smiled proudly and began to inch her way past the other girls until she was right beside the warlock.

"But if you know so much, how could you be so stupid?" he jeered and, with a wave of his hand, sent Matryoshka sprawling right on her backside with her heavy apron, skirt, and half a dozen petticoats thrown embarrassingly up around her waist.

The other girls might have laughed except for the fear that such humiliation might also happen to them. And so they remained silent.

"Anyone else care to venture a guess?" asked the warlock.

The young, black woman raised her hand.

"And what is your name?"

"Chantel, sir. Chantel Brown."

"Stand up, Chantel Brown, and tell us who you think it is that we must prepare for?"

Chantel stood. The front of her robe fell open and revealed large, youthful breasts that were completely bare. The warlock watched them rise and fall more quickly as the girl drew in one nervous breath after another. Finally, she turned to him and whispered, "Marla... Marla Morrison."

The assemblage fell silent. Most of the women thought they knew the story of Babcia and her battles with Marla. It was a war for Niko's very soul.

"She's dead," Matryoshka called. "Babcia killed her. She can't possibly return."

There was yet another long pause as most of the young witches nodded in agreement. This made the warlock look unhappily from one to the other to the other.

"Well, you're almost right, Chantel Brown," he said at last. "But almost is never quite enough is it?" And he let out a wicked laugh startling a flock of ravens that had gathered at the darkest edges of the circle. The birds launched themselves skyward in a single, ominous cloud. They flew in a great arch around the high tower and roosted on its topmost parapet. Their motion set off the braying of goats and horses penned in a nearby coral.

"I don't understand," murmured Chantel. "Tell us what's going to happen?"

"You're such a great storyteller," sighed Matryoshka. "You have to tell us."

Flattered, the warlock smiled and may have even blushed beneath the darkness of his coat.

"There's work to be done, young witches," he said. "But perhaps you will work harder if you have some understanding of what we're about... and there will be time enough to get things done... though you may end up working far into this night and the next and the next."

"Oh, we'll work gladly, Sir, for a bit of the story," said Megan. And the others echoed the sentiment.

"All right then," he answered. "I have your commitment, and believe me I'll make sure you honor it. But now, let me spin a tail as wicked as any you've ever heard... a cautionary tale to be sure: one that is not quite yet finished, and one in which you all may soon play a part."

The women in his coven murmured in astonishment. Illuminated as they were by starlight and firelight, they gazed in rapt attention at the warlock as he returned to the center of the circle, sat cross-legged in front of them, and began to tell his story.

Part One
Saint Joseph's

Chapter 1
The Birthday

Little Joy Madonie's face was crazy, comical with eyes bulging and cheeks puffed out. She looked like one of those suckerfish that attach themselves to the sides of glass aquariums. But that was only because she had pushed herself up against the opaque little window beside the front door to her home while she waited for her father. It was, after all, her eighth birthday.

Niko Madonie stopped on his way to the front door to inspect the stucco on the northeast corner of the house. It seemed to be coming loose. When he looked even closer, it appeared that part of the foundation was somehow beginning to crumble. It was something he'd need to take care of. He'd made the devil's deal, and he knew it. But he hadn't really agreed to anything, had he? He'd just accepted it all.

Niko sighed and walked up the three small steps to the front door. And that's when he caught sight of the silly face of that suckerfish girl pushed up against the window. He could see that his daughter was wearing a white party dress, white knee socks, and white tennis shoes. She was a miniature version of his wife, Holly, he thought, complete with long, blond hair, a pretty little nose, brilliant eyes, and that spectacular (though at the moment slightly twisted) smile.

Joy began to jump up and down with excitement. "Daddy's home!" she cried, and when Niko came through the front door, she ran up to him, threw her arms around his knees, and hugged him tightly for a long moment before looking up.

"Where's my present, Daddy?"

"Were you supposed to get a present today?" Niko teased.

"Daddy, this is my day, my birthday, and I want my present."

"But I thought that you were supposed to *give* presents to other people on your birthday."

"Daddy, did you get me the kitten or not?" Joy asked. "I want to know, now!"

"There'll be presents later," Holly said as she came walking in from the kitchen. "Now, get ready for supper, sweetie."

"Okay, Mommy," Joy answered, and she turned back into the suckerfish girl and swam her way out of the room.

"You're a bigger kid than she is," Holly said as she walked up to her husband.

"And you like kids, right?"

"Love 'em. I'd like to see a little more of this one, though." And then she put her arms around her husband and gave him a long, sexy kiss.

"Whoa," he gasped as he stumbled backward, "Is that what I've been missing?"

"That and more," Holly answered with a sigh.

"I don't get to play with Joy as much as I'd like to, either," he added wistfully.

"Did you get the kitten?"

"Got her. Put her in the garage."

"Great," Holly said and then she turned and led Niko into the kitchen where she immediately went to the stove and turned the Italian sausages that sizzled in a pan on the front burner.

"So why don't you put on something a little less business-like while I finish up with the birthday spaghetti?"

"Can't," Niko answered, and he couldn't help but turn a deep guilty shade of red. "Gotta go back right after the party."

Holly frowned. "For the fourth night this week?"

Niko walked up and wrapped his arms around his wife.

"It's gonna give us that swimming pool we've always wanted."

"I'd rather have you," she answered putting her arms around her husband and giving him another kiss. "Can't you at least stick around on Joy's birthday?"

"Only till eight thirty."

"I don't think it's enough for Joy... or for me," she sighed, and then she turned away from her husband rather decisively and gave her complete attention to the spaghetti.

#

Joy gobbled up the last of her licorice ice cream and banana birthday cake, which had been her choices. "Can I have my present now, Daddy?"

Holly jumped up and pulled a small, soft package from the cupboard behind her. "Here you are, sweetie," she said.

"Okay, Mommy," Joy looked a little unhappy. "It's not the right shape."

"It's the perfect shape for a T-shirt," Holly answered.

Joy let out a cheer when she opened the package and found a shirt with the words "Give a Friend a Hug" printed across the front. Above the lettering, CatMan Due, the famous saxophone-playing cat from the cartoons, was reaching out for an embrace.

"I like it, Mommy," Joy responded. "Can I put it on?"

"Of course."

Joy scrambled into the shirt and gave her mother a big hug. Holly hugged her back, and as she did she eyed her husband sadly. "Why couldn't you stay tonight?" she seemed to be asking.

Joy now turned to her father and stared him right in the eyes.

"Well?"

Niko looked from his little girl to the clock hanging on the wall behind her and saw that he had to leave in fifteen minutes.

"Don't know what you're talking about," he said.

"It's my birthday," Joy answered. "I wanted a kitten, and it was your job to get me one. Now, did you do your job or not, Daddy?"

"Let's find out," he answered with a grin and he led Joy into the garage leaving Holly to herself. She took another sip of champagne and noticed Niko's glass. It was almost completely full. Any party she planned for this evening was just about over.

She sighed and reached into her apron pocket. She pulled out a small piece of folded paper and read the note written in a very neat hand.

Please meet me tomorrow evening, Holly.
Sheraton Universal – Room 209 – 7:30
We were meant to be together, and
I know that I can end your loneliness.
John

Holly bit her lip and was about to read the words again when Joy came barreling through the double doors carrying a very sweet, but also very full-grown, gray and white cat that was almost as big as she was.

Holly just had time to crumple the note and jam it back into her pocket. She was blushing bright red by then, feeling guilty for just reading the message. Of course, Niko wouldn't notice her expression; she was sure of that. And, hopefully, Joy would be just too excited about her new gift.

"Mommy, look at Emmy!" Joy called.

"Emmy?"

"Yes, Mommy," she said. "I decided to call her Emmy because... look."

Joy hoisted the cat right up before Holly's eyes. For all the rough handling, the cat seemed quite content.

"See the letter 'M' in the fur over this eye? And here's another one. Two 'M's. That's why I want to call her Emmy. Okay, Mommy?"

"I think it's a great name, don't you, Daddy?"

"I do," he answered.

"But don't you think she's a little large for a kitten?" Holly forced herself to ask if only to get her mind off the crumpled note in her pocket that felt as large and explosive as a hand grenade.

"The people at the shelter said that she was the sweetest cat they'd ever seen," Niko said, totally missing Holly's expression, as usual. "They said that she would be better for a little girl than a kitten, and besides...."

"Besides what, Daddy?" Joy asked.

"Besides," Holly answered. "They're right. A friendly cat is probably a far better pet for a little girl."

"She's a kitten, Mommy."

"Anyway, I have to get back to work," Niko told Joy. "I'm sorry, sweetie. But the boss has things for me to do tonight."

"I see," the little girl answered sadly as she slung the cat over her shoulder. Emmy let out a soft meow and started to purr.

"Well, I don't see," Holly blurted out suddenly and rushed from the room.

"Holly, listen," Niko called but she was gone.

"You'd better stop this, Daddy," Joy told her father. "It's making Mommy very sad."

"I know that, sweetie," he answered. "But I have to go to work."

"Well, go then!" Holly shouted from the kitchen and, after a moment, added very softly... hopefully, "I'll wait up for you."

"I wouldn't do that," Niko said. "It may be two in the morning before I get home."

A long silence followed. Holly did not answer. Niko's expression was so pained that even Joy could feel it.

"Just go, Daddy," she said at last. "I'll talk to her."

"And what will you say?" he asked.

"That I love Emmy," she answered. "And that Mommy should find someone to love too, because she's very lonely now."

"No! For God's sake, don't say that!"

"Okay," Joy said with a shrug that almost dropped the cat from her shoulder. "I'll think of something nicer. Anyway, thanks for the kitten, Daddy."

"You bet," And he patted his little girl on the head before turning to the kitchen door. "Goodbye, Holly!"

Again, there was nothing but silence.

At last Niko gave up, gave Joy a kiss on the top of her head, and walked out the front door. As he did, he happened to glance at the corner of his home once more.

Yes, he thought to himself, somehow it's beginning to crumble.

Chapter 2
Joy's Room

Joy pounded up the stairs and made a sharp right into her room. It was painted soft pink with a white twin bed. Vines sprouting little blue flowers were painted up the bedposts and across the headboard. There was a matching white desk with a knick-knack shelf full of statues holding her favorite TV characters, and a dresser with a large mirror hanging above it. Huge posters from Niko's TV shows were pinned to all the walls. Above her bed, a teenage Gretel spread her arms graciously, inviting viewers to tune in and watch how she and her brother outwit the wicked witch. The TV show had deviated quite a bit from the original story but had been a tremendous success for Niko and his boss, Chuck Vaughn.

Other posters celebrated *Snow White and Rose Red*, another of Niko's successes. And then there was CatMan Due, jamming away on his sax. Chuck Vaughn himself, Niko's boss and the cat's creator, had signed this poster.

A bookcase at the far end of the room overflowed with every kind of children's book imaginable, many by Dr. Seuss, but there was also the *Doctor Doolittle* series, *Charlotte's Web*, *The Hobbit*, and the complete *Lord of the Rings*. Most importantly, tucked away in a far corner almost out of sight was THE book, *Grimm's Fairy Tales*.

It was a strange additive book that Joy's late grandfather had found in England during World War Two. Its gruesome illustrations had terrified Niko as a little boy. And yet Joy found it amazing, fantastic... especially the story entitled "Witch Girl" that told of an ancient witch who so loved her grandson that she took over the soul of his daughter so that she could be with him every day.

The books and posters were the furthest thing from her mind at the moment, though, as Joy scurried into the room and lay Emmy on the huge dresser across from her bed.

Emmy was not quite as relaxed now. She stretched out across the top of the dresser, raised her head, and looked at Joy with an expression that seemed almost anxious.

"Too bright in here for you, Emmy?" she whispered. "I'll turn the lights off."

Emmy meowed in what Joy took to be agreement. And so the little girl scooted over to the doorway and flicked off the lights. The room was now very dark except for the sliver of light from downstairs. It cut sharply across the center of the room leaving the space on either side very shadowy indeed.

"Would you like me to make a bed for you, Emmy?" she asked. The cat did not respond, just got to its feet and jumped from the dresser to Joy's bed where she lay down.

"Rather just sleep with me, huh?" Joy asked.

Emmy began to purr. Maybe it was the darkness that relaxed her or the thought of a nice place to sleep at the foot of Joy's little bed. But her closed eyes didn't detect the image that was forming in the darkness behind the little girl. It rose up out of the gloom, hideous and awful, an ancient crone, with saucer eyes, long, claw-like fingers, and a great pointed nose jutting out from under a dark gray hood.

Joy was still fascinated by the kitten, but something made her pause. She felt a chill and glanced at the mirror above the dresser where she saw her own reflection and behind her the hideous being. She blinked her eyes and shuddered.

"Babcia!" she called. "Grandma."

Chapter 3
Room 209

John Hunter lit the candle and placed it in front of the mirror in the hotel bathroom. Then he took a good long look at himself.

He had to admit he was handsome, with a strong jaw, bright blue, dreamy eyes, and broad shoulders. At six foot two in his stocking feet, he was the perfect figure of an ironman athlete. All he was wearing really was his white dress shirt and nothing else, not even socks. And his shirt was unbuttoned half way down the front.

Sexy!

He smiled as he ran his hand across his smooth face. Very close shave. Perfect! A perfect guy for a perfect gal! And this was a perfect place for their rendezvous: the Sheraton Universal Hotel on top of the mountain at the edge of the Universal Studios lot.

Why hadn't he ever brought his wife here? He wondered, and then he knew. In an instant, he flashed on that deadly conversation they'd had only two weeks earlier.

Susan had come into the kitchen wearing her shaggy, pink bathrobe. It was as though she didn't want to look attractive. Her hair was still in curlers; she had yet to "put on her face," as she liked to say.

"Good morning," Hunter had said as warmly as possible, he thought.

Susan just sighed. Her eyes still showed the effects of a night of lovemaking that was more labor than love.

"John," she said rather nervously while she sat down beside him and dumped some cornflakes into the bowl he had set out for her. "We have to talk about last night."

"We weren't at our best," Hunter answered quickly. He reached across for the coffee pot, grabbed it, and poured her morning's brew. "It happens."

"Well," she answered, and now there were tears in her eyes. "It's not going to happen again." She measured his reaction as she measured her words.

"What do you mean?"

Susan took a long swallow of black coffee, grimaced, and continued.

"I'm giving up sex."

Hunter almost dropped the coffee pot.

"What?"

"I don't need it," she answered quickly, as though she just had to get the message out there. "It's messy and uncomfortable."

"But we're married. We're husband and wife."

Susan's look turned cold. "I don't really love you anymore."

There was a long dead silence.

He was stunned. "Are you asking for a divorce?" he finally managed to stammer.

"Not at all," she said. "I don't want a divorce. I just don't want to sleep with you anymore."

"But it's my right!" Hunter insisted. He was now becoming furious. Why was she bringing it up this morning when he was getting ready for a very important day of work?

She laughed. Her tone was amazingly cruel.

"Don't talk to me about rights," she sneered. "Because I haven't had any for years!"

Hunter flinched; here came the same old shit all over again. But Susan didn't pursue the argument. She had a more immediate message.

"You have the right to live with me in this house if you want. I'll make a nice home for you. I'll do all those wifely

19

duties that you take for granted. I just refuse to, you know, do *it* any longer."

Hunter was flabbergasted by the finality in his wife's voice. He tried to speak but really couldn't. (Why now? Why was she telling him this now?)

"You can keep swooning over those cheerleaders, secretaries, and teachers-aides of yours," she continued. "Don't think I haven't seen the way you look at them. Well, let me tell you, Mr. Principal, they're all yours now, as long as you can be discreet about it. Jimmy can't know, not even for a minute. He has to feel that his home is safe and secure and normal."

Hunter's head was reeling. He didn't know what to say, so he just mumbled, "Gotta get to work."

"Yes, go ahead, Mr. Principal," she answered. "Go off to your crazy little empire, and when you get back here, you'll find all your things in the guest room. It'll be YOUR room from now on."

Hunter stood, and it crossed his mind to kiss her while he tried to think of something to say, but her energy was so negative that he just lowered his head and slunk out the door.

What the hell was wrong with her? Hunter wondered while he sat in the Sheraton Universal Hotel. It couldn't be his fault. Not John Hunter, principal of Mid-Valley Elementary School. He hadn't cheated on her, not yet anyway. She was frigid; that was all.

Bitch!

"Just don't embarrass the boy," she'd said. "Be discreet." And so he would be. Hell, no one was going to see him at this ritzy Hollywood hotel. It was the perfect getaway.

The problem was that he didn't need a getaway, some quickie, some roll in the hay just to prove that his wife's frigidity wasn't his fault. He needed a relationship with an intelligent and beautiful woman, someone worthy of a man as successful as he.

There was yet another reason for discretion: his career path. Next stop the school board. Everything was moving along nicely, he thought. So he'd play the faithful husband, just as Susan would play the perfect wife. And their son, Jimmy would probably never know. The school board would never know, his staff and teachers would never know, except for his new Librarian, of course.

He moved through the room one more time, checking the candles on each end table and the champagne chilling in the ice bucket beside the bed. He checked the slightly erotic Picasso print on the wall. Then he went back into the bathroom and checked his handsome face, his dreamy eyes, and the way he hung neatly under that white dress shirt of his: just a little bit of an erection to tease her.

AND WHERE THE FUCK WAS SHE, ANYWAY?

Hunter moved back to the bedroom and adjusted the little radio, re-dialed the soft sensuous mid-'70s rock station that he had been listening to. And in that moment of silence between stations, he heard something, a sound coming from right outside the door, the sound of a sigh or even of someone weeping.

He readjusted the music, keeping it very soft, readjusted his shirt to make sure he was properly covered up and went to the door to open it.

Holly Madonie was standing there sobbing. When she saw him, she blushed, smiled sadly, and reached for him as she stumbled in through the doorway. Hunter immediately closed the door behind her as she grabbed his face with her gentle hands and began kissing him on his lips, his cheeks, his eyes.

"John," she whispered softly and just pushed him backward onto the bed.

He fell easily, and she slipped off her shoes and climbed on top of him... still kissing him. She struggled to her feet on the bed and stood above him while she pulled off her dress.

Hunter looked up and could see her smiling through her tears above her beautiful breasts as she slid off her lacy, pink bra.

She brushed back her hair nervously. All she was wearing now were those panties. Hunter reached up to pull them down, and when he did a reservoir of her love spilled onto him. It splashed onto his shirt, seeping through it and trickling down between his legs.

Holly knelt so that she was sitting astride him. She began to slide herself up and down, feeling the sweet tingle of his touch while releasing more and more of her love.

"Oh, John," Holly whispered in a sadness filled with lust. And so the Principal of West Valley Elementary School rolled Holly over and gave her what she had been missing.

And when they were through...

The bed was soaking wet.

Chapter 4
Her Trip to the Store

"I'm going to draw you a sad nose," Joy said as she sat at the kitchen table with her father, and she did a quick circle for a face and then scratched a great hook into the middle of the circle creating a nose that did resemble Niko's large Polish-Italian beak.

"Why is it sad?" Niko asked.

"'Cause you are, Daddy," she answered with her usual directness.

"Maybe I am. But that shouldn't make my nose sad."

"Sure it should," she responded, and she drew a series of circle faces with sad noses on all of them. And then she asked, "Where's Mommy?" with a tone of great concern.

"She went to the store," Niko answered. He was sketching faces too, and all of his were frowning. "She'll be back soon."

"The store closed two hours ago," Joy said. "Is that why you're sad, Daddy?"

"Nope," he answered with a wistful smile. "Just trying to show you how to draw sad faces. Look..." He pulled her paper over to him and drew a circle face, two round eyes with lines pointing up above each eye to indicate eyebrows pulled up in sadness. "See," he said. "Sad eyes..."

"Or you can make a sad mouth." He added a frown to suggest a sorrowful set of lips. "But noses pretty much stay the same. They show who you are, not how you feel. So does your hair."

"Cool, Daddy," Joy giggled, and she grabbed the paper back and drew a series of images with different kinds of noses and hair but the same sad expression. Then she drew another face with a big frown, but the eyebrows turned down in the center.

23

"Now you look mad, Daddy," she said.

"Right. But turn the frown into a smile and what do you have?"

Joy drew another face with eyebrows arching down almost forming a V above the eyes, and then she drew a big smile.

"Wow!" said Joy. "Now you have someone who likes being mad." She drew the hooked nose into the middle of the face. "It's Babcia," she said.

Niko laughed. "You've seen her?"

"Of course, I have a mask of her in my bottom drawer, remember?"

And he did remember how Joy had somehow gained possession of the Mask of Babcia that had scared him so the first time he'd seen it at Leland University. But Joy had never told her father that Babcia appeared to her frequently in her mirror.

"Now, I'll make you happy, Daddy," Joy said matter-of-factly while she drew a classic happy face with the hooked nose she'd first created for him.

"Like it?"

"I do."

"Then why aren't you happy?"

He sighed. "I'm very happy when I'm with you."

"Actually, you're more like this, I think," she said, and she drew a sad pair of eyes over a slightly smiling mouth with the same hooked nose. The result was wistful. "That's you, Daddy, happy and sad at the same time."

The drawing caught Niko by surprise and made him laugh. He took the paper from his daughter and continued to chuckle while he scribbled out a whole series of creative sketches of his daughter's face: happy, sad, laughing, crying with tears flying out in all directions, sneezing, singing, giggling. They gave Joy the giggles, and the two were almost falling out of their seats with laughter when Holly walked in the door.

"What's this?" she said with a smile of her own.

"Look at these pictures," Joy said. "Here's Daddy, sad and happy the way he looks right now, and here's me...."

Holly looked at the pictures and smiled. "Very nice," she said. "But it's way past your bedtime, miss."

"I know," Joy answered. "Thanks for letting me stay up with Daddy for so long."

"Now, off to bed," Holly commanded.

"Right," Joy said with a smile, and then she ran up to her father and hugged him. Next, she hugged her mother, and then went to the corner and picked up Emmy the cat as though the creature was a bag of beans. She slung the cat over her shoulder.

"Night - night," she called as she headed upstairs to her bedroom.

Holly smiled. She turned to Niko, but he wasn't smiling at all. That was because he noticed the hours printed on the large striped shopping bag that Holly had set down right in front of him on the table.

Zodie's - Open 8 AM to 8 PM

It was now 11.

"Where have you been?" Niko asked with as much restraint as he could.

"I ran into Ginny Randolph at Zodie's," Holly answered. "So we just went over to the Pancake House and had some coffee, that's all."

Her quick response surprised him. "How is Ginny?" he mumbled at last.

"Oh, she's fine," Holly answered. "But, if you don't mind, I've had a rough day. I'd like to turn in too. Are you coming?"

"No," answered Niko with a finality that surprised him. "I think I'll just watch TV for a while." He moved slowly to the set and turned it on. Holly came up to him, gave him a quick kiss on the cheek, and left.

The more Niko thought about Holly's response, the more logical it seemed, so that when he finally did go to bed, nearly an hour later, he had convinced himself that his concerns were groundless. It was Joy who had planted the idea that Holly was out far later than she should have been. It was Joy who told him that he should be concerned about it. What did a little girl know about adult hours and adult feelings? Holly actually seemed happy when she returned home, far happier than he had seen her in weeks. So, everything was really fine, he decided. Until that is, he opened the hamper to toss in his grubby sweatshirt and saw Holly's clothing bundled tightly together. He lifted the bundle out of the hamper, and her pink panties fell out onto the bathroom floor. They were still sopping wet, and they smelled of her lust. As her husband, he knew that smell. It was one of the rare and special things about Holly that was such a turn on, that wetness and that scent of sex. But he and Holly hadn't had sex.

So what was going on?

Chapter 5
The Dream

The enormous, angry men snatched at Joy and chased her around the little cottage. Their faces were cold and evil. One of them seemed to be a priest because he wore that kind of collar, but he was the worst of them. He feinted toward her sending her scrambling away from him around the little table in the middle of the room and right into the clutches of another evil-looking man.

They were grunting at each other now in a language that Joy didn't understand. The man grabbed her, tossed her high into the air and then let her fall like a rag doll onto the hard, earthen floor of the cottage. She felt terrible pain explode through her shoulder and her hip when she pounded into the ground, and yet she tried to scramble to her feet in spite of it.

But the priest was too fast. He caught her leg and, jerking her up into the air; he flung her across the room to one of the other men. They were cheering each other on. The second man reached to catch her but pulled his hands away at the last moment so that the little girl fell and hit the floor again. Her face slammed hard into it. She felt her teeth shatter; her lips tear. Blood was pouring into her mouth now. Still, she was snatched up by one of the men who held her high in the air.

She was upside down, feeling the blood pouring out of her mouth, looking at the priest who had gone to the fire where a great caldron was burning. Beside it lay the battered and torn remains of her father with his throat cut and his blood spilled on the hearth and across the floor.

"No, Daddy!" she screamed hysterically, but that only incensed the men even more.

The priest grabbed a skewer from the fire, a long, thin spike and, still babbling in that strange tongue, he moved

27

toward her. The fire-red iron reflected in his eyes and across his hideous smile. He pushed it toward Joy, toward her battered face. She screamed. Her heart was pounding. She could feel blood-fear coursing through her veins. The priest was bringing the poker closer and closer to her. She tried to jerk away but suddenly another pair of hands grabbed her face and held it fast making her look directly at the skewer while the evil man brought it toward her eye. The heat radiating from it, scorched her cheeks, and seared into her eyeballs. The priest cursed her in whatever guttural language he was speaking and pulled the poker back so that he could thrust it into her eye, into her face, into her whole body, and drive it all the way through her.

Suddenly, a horrifying, mind-tearing ROAR split the air!

Joy jumped up in bed. Awake!

She was still trembling; her clothes, face, arms, hands, hair, and all the bedding were drenched with her sweat and tears. She could still hear that roar, that banshee wail, which tore through her mind like an earthquake. In the mirror was that sight again, too: the witch, Babcia, now even more of a monster while she took on the gray coloring of a beast, her fingers twisting into claws, her teeth growing and glistening into the fangs of a wolf.

"Babcia!" Joy cried. "Babcia, stop it! Stop it! Oh, please stop it!" And the little girl broke into a flood of tears and collapsed onto the bed still trembling, heart still racing, and sweat still pouring from her.

After a long moment, Joy pushed herself up with her arms and looked back into the mirror. The witch was still there, but her expression had changed. The grayness of the wolf had drained from her. Her eyes were no longer filled with rage, but with love.

"So sorry for dreams," Babcia whispered from the mirror.

"Horrible dreams, Great Grandma," Joy sighed. "They're killing me."

"But is not you," Babcia whispered softly.

"I know," Joy answered. "You told me. I'm dreaming your dreams, of when the witch-hunters killed your baby."

"Moj piekny chlopczyk," Babcia murmured. "My beautiful little boy." And suddenly the rage flooded back into her eyes and that gray wolf visage began to spread across her face.

"Stop it, Great Grandma, STOP IT!" Joy cried. "Your anger HURTS me."

A look of sorrow and fear now gripped the witch's face. What was she doing to her granddaughter?

"I fix," Babcia whispered. "I find way to go way from you at night time. Let you be little girl, alone. Let you dream little girl dreams."

Joy sat up in the bed.

"I'd like that, Babcia," she said still not daring to smile. "But how can you?"

"I find way; leave you alone," she said. "But not always."

"No," Joy answered. "Sometimes I like having you with me. You make me feel safe. Sometimes it's even cool, you know, so cool."

The image in the mirror smiled. That hideous old crone, a face that seemed impossible to look upon, let alone love, smiled, because this was a little girl who could look at her and did love her.

"But the dreams, Great Grandma," Joy whispered.

"I fix," Babcia responded. "Find somewhere else to go night. Let you dream as little girl, not as witch. Not horrible memories."

"But where can you go?"

At that moment, Emmy began to stir. She had been sleeping soundly at the foot of the little bed, but now she stretched and yawned. It was a funny, wide, cat's yawn.

Joy giggled and sighed a great soulful sigh for a little girl, and giggled again.

The witch was smiling too.

Chapter 6
Humiliation

Niko didn't want to be here; that was sure. Not on his first free Saturday in weeks. And yet it was so important to Holly.

"It'll be fun," she'd said. "You know Tracy?"

He nodded yes, even though he didn't. No point getting into another argument.

"It's the wedding of the sweetest, young teacher in my school. How could you not enjoy it?" Holly asked.

That was easy; he wouldn't know a soul there.

Holly had been acting very distant lately, and he was convinced that it was his fault, the fault of those long hours that he was spending away from her at work. So he would make this little sacrifice for her, why not?

They made their way into the entry to the little hall behind St. Finbar's church. She was wearing a navy polka-dot dress with a wide, white collar to match the dots. It was surely as short as the law or their Pastor, Father Rodriguez would allow. Just the thing to show off her perfect legs, though, Niko thought.

He followed along behind his wife carrying a huge box wrapped in white and silver wedding paper and topped with a silver bow. He could hardly see where he was going, and so, when he stepped into the entryway, he ran right into Father Tim Brennan, assistant pastor at the church.

Father Tim was young and handsome with short-cropped hair and the friendliest kind of Irish face. He wore a traditional black suit with a Roman collar. He was a very nice guy from all that Niko had heard, and it was confirmed when he smashed into him with that huge gift box and bounced back against the far wall.

31

Tim staggered for a moment and then rushed to catch Niko who was about to topple over. Tim grabbed the box and then Niko's arm to steady him.

Holly ran back to her husband, snatched the package from Tim, and began fussing with the bow and smoothing out the rather large dent created by the collision.

"Can't you watch where you're going?" she hissed at Niko. Unfortunately, her words said far more than that. There was a little bit of "Can't you ever do anything right?" and "Why did I ever marry you in the first place?" and other kinds of phrases that are unspoken when a marriage is headed into darkness.

Father Tim shrugged at Niko and then turned to Holly.

"Go on ahead, Holly," he urged. "I'll get Niko straightened out and then we'll find you."

Holly gave Niko another one of those I'm-so-disappointed-in-you looks, then nodded to the priest and headed off into the crowd.

"I don't think we did that much damage to the package," Tim said to Niko.

"No. It's not the package that's bugging her. It's everything else."

"Too much time at the office?" Tim guessed.

"For one," he admitted with a sigh. "Got a suicide deadline, but she doesn't seem to understand."

"Most wives don't," Tim answered. "Guess that's why I don't have one."

"Maybe you're lucky," Niko responded. He still couldn't bring himself to smile.

"I don't think so," Tim answered. "You've got Holly, and even on her worst days, she's wonderful."

"I hear that a lot," he sighed again.

"I'm sure you do."

Tim led Niko through the entryway and right up to the little bar that was set up at the rear of the wedding reception.

"Might as well stop and pick up a little peace offering," Tim suggested. "Maybe some champagne."

"Sounds good."

As Niko waited for the busy bartender to find him, Tim began to ask Niko about his work, the status of his latest TV show, and most surprisingly of all, about Marla Morrison. Though few people knew it, Marla was a witch. She had collaborated with him on his first film for Vaughn Visual Arts (VVA), but she secretly wanted to ingratiate herself to Babcia by trying to kill Holly. In the end, the great witch had turned on her and destroyed Marla instead.

"Tragic death," Tim said. "I read about it in the papers. Died when her bungalow burned down, right?"

Niko nodded at the story that everyone believed but he and Holly.

"I even attended her funeral," said Father Tim. "Though it was hardly the kind of thing a priest should have done."

"A witch's funeral," Niko said with an understanding nod. "We didn't go. Marla and I worked together and everything, but somehow I just couldn't."

"It was... interesting," Tim replied with an expression that suggested there were many less charitable adjectives that he could have used.

"How did you know her?" Niko asked.

"We grew up together," Tim responded with a broad smile brightening with the memory. "Right here in Burbank. I have to admit, I was crazy about her when I was about ten. She was, maybe, thirteen."

"Was she into ballet then?" Niko asked.

"You know it," Tim answered. "She had those ballerina legs even at thirteen. Kind of scrawny otherwise with freckles, but you don't do all that dancing and not get the legs. I used to follow her around all summer long, just to see her in her tight denim shorts."

Niko took a long look at Tim thinking this was a rather surprising attitude for a priest. But then they were both just men, weren't they?

"How about witchcraft?" Niko asked.

"She was definitely a teenage witch," Tim answered. "Maybe a little inexperienced, not what she ended up becoming after she went to Poland and studied with the pros. But still, she had some pretty spectacular moments."

"You saw some of her rituals, then?"

"One, anyway," Tim answered and blushed. "She lived right down the street from me. I was just a gawky guy and she was a freckle-faced girl with those amazing legs and a way of carrying herself that told you she intended to do something spectacular with her life."

Niko thought about the spectacularly gruesome final moments of Marla's life, how she had imprisoned Holly in a room and prepared to sacrifice both her and her unborn child to Babcia. Big mistake! Babcia was nothing if not loyal to her grandson and his family, and so she shredded Marla right there in front of the girl's own witch's altar.

Niko grimaced but said nothing. The priest didn't notice.

"I think about her a lot," Tim murmured. "Even now."

Niko collected his drinks, left a hefty tip, and turned from the bar. The last thing he wanted to do was reminisce about Marla. He didn't think Father Tim needed to know that his dream girl was into human sacrifice and murder.

"Sounds like you didn't get along with Marla," Tim said.

"We were supposed to be writing partners. But she always thought of me as a rival."

"She did like to be in control," Tim added. "I even knew that at the age of ten. Anyway, here comes your wife. Guess I didn't deliver you quickly enough."

Holly moved up to Niko and Father Tim. She was smiling at everyone in the room as she approached, but when her eyes turned to Niko, they took on a look that was decidedly cold and annoyed.

"I'll take him off your hands, Father," she said.

"I didn't mean to hold him up; we just wanted to get a little champagne for you," Tim answered.

Niko handed the drink to Holly and smiled. She took it without returning his smile or thanking him.

"I was on my way out of the reception when we ran into each other," Father Tim explained. "Got tomorrow's sermon to prepare. Better be going."

Niko and Holly nodded and smiled at the priest while Tim backed away, and then Holly ushered her husband into the reception, to meet that terribly sweet bride and groom, and her co-workers and, of course, her new lover.

#

Looking back on the event later that evening, Niko thought it was perhaps the worst experience of his entire life. Why would a wife who loved her husband at all allow him to be humiliated that way? Of course, he'd had no idea that it was going to happen. He didn't know she had a lover at the time, but as the afternoon wore on, it became clearer and clearer and, oh, so painful.

The first indication was meeting Rich Schubert, a teacher Niko knew Holly admired, a proud, handsome Aryan with a slight German accent.

Holly had said, "This is my husband, Niko." Rich had barely looked up, hadn't stood to meet him or shake his hand. He'd merely given him a quick look over his shoulder and turned away offering no sense of welcome or respect.

How could he think so little of me? Niko had asked himself at the time. He should know I'm a successful TV producer. It should count for something. But later, as he'd reflected on the incident, Niko realized that Rich did know him. Rich knew his accomplishments and failings through whatever stories Holly had told at work. Rich probably knew about his lack of attention to his wife and his unwillingness to take enough time away from his job to make their marriage work. Rich knew that Niko was a terrible husband. He had to believe it because Holly had to believe it if she was going to rationalize an affair with another man.

John Hunter, on the other hand, did not ignore Niko. On the contrary, he jumped to his feet to meet him, reached out to take his hand, squeeze it, and shook it over and over again. Sometimes during the afternoon, an afternoon that was full of the speechifying and ebullience of John Hunter, Holly's lover would reach over and grab Niko's hand and shake it maybe a dozen times for no reason at all.

Hunter was almost giddy. Why would he be? Niko wondered. The reason became clearer and clearer. Hunter was laughing at him.

You fool, I'm fucking your wife, and you don't even know it. You're willing to reach out and shake the hand of the guy who's turned you into a cuckold. And, you know what? I'm happy to shake your hand and laugh in your face.

What was Holly doing while all this was going on? Was she enjoying his humiliation?

Of course, she was!

Meet the man I'm fucking now; she seemed to be saying. He's handsome, isn't he... more handsome than you. This is what you get for ignoring me, and this is what you deserve!

Holly was laughing too hard at Hunter's jokes, talking too loudly to him, running her hand over his shoulder and down his arm, the way a wife or a girlfriend might. She was MARKING John Hunter as her possession.

Still, Niko never had the instincts for this kind of social politics. He was very uncomfortable, but he may never have figured it all out for himself. Until that is, he wondered how many other people in the room were tuned-in to the budding romance.

Everyone seemed to be: Rich, even the bride and groom. They were making John Hunter the life of the party, laughing along with him, giving him the floor over and over again: to tell jokes, to propose toasts, to make speeches. They were enjoying Hunter's boyish glee at Niko's humiliation, his total victory over the poor sad cuckold.

Niko looked around the room. It wasn't a wedding; it was a circus, and he was the clown. He was Dumbo, now stripped of his magic feather and left standing in the center ring wearing nothing but a rain barrel and a sad, painted face.

He turned and saw Susan, Mrs. Hunter. She wasn't laughing. She wasn't part of the happy crowd either. Her expression was one of absolute detestation. She hated him for being the kind of man who would drive his wife into the arms of someone else.

Niko stood. He couldn't take it any longer. Hunter stood, too, and shook his hand yet again. He looked Niko right in the eyes and smiled a great big, self-satisfied smile.

"We have to go," Niko said to Holly.

"I'm staying," she replied. "John and Susan will give me a ride home."

He turned to John who nodded in agreement.

He turned to Susan. There was no consent there. Her eyes were blazing. Her lips were moving. Anyone could read them, even Niko.

"You worthless piece of shit!" She hissed at him under her breath. He wasn't the only one who heard it, either. But he didn't protest.

It was an accurate description of the way he felt about himself at that moment.

Chapter 7
Father Tim Reflects

That very evening, Father Tim was pouring himself a glass of sherry and settling back in the darkness. He was reflecting on the conversation with Niko. At least, his thoughts started there. But, as they so often did, they soon returned to Marla Morrison... tall, freckle-faced Marla with her ballerina legs and her witchcraft.

There was more to his relationship with the young witch than he had told, just as he was sure that there was far more to Niko's relationship with Marla. Tim's memories began with those tight, denim shorts she wore all summer long in 1958, and they ended with the magical game she played with him.

Little Timmy, as he was called back then, had been following Marla and her friends home from the shopping center, enjoying the way they looked in their tight shorts and their new halter tops. Their breasts were just filling out, he remembered, just starting to have a shape, and he knew that the girls were as embarrassed and delighted with them as he was.

He followed a short distance behind Marla and her friends as they strutted down Hollywood Way. They didn't seem to notice him, or, if they did, they didn't care. After all, he was just a geeky ten-year-old kid, and they felt that they were entering womanhood.

One by one, the girls returned to their homes until it was just Marla walking alone down the broad sidewalk. She turned around. Timmy looked away. She went a little farther and turned again. He ducked behind a fence. When he came out, she was gone.

"Boogers!" he cursed.

He ran halfway up the block and looked down the side streets. No Marla. He ran a little farther, still no sign of her. Then he turned, and she was standing right there.

"Who ya followin', bud?" she asked.

"No one," Timmy answered. "Just goin' home."

"Come on, you were right behind us all the way, you know."

"I was just goin' home, is all. You just happened to be in front of me."

Timmy was staring at her hard, and he liked what he saw. Marla was even prettier up close, freckles or not. She had sparkly eyes and a wonderful smile. Then he looked down at her budding breasts, and that was it. He couldn't take his eyes off of them from that moment on.

"Gee!"

He actually said it out loud.

"Like my figure?" she asked.

"Sure."

Marla's smile broadened.

"I like it when guys look at me the way you are right now."

"Guys!" Timmy liked that. He felt geeky as hell, but she had just called him a guy.

"Well, you're so..." he started out strong, in his best "guy" voice, but he was losing his nerve as he whispered, "Beautiful."

Marla's smile glowed now. "Come on," she said.

He hesitated, but she motioned for him to follow. And so, they began walking home together.

She was thirteen and tall, maybe five foot six. He was ten, tall for his age, but still barely five feet. Marla moved with the stature and grace of a girl who had taken ballet from the age of three. He did his best to stand up tall and straight and look like he belonged with her. But he was still wearing ragged dungarees and a kid's T-shirt and a silly baseball cap. He grabbed it off his head and stuffed it into the back of his pants. That was better.

But something else was going on, something that Marla seemed to be very much aware of. As Timmy walked beside her, he looked up at her from time to time, and caught a glimpse of those small but amazing breasts, and those powerful thighs with the shorts stretched tightly over them. He was feeling very warm down between his legs, very warm, and very hard, maybe for the first time in his life.

After nearly two blocks of walking in silence with Timmy casting furtive glances at Marla's miraculous body, she started to giggle.

"Want to play a game?" she asked.

"I don't really play kid's games anymore," Timmy answered still trying to use his best "guy" voice.

"Oh, this isn't a kid's game," she whispered. "It's real grown up."

"Yeah?"

"REAL grown up."

Things were getting so hot and hard down below that Timmy could barely walk. Marla looked down at him and laughed out loud.

"Real grown up," she whispered again. "Wanta?"

His parents were very strict, hard-core religious and intolerant of anything that did not seem "age appropriate," as his mother always said. That made the invitation seem both frightening and wonderful.

"Can you get out tonight?" she asked.

"After dark?"

"Hasta be."

"I kin ask," he said.

"No, you can't ASK, you know," Marla snapped. She had stopped walking and was facing him directly, looking down at what she certainly must have known to be a very interesting, safe, and flattering erection that was nearly popping out of his pants. Timmy, of course, was too enthralled to do anything about it but pretend it wasn't there.

"You can't ask," Marla insisted. "NOT ASKING is part of the game."

"Okay," he stammered.

"Now, you know the big oak tree in the vacant lot off of Buena Vista Street?"

"Sure."

"Be there at midnight, just you, just me, and we can play the game."

"What kind of game is it?"

"Don't be a poop," she responded. "Just be there. Just us. Don't bring anyone or anything."

"Nothing?"

"Well, you can bring THAT!" Marla said with a sudden giggle, and she pointed right between Timmy's legs. Then she ran off down the street looking absolutely breathtaking, with her long red ponytail bobbing behind her.

Father Tim took a long sip of his third glass of sherry.

"The game," he murmured with a guilty smile.

And he fell asleep.

Chapter 8
Harry Rodgers Returns

"But I'll lose my job," Ramirez kept saying to Niko as they walked down the antiseptic corridor of the old sanitarium.

"Five thousand dollars, cash, right now, today, before I leave the building," Niko responded. "You've taken my money before."

"But not that much, and you've never asked for this," Ramirez answered. He was a fat man who waddled as he made his way through the hall. His guard's uniform was too tight. His shoes squeaked as did his holster, gun, and nightstick. He worked in a sanitarium, but he was armed like a guard in a penitentiary. Credit the quality of the clientele.

"Do you want the job and the money or not?" Niko asked. The guard did not answer, just led him into a small, gray room where he'd be allowed to talk to one of the full-time residents.

The heavy door slammed shut behind them. The room was barren, no pictures on the walls, just a small metal table with four chairs around it. The two men approached the table and sat together on one side, and almost as soon as they did, the door at the opposite end of the room opened, and a third man stepped through it. He was tall and gaunt with sandy hair and horn-rimmed glasses. He wore tennis shoes, gray sweatpants, and a black T-shirt with a picture of Marilyn Monroe silk-screened on the front of it.

"Niko," he said with the biggest smile he'd been able to muster in years.

"Sit," Ramirez said.

"How have you been, Harry?" Niko asked.

"Pretty good, pretty good," Harry Rodgers responded. "They let me use the darkroom now. I like that. I can take all the pictures I want, and develop them. No witches in any of the pictures either."

"Good," answered Niko. "I haven't seen any witches in a long time myself."

"I'm glad. Because they can drive you to... you know."

"What?" the guard asked. "Witches can drive you to what?"

"Harry and I were just reminiscing," Niko answered. "About the time he was the manager of the apartment where we lived. He liked to take pictures of the pretty girls in the building, even took some of my wife, didn't you, Harry?"

"A peeping Tom?" Ramirez asked. "Or worse?"

"Worse," Harry answered, and suddenly his hands began to tremble.

"Only in his mind," Niko said. "Harry fancied himself a serial killer."

"I wanted to punish them," Harry added.

"But he never really killed anyone, just took pictures, developed them and then put them into scrapbooks."

"My victims," Harry added nervously.

"Sounds sick to me," the guard said.

"That's why I'm in here," Harry answered. "To get well."

"But didn't you say something about a witch?"

"We gave Harry a witch mask," Niko continued. "It was a mask that had been made of my Grandmother when she lived in Poland."

"Babcia," Harry interjected.

"A friend had gotten it for me at Leland University," Niko continued. "And gave it to me as a scary sort of gift."

"What happened to the friend?" Ramirez asked; he was getting a little spooked.

"Let's just say he fell in with the wrong crowd," Niko answered.

"Were they witches?" the guard whispered.

"Maybe some of them were," Niko said. "Not sure."

"They killed him, though," Harry added. Ramirez jumped at the words.

"Does this job have anything to do with killing and witches?" Ramirez asked.

"Calm down," Niko said to the guard. "This is just a case of marital infidelity."

As he said those words, Niko's whole body went limp.

"You want me to take pictures of Holly again, don't you," Harry asked stoically. "Is she being unfaithful again?"

"She was unfaithful, and you're still married to her?" Ramirez asked. "What happened to the guy she was fooling around with?"

"The guy who gave me the mask of the witch?"

"The guy was fooling around with your wife; that guy was killed by..."

"Witches," Harry concluded.

"Same guy," Niko said.

Ramirez jumped to his feet. "I don't want any part of this."

"I have five grand cash in my pocket right now," Niko repeated. "All you have to do is take Harry out for a little ride next Wednesday afternoon. You've done that before. Let him track my wife, take a few pictures, develop them, bring them over to me; that's all. You get the full five grand up front and another ten when you're done."

"And what do I get?" Harry asked.

"You get to do your favorite thing, Harry," Niko said with a grimace. "Take pictures of my wife screwing somebody else, you son of a bitch."

Harry smiled.

"But what if she's not doing anything?" Ramirez asked.

Niko smiled for the first time in days. "I'd love that," he answered. "And you'll still get paid."

Interlude One

The warlock stood and marched up among the seats. His teenage witches were captivated.

"Does he find out what his wife is doing?" Megan Cummings asked the warlock when he moved close to her.

"Of course he does," answered her sister. "It's a foregone conclusion."

"Nothing is a foregone conclusion when witches are involved," said the warlock. "And in Niko's case there is a very unusual witch who plays a part... his grandmother yes, but someone with a very unique perspective for a witch."

"Is it because she lost her baby to the witch hunters?" asked Matryoshka, who was feeling quite self-satisfied in knowing more of Babcia's story that the other young witches.

"Actually, in this case, it had much more to do with her relationship with her father," he answered.

"Her father?" Matryoshka asked with a troubled expression. This was a part of Babcia's story that even she did not know. "Tell us about it," she said quickly.

"I'd rather hear about Holly's affair and what Niko does about it," said Megan Cummings. "I'll bet he murders John Hunter."

"We shall see," said the warlock. "But I think it would be helpful if you did know a little more about Walter Sapalski, Babcia's father. Let's take a minute to see what happened to him so many hundreds of years ago. Shall we?"

#

Walter Sapalski reined in his horse before allowing her to charge across Dearth Bridge. It was a high, narrow crossing that spanned Dearth River on the outskirts of his village, a perfect place for brigands to hide. They could crouch on either end of the bridge and rise up to catch unsuspecting travelers, steal their goods, slit their throats, and take their horses, too. And with a prize like Arra, Walter suddenly realized how alone and vulnerable he was.

"Shall we chance it, girl?" he called to his horse.

Arra reared up on her hind legs and whinnied loudly. She was ready for the challenge.

"Go then," Walter called and dug his heels into the horse as they lit out for the bridge.

He was doing just what they'd wanted him to do, the Wynofski brothers, fun-loving lads from the village, jokesters and brigands more for the joy of it than anything else. Yes, they were apt to slit a throat or two in a night's work, but it was all in good fun, nonetheless.

The only problem Walter presented to the brothers was one of ownership. Which one of them would get his horse after they slit his throat?

No matter. It was something they could settle later, Charles Wynofski realized as he rode his horse up out of the rushes along the side of the bridge and out onto the span. He was facing the oncoming rider now, and he lowered his lance. It was a battered version of something a knight might carry into a joust, the perfect tool to unseat a foolish rider whose steed was perhaps mightier than he deserved.

Walter saw the rider come up on the other side of the bridge and the lance he carried knowing that it was meant to be his undoing. He pulled back on the reigns. Arra reared, spun in her tracks and turned to light out in the opposite direction, but by then, it was all too late. Charles was suddenly upon them, swinging the lance like a club, nearly splitting Walter's skull with the power of his blows. He spun in his saddle, almost falling off his mount. That's when Fredrick Wynofski charged him on foot. He grabbed the old man and pulled him from the horse, nearly breaking his leg in the process.

Michalina caught up to the action just as Charles raised his lance above Walter's head. He was prepared to do the old man in with one last deadly blow.

But Michalina screamed then. SHE SCREAMED! A witch scream, a banshee wail that was horrible and bone chilling!

It cut through the night air with a power that split the boulders beside the road. It dashed down the branches of high trees, momentarily turned the flow of the river forcing the current back upon itself. It set off the cries of wolves deep in the forest as they added their calls to the witch's lament. It was a deafening, high-pitched, piercing sound that caused Charles to drop his lance and put his hands to his ears at once. He felt dizzy, sick to his stomach. The world seemed to be spinning in rhythm to the monstrous roar all around him. Fredrick closed his eyes so hard that they twisted his face in pain. He began pounding on his head as if he could somehow beat away that banshee cry.

Then all was silence.

"Leave him!" A deep, unearthly voice echoed with the power of the witch's wail.

The brothers looked at each other. They were frozen with fear. And then they saw it, the vision: Arra, the pale horse that now seemed like a ghostly apparition as she trotted back through the mists toward her fallen rider.

Astride her was a being like no other in this world, a girl dressed in black: young, beautiful, but with a rage in her eyes and across her face, a look so twisted with anger and pain that the sight of her might have murdered the two jovial brothers on the spot.

The men exchanged horrified glances. And then they jumped to their feet and ran back to their horses. They were on them in an instant, racing from Dearth Bridge and the road, *racing from the old man they'd left nearly dead and his pale horse, racing from the dark figure of the young girl...*

Michalina, the witch.

Chapter 9
Guns and Pictures

Niko Madonie rushed into the room almost knocking over a large chair as he made his way to the dining room table. He emptied his pockets, pulling first a large metal object from his coat and dropping it onto the surface with a terrible thud. It was a gun.

Next, he flung dozens of pictures out onto the table, the evil pictures, the damning nine-year-old pictures of his wife, Holly, in the arms of Billy Bright.

Emmy recoiled from the noise and commotion. The cat had curled up in her customary place by the fire. Then she stretched, yawned, dug her claws deep into the carpet, and narrowed her eyes. Across the room the master was behaving most unusually, she thought.

In faraway bedrooms, Holly and Joy hardly stirred in their sleep.

It was late, almost midnight, Emmy realized. She didn't know much about human time, but she did know about midnight; she could feel it buzzing through her whole body. It was time to make some mischief. But she did not move. She just sat there motionless, staring at the master through her narrow eyes. He was agitated enough for both of them.

Niko Madonie! Master! Why did she call him that? Emmy wondered when no one else in the family had a title. Holly was Holly, Joy was Joy, but Niko was the Master. It was some kind of deference, wasn't it, because he was so important? The title came to her with so many feelings when that presence took hold of her, as it had this night… the presence of Babcia.

Niko drew his trembling fingers across his brow and wiped away the heavy sweat that had accumulated there. Then he sat forward, reached in front of him, and began arranging the pictures: Holly and Billy Bright having passionate, dirty sex! Why hadn't he thrown the pictures away?

"Because I knew it would happen AGAIN!" he said out loud.

An envelope beckoned from across the table; it was still sealed, the new envelope from Harry Rodgers.

Harry had delivered the pictures he'd requested the day after their meeting. Ramirez had done his part, too, by taking Harry on a ride to the Sheridan Universal where Harry had found a way to hide in the very room where Holly and John Hunter had their rendezvous.

Niko ripped open the envelope and pulled the stack of pictures from it, a perfect sequence of seduction and submission, another perfect set of pictures of someone else fucking his wife.

In the pictures, Holly had that look in her eyes again, the look she had in the pictures with Billy, as though some other being had taken hold of her.

Niko's hands trembled while he arranged the latest pictures in a neat row just below the images of Holly and Billy. Together both sets made a perfect display of his wife's obscene infidelity.

He reached into his pocket and pulled out a handkerchief to dry his hands and his face. The ticking clock behind his head seemed to grow very loud, and soon his whole body twitched in counterpoint to its rhythm.

Slowly Niko took the gun and brought it up before him. He closed his eyes and held them closed for a long moment. He was going to kill John Hunter in a few hours, kill Hunter and leave Holly to suffer the rest of her life with the knowledge that her infidelity had cost the man his life.

Niko had purchased the gun, learned how to use it, and plotted a way to get John Hunter alone so he could blow the bastard's brains out. All he needed to set things in motion was the final proof, and Harry had provided that.

It wouldn't be easy. Hunter worked in a school. Confrontation there could be dangerous to the students. Confrontation at his home was impossible. But he did take those longs walks, didn't he, early in the morning, before work.

Niko had scoped it all out. In a few hours, Hunter would begin his walk, and Niko would just drive right up beside him, roll down the window and....

In the meantime, he would just sit there at the table, think about what had happened to his life and his marriage, and he would wait for morning.

Niko closed his eyes and held them closed again. Then he brought the gun up before his face to study its deadly features. It was beautiful.

He'd rehearsed this all in his mind a thousand times. Strangely, he had an erection. The images of Holly were erotic, weren't they? She was so beautiful. He'd almost certainly never touch her again, never hold her, never be able to give her the pleasures that John Hunter was providing now.

"No more!" Niko grunted between clenched teeth, and as he did...

He accidentally squeezed the trigger.

Chapter 10
Holly's Night

Holly's sleep was troubled that night. She and John had made a pact. As much as they loved each other, they would stay with their spouses. John loved his son Jimmy and couldn't bear the thought of losing him to what would surely be the verdict of any 1970s divorce court.

Holly just wasn't sure about anything anymore. She couldn't swear that she still loved Niko. And now, with his intense work schedule, it was as though she didn't even exist for him. He seemed so distant and indifferent to her. As though everything she said and did was meaningless.

She hated him for that.

When John mentioned his son, Jimmy, and her little girl, Joy, it just seemed much easier and more prudent to maintain their marriages. Besides, they could have all the fun they wanted in the evenings whenever she could get away and visit him at the Sheridan Universal. Niko wouldn't know or care. He was too caught up in his own private little world where she no longer had a part.

Because BABCIA was in her dreams: Niko's ghost witch of a grandmother, for the first time since it happened, Holly was reliving the most terrible night of her life. It was a night filled with madness: Witch ballerina Marla Morrison summoning Babcia, only to have the ancient crone turn on her and destroy her. Then the door had opened, the one to the little room where Holly was being held captive. The hideous crone was advancing on her, pointing her twisted finger at the girl, and calling out, "She's mine!"

But it was what happened next that Holly suddenly remembered for the first time. Babcia had seemingly just disappeared, except that hadn't happened at all. She'd actually

52

become sparkly little wisps floating in the air right before Holly's eyes. And when Holly had drawn her next breath, Babcia had entered her, found her womb, and taken possession of her baby. The dream grew more terrifying still.

Holly was giving birth, a twisted painful birth without any anesthetic whatsoever. She lived it all over again, but now she was pushing out a mangled mass that felt like a gaggle of coat hangers. They tore at her as they emerged. And why shouldn't they? It wasn't a little girl that she was giving birth to in her dream. It was the scrawny, sharp-boned, hideous body of BABCIA!

"SCREE!"

The piercing cry of an animal cut into her dream and awakened her instantly. The roar of a gunshot followed immediately. Holly jumped to her feet.

Yes! It was a gun. She was sure of it, and it was not in her dream.

"Mommy! Mommy! What's happening?"

Joy came running into her room and wrapped her arms around her mother.

"I don't know," Holly whispered. "Maybe it was a burglar, and Daddy shot him. But," she added in terror, "Daddy doesn't have a gun."

"Yes, he does, Mommy," Joy answered. "I've seen it."

"NIKO!" Holly screamed and rushed down the stairs and into the dining area, and, oh, what she saw there!

Niko's blood was splattered across the wall, his body blown back in the chair with a large chunk of the side of his face torn off. Claw marks scratched across the table as though Emmy had tried to do something.

Holly turned to Joy who stood behind her with a look of heartbroken horror.

"Daddy!" the little girl called rushing past her mother and throwing her arms around the bloody mess that had been Niko.

"Be careful. Don't make it any worse," Holly called. "Don't hurt him."

"Mommy," Joy hissed as she pulled away and looked at her mother, "I think we both know who hurt him."

Holly stumbled backwards, away from her daughter and her awful, grown-up words. Her hand hit the sideboard with the phone. She grabbed the receiver and pulled it to her mouth. The emergency number was plastered on the wall behind the phone, and she dialed it.

From deep in the corner of the room, Emmy looked out at the scene. Somehow she had managed to sweep the pictures off the table and gather them for herself, these incriminating pictures of Holly and her lovers that had made the master...

Want to commit murder!

Chapter 11
Marla's Game

Father Tim Brennan heard Niko had been taken to the Emergency Room, an attempted suicide, someone said. Could that be right?

Father Tim was feeling guilty as he did about almost everything, thinking that he should have recognized the signs when he and Niko had spoken at the wedding reception. He'd known that Niko's marriage was going wrong. But how wrong?

Tim slipped on his shoes and hunted around for his collar. That damn Roman collar! He had to wear it, had to visit Niko in his official capacity.

Niko and Holly. Maybe she would be there.

Tim could imagine that being married to such a flirtatious and beautiful woman would be difficult. There weren't a lot of women like her, not that beautiful, anyway.

But there was Marla, wasn't there?

Niko and Marla. The guy sure attracted some exciting women, Tim realized. An image of Marla came floating to him, and just like that he was plunged into his old memories of the ballerina.

Tim had just found his Roman collar and was about to put it on, but it just fell from his hand as he stood there, his mind returning to that night...

The night of the game!

#

Little ten-year-old Timmy knew the tree Marla had described, an enormous old California live oak that inhabited a vacant lot off Buena Vista Street in Burbank, California. Behind the tree, there were still wilds and underbrush. Brambles twined around each other seeming almost intentionally to turn their sharp thorns out to prick and grab at anyone who ventured too close. White and pink roses from some long-forgotten, endangered variety were gigantic and so fragrant that the air around them was absolutely intoxicating. Police patrolled the place regularly to keep the vagrants away, so it seemed fairly safe for children... but not at midnight, Timmy thought.

Still, Marla had instructed him to meet her amid the roses under that tree, and so he did, sneaking out the back door after his mother had gone to bed. His father was away on business. That made it easier. The moon was full, casting long shadows across the back yard and tinting everything with a strange, silvery glow as he hopped over the fence and jogged down Hollywood Way to Buena Vista Street. Then it was on to the vacant lot and the tree.

There, standing under the tree, drenched in the intoxicating smell of the roses, illuminated by the silver moon, was the hunched over shape of a woman clothed in long robes that were black and frightening.

"M... M... Marla?" Timmy stammered.

The figure didn't move. Timmy backed away slowly without taking his eyes off the apparition.

"Marla?" he whispered, and then he tripped and fell right on his seat.

The figure turned. It was a crone, a hideous old crone with a great hooked nose with a wart on the end of it. Outlined in the moonlight, her whole awful face seemed to glow. She staggered zombie-like toward Timmy, who was now scuttling away backward, still facing her, not daring to take his eyes off her.

"D... don't hurt me!" he cried, but the crone moved closer, reaching out a hand for him, a horribly disfigured, green hand with great claw-like nails.

AND THEN THE HAND FELL OFF.

It fell right into Timmy's lap. He screamed and jumped away only to see that it was really a rubber hand painted florescent yellow and green. And where it had been attached to the body of the old crone was the young, freckly arm of Marla Morrison, who now reached up and yanked a horrifying rubber mask from her face.

"You look so silly, you know, bud," she said and burst into laughter that was so fresh and happy, it made Timmy start laughing too, even though only a moment ago he'd been about to pee his pants.

"Come on!" Marla called, and without looking back, she turned and marched into the woods behind the great tree.

Timmy jumped to his feet to follow her, not wanting to be alone in the scary moonlight.

Marla led Timmy to a tent that she'd pitched there in the wood. She stepped out of the moonlight and into the tent, lighting a small lantern the moment she was inside, so that her silhouette loomed within the glowing tent. From the outside, she now looked like the ominous creature she'd portrayed before, and Timmy had to duck inside quickly to see that she was not. She was still ballerina Marla, but now sporting a very haughty expression. Her eyebrows arched and her mouth twisted into a regal sneer as she watched Timmy enter.

"Sit," she commanded pointing to a small chair in the corner of the tent. And he obeyed.

"Now, bud," she began. "Let's get to the game."

There was a small table and another chair in the tent. Across from the table, a large kettle rested on the floor. The kettle was half full and smelled of strange, swampy things that even choked off the aroma of the roses. Timmy found it most unsettling. In center of the floor in front of the table were several bundles of twigs twisted into rather frightening shapes. On the table in front of Marla, many strange bottles held brightly colored liquids and powders and a squirmy thing or two. A thick book lay open to a page almost at its center.

"Is your chair acceptable?" she asked, still with that haughty expression.

Timmy nodded. He sat forward and leered at Marla who, in the lantern light, looked regal and much, much older than 13.

"First things first, you know," Marla said, and she pulled a large pin from her hair and brought over to him.

"Stick out your finger. I need a drop of your blood."

Timmy immediately pulled his hand back behind him.

"Come on, bud," Marla insisted. "It's for the game. And for the spell, you know."

"The spell?" he asked.

"Right, it's a witch's spell and a witch's game. You aren't afraid, are you?"

Timmy didn't answer.

"Cause if ya are, you know..."

"Are you really a witch?" he asked.

"Of course, I am," Marla answered. "Now, play or go home?"

"Play," he said with sudden excitement and stuck out his hand. Marla immediately seized one of his fingers and drove the pin deep into it. He winced but didn't cry. He knew that was important.

Marla squeezed several drops of blood out of his finger and caught them in a clear glass dish that she held in the palm of her hand.

"Good! Now for a little of your hair," Marla added, and she set the dish on the floor of the tent. Reaching around behind Timmy, she grabbed several strands of his hair and yanked them from his head.

He didn't even cry out when she did it, even though it hurt terribly.

"Good guy, bud," Marla said, and then she picked up the dish and marched back to her table.

"Now, here's the fun part."

She pulled a match and a candle from a drawer in the table, lit the candle and, flipped off the lantern when candlelight filled the tent. The candle flame gave a warm, flickering glow to Marla and every thing else in the tent.

"Tell me your favorite color, bud," she called as she produced a box of crayons from the drawer under the table.

"Blue," Timmy answered immediately. He stood and moved toward her.

"Back in your seat!"

He obeyed.

Marla removed a blue crayon from the box and held it up for his approval. Timmy nodded, and so she peeled the paper off the crayon and dropped it into a beaker that was sandwiched in between the bottles on the table. She placed the beaker on a little burner and turned it on, its flame enhancing the brightness in the tent.

"Hot in here, you know," Marla said.

Timmy nodded.

"Wouldn't you like to take something off?" she asked with a smirk.

"Like what?"

"Like maybe your shirt, you know?"

Timmy didn't feel especially warm, but what do you do when the most beautiful girl you know asks you to take something off?

"Come on, come on," she urged with arched eyebrows. Her lips were twisting into another of those haughty sneers.

"Will you take something off, too?" he finally blurted out.

Marla was surprised by Timmy's boldness.

"All I have on is this robe, bud."

"So take it off," he responded. He didn't realize he could be so quick. It was just the first thing that popped into his mind, but he thought it was a very cool response. Maybe he WAS a big guy.

"I can lower the robe to my waist if you like," Marla teased.

His jaw dropped.

"You'll see my breasts," she continued. "I've never shown them to anyone before, you know."

"No one?" He could barely get the words out.

"Well, my mom," Marla confessed. "But forget your shirt. You'll have to take off something more, you know, interesting."

"Like...."

"Your pants, of course."

"Deal," he answered enthusiastically. "And I'll take my shirt off, too."

Timmy scrambled out of his clothes, down to his shorts, anyway. That seemed to satisfy Marla because she pulled her arms out of the robe and let it fall around her waist. He spun around and took his seat, and as he did, he saw her budding breasts, and his mouth fell wide open.

"They're so...."

"Yes, they are, bud," she answered proudly. "Now, close your mouth."

He did and sat back and watched Marla, who was taking a good long look at what was going on inside his shorts. Then she snickered.

The blue crayon was fully melted by now and hissed and bubbled in the beaker. She pulled it away from the flame.

"Your blood," she murmured while she poured the droplets from the little dish into the beaker. "A pinch of Jasmine, a few pine needles and guess what we have?"

Timmy was too astonished by the vision of Marla to know or care. How could this be happening to him, a ten-year-old geeky kid who was suddenly playing some kind of sex game with a beautiful, half-naked teenage witch? Was she brewing up a potion just for him?

"Almost got it, bud," she said as she poured the beaker full of hot blue wax onto the tabletop. She wet her fingers in a little bowl and began to form the wax into a figure that was shaped like a boy.

"Is that me?" he stammered.

Marla didn't answer; she just smiled and added other ingredients to the figure.

"Cassia rose oil," she whispered. "And now the most important ingredient of all."

Marla took the strands of hair that she'd pulled from Timmy's head and pressed them into the figure, this doll, this witch's poppet. And the moment she did, Timmy could FEEL her fingers touching the doll. She tickled the poppet around its neck, and he squirmed and giggled.

"Stop it!" he yelped.

Her fingers moved down the poppet, tickling under his arms as she went.

"Oh no!" he said and doubled over with laughter, "Please stop! I'll wet my pants!"

"I don't think so," Marla answered and slid her fingers across the poppet and....

"TIMOTHY BRENNAN!" his mother called.

"TIMOTHY BRENNAN! WHAT ON EARTH?"

His mother marched into the tent and grabbed her son by the ear. She yanked him to his feet.

"LOOK AT YOURSELF, YOUNG MAN!" she shouted.

Timmy didn't bother; he just looked up at his mother and grinned. In embarrassment or pride or he didn't know what, but it seemed to infuriate her even more, as she dragged him out of the tent.

"WHEN YOUR FATHER GETS THROUGH WITH YOU, YOU'LL WISH YOU HAD NEVER BEEN BORN!"

Mrs. Brennan screamed. "AND, AS FOR THAT STRUMPET...."

The strumpet laughed. Timmy could hear her laughing while his mother dragged him away from her, across the lot, down the street, through the wicked smell of roses, and all the way back to his home. Marla's laughter rang through the night. It haunted him; he seemed to hear it for hours, almost until dawn.

It haunts me still, Father Tim realized. She's dead, and she haunts me still.

Luckily, Timmy's father was out of town. There was hell to pay when he returned, of course. Tim was immediately sent packing. Within a week he found himself in the most repressive Junior Seminary that his devout Catholic parents could find, thousands of miles away from Marla and her witch games.

Tim never saw her again, alive anyway. But he knew that she'd never face any repercussions. Her parents wanted a prima ballerina, and if they had to put up with a little madness and a little witchcraft to get her?

Of course, they would.

Chapter 12
Emergency Room

Father Tim stuck his head through the hospital room door to look in on the patient. Everyone was saying that Niko Madonie had attempted the unforgivable sin: suicide.

He was so strong, said the surgeon who had put his face back together. And he was lucky. Father Tim was certain about that last part, or he'd be burning in hell right now.

Holly sat beside Niko holding his hand. She wore no make-up, yet her lips were full and red and her cheeks were warm. Even her sadness was beautiful.

"How is he this morning?" Father Tim asked.

"Getting better," she answered. She sniffed back a tear and smiled.

"The nurse said she thought she saw some alertness in his eyes."

"Thank God," Father Tim answered.

"Yes, thank God," Holly said and stared at the priest.

"Father, I'd like to...." she began and then paused, not knowing exactly how to say the words.

"Go to confession?" he volunteered.

"I need to talk to someone. Is it too late for me, Father?" She was starting to sob.

"Of course not," he answered. "The chapel is right down the hall to the left. There's a confessional. Just go into it, and I'll be right there. I just want to say a prayer for Niko."

Holly nodded without a word. And then she moved silently from the room.

Father Tim approached the bed. He looked down at the young man who'd shown no sign of regaining consciousness despite what they'd told his wife.

Father Tim bowed his head and began to pray, asking a God he believed in less and less to save this young man who had so much to live for.

#

"Bless me, Father, for I have sinned," Holly whispered through the plastic partition in the confessional wall. She could barely see the outline of Father Tim nodding there on the other side.

"It's been two years since my last confession. Since then..." she began and broke into tears. Father Tim could barely stand it. And yet what was his vocation if not helping sinners such as Holly?

"I can't do it, Father," she suddenly blurted out. She was crying openly now.

"Is it another man?" Father Tim whispered.

"How could you know?"

Father Tim actually smiled. He could sense her beauty through the partition, and it was overwhelming.

"It's a pretty simple puzzle," he said.

"I'm not a puzzle," Holly answered in anger. "I'm just a girl who got married too young, whose husband is too busy for her. Who needed someone to talk to and who...." And then she was crying again.

"Do you want God to forgive you?"

"Of course I do, Father."

"And your husband?"

"Niko will never forgive me."

"I think he will," Father Tim answered.

"How do I..." again Holly's sentence trailed off.

"First you have to end the relationship with that man. Can you?"

"I don't know, Father," she answered in abject misery. "John means so much to me now."

"You'll have to pray, Holly."

"I have been."

"Good," said the priest. "Think of the good things about your life with Niko. Meditate on the reasons you love him."

"Loved him," she corrected.

"Then try and find that love again. Next time you visit, come back and see me. I'll help you."

"But what if he dies?"

"I'll help you with that, too," Father Tim said softly. "Now, say three Hail Mary's as penance for your sins and promise you'll try to find a way to end your sinful relationship."

Hard silence came from the other side of the confessional. Holly murmured something Tim could not understand, and then she hurried out the door, out of the chapel and away from the hospital.

Father Tim sat there for a long moment. There were tears in his eyes. Then he stood and walked into the chapel, made his way to the front of the altar, and bowed his head.

"Heavenly Father," he prayed. "Please help that poor girl. Please forgive her for this terrible sin, and please help her husband recover."

He paused for a very long moment and then added, "And please, Father, protect me from the feelings that...

"I'm starting to have for Holly."

Chapter 13
Chuck and Sally

It was the new Sally Fukes who sashayed into Chuck Vaughn's office that day.

"Well, look at you," the world's greatest animator said as he chomped through four sticks of Juicy Fruit Gum. He was a short man who had put on a few pounds in the last few years. He looked like a rather plump little leprechaun. He still wore those round glasses, but now they were shaded slightly pink to go with his kaleidoscopic attire: shiny black slacks, a colorful vertically striped shirt, and a mint green tie that clashed violently with the rest of it.

He'd managed to keep his hair through those last few desperate years, the little hair there was, anyway. Now totally silver, it was combed directly forward and sharply cut at the edge of his forehead. On the desk behind him, a huge black cat (the latest version of CatMan Due) lay napping. But when Sally appeared, the cat popped his eyes wide open just the way Vaughn did when he saw her.

"How the hell did you do it?" he asked.

Sally was proud of herself. She' had lost over one hundred and twenty pounds and was down to half her previous weight. Of course, she couldn't tell how she'd done did it because it was witchcraft, pure and simple.

After the horrible events that had led to Marla Morrison's death, her coven had dissolved. Most of her Hollywood witches were only pretenders, wannabe witches who couldn't cast a spell if their lives depended on it. They were just there for the aura, the camaraderie, and the sex. And they couldn't keep things going without her.

Sally, however, was different.

She'd been a witch long before she'd come to Hollywood from the hills of Tennessee where she'd been trained in The Craft by Mother Black who saw that her instruction was strong and her commitment solid.

Marla Morrison recognized it. That's why she gave Sally her Ladanki, her bag of charms. On the night she was to die, Marla must have known the danger she was facing because she handed the Ladanki to Sally. It was her most valued possession and had been brought from Poland where she'd learned her witchcraft from a pupil of one of the greatest witches who had ever lived. The pupil was Clara Goriki, student and eventual enemy of Babcia. Clara should have protected Marla from the she-wolf that Babcia had become and should have saved her when the beast tore the beautiful witch ballerina to nothingness. Or *had* Clara really betrayed her? What had actually happened in Marla's last seconds alive?

Sally didn't know, had wondered, yes, but was quite unsure of it all, except that now she understood that it was her job to use those tools to do many things for Marla. Foremost among them was to gain revenge against Niko Madonie and his witch grandmother.

Sally had quit her job as a receptionist at VVA (Vaughn Visual Arts) the day after Marla's death and had taken the Ladanki back to Tennessee to find Mother Black once again. In spite of the warnings, and even threats from local authorities, the two women worked together to contact Marla's spirit, to find out exactly how and when she wanted revenge.

The first priority they decided, with Marla's evil blessing, was the spell of BECOMING, the spell that in three short minutes slimmed sweet, chunky Sally Fukes into a lithe, sexy witch who could easily have her way with any man. This was the knockout babe who now greeted Charles Martin Vaughn.

"Kin ah have mah ol' job back?" she asked. She hadn't lost a bit of that Tennessee twang.

"Still won't let you play that country music crap," Vaughn insisted.

"Ah kin do without it."

"Same salary?"

"Dontcha think mah new look will brighten up the lobby a little bit more?" Sally said and wiggled her ass invitingly. "That's gotta be worth somethin'."

"Ten bucks more a week."

She slid into a chair and crossed her legs, letting her mini-skirt ride up high upon her thighs.

"Twenty?"

"Okay, twenty," he groused.

She crossed her legs the other way kicking them up a little as she did. The mini-skirt did its work.

"Nice, but you'll never beat Marla in the leg department," Vaughn responded.

"Nope, guess ah never will," she answered. Then, to change the subject, she asked, "How's Niko?"

Chuck suddenly slumped in his seat and lowered his head. At least Sally had been a distraction from all that.

"Stupid son of a bitch tried to kill himself," he whispered.

Sally fought back a smile. Well, that was a step in the right direction, she thought. But what she said was, "Poor dear. It was that unfaithful bitch-wife a his, wasn't it?"

"Couldn't come at a worse time," Vaughn continued. "The MikleyToon folks are trying to buy VVA, and our biggest asset is Niko Madonie. The kid was halfway through the storyboards for our latest show, Rapunzel. It was going great, and then he goes and blows half his face off. Fortunately, he survived."

"Aw, that's too bad," she sighed unwittingly.

Vaughn blustered in amazement. "What was that, girl? Are you saying that it's too bad he didn't kill himself?"

"Course not. I was simply sayin' that it's too bad that he *tried* ta kill hisself at awl. Is he gonna be okay?"

"Not so far," he answered. "But we'll see. Hell, I'm even going to church these days, for Christ sake, and you know how I feel about all that nonsense."

"About the same as me, ah reckon."

"Ah reckon," he repeated.

"When will ya know more?" she asked.

"Can't say. But if Niko doesn't come out of it fast, it won't matter. The longer he stays unconscious, the less likely he'll be able to function like a normal human being." Vaughn put his head in his hands. "Boy, do we need him."

Sally sat there for an awkward moment just looking at him. Finally, after a few more tragic moments passed, she spoke up.

"Want me ta start tamarrah?"

Vaughn eyed the sexy witch. Who knew that under his sweet, chunky receptionist from Tennessee was this babe?"

"That'll be fine," he answered and motioned as though he were shooing her away. He picked up the sketches sitting on his desk, sketches that Niko had done in that quick and cartoony hand of his.

Son of a bitch, why did Niko have to try and blow his brains out two weeks before the Mikley people were to sign the deal? Now Vaughn's only hope was that Niko would somehow show some signs of recovery before the next and most important meeting with the monster animation conglomerate, MikleyToons.

"You want me to go now, right?" Sally asked.

"I do, doll, nothing personal."

"Course not," she answered.

"I'll see what I kin do about these legs," she added.

"Twenty-five years of ballet should do the trick," Vaughn grumbled through his chewing gum.

Sally's smile broadened.

Right, twenty-five years of ballet, she thought...

Or five minutes of witchcraft.

Chapter 14
Holly's Nightmare

"You unfaithful bitch."

The words were whispered ever so softly, as though they were a dark, muted curse, but they woke Holly Madonie from a sound sleep.

It was exactly midnight, and she was sure that the words were not spoken in her dream. Someone had uttered them to her from out of the darkness on the far side of the room.

She was terrified, and yet she forced herself to look into the corner... at that low, disfigured shape that might be a bundle of newly washed clothes piled high on a rocking chair, or Babcia herself.

"Die, you unfaithful bitch!"

And now that shape started moving toward her.

Holly jumped to her feet, pressed herself against the opposite wall, and slid carefully away. Was it moving, that shape? Was it talking to her?

"Die, you whore!"

Holly seized the handle of the bedroom door, jerked it open and stumbled out into the dimly lit hallway, moving as quickly as her wobbly legs would take her toward the room that contained the only other living person in the house.

She opened the door to her daughter's bedroom and rushed to the bed where Joy lay sleeping. But the figure that was curled there was someone far too big to be Joy. And suddenly, the creature jumped bolt upright in the bed.

IT WAS BABCIA! IT WAS THE WITCH, all hollow-eyed and decaying with the stench of rotting flesh and death, pointing her terrible claw hand and shrieking out, "DIE! YOU UNFAITHFUL BITCH!"

Holly let out a scream and fled back toward the bedroom door and the stairway beyond it. She rushed away without looking back, through the door, down the stairs and into the dining room where the walls were once again splattered with the blood and brains of her dying husband. Somehow, his figure was again slumped over the dining room table, drowning in the blood that was splattered everywhere, flooding the table and seeping into the carpet.

"DIE! YOU UNFAITHFUL BITCH!" Niko's half-face screeched when it jumped up for a moment and leered at her. Holly screamed again, clutched at her hair, tangled her fingers through it, and turned this way and that to find some means of escape.

"DIE, YOU UNFAITHFUL BITCH!" The words echoed down the hallway from the bedroom, spinning through her head, pouring into every muscle of her body tingling, tightening, drenching her face and her body and everything she wore.

"MOMMY!"

Joy's voice came screaming at Holly, and the woman spun to see her daughter running toward her with outstretched arms. And then Joy's arms were around her mother, and the little girl was consoling Holly, sobbing with her, then pulling her, leading her into the living room where they both collapsed onto the couch.

"DIE, YOU UNFAITHFUL BITCH!" The devil's own voice called in a deep, awful rumble, and it was almost as though the voice were coming from Joy, but then she was shouting in her own voice, insisting that something or someone be the cat. Yes! That was it; those were the words: BE THE CAT!

Emmy then came into the room. But she was larger and darker than Holly remembered, and her eyes were sharp, almost human.

Little Joy held out her hand against the cat, and it arched its back, snarled and stopped. She held her mother even more tightly, and Holly could feel the little girl's protection.

The cat began to pace back and forth whining and growling like some otherworldly animal. And then she grew. Her shape morphed until she was no longer a cat at all, but something larger, more vicious, more evil, with great, sharp claws and huge, terrible teeth (all the better to eat you with, my dear.)

"A grandmother who's a witch, a witch who is a wolf." Niko's very words came boiling into Holly's brain. And she screamed again!

A monstrous she-wolf now paced back and forth before the mother and child, drawing closer and closer with every pass. She bared huge yellow fangs and flashed her claws at the two of them.

Little Joy looked directly into the eyes of the wolf and shouted her powerful command once again.

"BE THE CAT!"

The monster raged at them, came closer, roared with its rotting breath, slashed the air with its claws but did not touch them. Instead, after an almost unbearable few moments, it turned slowly, hissing more like a cat now and then slunk off toward the other room transforming completely back into the shape of Emmy, the cat while it retreated.

Just as little Joy had commanded it to.

Chapter 15
Be the Cat

Joy tottered back to her room. Was it a dream she and her mother had shared? Then why did she find herself alone downstairs? She pushed open the door and trundled in. Emmy came scurrying beside her brushing by and hopping onto the bed.

Joy sat down on the edge of the bed and pulled the cat to her. She buried her face in the cat's soft fur and began to sob.

"I don't like this, Great Grandma," the little girl sighed. "What are you doing to me?"

Slowly the witch's image formed in the mirror across from the bed. Babcia's expression seemed gentle. Still, a touch of anger lingered in her eyes.

"Why you protect her?" Babcia asked.

"'Cause she's my Mom," Joy sobbed. "Can't you go away; just leave us alone? Please?"

Babcia smiled. It was as loving a smile as had ever crossed that ancient face.

"Someday, Moje dziecko," she murmured.

"But you're killing me," Joy insisted.

"No, little one," Babcia answered. "You strong. I not hurt you, not hurt mother."

"But you ARE hurting her," Joy cried. She was clinging to Emmy, almost squeezing her in half. Of course, Emmy was fine. She didn't care; she just purred softly.

"She need to understand what she does," Babcia added.

Joy shook her head no, but then nodded a soft assent.

"Must save Papa," Babcia added. "Is difficult, very difficult. You help."

Joy's look turned far more purposeful.

"Save Daddy?"

The witch nodded.

"I will, Great Grandma. Can we?"

"Must be brave, Moje dziecko."

"I will, Great Grandma," Joy said. "But please, no more nightmares for me or my Mom."

"Will try," Babcia answered.

"Only pleasant dreams, okay?" Joy said and smiled at the ugly old crone.

The witch smiled back and nodded.

"Thanks, Great Grandma," Joy whispered as she slipped under the covers.

Emmy curled up at the foot of the bed and went immediately to sleep.

"Only pleasant dreams," Babcia answered as her image faded slowly from the mirror.

"Will try."

Interlude Two

The sad clip-clop of horse's hooves drew Julia Krawkowska to her window on that moonlit night so many centuries ago. And what she saw was something that would forever be held in her memory, something that would someday become legend thereabouts. For there was Arra, Walter Sapalski's handsome mount, mournfully trudging along the dusty road with a rider slumped over her back. It was Walter himself, bobbing from side to side. Blood had drenched his tunic and his britches. Surely he had been the victim of a terrible beating.

Julia might have rushed out to aid her neighbor were it not for the figure leading the horse. It was an unfamiliar young man, tall, broad-shouldered with a countenance so handsome, and yet so mournful, that it nearly broke her heart to look at him.

Still the old woman determined to follow the youth regardless of the dangers of the night. And so she did. Snatching her cloak, she moved out into the darkness relying only on the moonlight to guide her way.

She followed the sorry procession to Walter's home, where the sturdy youth lifted the man easily from his horse, carried him across the threshold and inside. Julia saw the handsome, young man place Walter gently on his bed. She watched through the window while he undressed the wounded man, built a fire under the kettle, boiled water, and tended to the old man's wounds.

Walter was nearly unconscious, perhaps hallucinating, for he kept calling to the young man, "Save yourself. Make your getaway! Leave these ruffians to me."

And yet the young man cared for Walter with great purpose, calmed him, bathed him, talked him sweetly to sleep.

The youth sat that whole night with him mopping his brow and praying over him.

"Michalina, is that you?" the old man called in the deepest part of the night.

"It is, Papa," the voice returned and the old man opened his eyes and saw that it was not a strapping youth who had rescued him, but his own little girl no more than twelve years old.

"I've come to be with you, Papa," she said "To cheer you up. Would you like me to sing to you?"

"Aye," he answered. "Sing, sweetheart."

And little Michalina opened her pretty lips and whispered a song, a song that only Walter could hear, about the warmth of sunshine and bright mountaintops looking down on fields where soon she and her father would walk among the flowers and be at peace forever.

Little Joy Madonie had this vision, felt that same love, heard the same song in her dreams, and knew the happiness that Michalina had felt for those few brief days while she tended to her father and shared his love...

So many centuries before.

#

The young witches were bawling like babies now, heartbroken over the tragedy that engulfed Niko and his family as he lay in the hospital still unconscious.

"Flirtation," grumbled Matryoshka.

"The warlock walked up beside her and rested his hand on her shoulder. "You say that as though it were a bad thing, sweetheart."

Matryoshka spit on the ground and cursed in Polish. "Look what it's done to Niko and his little girl," she said bitterly and then she looked up and unconsciously fluttered her eyes at Wicktor.

"Ah, but look what it's done for us," answered the warlock.

"I never flirted with you," said the girl defensively.

"Oh, is that right?" The Warlock laughed. "Did you know that all women are descendants of witches?" He raised his voice and addressed his entire coven. "Some bit of witchcraft runs through the blood of all your sex. Those brews you cook up on cold winter nights to warm and cure yourselves and your loved ones... that's witchcraft. The way you bat your eyes, push out your breasts, and smirk with pretended innocence? You are using your powers to bewitch even the strongest men... to reduce them to babbling little boys. The way you caress, apply salves and lotions to cure and strengthen those you love... the salves may come from the pharmacy, but the caress....

"Babcia, the greatest of all witches had within her the power to heal and to destroy... the problem is her mix of instincts, those of a woman, a witch, and a she-wolf. She can torture and brutalize anyone, but she can also love and cure.

"Ah, and that tenderness is there even in this most evil of women, my young witches... as in all of you...

"As in all of you."

Chapter 16
Awakening

"Niko, come play me."

The words were little more than a whisper, but they screamed through the dead silence in Niko's soul like the screech of a huge bar that is suddenly lifted from a gateway that no one thought could ever be opened. The slamming of the gears into place, the grinding of the chain that lifts the bar, the awful squeal of the bar itself as it wrenches free allowing the gate to open at last... those simple words affected Niko in that way. And then light poured in everywhere.

Niko saw an image forming. It grew clearer and clearer. It was an angel, a little angel with soft choirgirl hair and a hopeful smile. It was Joy.

But in another moment, a shadow passed before it, the face of another little girl from centuries before: Michalina, the child who had so loved her father. And then those features also changed, transforming themselves into yet another face, the frightful visage that Michalina had become in her ancient age: Niko's grandmother, Babcia.

She startled Niko, terrified the young man, but more than anything else...

SHE WOKE HIM UP.

Holly had left her little daughter alone in the room with Niko when she went for her counseling session with Father Tim. She'd dropped Joy off not at all sure that her experience the night before had been a dream or reality. (It was only a dream. It had to be.)

That next morning the little girl gave no indication that she'd participated in the horrid event either. (So it had to be a dream, Holly realized.) In reality, the little girl was so calmed by the sweet dream that Babcia had given her later that same night that she determined that the best thing to do was ignore the witch dream, act as though it had never happened, and make her mother think that it was a conjuring of her own guilty imagination.

Joy was now grateful that she could spend time alone with her father, a man who was quite unconscious, whose face was wrapped tightly in so many bandages that he was hardly visible, a man who at that point was little more than a breathing vegetable.

Joy had carried a large satchel into the room with her, a satchel with just enough air holes in it to allow Emmy the cat to survive.

Joy had brought Emmy with her so Babcia could leave her body and move into the soul of the cat. At this point, little Joy felt she actually had the power to send the witch away at will, to send her into the cat, and get the witch to leave her alone so that she could be herself.

The longer Joy looked into the closed, dead eyes of her father, the more powerfully she felt Babcia's presence grow in her mind. She now understood how, so long ago, Babcia had looked into the dying eyes of her own father and felt the same terrible longing. And so she spoke the one sentence that had been the witch's call to Niko throughout his life: "Niko, come play me." And in the depths of his unconsciousness, Niko heard the words and responded.

He opened his eyes.

"Daddy," little Joy called and threw herself at her father.

"Joy," Niko whispered through his bandages and felt the pain of the effort shoot through his entire being. What had he done? How could he have ever been so foolish? All he wanted in his first moment of consciousness was to recover, to be with his little daughter, to be with Holly again.

Holly! Niko felt a different kind of pain tightening his entire being.

Babcia saw it through Joy's young eyes and read it in what little there was to see of his face. She blazed anger in the little girl's eyes that terrified him.

Joy read her father's reaction.

"Babcia," she cried suddenly. "Be the cat!" And in a moment, Emmy let out a wicked howl, and she knew that the witch had done as she was told. Now the little girl smiled brightly at her father...

A man who was suddenly very much alive!

Chapter 17
Confession

"Bless me, Father, for I have sinned."

Holly was in Father Tim's office now. It was part of his apartment in the rectory, which was attached to one wing of the hospital. He had a little kneeler that conveniently swung around so that he could hear confessions while sitting at his desk. A small latticework panel could be pulled up to provide a modicum of privacy for both parties.

"It's been a week since my last confession," Holly continued. "Since then I have...." Suddenly she broke into tears.

Father Tim realized at once that the girl had not been able to break off her relationship with her lover, even when her husband's prognosis had become so grave. She had turned more and more to John Hunter. He was her savior.

Holly hoped that somehow she could convey that feeling to the priest, but sitting there in the same hospital where her husband was showing no signs of improvement (at least as far as she knew), she felt accused, dirty, and ashamed.

Father Tim reached around the side of the small latticework partition. He took her hand. The partition was only there to avoid the embarrassment of eye-to-eye contact during the telling of sins, and so he felt no compunction now about reaching around and giving Holly the strength of his touch.

"What am I supposed to say?" she sobbed.

"Why don't you tell me about the relationship in your own words, from the beginning."

Holly heaved a heavy sigh, brushed her hair back with her free hand, and held even more tightly to Tim with her other. Yes, that was a good idea, she thought. And so she began.

"It all started when Chuck Vaughn gave my husband this great opportunity," she said. "He wanted Niko to write and direct a new TV show about Rapunzel. You know the story?"

"Yes," Father Tim whispered.

"Niko was going to have to work longer hours because there was so much that Chuck had to teach him about directing.

"Chuck can be a very grumpy guy, Father, and Niko was really feeling the strain. But instead of confiding in me, or using our weekends to get away, he just stayed at work. I'd make supper, and he wouldn't come home; he worked all weekend, every weekend; I was completely alone.

"I'd taken a job at Joy's school at the time, just volunteering and picking up a little extra money as an assistant librarian. Then, one day the principal called me into his office. I thought he was going to reprimand me or something. I really did."

Holly pulled her hand away from the priest, took a handkerchief from her pocket and dabbed the fresh tears from her eyes. Though Father Tim had removed his hand, she reached for it again. Father Tim obliged and Holly clasped it tightly.

"The principal didn't want to reprimand me, Father," she continued. "Instead he told me that he was in love with me. Can you believe that? He said that he had been watching me and the way I did things, how I interacted with the children and all, and it made him love me.

"My God, Father, LOVE, the thing I was missing the most."

Father Tim looked up at the young woman; the latticework could not hide her beauty in spite of her look of terrible guilt.

"Like a fool," she continued. "I thought I could talk him out of it. God knows I tried.

"I prayed a lot, Father, and then one day I went into the principal's office, John's office, and he started talking about his wife, and how cold she'd become. I could relate, you know, Father, because Niko..." Holly choked back a sudden sob, "...was becoming the same way." Suddenly, her sobs turned into a torrent of tears.

"Oh, Father, we were crying together, for the loss of the people we loved, who were replaced by these imposters!

"Am I making any sense?"

Tim nodded and smiled a little for her. Holly couldn't see the smile. She was looking down at her hands and couldn't meet his eyes when she began speaking again.

"That's when it happened for the first time, Father."

Tim pulled his chair closer to Holly and felt her grip tighten.

"John was crying; I was crying, and then he took me in his arms, and he began to comfort me. He held me. He kissed me and...."

Holly looked up at Father Tim with a look of desperation on her face.

"That's when I did it, Father. I did it. He was kissing me and hugging me tightly and telling me that everything would be all right, and then I did it, I opened my mouth and kissed him. I pushed my tongue into his mouth, and he let me, and he responded, and, oh, Father, it was like the first time Niko and I shared our first wild kisses, only John and I didn't stop kissing."

She closed her eyes and brought her hand up to her soft, beautiful neck.

"He began kissing me on the neck and then on my shoulders. I opened my shirt for him and let him kiss me all over, on my breasts. I pulled my bra open." Holly's hand cupped her breast as she remembered the experience, her fingers squeezing her nipple through her soft, cotton blouse.

Even with the latticework between them, Father Tim was aware of what she was doing. He also knew he should stop her or at least refuse to listen to her anymore. Somehow, he had to try and control the desire that was building within him. But he did none of those things. Instead, he slid his fingers down below the edge of his desk.

"Father," Holly moaned. "He was so passionate, and yet there was sweetness in his kisses. All my loneliness was flowing from me. He was drawing it out of me. It felt so wonderful, and I knew that I had to do something for him, Father. I had to reward him and show him that I accepted his love."

Father Tim leaned closer to Holly. She could barely make out the look in his eyes, a look of compassion. She felt his hand trembling in hers. She hesitated and looked at him questioningly.

"I shouldn't go on, Father."

Father Tim hesitated for a moment, knew she was right, but couldn't stop himself from saying, "You have to, Holly."

His free hand had made its way inside his cassock, but Holly couldn't see it and, though she could feel the desire in his touch, she chose not to believe it.

She squeezed the priest's fingers even more tightly and did not question him again.

As with so many other men in Holly Madonie's life, she simply did what he wanted her to do.

"John told me how cold his wife had become," she continued. "That she refused to have sex with him ever again. That's how I repaid him, Father.

"My breasts were so hot from his kisses that I...."

SLAM!

Someone pushed the door open so forcefully that it smashed against the wall.

It was Joy. The little girl stood before Holly and the priest. Their hands said everything. One of Holly's was on her breast; the other was intertwined with his. Father Tim's other hand was buried deep in his cassock performing motions that fortunately meant nothing to an eight-year-old girl. But they said everything to a five-hundred-year-old witch.

The face of Babcia flitted across that of the little girl. It was a face horrible in its accusations and anger. Holly pulled her hand up as though to shield her eyes. She turned to Father Tim. His expression was a strange mix of horror and fascination. It made no sense to her at all, or perhaps even to him at that moment.

"Mommy! Mommy!" the little girl called as soon as the horrid visage of Babcia had passed from her face. "It's so great, Mommy!'

"What is?" Holly somehow found a way to ask.

"It's Daddy!' Joy cried.

"HE'S AWAKE!"

Chapter 18
Mother Black

"Nasty stuff," grumbled Mother Black as she peered at the four of them (yes, four) through the swirling mists of her scrying ball. A shiver twitched its way down her back and out across her shoulders. She had seen the evil presence boiling behind the child's eyes, and she was terrified.

"Sure doan' wanna tangle wit you, Bot-cha," she mumbled through a mouthful of missing teeth. "Guess we's destined ta fight anyways, though, ain't we?

"It's sad, old grandmother," Mother Black added respectfully. "Damn-cursed sad."

She'd watched Holly's confession and seen everything that had happened through her orb, that great, dark scrying ball that she'd brought with her from the backwoods of Tennessee. She had smiled a toothless grin.

"No more funnin' fo' you two," she'd cackled. "Not no more taday, anyways. You'll have another chance ta tease yo holy boyfriend later, though. That's what yer doin', ya know, chil'. Confessin'? What rubbish. Yu's jus teasin' him!

"Best mind yer kid, now, girl. Go see if 'at husband a yours is really come back ta life. Bet he is. Too bad fo' you, chil'. Cause he is."

Mother Black had a hand in Holly's funnin'. She' had picked up the poppet that Marla Morrison had fashioned from strands of Holly's hair years before.

"Coochy coo," the witch had murmured while she'd rubbed her thumb across the large breasts that Marla had given the doll. Miles away, Holly had reacted immediately, moving her hands toward her breasts, reaching to caress them when she made her confession.

Mother Black had been laughing and enjoying herself before Joy had entered the room with her message and that hideous presence had shown behind the little girl's eyes.

"Joy, is this a joke?" Holly asked.

"No joke, Mommy," she answered. "Daddy woke up just now and smiled at me. Come see."

"Thank you, Lord," Tim said. But he could see the conflict darken Holly's face. Joy could as well, and she hated her mother for it. At that moment, Joy was part child and part all-knowing witch, and the combination was devastating.

"That's wonderful news," Holly lied to Joy.

The full fury of Babcia suddenly gleamed across Joy's face, and the little girl turned and darted from the room. That was the moment Mother Black recognized what she was up against.

"Ummm, Ummm, Bot-cha! Yo' gonna be some tuff en'my!"

Damn kids, she thought, always meddling with things they know nothing about. Always leaving it for the grown-ups to clean up afterward. Hell, she and Bot-cha were going to have to try and destroy each other when they rightly should be friends.

She set the poppet down next to the orb and pulled a black velvet cloth over both of them.

"All fer what?" she asked aloud. "Fer greed, mostly, greed an ambition."

She pushed the table holding the orb and poppet back against the wall. Then she grabbed an old corncob pipe and stuffed it between her gums. Her twisted fingers snatched a long wooden match from the table and struck it on the fireplace.

"Nasty work's a comin'," she added as she drew in the pipe smoke and held it in her lungs. "NASTY!" She blew a twisted smoke-ring that drizzled away into the air, and that's when another apparition stepped toward her out of the shadows. It was an ancient woman almost as dark and wrinkled as Babcia herself, although this woman actually seemed somehow to be alive despite being hundreds of years old. Who but a witch could have lived that long? No one else, Mother Black was sure of that.

The woman was gaunt-faced with a deep scar running from her left eye down to the corner of her mouth, and that eye, that left eye was terrifying... a white filmy thing with some obscene dark cancer roaming uncontrollably behind it. Mother Black knew that watching it, just being in its presence, in fact, would drive most humans to madness.

"So, who're you then?" asked Mother Black.

The old woman shuffled all the way up to Mother until they were almost nose-to-nose.

"Someone who knows what this is really all about," said the other witch. "And it's time you knew all of it, too."

The women stared at each other neither blinking nor flinching for as long as a minute until at last Mother Black spoke up:

"And yer name, gal..."

The old witch cackled at that. No one had called her gal in at least three centuries. "Clara's my name," she said. "Clara Goriki... an old enemy of that bitch-witch Bobcha you've been looking at."

Mother Black took another long drag on her pipe and blasted a cloud of smoke right at Clara. The old witch smiled and sucked the smoke deep into her lungs as though it were a generous gift, not some kind of test or insult.

"An just wha's yer beef wi' ol Bot-cha," Mother Black asked as she hobbled over to an old cane chair in the corner and sat. She motioned for Clara to do the same.

"Don't suppose you have any tea, do you?" Clara asked while she settled into a high back chair across from Mother Black.

"I'm a witch, ain't I?" Mother replied with a chuckle. "Course air's tea. Let me make us a pot while ya fill me in on wha's really goin on here. Obviously, it's more'n at scatterbrain Sally's tellin' me... if she even knows, at is."

And so the old black witch shuffled into her kitchen, where she took out an iron kettle and a couple of chipped pewter mugs. She spooned some tea into a tea cradle while Clara took a deep breath and slowly began to unravel a tale of hatred going back centuries, back to a small village in Poland where Babcia had transformed herself into a youthful beauty and stolen the heart of the only man Clara had ever loved.

"She broke my heart and killed my mother in the process," said Clara. "And she did *this* to me." Clara jerked her finger angrily to her dead eye and the hideous scar that ran from it to the corner of her mouth. "And now it's payback time."

"So, it's revenge yer after," Mother Black said with a cheerful smacking of her lips.

"Oh yes," Clara answered. "Revenge too for my pretty ballerina Marla who maybe tried to play both of us a little too much."

"Don't quite git yer meanin' there," Mother Black said as she brought the heavy teapot over and poured a thick serving of good black sludge into each mug.

"Well, I gave the girl many secrets," said Clara. "And in return, she was supposed to undo Babcia once and for all. But you know youngsters. Marla had other ideas. She wanted to make friends with the bitch-witch, see if old Babcia could advance her career a little. Then, once she'd gotten as much as she could get from the bitch witch, she'd kill her for me, and I'd have my revenge. But the girl was just too impulsive and too damn evil. She thought she'd please Babcia by murdering Niko's lovely wife, Holly, in order to gain a few favors."

"That Holly's a ho," Mother Black said. "I been watchin' her in action. She's even flirtin' wi a God-blessed priest."

"Well, she is slutty," said Clara. "But Niko asked Babcia to protect the girl, so when Marla invited Babcia in to witness Holly's execution... and her baby's along with her... Babcia showed up, and it was Marla that got taken down."

Mother Black nodded and smiled at the tale. "So you wants vengeance. Always liked at," she said. "Makes me feel real good ta get even with someone fer some harm they did... even if it weren't done against me."

Clara nodded and sipped her thick black tea. She was deciding she liked this old backwoods witch very much.

"So, this Babcia stole the man you loved," Mother Black summarized. "An somehow killed yo mama in the process."

Clara nodded.

"Then she undid the pretty little ballerina you sent to get even with her."

"Turned herself into a she-wolf and tore the poor girl apart," said Clara.

"Oooo, thas nasty!" Mother Black's whole body shuddered at the thought. "Guess yo is due a good piece a revenge, then, Clara. And Sally and I will be glad ta help ya."

"Thank you," said the Polish witch as she guzzled her tea. "But you know, it gets even better, old Mother. There are an awful lot of young witches who pay allegiance to Babcia. Witches everywhere want to be on her side because of the power she commands. Now, if she wasn't around, who do you think they'd have to lead them?"

"You, yerself," answered Mother Black.

"Us!" Clara added with a greedy smile.

Mother Black didn't say a word or give any hint of her reaction to the tempting suggestion. She just sat there for a long time. Then she took her cane, gestured for Clara to follow, and hobbled out into her sunlit garden.

Mother Black's garden was not unlike other witch's gardens hidden away in the San Fernando Valley. There may have been as many as a hundred of them at that time, planted mostly by witches who were forced to accompany their families into the California sunshine. Occasionally, a young woman of Marla Morrison's coven succeeded in making things grow and using them to expand her knowledge of The Craft. But the real successes were the old crones who took their work seriously and limited their ambitions.

That's how it was with Mother Black. Sally Fukes had found her deep in the mountains of Tennessee and told her all about her adventures in Hollywood and Marla and how she'd died at the hands of Witch Babcia who now inhabited the body of Niko Madonie's daughter.

Mother Black hadn't known much of Babcia's long history and so she wasn't concerned. Until now! Suddenly she had seen Babcia in the eyes of the little girl and heard Clara's story.

These were crazy times for witches; that was evident. In days gone by, there were deep forests where an old woman could hide out for decades, even centuries if need be. She could raise her cats, cast spells, and drink a little brew from time to time. It was a hard life, simple, lonely, but good. Today's witches wanted to get out into the world, not away from it. They wanted to use their powers to achieve goals other than their own personal survival.

"New kinda witches, they is," Mother Black mumbled.

Sally had had two goals, and Mother Black agreed to share them. The first one was easy: success at VVA. The Spell of Becoming had gone a long way toward achieving that. Chuck Vaughn, after all, was just another man with all the weaknesses and failings of his sex, ruled by his cock as much as anything else. He would soon be under Sally's spell, country music or not.

The second goal seemed just as easy at first: revenge. It was something Mother Black knew and understood. Get even with Niko and Holly for the terrible fate that they had brought upon Sally's mentor, Marla Morrison.

The usual revenge wasn't difficult for Mother Black. To single out victims and watch them pay for their crimes was something she'd loved doing for over a hundred and fifty years.

But now here was Clara Goriki with an even more ambitious goal, not just to exact revenge, but also gain control of the followers of the great witch herself.

"Nasty business!" Mother Black said to Clara, and the Polish witch nodded in agreement.

"But with quite a payoff," Clara added.

"Never wanted fame 'n fortune," Mother Black said.

Clara shrugged.

"Never wanted those, whatchacallems?" said Mother Black.

"Minions."

"Yeah, never wanted none a' them," But power... thas another story entirely. Might be nice."

Mother Black suddenly remembered a request she'd gotten from Sally, so she hobbled over to the little patch of rosemary that grew in the corner of the garden.

"A spell fer sexy legs," she cackled. "There's a'good en. Know that spell, Clara?"

The Polish witch smiled. "Sure, it's a popular one in Poland these days."

Clara snatched up some of the rosemary and turned toward the other end of the garden. "Let's just grab some of that milkweed over there," she said.

Mother Black hummed to herself as she plodded along after the Polish witch. She had felt so good. These little spells for Sally had been just the thing she needed to help loosen up her creaky old head-bones and brighten up her toothless smile. And toying with that strumpet Holly Madonie (tweaking the knobs of her sexiness) that was a real hoot, too, wasn't it?

Mother Black had been having the time of her life. But in the last few minutes, in her visions through the scrying ball and her conversation with Clara, she began to realize the power of her adversary and the gravity of the conflict she would soon be facing.

"Nasty stuff," she grumbled to Clara.

"Gruesome!" her guest answered, but with an eager smile.

Chapter 19
Niko Awake

Holly walked slowly to Niko's bed and sat down beside him. Except for his sad, painful eyes, his face was a mask of bandages. Yet, she didn't need to see any more. His eyes said it all. They were tragic!

She brushed away her tears. She didn't mean for this terrible thing to happen, even to a man who had acted as though she wasn't even there, who said he loved her and then ignored her completely. And now, everyone was calling it "attempted suicide"! It was just the kind of thing that she would have expected from Niko, Holly realized. He had made himself a martyr to his own selfishness.

Father Tim walked up behind Holly. For a moment Niko had no idea who he was. (John Hunter?) Niko's fists tightened, his eyes glared back at her.

"What's the use," she murmured. "I don't love you anymore, Niko. I don't," and she stood and fled from the room.

Niko reached out to catch her and stop her. He had to explain, bring her back to him. He struggled to get to his feet, but his body simply did not have the strength, and so he fell back in utter despair.

The man who had stood behind her approached him then, put his hand on his shoulder. (John Hunter put his hand on Niko's shoulder. Only, what was he doing wearing a Roman collar?) That's when Niko realized his mistake.

Anguish filled his eyes, anguish that was a crucifixion for Father Tim who knew that he, too had lusted after Niko's wife, and he still wanted her.

What kind of man am I? Father Tim wondered. What kind of a priest?

He did the only thing he could think of doing. He pulled the crucifix from around his neck and placed it into Niko's hand. The young man grabbed at it as though it were the edge of a life raft in his sea of misery. Father Tim nodded, smiled a little and stepped away making room for little Joy to approach Niko's bed.

"I'm here," Daddy," the little girl said sweetly. "And I'll take that." She pulled the crucifix from him and set it on the bedside table. "You don't need that; you have me."

Father Tim stepped forward to object, but Joy quieted him with a look that somehow reflected five hundred of years of persecution and hatred.

"I love you, Daddy," she continued as she turned back to her father. "I'll take care of you."

Niko's lips tried to form a smile beneath his bandages. His eyes brightened if only a little. Joy smiled, too, and then she glanced back at the door through which Holly had made her dramatic exit.

"I'll take care of Mommy, too," she continued. Somehow the voice of the little girl shifted with those words.

It had become the voice of Babcia.

Chapter 20
Confusion

Holly rushed from the hospital to the room at the Sheridan Universal Hotel, to the room where she and John Hunter always met. He was already there and had the champagne chilling. He looked out through the front window and saw her coming.

Holly flung opened the door, hurried in, threw her arms around him, and wilted.

She pressed her head deep into his shoulder and felt the fabric of his sports coat soaking in her tears.

"I can't stand this anymore," she called. "I can't stand HIM. He's coming back. He's awake and recovering. He's going to get well."

Hunter winced at those words.

"How can he?" Hunter asked. "He was practically dead."

He held her tightly to him. He let her pour her sorrows out through her tears. But it was all so damn wrong. What a way to fuck up a perfect situation.

"Not good," Hunter whispered to Holly. "Not good at all."

He leaned forward and pressed his lips gently against her neck. She pushed him away.

"Not now, John," she said firmly. "I can't."

Since their first encounter, Holly had never refused his advances, especially ones offered as sweetly as these. He smiled pleadingly.

"No!" she said firmly. "Not after all I've been through today."

Hunter walked across the room, turned and looked at Holly. God, he wanted her. She read the look in his eyes.

"NO!" she repeated. "I'd better go," and she stood and made her way to the door.

"Holly," he began.

"I don't know what's going on," she said suddenly. "But just now, when you tried to kiss me...."

She looked frantically for her purse, found it on the table by the door, and snatched it up at once.

"Shit! Niko is suddenly coming back into my life. I hate the idea, but...."

Hunter's face twisted as though he were longing to understand.

"I just don't know." She shook her head. Then she turned and made her way out of the door, leaving her lover to contemplate the untouched champagne...

And his unfulfilled desires.

Chapter 21
Challenges

Sally Fukes sauntered into Chuck Vaughn's office sporting a new miniskirt and legs to rival those of Marla Morrison.

"How'd ya get them pins?" Vaughn growled.

"Found a great new exercise routine," she answered swinging her hips while she showed off her shapely new legs.

"It's so intense, hard work, real hard work, but it sure is worth it. Dontcha think?"

"Sure do," Vaughn rasped eyeing her up and down with a big grin. "And not a moment too soon, either."

In spite of his gruff exterior, Charles Martin Vaughn was as happy as he'd ever been in his life.

"Niko's making a miraculous recovery," he said with a big grin. "That's all it'll take to have those MikleyToon guys close the deal and buy the place."

"Niko's recoverin'?" Sally asked trying to hide her impending panic.

"Recovering as if by magic, babe," Vaughn answered. "Or even..."

"Witchcraft?" she suggested knowing full well what it meant. He didn't like the word, didn't like the idea, but he knew that he owed much of his recent success to witches.

"We girls gotta have our fun," Sally cooed in her sweet, Southern drawl. "How kin ah help?"

Vaughn grinned. A hundred possibilities flashed through his mind, but one practical matter was paramount.

"I'm planning a big meeting with the guys from MikleyToons," he answered. "As soon as Niko recovers enough to join in a phone conversation, we're gonna do it. Haven't seen him yet. Scheduled to go down there tomorrow.

Know it'll be great. The doctors all say he's alert and ready to think about work."

"Is he?" Sally cooed as she pulled herself up onto the very edge of Vaughn's big animation desk. Her skirt rose with her, sliding high up on her thighs.

She'd never gotten a leer from any sober man like the one he was giving her now. She giggled and crossed her legs.

"How do ah fit in?" she asked.

Vaughn didn't answer for a long moment. He was transfixed by Sally's exciting new shape. Then he caught himself, blushed, cleared his throat, and continued.

"Pull the whole meeting together for me," he said. "Make all the arrangements. Then come in looking just the way you do right now. That ought to seal the deal, doll. You're gorgeous!"

"Thank ya," she answered as she slid off the desk and sashayed right up to him. "But I can do even more if ya want me to."

She leaned forward and ran her fingers across his chest and up the side of his cheek. The great animator closed his eyes and held his breath. This was going to be a beautiful relationship. Of course, there was one more thing he needed badly: a way to hedge his bets, just in case Niko wasn't quite a hundred percent. He swallowed hard. He'd figured it all out during another one of his sleepless nights. All he had to do was put it into words.

"Want to try the impossible?" he whispered.

"Love to," Sally answered.

"Then find a way to bring Marla Morrison back."

Sally shrieked and took three large steps backward. "But she's DAID!"

She'd hoped for an invitation into his bedroom, of course. But after only a moment, she realized this was okay, too. This was an intriguing new challenge. Mother Black might even be able to find a way to do it, sort of.

"Maybe ah kin do that fer ya," she whispered at last. "If ya'll will do one little thing fer me."

"What's that?" he asked.

She cocked her hip and grinned. "Let me come with ya when ya visit Niko."

Chuck Vaughn was actually sweating. He was not a great womanizer, but he'd had his share of admirers and here before him was one of the most beautiful staring him right in the face.

"How can I say 'no,'" he answered. "After all, I...."

He was unable to finish the sentence. Sally was on him, mounting him as though he were the kind of mechanical bull she was used to riding at those damn cowboy bars of hers. And she did ride him, on that great animator's chair, swiveling and bucking like some hot little cowgirl on her first big night at the rodeo.

And Mother Black watched it all from miles away. She saw everything through her scrying ball. Oh, she wished that she had a less impulsive, less wild pupil, one who thought for a moment before she made rash promises that would take caldrons of witchcraft to fulfill.

But then, she did provide interesting challenges, didn't she? Mother Black realized with a smile.

"Bring 'em on," she muttered. "Even that bitch-witch Botcha.

"Bring her on, too."

Chapter 22
Tim and Niko

Father Tim peered through the doorway into Niko's room. The young man was sitting up in bed. Most of the bandages had been taken from his face, though a large gauze pad was still taped firmly over the worst part of his wound. Still, his expression was far from healthy. He looked as though he were in anguish. Father Tim thought he should be as positive as he could.

"You're looking much better," the priest said as he stepped into the room.

Niko grimaced.

"Not feeling it, Father," he said.

"It'll take a little time."

"More than a little," Niko moaned. "Everything is coming back to me now. I'm starting to think about Holly and her lover."

"Is that why you tried to kill yourself?" the priest asked.

"You think I tried to kill myself?" This was the first Niko had heard the rumor that everyone else believed.

"Didn't you?"

Niko smirked and shrugged. It was almost funny, he thought.

"I bought the gun to kill John Hunter, planned to find him on his morning walk, stop him along his way and then I would...."

Niko popped off a shot with his finger. It was pointed right at the priest.

"That night I was just waiting for dawn, absolutely certain about what I had to do. I was just looking at the gun, sort of playing with it. I was certainly tense, but I never planned to do anything but get the bastard."

His entire body tightened as he remembered. "And the next thing I knew, I... was here."

"So, it wasn't suicide?" Tim asked as though murder was far less of a crime, and according to his church, it was.

"Next time," Niko murmured.

Father Tim flinched.

"Maybe we can get you headed in the right direction instead," he said softly. "Holly loves you."

Niko shook his head. "Sure doesn't seem that way."

"I've talked to her, prayed with her. I know she wants to try and work things out."

Father Tim was lying, and he knew it. But it was for a good cause. In spite of his frustration with Holly, in spite of the things she said, in spite of his own sinful desires about her, he believed that she really did love her husband and that he could bring the two back together. It would be difficult and painful, but that might make it something of a healing penance for them all.

In that instant, the priest suddenly saw himself in confession fifteen years ago. It was the confession that had changed his life.

He was in his last year at the junior seminary, as obsessed with girls that year as any other sixteen-year-old boy.

Still, his obsession was different. It had a very dark side to it, and that dark side was Marla. She came to him in his dreams to seduce him. Little Timmy never saw Marla again after he was sent to the seminary, but Tim Brennan did. He saw a perfect image of the girl who would be nineteen years old by then.

Sometimes she slunk into his dreams in the dark robes of a witch looking very much as she had under that tree on Buena Vista Street. And as she drew closer to him, she'd peel off the robes until she wore absolutely nothing. Sometimes she would reach behind her and pull out a bright red shiny apple. She'd bite into it and let the rich juice moisten her lips and drool down her chin.

"Join me, Timmy," she would murmur. "Your mother can't reach us now." Then she would burst suddenly into his worst concept of a witch, a withered old hag with claw-like hands reaching for his eyes, and he would wake up sweating bullets.

The witch/apple dream wasn't the worst of it, though. There were others. Sometimes he would envision her dancing, just for him.

"Do I excite you?" she'd ask. "It's a sin, you know, a mortal sin, and you'll burn in hell for it!"

Then the freckle-faced witch would smile her saucy little smile as she produced the poppet. She'd begin stroking it, though not in the soft tickly places she had when Timmy was just ten. Her goal now was to drive him wild, and she did: teasing, stroking, sometimes rubbing the poppet over her own body, which was so wickedly alive before him.

Another wet dream, Tim would realize when he awoke in a puddle of milky ooze. Maybe it was her gift to him. If so, there were hundreds of those gifts over that year.

"It's Satan speaking to you," old Monsignor Donavan would whisper from behind the confessional latticework. "The devil created women's bodies to tease and torment us and lead us away from our intended work."

Even Tim Brennan as young, impressionable, and tempted as he'd been since that first midnight visit with Marla, did not believe the old man. And yet there was something exciting about the idea, wasn't there, something very thrilling about the concept of witchcraft and women using their beautiful bodies to lure men to their doom.

#

"Father," Niko called, and the young priest suddenly snapped out of his reverie. It took him a moment to remember where he was and what he had to do.

"The doctors tell me you're getting better," he said to Niko. "So why don't we just start focusing on the good things in your life."

"There are no good things," answered Niko solemnly.

"There's Holly and the fact that we can save your marriage."

Niko just shook his head sadly.

"And your daughter," said Father Tim. "Think about her."

Niko just sighed: his daughter...and his grandmother. "She's a witch, you know," he whispered.

"Your daughter?"

"Her great grandmother lives inside her. She was a witch who lived in Poland hundreds of years ago. She has that kind of power."

Father Tim shook his head. He searched Niko's eyes for some sign that he was joking but saw none.

"My grandmother, my Babcia, as I used to call her, has haunted me all my life," Niko continued. "And here's something for you, Tim. She killed Marla Morrison."

"She started the fire that killed Marla?"

"Marla was dead before the fire ever started, mauled to death by Babcia who had turned herself into a wolf.

"A grandmother who is a witch, a witch who is a wolf..." Niko murmured.

Tim again looked at the young man for some sign that it was all a joke. Again he saw none and shook his head in disbelief.

"Want me to prove it to you?" Niko asked. "Holly and Joy are coming to see me in a few minutes. She just called to tell me. I can almost guarantee that Babcia will be with them. I may be able to make her show herself. Would you like to see that?"

Tim was amazed. And yet, to see another witch! He nodded hesitantly, and Niko smiled. He liked the idea of challenging this uptight priest.

"You'll have to hide, though," Niko continued. "She'll never show herself if she knows you're here."

"Not my style at all," Tim began, but then they heard Holly and Joy coming down the hall. Tim looked around in confusion, and just as the little girl and her mother reached the door, he ducked into the small closet at the back of Niko's hospital room.

Chapter 23
Reconciliation

Joy felt as though there were a caged animal inside her, scratching wildly at every corner of her being, trying desperately to escape. She was immediately sorry that her mother had told her not to bring Emmy. At least Joy could have exiled Babcia to that poor creature. But now she could not, and so she felt the witch's desperate effort to break free. Something was very wrong in her father's hospital room or was about to be.

Joy could feel the sense of impending doom.

Holly's emotions were almost as unsettled. The thought of Niko coming back to her was suddenly a good thing, as though she'd realized that what she'd assumed was a suicide attempt might have been his way of reaching out to her. He'd survived, after all, hadn't he? Maybe now he could become the husband she remembered loving so much.

She had made herself as radiant as she knew how, had put on her most enticing dress, the latest style of the sexy yet innocent clothing she'd worn when she and Niko had first met. She'd even worn her sexy wedding lingerie. If things worked out well enough, she thought, she might even tease Niko a little. Still, she was very nervous.

"God, please make it go well," she pleaded.

Somehow she'd managed to put off all contact with John Hunter. He'd called her a dozen times a day, but she'd ignored every call. She wasn't even sure why, except that the hope she could rebuild her broken marriage was becoming stronger and stronger.

"Hi," was all she said when she finally came face to face with her husband. He had lost about twenty pounds during his hospital stay, but his face looked good, clean-shaven, handsome, cute anyway, except for that horrible mess of bandages on the right side. She could only imagine what it covered.

Niko smiled up at his beautiful wife, still as sweet and innocent-looking as the day he'd met her, still sporting that choir-girl blonde hair tucked neatly under at the ends, still looking at him with those starry green eyes, still with a clear, smooth complexion and full lips that he longed so desperately to kiss. And then she was kissing him, softly, lovingly and suddenly passionately. He reached around behind her and pulled her to him. God, he wanted her.

Holly wrestled away from Niko though her eyes flamed with passion. She glanced over toward Joy. Niko nodded. Not in front of his little girl, he realized. Joy smiled. She would have been delighted at the sight of her mother and father kissing, but she still had a horrible feeling that something very wrong was about to happen, and as a result, the witch within her was going absolutely wild.

"I'm so sorry," Niko whispered.

"So am I," Holly answered. She reached into the shopping bag she'd brought with her and pulled out a little pink plaid stuffed elephant. Niko recognized it at once. He'd won it for her on their very first date. Beside it, she placed another familiar item; a portrait he'd taken of her when they were first going out. She looked so very young, so very sad. She had written something on the back of the photo:

"Thank you for finding me and loving me,

"Your lost little girl."

Holly sat down on the bed beside her husband. She took his hand and held it tight against her chest. Together they cried tears of both sorrow and forgiveness. From inside the closet Father Tim smiled and cried a little himself. And then an evil thought crossed his mind. He was losing her.

Holly pressed Niko's hand tighter against her breasts. He tried to move his hand.

"Don't get any ideas," she whispered with a little grin, and the two of them burst out laughing.

In the corner of the room, Joy watched happily, but the witch within her did not. Evil was yet to come. That much was certain.

Would it come from the being in the closet? Babcia wondered. She sensed his presence. Was he the threat? That... priest! Babcia felt contempt for him.

Holly reached into her purse and pulled out a greeting card. It was one of those touchy-feely message cards that had recently become so popular. She handed the card to Niko. He took it and pulled the card from its violet envelope.

It featured a saccharine illustration of lilac sprigs, the kind that they'd grown up with in Rochester, New York. Between the lilacs were the words,

"Please forgive me."

Niko reached up and touched the side of Holly's face. He pulled her to him, and she kissed him again.

"Open it," she whispered. And so he did.

Inside the card were the words:

"...For all my weakness and for all that's happening."

Niko winced when he read it.

If he could only have understood that it was just a bad choice of words. If only he could have pulled the greeting card writer up before him and used the gun he'd purchased to blow the writer's brains out. "Bad choice of words" should be a capital offense for greeting card writers punishable by death! But it's not. They go on with their lives; they're as happy as can be with little thought of the effect their crime has on the poor unfortunates who misunderstand.

"All that's happening?" The words were like a fire igniting in Niko's brain. Did that mean "all that's *still* happening" is STILL GOING ON? Was his wife still fucking John Hunter?

Niko's face twisted with sudden and irrational fear. Holly's hopeful smile faded.

"All that's happening? What do you mean by that?" was the accusatory question Niko threw at her. It was another bad choice of words, a very bad choice. Holly recoiled in disbelief. Her eyes shot the accusation back at her husband. His eyes were firm and hateful, and just like that, the attempted reconciliation had ended.

Holly stood. She snatched the card from her husband and shoved it back into her shopping bag. Then she grabbed the little elephant and the photo and did the same.

"Why do I even try?" she sobbed. "Come on, Joy. We're going!"

Little Joy jumped up. "But Mommy."

"WE'RE GOING!"

Joy sobbed as her mother grabbed her by the hand and marched her toward the door.

"Goodbye, Daddy. I love you," she called as Holly dragged her from the room. The beautiful woman did not even look back. As far as she was concerned, everything was settled.

That son of a bitch husband of hers! She had tried. Oh, how she had tried. And now all she wanted to do was get away from him and never see him again. She wanted to find John, hold him in her arms, bury her head on his shoulder, and cry her heart out.

Joy, for her part, felt the witch scrambling desperately within her. This broken reconciliation was bad enough, but it was hardly the evil that was to come. That would be so much worse. Babcia had to escape so she could stay behind and protect her beloved grandson, but through whom? In that closet, that thing, that priest in the closet? Could she enter *his* body?

Never!

Possess Holly, then? Turn her around; go back to Niko and save him. NO! The whore who had nearly destroyed the most precious thing in her entire eight-hundred-year life? That idea brought an even more emphatic NEVER!

And so the witch stayed within the little girl. She snarled and raged like some wild wolf, letting her own evil pride prevent her from protecting Niko. Hopefully, he would survive what was to come. She could restore his health once again, as long as he lived. But raising the dead was not within Babcia's ken, and she knew it.

Holly's high heels echoed as she marched down the empty corridor. The soft patter of Joy's little sneakers accompanied them.

The corridors were so empty; no other living soul was present, no being that Babcia could inhabit. And so she left the hospital, and within only a few seconds, before Father Tim could safely extricate himself from the closet...

The horrible danger arrived.

Chapter 24
Witch Sally

Chuck Vaughn strode proudly into the room with the sexy witch on his arm. Sally was done-up in a sweet Southern sizzle that she knew would keep Chuck (perhaps even Niko) under her spell.

Her jeans were powder blue and fit so tightly that every curve of the girl's shapely body was "tricked out" to perfection. She had unbuttoned her country-white cotton blouse with little eyelets in all the right places just enough to reveal the traces of her sexy lace bra. The heels on her black cowgirl boots were so high that she towered over the famed animator. And he seemed to love it.

Chuck Vaughn expected the best when he entered Niko's room, yet he found the worst. When he caught sight of the young man, he stopped dead.

Niko's eyes were dark and teary; his shoulders sagged under the weight of utter hopelessness. His lips were drawn into a thin, tragic line. His hands were shaking. He looked up at his mentor and at the wondrous apparition beside him and said absolutely nothing. He just stared at them as though they weren't even there.

"Niko," Chuck said as he stepped to the bed, "What the hell's goin' on, boy? You're supposed to be doing great; the doctors say so, say that you'll be out of here in no time."

Niko looked up at the great man, recognized him, let a thin smile tease the corners of his lips, and reverted to that look of absolute despair.

"Niko," Vaughn called, grabbing the young man's arm. "We need you! Got a great deal cookin'. You and I will be working for MikleyToons. Think of that! Think of the great things we can do, the money we'll make. Hell, with the stock you've got in VVA, just signing the deal will make you a millionaire."

Niko's eyes were as tragic as ever. They searched Vaughn's face for a look of understanding and perhaps acceptance. They found none.

"Holly," Niko whispered.

Vaughn rolled his eyes and looked back at Sally in exasperation.

"Hell with that bitch," he responded and started to pace around the room. "You'll be so damn rich by the end of the month that you'll have women draped all over you, women sexier than Holly, women more beautiful than she is. Whoever you want, we'll find her for you.

"Remember Sally, here?" Vaughn asked and gestured toward his new/old receptionist.

Sally stepped forward. "Hi, howdy," she called.

Niko looked at her for a moment, looked her up and down, then rolled over with his face to the wall, turning his back on both of them.

"Motherfucker!" Vaughn shouted and grabbed an entire pack of gum, unwrapped it in a wild shuffle, and crammed all five sticks into his mouth.

"Listen to me, Niko," he slobbered, "We need you, boy. You can be out of here in a week. We can be talking to Mikley in two. You and I can be rich as kings in three. Hell, if it's sex you want, Sally will give you the best blowjob you've ever had in your life, right now."

"Love to," Sally cooed and she sidled up to Niko and ran her hand up and over his arm.

Niko pushed her away in anger. And then just a moment later, his whole body began to quiver with deep sobs.

"Shit!" gummed Vaughn. "You can't do this to me, Niko!" He ran his trembling fingers through his hair, mouthed a few terrible words at Sally, and stormed out of the room without a backward glance.

Sally stayed behind, though. She made no attempt to follow the great animator. Why should she? She had work to do.

"Niko," she whispered. Her voice had transformed into Holly Blue's. Niko lurched around in the bed and stared at his beloved. Only it was Sally that he saw, of course. But in Niko's troubled mind, she looked exactly like....

"Marla!" he screamed out loud and drew back in terror.

Looking on from the closet, Father Tim saw another view of the transformation. He saw Sally become Marla, and somehow his old love turned toward him for just a moment and flashed a sexy smile. But then she turned her attention back to Niko and a further transformation ensued.

"Oh, I'm not Marla," the beautiful witch hissed when she moved toward him. Slowly, hideously, she began to shift into the evil personification of the darkest powers of witchcraft and of death itself. Her left eye clouded and a deep scar stretched from it to the corner of her mouth. Her hair was brittle gray straw, her face gaunt. She became Clara Goriki!

Sally's boots became low, dust-worn scraps of shoes that soon disappeared under baggy stockings that drooped down over them. Then they, too, were completely hidden by the long rags of her skirt.

The curvaceous figure that Sally had gained through The Spell of Becoming was changed once again. This time it became the stick-figure form of an ancient woman.

Sally raised her hand, and Niko could see her knuckles swell with arthritis, her fingers twisting until they became claws. Pockmarked skin sagged from them. The bones in her arms and legs twisted as well, bending her, stooping her over into a haggard, broken shape that was Clara in her most horrific persona.

Somehow this evil manifestation of witchcraft eluded Father Tim while the witch's back was still to him. He could not see the horrible transformation that was taking place on the countenance of pretty Sally Fukes. But Niko could. And he didn't care.

"Yes, kill me," Niko said and smiled into the face of Clara Goriki. "KILL ME!" And Clara attempted to oblige. She stretched her long, gnarled, decomposing fingers toward the wound on Niko's head. She smiled a cold, rotting smile. He smiled back bravely before feeling the knife-sharp slash of her claws into his wound, down his cheek, and across his throat.

Blood erupted at once. It squirted wildly all over his face. Niko continued to smile in defiance as blood flowed over his cheeks and across his lips. He laughed in the face of the witch as he grew weaker. But soon his eyes rolled up into his head; his body went limp, and he fell back upon the bed. A hideous cackle burst from Clara.

"My God," Father Tim screamed. He burst from the closet, grabbed the witch and spun her toward him.

The sight of her face made him pull his hands up to shield himself. It was now a seething mass of maggots swarming out of her eye sockets, spiders crawling through the tangled clumps of her hair, and snakes boiling up through her ears and out of her mouth.

This deadly Clara gave the priest a hideous smile and breathed the stomach-churning stench of a thousand rotting corpses into his face.

"Noooooooooo!" Tim cried.

It was a loud, desperate, wretched call that echoed through the halls of the hospital reaching nurses' stations where they knew Father Tim's voice. They could tell he was in trouble and came running.

Father Tim gasped for breath. He fell to the floor clutching his throat as he suffocated. Across the room, Niko was dying from the loss of blood.

Clara let out another wild cackle and spun from the room, transforming once again into the shapely form of sexy Sally.

Oh, Mother Black would be so proud of her now, Sally thought. The old southern witch would surely be viewing it all in her scrying ball and would be elated. She'd gained the revenge they both had sought on Marla's behalf. And by letting the spirit of Clara participate...

MARLA WAS TRIUMPHANT!

Interlude Three

The young witches were gasping for breath. Some were in tears. Chantel Brown gaped back at Wicktor, her eyes bright with terror.

"That can't be possible, sir," she begged. "Not that."

The warlock insinuated himself up to her, his mouth curled into a heartless snicker. "Too cruel for the likes of you, lovely Chantel?"

The girl pressed her hand hard against her chest and nodded breathlessly.

"Then what the hell are you doing here?" he shouted and turned on the rest of his coven. "What are you all doing here if you're not ready to shed a little blood... spin a little terror?"

"But Mr. Warlock," began Morgan Cummings. "I don't think that it's right that...."

The Warlock roared his disapproval.

"Not right? Not right, young witches? Don't you know why you're here? Aren't you aware of the evil business we're preparing? Why, before we finish with our session, all of you will share in an act that is every bit as heartless as the one Mistress Goriki carried out against Niko Madonie.... Only it will be upon a far more innocent subject, believe me."

The girls looked at each other in horror.

"But, Wicktor, who would that be?" asked Matryoshka.

"You'll know that soon enough," answered the warlock. "Before my tale is finished, you'll know who, and you'll have learned to be as bloodthirsty as any raving maniac who ever tore the arms off of an infant."

"Murder an infant?" gasped Chantel.

Megan Cummings suddenly darted from her place on the steps and ran to the edge of the woods where she stooped in the darkness and vomited. Her motion set off bleating from the

116

goats penned up in the outer edges of the circle. Fortunately for the girl, their noise covered up the terrible retching and choking and gagging that accompanied her sickness.

"But surely you're not saying, sir," Chantel begged. "That there's no room in a witch's heart for tenderness."

Wicktor turned to see the innocent, black girl almost pleading with him for a hopeful answer. He shrugged.

"Yes, sure, certainly there are moments when a witch can be as kind and gentle as anyone," he said, perhaps realizing that he needed to sooth his brood a little if only to better indoctrinate them into the ways of witchcraft.

"Then tell us of those tender moments, Mr. Warlock," said Morgan Cummings. She was clearly the stronger of the two highborn sisters.

"Yes, Wicktor," said Matryoshka. "Give us an example."

"An example right from Babcia's own life… would that serve the purpose?" Wicktor asked.

Megan Cummings finally made her way back out of the shadows and was able to sit beside her sister again. She'd managed to wipe the vomit from her lips, but her skin was still as green as witches' brew.

"Yes, an example of the tenderness of witches would be splendid," she croaked.

Wicktor chuckled. "You want an excellent example of how tender a witch can be?"

"Oh yes," came a collective sigh from the entire coven.

"Very well then," said the warlock as he made his way back to the center of the circle and sat down again. He pulled an obscene cigar from out of his shirt pocket, pushed it half way into his mouth and sucked on it for a moment before pulling it out, biting off one end, putting that end into his mouth and lighting the other with a bit of a twig that he pulled from the fire.

"Now. Listen."

#

Julia Krawkowska, kindhearted neighbor of Walter Sapalski, oh so many centuries ago, watched and listened to the songs that the handsome young man sang to the dying old man every day for weeks. But what did she hear, really? What did she see? Not much of it, except for that one brief moment, when the youth passed in front of Walter's small looking glass, and Julia caught an uneven reflection. It was not really a young man at all, but Walter's own little daughter somehow cloaked in a dark shroud that brought her to the size of a strong and hale youth, the one shape that no one would challenge on a dark and evil night.

Yet that reflection was so true: the look of little Michalina, the tears of the little girl, the love and the kindness in her eyes, and the whispered songs meant to bring joy to the old man's heart.

But of course, Julia could not breathe a word of this to anyone. For she understood its meaning and its consequences. There was only one way that little Michalina could take on the shape of so vital a youth, wasn't there? There was only one way that she could minister so lovingly and expertly to her father. There was only one way that she could fill his failing heart with such vivid images of peace and hope, and there was only one way that she could have survived after being taken from her home as a child:

WITCHCRAFT!

Julia Krawkowska knew the penalty for consorting with witches, and so she kept her knowledge a secret, even as she watched every day as Michalina (in the guise of a hearty young man) rode Arra out into the woods to capture game to feed her dying father. Even as Julia smelled the delicious stews that scented the soft evening air as Michalina prepared meals that she hoped would somehow restore the old man's strength. Even as Julia saw Michalina (still as a young man) emerge from the home with her arm around old Walter, as though she were giving him one last taste of sunlight, bringing to life the visions that she had sung about so sweetly. And though there was pain in the old man's eyes and in his every movement, he spoke with joy and hope in the tone a father would take with his precious little girl.

#

Julia was startled only four weeks later by the mournful call of a great wolf that circled through the forest and around old Walter's home. She ducked away from her own bedroom window lest it see her and attack, but the wolf had no interest in her. It approached the front door of Walter's home where Michalina, still dressed as a young man, soon emerged carrying a sack, which must surely have been the remains of Walter himself.

She set out at once digging in the yard in back of the house, creating a long, deep grave in which to deposit the body of her beloved father. The wolf stood nearby and filled the night with such sorrowful wailing that even Julia was moved to tears. The cacophony went on for hours as the girl, (who seemed so much to be a powerful young man) dug the grave so deep that it was well over her own head when she finished.

Then slowly, gently she lowered the old man's body into it. She tossed a handful of dirt in after the body and began refilling the hole. The wolf increased its wailing and soon other wolves in the woods around joined in until the entire world seemed filled with a deep animal mourning that would have sent chills through the souls of the Wynofski brothers if they were only sober enough to understand.

At last, the grave was nearly filled when Michalina pulled the large cloak from her shoulders and thrust it into the grave as well. She was once more a little girl, a little girl who added the final shovelfuls of dirt before she fell down on her knees and wept uncontrollably.

The great wolf approached her, pawed softly at her as though trying to comfort her, and whimpered tragically. And with that whimpering, the whole forest of wolves took up the chorus until the night became filled with universal sorrow.

Little Michalina put her arms around the great beast and hugged it. She took two sticks and bound them together into a cross and placed it at the head of the grave.

"As you wished, Papa," she whispered.

She turned and gathered a handful of flowers from the garden nearby and scattered them about.

"Goodbye, Papa," she whispered. Then she turned and set off into the darkest part of the woods...

With the wolf walking slowly beside her.

Chapter 25
Rootin' Tootin'

Emmy, the cat, scurried through the nighttime, aware that there was very little time. She had to collect the necessary ingredients if she were to save Babcia's grandson. Of course, the most important ingredient was the most difficult to obtain: blood from the witch who had destroyed him.

Babcia needed the cat to help her traverse the distance from her home with Joy and Holly to the run-down bungalow where Sally Fukes lived.

Emmy (Babcia) stopped cold with a sudden realization. Sally was not the only witch involved in these matters. There were others, ancient and far more malevolent creatures helping Sally along. And with that understanding, the images of Mother Black and Clara Goriki poured into Babcia's consciousness. Within the sleek body of the cat, Babcia trembled. The last thing she needed at that moment was a confrontation with an ancient enemy.

Sally was a wannabe; she knew a few simple tricks, but she hadn't lived in dark forests for hundreds of years. She was no match for Babcia. But Mother Black was an entirely different matter, and Clara Goriki was even worse.

Of course, Babcia faced more obstacles than a trio of witches. Transportation had become a major issue. Since entering Joy's body, Babcia found that she no longer had the freedom to move about as a spirit. She had to possess someone or something and move that being to get where she was going. She'd actually known the trade-off before she'd become part of Joy, but what a limitation it had turned out to be. Now she couldn't return to the spirit world or escape the bounds of Joy's or Emmy's or ANYONE'S body until that vessel was broken, until whoever she possessed had died.

Emmy cut in front of an oncoming truck as she skittered across the highway. The cat had no desire to make things easier for Babcia by becoming road kill. She'd have some say in the matter. After all, it was her body.

Babcia felt a rush of pain; it was Niko. The witch was desperately tuned-in to the boy's feelings, and she knew how close he was to death. The doctors were working feverishly to save him. But they had no magic at all, just science and medicine.

What chance did he have?

As Emmy approached Sally's home, she could feel the eyes of Mother Black staring at her. The old woman knew she was coming and was waiting for her. What to do?

Babcia (Emmy) needed buckets of blood, Sally's blood, and even worse, Clara's blood, and she needed it in a hurry. She had to get it back to her home where she could brew up the potion that would save Niko's life. It would all take time, especially when she was traveling by CAT!

A head-to-head confrontation with the trio of witches would be time-consuming and destructive, and Sally might just escape in the process.

What to do?

Trick Mother Black maybe, trick a one hundred-and-fifty-year-old black witch-woman from the hills of Tennessee, a woman who was watching her every move through her scrying ball. Confront Clara and; get into that same old awful argument about Clara's love for the man Babcia eventually bewitched and married.

It wasn't going to be easy to outwit a pair of ancient crones, Babcia thought while she directed Emmy to jump up into the tree that grew beside Sally's home. And, just like that, the tree began to twitch and close its branches around her attempting to cage her in. The witches were already at work. Emmy leaped from the tree's clutches high up into the air, then down through the chimney, and what a dark, sooty mess that was. She coughed and choked her way through the chimney and out of the fireplace.

Rootin'Tootin', Sally's huge bulldog, named for Sally's idea of her exciting lifestyle and the dog's disgusting ability to break noisy and noxious wind, spotted the cat and at once gave chase. Emmy shook the soot from her as she dodged across the room just beyond the jaws of the clumsy bulldog. She raced down the hall and through a door that was only slightly ajar. It was the door to the bathroom. Emmy kicked it closed behind her, right in Rootin' Tootin's face. The dog responded with an ear shattering, deadly fart that Emmy was glad to know was on the other side of the door.

The whole thing was a bit of nasty good fortune though: good fortune for Niko and Emmy, nasty for Sally Fukes.

The now-beautiful cowgirl-witch was up to her eyeballs in bubble bath, washing off the last vestiges of the Crone, masturbating just a little as she thought of the effect her new looks were having on men. Even Niko had had a little glint in his eye, she decided.

She was luxuriating in the sensuous warmth, singing along with old country and western songs on the radio.

She was totally unaware of the danger about to pounce upon her. And pounce it did.

Emmy took one look at her intended victim, opened her claws, and dove headlong into the mountain of bubbles.

"OH MY GOD!" cried Sally as she felt the cat's talons dig into her. Then there was violent screaming and snarling and tearing of flesh as cat and witch tried to claw each other to death in the slippery wetness.

Half the bathroom was a churning mass of blood and soapy water and bubbles when Mother Black and Clara Goriki pushed open the door and hobbled into the scene in their stocking feet. Just as awkwardly, Rootin'Tootin' followed right behind the witches and immediately lost his footing when he hit the soapy foam. Tootin' slid past Mother Black and crashed into the wall with yet another noxious fart; then he bounced directly back into the old women and pitched them both headfirst into the tub.

From that moment on, it was a tangle of claws and teeth and arms and legs and stringy hair and twisted witch-rags and bloody eyeballs and torn flesh, and screams and curses all set to the best country tunes.

Then suddenly everything stopped. The water settled. There was not a breath, not a movement, not a sound of any kind except for the blaring radio.

Emmy scrambled from the bloody foam and fell to the floor, panting desperately. Lucky for her that Rootin'Tootin' had been knocked unconscious.

Slowly then, the torn body of Sally Fukes rose from the slimy tub; blood pouring from the wicked scratches across her chest and face and especially from her neck. Her skin was now a shriveled, pasty white, and her hair hung in ugly ropes around her face. Her eyes held the blankness of the possessed. In her hand, she held the entire severed arm of Clara Goriki shriveled with age and bathwater yet still gushing blood.

Sally marched like a zombie down the steps into Mother Black's room where she leaned over the great caldron that was sitting in the corner. She rang out the arm and let its blood squirt into the pot. Then she opened her mouth and let another half bucket of her own blood and slime spew into the caldron.

Sally then turned toward Mother Black's shelves-full of ingredients, and still zombie-like, she gathered herbs and potions and slithering creatures to add to the mix.

Soon a great black cloud rose above the caldron. Sally summoned up winds to carry it to the hospital where Niko Madonie lay on the operating table. He breathed in the cloud and regained his strength almost at once. The doctors would credit his miraculous recovery to their great skill and science. Babcia, of course, knew better. It was she, after all, who had taken over the body of Sally and used it to do her work.

Now she navigated Sally back into the bathroom, right up next to the panting body of the cat. Babcia stepped from Sally's body to that of the exhausted feline. She forced Emmy to pull herself out into the darkness where she could lick her wounds and recover, much as Sally and Clara and Mother Black would soon recover from their soggy battle and horrific dismemberment.

Sally would require major witchcraft to restore beauty to her disfigured body. Clara would need even more magic to become whole again. And Mother Black, without that lovely coat of grime that felt so gosh awful comfertin', would be left to further ponder the power, the cunning, and the amazing luck...

Of Babcia the witch.

Chapter 26
Goodness

Everything was darkness, then a little sliding sound, and sixteen-year-old Timmy Brennan found himself looking into the illuminated latticework of the Junior Seminary confessional.

"Bless me, Father, for I have sinned," Tim began. "It's been a day since my last confession."

"Not very long," said the soft, clear voice on the other side of the latticework. "Maybe you shouldn't come so often."

Timmy was stunned. It was a voice he'd never heard before, certainly not the raspy, judgmental drone of old Monsignor Donavan. Must be a visiting missionary, Timmy decided, called back from some remote village in Africa for a little R & R, and probably damn glad of it. Timmy almost felt that he was talking to a friend.

"Problem is, I have this terrible addiction," he continued. "Impure thoughts, impure touches. It happens all the time, even when I sleep."

"That's not really an addiction," the voice responded.

"But there's this girl," Timmy said, "I think about her all the time. I know her, and she comes after me in my dreams. She told me once that she was a witch. Father, she wants me, and she's incredible."

"An incredible witch," came the bemused response from the other side of the latticework.

"An incredibly sexy witch."

"That's how the devil works," the voice answered after a moment. "He fascinates us."

"Good word. That's how it feels."

"The trick," the voice continued, "is to turn away from Satan and all his fascination, start believing in your own goodness. Start accepting it, building on it."

Timmy liked that idea. And in that instant, another idea came to him, and this one was so amazing, so uncommon to his experience and so original that he felt it must have come directly from God himself. At that moment, he suddenly believed, even knew, that he was GOOD and that someday he could do great and wonderful things. Timmy knelt there basking in the warmth of the idea. He would become a priest. That's how he would make it all happen, preserve his goodness, share his experience, and accomplish wonderful things.

In a hospital room sixteen years later, with witch-horror darkness all around him, Father Tim opened his eyes.

Even more than the horrible Crone who had thrown him into unconsciousness, he remembered that confession and knew suddenly that believing in his own goodness would not be easy at all. From now on, it would be a terrible challenge. And that was simply because he was aware of the very first word he'd spoken upon awakening from the witch attack in Niko's hospital room.

The word was "Fascination."

Interlude Four

"I don't like it," said Chantel Brown as she sat on the stone bench two rows up from the circle where the warlock sat telling his story. Behind him, the great fire smoldered. It was now only a poor shadow of the blaze that had so filled the night with flickering images and frightening shadows.

"My story's all true," said the warlock.

"Maybe so," said Chantel. "But for Mother Black to be defeated so easily...."

The warlock laughed. "You think it was easy for the cat to dive into that tub full of dirt and slime and allow Babcia to shift into the body of Sally Fukes? You think it was easy for Babcia to rip off the arm of a witch at least four hundred years younger than she was, then reattach it after she'd drained enough blood to create the potion that would save her grandson's life?"

"I didn't say those things were easy," protested Chantel.

The warlock stood and glided up to the row where the young ebony witch sat, robe fallen away from her long legs, back arched, breasts upturned, eyes wide with anger. He was still puffing on his obscene black cigar, still basking in the attention of all the young witches who followed him with their eyes as he made his way to Chantel.

"Mother Black should have put up a far greater struggle than that," said Chantel.

The warlock pulled the big cigar from his mouth and pointed the fiery end at her face as though he meant to brand her right in the center of her forehead.

"This is about solidarity, isn't it?" he asked. "Black Power or something like that?"

"We don't use those words anymore," Chantel answered. "I'm merely questioning the fact that a strong black woman could be bested by an eight-hundred-year-old witch trapped in the body of a drowning cat."

The warlock shrugged. "Well yes, when you put it that way." And he broke into roaring laughter that was immediately echoed in the cry of ravens and the bleating of goats. Then his eyes turned cold again. He moved the cigar even closer to the beautiful young witch... brought it just below her left eye.

"You're questioning the word of the leader of this coven," he said.

Chantel stared at the glowing end of the cigar, looked back at the powerful beast that threatened her with it, and didn't even flinch when he brought it closer still.

"Go ahead," she growled. "You want to brand me?" And she reached up, pulled open her robe, and dropped it to the floor. "Burn me! Anywhere you like!"

Now it was the warlock who was shocked and not just because the girl's body was absolute perfection. It was her bravery, her total unwillingness to be intimidated by the burning end of his cigar that caused him to stuff the ugly thing back into the corner of his mouth. Then he patted her gently on the shoulder and murmured, "You're a damn tough one all right, Chantel. Good girl."

Then he turned and marched back down to the center of the circle, and, as he went, he flashed his hand at the dying fire, which erupted into monstrous flames once again. Heat blasted from it, raising the temperature in the small amphitheater another twenty degrees.

"If any of you young witches are feeling the least bit uncomfortable," said the warlock as he spun back to face his coven. "Please don't hesitate to remove your robes just as the lovely Chantel has done." He eyed the proud woman and was thrilled to see that she had not slid back into her robe but sat there stark naked with her garment puddled at her feet.

"We're all witches here," he continued. "Nakedness is a beautiful thing that we can share. Isn't that right, Matryoshka?"

Wicktor's youngest convert stood and smiled at the warlock. In truth, she'd been hoping for a moment like this for quite some time. She'd been fasting and exercising for weeks, and she was eager to show off the slim and shapely body she'd worked so hard to achieve.

"Nakedness is simply fantastic, Pan Wicktor," Matryoshka answered, and she immediately raised her hands to her shoulders and pulled her robe from her. She folded it quickly and set in on the hard stone seat making a comfortable looking cushion.

"I agree," said Morgan Cummings. "Nakedness is wonderful," and she dropped the robe from her shoulders and let it fall from her pale white body. She too took advantage of the thick fabric and folded it into a cushion.

"I want to be naked, too," added her twin. And she opened her robe and let it fall from her shoulders as well. Her words were the beginning of a free-for-all as all the young witches then pulled the robes from themselves or their sisters giggling and shrieking, sometimes tossing the robes across the space, other times stealing from one another to create comfortable seats for themselves.

"Well now," said the warlock, as he eyed his entire coven now sitting naked in front of the sizzling fire. "I guess it will be my job to keep the flames burning warm enough so that none of you will catch the slightest chill."

The girls nodded eagerly, and several of them moved into the lower seats to be closer to the raging bonfire and its warmth.

"Now look at yourselves," said the warlock. "Look at how beautiful you all are as you sit there, so attentive, so eager to hear of the witchy adventures that we will soon have."

The twenty young women looked around taking in the sight of the other naked young witches, all in their prime, all as beautiful as a springtime garden, all lit by the perfect golden light of the fire. It was both erotic and empowering. A few of the girls giggled nervously, which soon gave way to confident sighs and smiles of pride.

"You are all breathtaking. I want you to know that," said the warlock. "And I do have to tell you, Mistress Brown that you don't have to worry about Mother Black. She proves to be a powerful adversary for Babcia and her friends.

"But do you... do any of you remember the request that Chuck Vaughn made of Sally the last time she left his office... the miracle that he asked her to perform?"

The girls were stunned. None of them remembered. The warlock, for his part, looked out at that sea of witches and smiled. "Well, then you'll all be surprised when you learn just how formidable the trio of Clara Goriki, Mother Black, and Sally Fukes was in the bloody struggles that followed."

Part Two
Returning

Chapter 27
Marla Returns

Marla Morrison did a pirouette as she danced across the front room of the little bungalow that Sally and Mother Black shared. Marla was feeling very much alive, and what a wonderful feeling it was. She was heading for the front door to answer a knock by the woman whose body would soon be her host, whose soul she would inhabit just as Babcia had taken over the body and soul of little Joy Madonie.

Marla shuddered as she passed by the fish tank that sat at the front corner of the room. It was a perfect place to breed eels, piranha, and other deadly creatures that Mother Black used for her potions. But it wasn't really the eels that bothered Marla when she passed the tank. It was the reflection that the water gave, not the mere image of an ordinary mirror, but the bold truth about the being that passed before it.

And so, though Marla was nothing but a spirit showing the outward appearance of youth, she was still, in reality, a ghoul, a burned-out husk of a corpse with charred, blackened flesh, half melted eyes, death-tangled hair, and rotted teeth.

Sally, when seen in the reflection from that same fish tank, suffered from a representation almost as alarming. She was not the lithe, curvaceous young witch that Chuck Vaughn had fallen for, but a morbidly obese creature who had not really shed any weight in her transformation. She'd just made it invisible. And because Sally no longer had to account for her eating habits, she was still gaining weight, now approaching four hundred pounds and not even aware of it, unless she looked into the fish tank, of course, which she decided never to do.

Marla danced to the door on those beautiful, phantom ballerina legs. Behind her was a dark room filled with candles, where the flickering light illuminated the faces and often naked bodies of many members of her coven. The Hollywood witches had come together in the little bungalow for Marla's return.

At the back of the room, Mother Black smiled as she stirred a great caldron that bubbled away over a monstrous fire. Clara Goriki stood beside her, and every now and then, the Polish witch would grab a newt or a rat from one of the cages beside the fireplace and toss it into the gurgling foam. The two witches delighted in the pop, sizzle, and desperate high-pitched death-cries that they heard when the poor creatures hit the boiling liquid.

"Welcome!" Marla cried as she flung open the door. And then she stopped cold. Standing before her was simply the ugliest woman Marla had ever seen in her life. As ghoulish as Marla was, as dead as she was, as familiar as she was with the visage and shape of the Crone (who was, after all, the witch's representation of all the horrors of death), this woman was worse.

Marla swallowed hard. Then she called, through a very false smile:

"Rosie! It's so good to see you."

Chapter 28
Rosie Part 1

Rosie Osborn was not a feminist. But she was, in many ways, a poster child for feminism, not in her appearance, of course, but in the terrible life she had led because of male prejudice and injustice.

The truth was that Rosie would never appear on any poster. Her back was curved and her old skin was baggy and wrinkled like an oversized bathrobe. Below her lips, there was no chin at all, just a sharp descent into a bulky, uncomfortable neck. She always wore a long, floral dress that never matched the mottle of her skin. Her breasts were enormous and of unequal size, so that one drooped down far below the other. Her teeth were rotting and crooked, and her voice was raspy. Her hands trembled with every gesture. She was too disorganized to be Babcia, though she sometimes reminded Niko very much of his grandmother.

The thing about Rosie, though, was that when you put a pencil between her fingers, she could use it like a fine sculptor's knife to render a perfect image onto a piece of paper.

Rosie was able somehow to see into people's souls and capture their essence with a few, deft, artist's strokes. She might have become one of the great portrait painters of the mid-20th century if her luck had been better. But it hadn't.

One of Chuck Vaughn's more insightful ideas was to apprentice Niko to Rosie during the slow time between his projects. This would give the kid a thorough indoctrination in the art of animation, Vaughn reasoned. And he was right.

Niko immediately took to the old woman. He was no stranger to scary old faces, but he'd learned to look beyond surface appearances into people's eyes, and he liked what he saw in Rosie's.

Rosie Osborn had been a sweet-looking girl in her youth, almost beautiful actually, with a gentle nature to match. And that sense of sweetness was something that young men found quite attractive in the late 1940s. Rosie was modest too, kind and humble, with a soft, musical voice and an innocent, inviting appearance. Maybe it was a little too inviting.

Rosie married young and had four children before she was midway through her twenties. Her husband was an alcoholic who abandoned her after only a few years. How could she feed and care for growing boys when she was totally on her own? There were virtually no jobs for women at the time. What talent could she exploit?

Well, she could draw and had begun to make a little money drawing portraits of friends and family. That was when she heard about the animation industry. There was a specific role for women in the business.

Men, called animators, did the original animation drawings; women did ink and paint. That is, women traced the men's drawings in fine ink lines onto clear plastic sheets called cells. Once the drawings were traced onto the cells, they were then turned over and painted on the reverse side.

Rosie was an excellent inker, and she readily found a job at the MikleyToons Studio inking and painting, though she was capable of much more. She was capable of doing what was thought of as the man's work of animation, and she desperately needed the pay that came with this increased responsibility. Rosie appealed to the head of Mikley's animation department, and he allowed her to stay late and study the daily work of the animators so that she could eventually become one.

Rosie's problem was that the male animators didn't want their work done by a woman, even a sweet and self-effacing one. They didn't want female competition for the few jobs that existed at that time. More insidiously, they resisted a woman's entry into the men's clubs that were the animation offices and bullpens... assuming it would limit the things they could say or do. They didn't want to feel uncomfortable. And so, when Rosie was able to gain a job as an animator, they made her life miserable. They played cruel jokes on her, told stories about her, and did everything they could to get her fired. And eventually, they succeeded.

Rosie ended up going from one studio to another encountering resistance on all sides. In some of the shops, the men actually got quite physical with her. If sexual harassment had been called a crime at the time, she could have named many perpetrators. Instead, she began to believe that her good looks were far more of a liability than an asset, and that's when she began to over-eat, almost to hide the attractive appearance that seemed to invite abuse.

Fortunately, miraculously perhaps, it was about that time that Rosie applied for a job at Vaughn Visual Arts and found a sympathetic mentor in the person of Chuck Vaughn.

Vaughn moved her into the ink and paint department so that she would not be exposed to the jokes and the ridicule of the male animation establishment. But he gave her animator work. And he paid her animator pay. Rosie was saved financially, at least for the time being. But soon the men in the company heard about her arrangement and began lobbying to have her fired again. Vaughn flatly and simply refused. And so Rosie was able to hang on at VVA until the more enlightened age of the 1960s when she could rightfully take her place beside the men in the animation rooms. Her children were now fully grown and had moved away. But it was then that her body betrayed her.

Rosie's alcoholism, which had begun as a way to cope with the difficulties of her life, took over her evenings, pickled her liver and large parts of her brain. Her pretty face was buried under dark, alcoholic eyes and mounds of puffy fat that came with the Twinkies that accompanied her nightly bottles of Thunderbird. Arthritis attacked her as well. Her body became bent and twisted, and she could barely move. But fortunately, she could still draw.

And it was at that time, as an ugly cripple, that she took on the challenge of teaching the art of animation to the new wunderkind at VVA. Even though she'd made it a point never to consort with or even befriend the writers and producers of Chuck's shows, she made an exception for this rather "cute" young talent.

The relationship was very close and extended through an entire summer, long enough for Niko to learn a great deal from the "ugly old cow," as the male animators still called her behind her back. But soon enough, Niko was yanked back into his position as head writer at the studio so he could begin piecing together a new story for Rapunzel. He still visited Rosie regularly, still talked to her and asked her advice. He shared the joys of his new little girl and the pain of his wife's infidelity. Rosie felt heartbroken to hear that Niko had nearly killed himself. It was just more proof of the absolute unfairness of life, she thought.

More drinking followed. Niko's near-death set Rosie off on another downward spiral. She had just about given up hope and decided to kill herself with alcohol once and for all, when one day the new and improved Sally Fukes came sashaying into her office with the most enticing offer she'd ever received in her life. But this offer wasn't from Chuck Vaughn. This offer came from the dark and twisted minds of Clara Goriki and Mother Black.

And it was all about witchcraft and revenge.

Chapter 29
Rosie Part 2

Rosie took the small flask from her purse and raised it to her lips. Yes, she was drinking at work. She'd never done it before, until yesterday. On that day the accumulated pain of her life had just been too much for her. A little nip, she thought, why not? And she'd taken one as soon as she arrived at the office and slid behind her big animation desk.

The drinking didn't seem to hurt; actually, it steadied her hand. She felt better all day, and no one had come into her office to notice that the room smelled like a distillery.

It worked well yesterday, Rosie told herself. So, why not have a nip or two today?

She pulled off her light, morning coat, hung it on the rack by the door, and waddled over to the big desk in the corner, past the much smaller desk that Niko had occupied when he was her apprentice. She dropped into the swivel chair and propped her slipper clad feet up on the little stool that she'd purchased to help make herself a bit more comfortable. Then she opened the big purse that she always carried with her and pulled out a flask of the cheapest gin money could buy.

A poster of CatMan Due looked cheerily down on the old woman as she dropped her purse to the floor, twisted off the cap on the flask, and raised it to her lips.

"Stop that, ya'll," someone called suddenly. It was Sally Fukes. The loud words came from right behind Rosie, and they startled the old woman so much that she dropped her flask and watched it bounce across the hardwood floor spilling cheap gin everywhere. Certainly, there would be no hiding her affliction now, or would there?

"I'll have Sam take care of it," Sally responded. "He'll be discreet, ah promise."

NICK IUPPA

Of course, he would. Sam Appaloosa, the muscular young janitor, was fascinated by the curvaceous new Sally. He'd do whatever she asked without question. And he'd certainly never mention it to anyone if she told him not to.

"Why'd ya wanta drink that nasty stuff anyways?" Sally asked. "I got somethin' much better for ya right here, whipped it up special mahself." And she produced a tiny bottle from her pocket.

"What is it?" the old woman asked.

"Somethin' that'll make ya'll feel jes peachy," Sally cooed.

As much as Rosie tried to avoid any interaction with her coworkers, she knew that Sally had undergone a miraculous transformation. It was the talk of the studio. And the fact that Sally's change was so complete gave Rosie a sudden sense that the girl might know some secrets that could help her.

"Have a swig," Sally whispered as she sidled up to the old woman. She wiggled her hips just a little, almost as though she was attempting to seduce Rosie. And, in fact, she was.

"You'll jes love it! Girl Scouts' honor. It's the same kinda stuff that helped me slim down. Jes a slightly different mix is all."

Rosie took the little bottle from Sally, raised it to her lips, and sipped it tentatively.

A soft tingle spread through her body bringing warmth especially to her breasts and her most secret places. There was a sudden sense of feeling alive, of wholeness, and, better than all of that... a sense of youth.

Rosie turned to the mirror beside her desk and saw the countenance of another woman flit across its face. It was she as a young girl, as beautiful as she'd ever been. The image danced out of sight and returned growing sweeter and younger, filling Rosie with a sense of who she'd been, a girl that many men wanted, who had the whole world and a wonderful life ahead of her.

141

She began to raise the little bottle to her lips again, but this time Sally snatched it away.

"No more fer taday."

"But I'm losing the feeling," Rosie said with a touch of panic in her voice.

"Well, there's a way ta make it come back, ya'll," Sally added. "Ta make it STAY."

"What do I have to do?"

"Not much. Help me out with a little project I'm cookin' up at home, thass all. Interested?"

Rosie turned back to the mirror. The image of the youthful girl flitted before her eyes one last time, just enough to tease her, to let her know that it was indeed possible.

"I'm very interested," she said trying to appear to be a serious businesswoman and not just a desperate old wretch.

"Can ya get over ta mah place this evening, around ten?"

Rosie nodded with no hesitation.

"Then do it," Sally said cheerfully.

And that is how a truly fine artist, a woman who knew almost everything about animation, a woman with the talents needed to provide the proper host-body for Marla Morrison, ended up standing just outside Mother Black's door that evening as Marla's dolorous spirit studied her in all her ugliness.

Marla twisted and turned with uncertainty. Then suddenly shouted:

"Rosie! You're the guest of honor, you know!

"Come on in and join the party!"

Chapter 30
Billy

The great gray billy goat let itself be led out of its pen at the very back of the garden. He'd been scrubbed cleaner than any billy goat ought to be, but he didn't mind, not today of all days. He knew what was in store for him.

Sally led him on a very short leash; the bell around his neck clanging joyfully as he stomped along the garden path right up to the back door of the bungalow.

Inside, Rosie Osborn had already exchanged her hideous flowered dress for the simple black robe of the Hollywood witches. It was black velvet with a white cord that could be drawn around the waist if desired. Rosie had tied hers tight, but the other members of the coven, those Hollywood witches, those librarians and school teachers and waitresses, those wannabe starlets, all had theirs hanging open if they wore them at all.

The young witches were sipping wine and herbal tea while munching on soy crackers, fried insects, and beetle-nuts, but they stopped their conversation for a moment to stare at the billy goat as he stomped through the doorway and into the room. Mother Black made her way from the fire and knelt directly in front of him.

"Handsome Billy," she crowed. "Yer handsome, ya knows." And she scratched his horny head, raised his face to hers, and kissed him right on his lips.

Rosie, watching from the corner, wondered who got the worst of it, the old witch or the goat.

Billy must have liked it because he responded by sticking out his long, sandpaper tongue and taking a good swipe at the witch's face. The old witch smiled and stepped away. That allowed Sally to lead the goat farther into the room where he slammed into tables and knocked over lamps as he went. Occasionally, he would tilt his head sideways and stuck out his hideous tongue to slobber up some of the goodies that were set out in little dishes on every available surface.

The young witches oohed and aahed at his every move, as though he were a rock star who had just thrashed his way into their presence.

Sally led the goat to a small group of witches who stood at the front of the room. Billy immediately poked his snout under the robe of the blonde, long-legged woman at the very center of the group. Rather than recoiling, the woman pulled back her robe and allowed the goat to sniff and nuzzle her between the legs. She rolled her eyes in happy surprise, and Rosie could just make out the creature's tongue at work on the beautiful witch.

Rosie wanted to turn and run. She wanted no part of the beast, and yet she supposed that he was there just for her.

Another young witch hopped on the goat's back and rode it as Sally led it around the room and then finally right up to Rosie Osborn.

"Rosie, meet my friend Billy. Ain't he handsome?" Sally asked.

"Nice to meet you, Billy," Rosie said tightening her robe about her. Billy lowered his head and gave her a butt right in the crotch. It almost knocked the old woman over, but Marla was there to catch her and bring her back to her feet again.

"Don't worry," she whispered when Sally led the beast away. "He's Sally's pet, and she feels she has to bring him out at every gathering we have. Not very civilized, you know."

"Will I have to..." Rosie began.

Marla giggled. "FUCK him? You and the goat? We're modern witches here, you know, and this is Hollywood. But still, we'd never do anything like that."

Rosie sighed with relief and downed her entire glass of Chablis in one gulp.

"We've got a much more handsome lover for you," Marla cooed. "You'll like him a lot."

"A lover?" Rosie asked, not sure if she should be worried or excited and feeling a little of both.

"First we cast the spell, and then we all make love."

"The spell?"

"The Spell of Becoming. You become the young beautiful 'you' just as you did when Sally gave you a taste of the potion this morning. The two old witches and I watched it through our scrying ball, you know."

Marla gestured to the great, crystal globe that sat on the huge coffee table in the center of the room. Many members of the coven had gathered around it and were taking turns staring into it, watching old friends and lovers. Sometimes, one of the witches would pull out a small poppet and begin jabbing at it with sharp pins. The subject within the ball would begin thrashing about in pain in response to the pricks. The other witches looked on and laughed and talked about how much control the poppets gave them over their victims.

Sally, having returned the goat to his pen, joined the group, and pulled out the poppet that Marla had made of Holly Madonie. She swiped her hand over the ball and Holly's image suddenly appeared. She was with her lover, John Hunter, at the Sheridan Universal Hotel. Holly was just entering the room and removing her coat.

Sally began stroking the poppet on her breasts and thighs and, through the ball, she could see Holly reacting, moving to John, kissing him, directing his hands to the same sensuous areas that Sally was arousing with the poppet. The Hollywood witches laughed and cheered as the couple began undressing each other with growing passion.

"YOU did it!" Rosie shouted accusingly at Sally. "YOU made Holly unfaithful!"

Sally turned toward Rosie, smiled and nodded. "With a little help from my friends," she said.

"Let's face it," Marla added, "Holly was moving in that direction anyway; we just made it a little easier for her."

"I don't like this," Rosie responded. "It's evil."

"Of course, it is," Marla answered. "We're witches, you know, evil fucking witches. But then think of what we are offering you: permanent youth and beauty."

"I'll have to hurt Niko, won't I?" Rosie fretted.

"Probably," Marla teased. "I hate him, you know. He killed me. I want revenge."

"You mean you're dead?" Rosie asked in astonishment.

"I am," Marla answered as she gave Rosie a long serious look, and the shadow of her ghoulish corpse faded into her phantom body.

"But not for long," she added with a smile when the ghoul disappeared. "I'm going to hitch a ride on the next person who undergoes the Spell of Becoming. Know who that will be?"

One of the Hollywood witches stepped up to Rosie and handed her another glass of Chablis. Rosie downed it at once.

"I think Niko's sweet," Rosie said ignoring Marla's question. "I like him very much."

"Really," Marla cooed. "That's interesting. Maybe we can arrange to have you become his lover. Would you like that?"

Rosie didn't answer, but her eyes shown a mix of horror and enthusiasm.

Marla leaned forward and whispered into Rosie's ear, "I think you're ready for the spell."

"I am?" Rosie asked softly.

"Yes, I am."

Chapter 31
The Spell

Rosie trembled as Marla led her to the center of the room. The other witches formed a circle around them. Mother Black brought two large candles and placed them on either side of the scrying ball. Then Sally stepped forward and removed the ball from the table. She carried it to the far corner of the room where she covered it with a velvet cloth.

The room was thick with sandalwood incense and now Mother Black anointed the candles with rue oil. Then she lit them while Sally extinguished every other source of light in the room.

Mother Black smiled her toothless smile. She reached behind Rosie and opened her robe. "Here ya go, sweets," she croaked as she pulled back the robe and let it fall. The act revealed the old woman's monstrous, naked form.

Marla brought forward a container holding a myriad of spices and herbs and began adding pinches of the herbs to the candle flames, which crackled and sparked.

Now Marla stepped behind Rosie, running her fingers through the old woman's nasty hair. Finally, she grabbed it and pulled it tight. Clara Goriki slowly stepped out of the darkness and raised one of the candles above Rosie's head, tipping it forward to allow the hot wax to spill onto Rosie's hair, and then down her forehead, and onto her face. Rosie let out a sharp cry of pain when the molten wax touched her flesh, but then she stopped abruptly.

As she felt the melted wax spread through her hair and down her cheeks... far more wax than should have ever been able to come from a single candle, Rosie realized that the skin on her face was becoming firm and fresh and that her hair was no longer coarse, but soft and beautiful.

Clara reached for the second candle and raised it over Rosie's sagging breasts. The wax dripped over those sad, misshapen things, and this time Rosie did not say a word as she immediately felt her breasts tighten and pull upright. She welcomed the sting of the wax when it poured over her belly and down between her legs.

Clara now dripped wax over the small of Rosie's back, over her shoulders and arms, onto her huge lumpy buttocks, all of which tightened and, once again, became firm and fresh and young. And all the while, the Hollywood witches watched with wide, wondering eyes as they chanted a simple mantra:

Becoming beautiful,

Becoming healthy,

Becoming victorious!

They repeated the phrases over and over again. And, as Rosie felt her body move to perfection beyond her greatest expectations, she became more and more intoxicated by the smell of the candles, the incense, and the chant.

The Hollywood witches stepped aside for just a moment as Sally came forward with a full-length mirror that showed Rosie how beautiful she had become. At the same time, it revealed a very tall, handsome young man who had entered the door at the back of the room. Though Rosie could only see his head, shoulders, and chest reflected in the mirror, she sensed that he was entirely naked.

If she'd bothered to learn a little more about the goings on at VVA over the last decade and hadn't hidden in her office in long years of melancholy, she would have gasped in astonishment. It was Billy Bright!

Billy Bright! Marla and Holly's lover! Dead at Marla's own hands on that terrible night so many years ago. But now he seemed to be very much alive, and he was quite excited. He smiled and winked at Marla, and she beamed back at him. No affection lost there, apparently.

Sally removed the mirror when Billy moved up behind Rosie. The transformed woman could no longer see herself or what was behind her, but she could feel Billy as he slid his hands up and over her youthful body. He kissed her neck. His fingers caressed her shoulders, her breasts, and belly. He pressed himself tight against her, and Rosie gasped at his growing excitement, now standing tall against what was surely a most curvaceous, young bottom. She loved the thought of her newfound beauty; it made her smile.

Would he take her? As intoxicated as she was? Rosie hoped so.

Marla suddenly stepped in front of Rosie, put her hands on her shoulders, and gazed into her eyes.

"I would become you," she whispered. "Will you receive me?"

"So shall it be," chanted the witches closing in to form a tighter circle around the trio. "So shall it be."

Rosie was confused and wasn't sure what to say, so she did the easy thing, the obvious thing.

"So shall it be," Rosie repeated softly, and at that very moment, Marla pulled Rosie to her and kissed her passionately on the mouth, and just as quickly, Billy thrust himself into the youthful old woman.

Lightening flashed suddenly. It brightened the entire room, and as it did, Marla dissolved into thin air.

Rosie screamed, closed her eyes and felt the wonderful, powerful thrusting of Billy as he pounded into her.

"Oh, yes," she called breathing in deeply, consuming the tiny wisps of energy that had been Marla Morrison, just as Holly had taken in the spirit of Babcia so many years before. But this spirit was not to become any child within Rosie's womb. This spirit would become part of Rosie herself, creating a whole new being, a mixture of Rosie and Marla, a creature bent on total revenge. And yet there was a secret ingredient added too, wasn't there? It was the love that Rosie felt for

Niko Madonie. Marla sensed it as soon as she became part of the woman.

Could she use it to her advantage? Marla wondered. Perhaps so.

The Hollywood witches smiled with delight as Billy had his way with Rosie. He now placed his hands on the table and leaned forward, taking her with every ounce of energy he had, which was considerable because this was not the ghost or even the spirit of Billy Bright that was taking Rosie Osborn.

If she had turned her head even slightly, Rosie could have looked into that fish tank with the all-too-revealing reflection, and it would have shown not the gorgeous new Rosie Osborn that all the Hollywood witches admired, but the hideous rotting corpse of Marla Morrison. And, worse than that, it wasn't the monster manhood of handsome Billy Bright that was thrusting into her. It was the huge, ugly, animal thing of that horny billy goat.

Or perhaps something even more monstrous than that.

Chapter 32
Here's Jeannie

Charles Martin Vaughn was shit-kickin' sad, (his words.)

Rosie Osborn was dead, an apparent suicide. No trace of her body had been found. But a note left in her apartment indicated that she'd intended to drive her clunky, old Plymouth Valiant out to the Malibu coast and floor it, sending herself and the old rust-bucket flying out over the biggest cliff she could find. Apparently, she'd launched her car so far into the air over the ocean that it was unlikely it would ever be recovered.

Given the hard life she'd led and her terrible state of mind after hearing of Niko's relapse, who could argue with any of it. Niko was, after all, one of the only friends she had at the studio, maybe in the world.

Chuck felt he hadn't done enough for the old woman. It was more than anyone else in Hollywood had, of course, but still far from the kind of generosity he could have shown her.

Christ, he felt guilty.

The irony of it all was that during those last few days when everyone was looking for her trying to figure out where she was, deciding, at last, to break into her home, find her note and confirm her suicide, Niko had made a miraculous recovery. Hell, he was going to be released from the hospital this very day, and Chuck should have been ecstatic about it. But how could he be with the complete sadness of Rosie's death overwhelming him?

If there were only some way he could bring her back, he vowed he would make it up to her. But what was the use in thinking that way? That kind of second chance never happened to anyone.

#

"Got someone for ya ta meet," drawled the sweet southern voice of Sally Fukes. Vaughn looked up and smiled at his newest protégé.

Sally strode into Chuck's office in the sexy, black mini skirt and rib-knit top that had pretty much become her uniform at VVA. She wasn't hiding those Marla Morrison ballerina legs of hers either. She smiled like someone who had found the perfect gift and couldn't wait to deliver it.

Chuck wasn't in the mood, not at all, but what the hell, he decided. It was time to start being nice to everyone, in memory of old Rosie.

"What ya got?" Chuck asked.

Sally gestured toward the office door and in walked the sweetest, most beautiful young woman Chuck had ever seen in his life. She looked very much like the old-time actress, Janet Leigh, Vaughn realized, maybe from her earlier movies, *My Sister Eileen* or *Little Women*, not that new piece-of-shit Hitchcock flick where she got hacked to death in the shower.

"Chuck," Sally began, swaying back and forth almost coquettishly. "You wanted me to find you another Marla Morrison, and I did. This is her sister, Jeannie."

Chuck seemed to stare at the beautiful, young woman forever. She wore a silk dress with padded shoulders and a wide belt. The skirt was cut short in the current style revealing attractive legs that matched a classically understated figure.

A slim waistline, Vaughn thought, and a perfect smile. She was just the person to star in an executive presentation to the MikleyToons Company.

Then something miraculous happened:

She spoke.

"How do you do, Mister Vaughn," she said in a voice that was strong yet feminine, clear and precise yet gentle at the same time. It was as though she were singing her words, Vaughn thought.

Jeannie held out a gloved hand for the great animator to shake. Vaughn took it and kissed it. It just seemed like the thing to do.

Jeannie sighed.

"Thank you, Mister Vaughn," she said. "Oh, and I've brought you a portfolio of my work. I knew you'd want to see it."

"You're applying for your sister's job?"

"The head writer's job, yes," she answered. "I know it's a very important one. I'm not as clever as Marla, but my work is good, I assure you."

Jeannie went back to the doorway, lugged a huge portfolio into the room, and hoisted it onto Vaughn's desk. The animator moved quickly to help her, and the act drew them close. Vaughn's hand grasped the handle of the portfolio right beside Jeannie's. She turned to him and smiled as they lifted it together. For a moment Sally didn't like the scene at all, her man and this classically beautiful woman so very close. But, of course, when he turned toward Sally, she was all smiles again.

"I have it now," Vaughn said and opened the portfolio to the most chilling image of a witch he'd ever seen in his life, the Crone in all her deadly powers.

"Christ!" he shouted.

"Don't you like it?" Jeannie asked.

"You drew this?"

"Yes, I did. It is a little overpowering, isn't it?" And with that she snatched a sheet of animation paper from Vaughn's desk, took a pencil, and sketched up another image of the same deadly crone, but this time with a smile on her face and a twinkle in her eyes. The combination was arresting. Chuck Vaughn hadn't seen that kind of quick sketch artistry since Marla and hadn't seen that ability to inject personality into an illustration since Rosie Osborn.

Jeannie handed the drawing to the dumbfounded animator, and they both turned back to the portfolio. In addition to the horrific pictures of the witch, there were lovers, a boy and a girl, drawn with surprising sweetness and care.

"These are some things I whipped up for Rapunzel," Jeannie said. "I heard you were doing it. I thought this might work for the lovers."

"Yes, well," Vaughn began nervously. "Niko Madonie is responsible for that."

"Niko's getting better?" Jeannie responded with the interest of someone who knew him very well. "But that's wonderful. I heard that he was..." She turned away, and Sally could see that tears were forming in her eyes.

"He managed to pull through the latest setback, thanks to the work of a brilliant team of surgeons," Vaughn said. "He should be back tomorrow, in fact."

"Do you think he'd be willing to work with me?" asked Jeannie with disarming humility.

"If not, I'd say he hasn't gotten over that gunshot wound in the head," Vaughn chomped through his gum.

Jeannie giggled, "Thank you."

"Can you start tomorrow?"

"But we haven't even discussed terms of employment or hours or salary or anything."

"Okay, let's do that," Vaughn said tossing a few more sticks of chewing gum into his mouth and turning to his assistant.

"Sally, give her whatever she wants."

"Will do," Sally said doing her best to hide a sudden sense of alarm. This mixture of Rosie Osborn and Marla Morrison had produced something totally unexpected, a sweet, self-effacing young woman with seemingly limitless creative talent whose stated purpose must surely be the total destruction of Niko Madonie, and yet somehow she had become someone...

With whom Niko would almost certainly fall in love.

154

Chapter 33
Waking with Holly

Niko woke up with a song pounding in his head:
She was sweet seventeen with soft green eyes
And a willing smile she could not disguise
Then she looked my way, and it was clear to see
That no other girl would ever matter to me

For a long moment, he didn't know where he was. And then he recognized the strange, crooked plaster pattern in the ceiling and the new chandelier that he and Holly had hung in their bedroom.

Then the song came crashing back:
Then she looked my way, and it was clear to see
That no other girl would ever matter to me
As long as her green eyes smiled at me

Niko turned toward Holly. Her back was to him while she slept. He slipped from the bed and made his way around to the other side. He knelt down in front of Holly to look at her as she lay sleeping. Every woman looks angelic when she's asleep, he thought, but Holly's beauty had elevated her to a higher order of angels.

His lost little girl!
No other girl would ever matter to me
As long as her green eyes smiled at me

As Holly lay there in angelic sleep, Niko's was filled with such longing that he just had to reach out and touch her. And he did. He slid his hand up to her face and pushed her golden hair back from her eyes. It was enough to wake her.

"Niko!" she called as though she were surprised to find him there.

"Hi," he answered with a silly smile, wondering how he could express the flood of emotions he was feeling.

"Is it really time to get up?" she asked.

"It's 7 AM."

"Wow," she answered and struggled to sit upright in bed. Doing so revealed her cute pajama top covered with images of roller-skating teddy bears.

"Why are you up so early?"

Niko shrugged. "Thought I'd make you breakfast."

"But you don't know how to make breakfast," Holly teased.

"That never stopped my mother," Niko surprised himself by answering. Holly grinned.

"If I had time, I'd make breakfast for you," she said as she pulled herself from the bed. "But I've got to get rolling."

"How 'bout we take a shower together first?" Niko asked. He cupped his hand around Holly's breast. "This one seems in dire need of a scrubbing."

Holly gently took his wrist and pulled his hand away.

"Not this morning," she murmured.

The young man lowered his hand sadly.

Holly brushed by him and grabbed a stack of clothing that had been sitting on her dresser, the day's work outfit. As she turned around, one small article fell from her arms, a single nylon stocking, not pantyhose, which every woman wore to work those days, but a single nylon stocking. Niko reached down and picked it up for her. She took it and looked carefully into his eyes before kissing him quickly on the cheek and rushing into the bathroom.

A nylon stocking! Why would she be wearing it to work? Niko wondered. No one wore nylons anymore except in the bedroom as part of some kind of sexy outfit: push-up bra, bikini panties, nylons stockings, high heels; the ensemble already had a name, "fuck me clothes."

Why would she want to wear her 'fuck me' clothes at work all day?

The answer was obvious, wasn't it?

Holly was going to wear them for John Hunter so that she could be sexy as hell when they slipped away for a little lunchtime tryst. And suddenly a set of memories that Niko had suppressed after recovering from his latest relapse came flashing into his mind: John Hunter, the obscene pictures, the affair, the gun, the murder plan.

Niko sank to the floor. Was this what he had come back to? More infidelity?

Why should he have thought otherwise? he wondered. Because he'd been given a third chance at life and had hoped in the time it had taken to recover that Holly'd realize that she still loved him?

Father Tim had sure encouraged that belief.

Holly came out of the bathroom showered and dressed in a most modest outfit, knee length skirt and high collared blouse, a perfect way to hide all that sexy lace and nylon.

She reached for Niko, pulled him to his feet, and looked into his troubled eyes.

"I have to go now," she said firmly and gave him a kiss on the cheek. "When's your appointment at the studio?"

"Two," Niko answered. "Just a half day at first, seeing Chuck again and talking about getting back to the show."

"Take it easy, okay?" Holly said. "Don't do anything crazy."

Niko studied his beautiful wife for a long time (unfaithful bitch) and then nodded.

"Gotta go," she said and turned to leave. Then she hesitated, came back to her husband, and put her arms around him.

"These clothes are for you," she said. "My sexy wedding lingerie, remember it?" Niko nodded. "They're for later this evening. I was hoping to surprise you because I wanted you to, you know...

"Make love to me."

Chapter 34
Marriage

"Why can't we get married, John? Why can't you just leave Susan and marry me?"

Holly pressed a cigarette to her lips and took a long, slow puff. Smoking wasn't the first vice she'd learned from her lover nor would it be the last.

John Hunter didn't answer Holly's question. He lay on the bed beside her and said nothing.

"Damn him," she said. "He's back, and he's telling me that he loves me. He wants to start over."

"You know you can't believe him," Hunter responded.

He pulled his muscular body up from the bed and looked down at her as she lay on top of the covers in those stockings and garters and sexy bra. He took the cigarette from between her fingers, took a puff, and returned it to her.

"He's acting as though none of the past year even happened," she said with a sudden catch in her throat.

Hunter was in the bathroom now pulling on his trousers and shirt. Holly walked up behind him, put her arms around him, and leaned her head against his shoulder.

"Leave Susan. Marry me."

Hunter turned. "It's a little more complicated than that."

"But he's making plans. I'm sure he'll be promising things to Joy. And he wants to make love to me tonight."

Hunter put both arms around Holly.

"Of course, he does," he said. "You're his wife, and you're beautiful."

"Doesn't it make you jealous?" Holly asked as she pushed him away.

"It's all part of the game," he answered. "We have to play along for the sake of our jobs and our children."

Holly looked at him with disgust.

"I have to fuck a man I don't... may not... am not sure I...."

"What are you talking about?"

"I want to marry you now, John, that's all. This morning Niko was acting as though we could go back to the magic times when we were first married. And..." Holly bit her lip then whispered, "For a minute it actually seemed possible."

"You know better than that."

"I should," she answered sadly. She walked from the bathroom into the sitting area of their suite. She was still only wearing her white lace bra, a garter belt, and those nylons.

It wasn't an easy outfit to put together in the mid '70s. Every item was out of style. But Holly liked it. She knew it turned men on, and maybe for no other reason than that, she felt comfortable wearing it.

"This afternoon, he goes back into work," she added. "Pretty soon he'll start feeling the pressure, get caught up in the routine, and he'll forget all about me again. Then the silence will start."

Hunter walked into the sitting room, took his suit coat off the arm of the chair and pulled it over his shoulders.

"If that's the case, you won't have to worry. We can go on as we have."

"But I don't want that either."

"Okay then, maybe it'll be different this time. Maybe he's learned to be an attentive husband."

"Is that what YOU want?"

"I want you to be happy."

"Even if it means that I end up falling in love with my husband all over again? Can't we just get married and settle all this, before I...."

John Hunter stared at Holly for a long moment. She returned his look with stony defiance.

"Marry me, John."

Hunter started to answer but just shook his head and walked from the hotel room.

Holly sank into the couch.

"You don't even care, you son of a bitch," she yelled after him. "You're just using me. I'm just a hot, easy fuck." And then she murmured the rest of her thoughts to herself.

"You're never going to leave Susan, are you? And in the meantime...

"What kind of a fool does that make me?"

Chapter 35
Niko Meets Jeannie

Charles Martin Vaughn jumped up from behind his desk and ran to greet Niko as he arrived. He wrapped both his arms around the young man and held him tightly.

"Son!" he cried. "My son!" He stood back, held Niko at arm's length, studied him up and down, and then slapped him hard across his face.

"If you ever do that to me again..." he blustered and fell back sobbing.

Niko brought his hand to his jaw, gave it a gentle rub, and smiled back at the great animator. He was glad to see him, and Vaughn could tell.

Then Niko turned and saw Sally standing in the corner. She looked wary.

Does he remember? She wondered. Does he realize that I was the vessel Clara Goriki used to attack him, reopen that terrible wound, and almost send him to Hades?

Niko smiled at her. He did not remember.

"Lookin' great, Sal," he said.

She nodded while Chuck continued to blubber away. And it was at that moment that Niko saw the other figure in the room: a very young woman with a sweet smile.

"Perhaps I shouldn't be here," she said softly.

"Oh, but you should," Vaughn answered sniffing in a nose-full of tears and snot.

"Niko, this is Jeannie Morrison."

Niko's eyes darkened only slightly at the name Vaughn spotted it.

"Right. Morrison. Marla's sister," he continued. "She's a crackerjack artist with a lot of ideas for our new show."

"Oh, please," Jeannie protested. "I'm not as talented as Marla. And my ideas aren't really worked out. I mean, she was the ballerina, and I'm just a..."

She couldn't finish the sentence. Niko had walked directly to her, taken her pretty gloved hand and, after a moment, kissed it. Jeannie blushed.

"You people have a very strange way of greeting a girl," she said nervously.

If Vaughn had been able to jump up and click his heels in mid-air, he would have done it. "You two are going to make quite a team," he said. "A writing team! You and Jeannie! And next week, when the gang from MikleyToons gets here, you're gonna blow 'em away."

Niko didn't respond at all. He was staring at Jeannie totally captivated.

"Sally," Vaughn snapped. "Get the witch room ready." He stuffed a handful of gum into his mouth and slobbered through the rest of his instructions. "Bring in all the usual supplies, drawing paper, lots of it."

"Oversized," Jeannie added without taking her eyes from Niko.

"Good," Vaughn added. "Lots of big sheets. Then go out and get some brand new Magic Markers, all the colors, and the grays. Get storyboard tablets, pencils, and sharpeners. Anything else?"

"The cage," Jeannie added still focusing completely on Niko. The young man didn't pay any attention to the conversation. He hadn't taken his eyes from his beautiful new partner since the moment he'd noticed her.

"The cage!" Jeannie repeated with a sweet smile.

Chapter 36
Nylon Stockings

"Joy is visiting next door. Please come in, Niko."

That was the message that he found taped to the front door of the Madonie home. The words were spelled out in Holly's neat, childlike printing. He smiled. He understood the possibilities.

When he pushed the door open, Niko saw a single nylon stocking tossed almost haphazardly inside the doorway. She hadn't been kidding, he realized, and he began to feel a growing excitement.

A little further into the living room, a second nylon had been flung just as randomly, as though Holly had simply peeled it off and dropped it as she'd rushed ahead. Then, almost at the steps, Niko found another stocking draped over the banister. This one was a slightly darker color.

Halfway up the stairs, she'd dropped three more stockings, each one a progressively darker shade, until, at the very top, just outside the bedroom door, a pair of black nylons were displayed invitingly.

Niko followed the trail laughing as he went along. Guess it was going to be a nylon stocking evening, he thought. What could be better?

Inside the darkened room, he saw her standing in the far corner near the mirrored closet doors. A few candles were all that illuminated her perfect form. She wore nothing but one of Niko's starched, white dress shirts and a pair of white nylon stockings.

The shirt was unbuttoned and open. Her feet were tucked into a pair of white high-heeled pumps. Her hands were trembling, even though they were folded up in front of her as if in prayer. She looked more anxious and uncertain than Niko had ever seen her look in their entire life together.

This was his lost little girl, he realized and smiled lovingly at her.

"Oh, Niko," Holly sighed and opened her arms to him. As she did, the shirt opened fully revealing her perfect breasts and hips and thighs. So that, when he rushed to hold her, he was hugging the nearly naked body of his wife. Holly kissed her husband at once, with passion, love, and no small amount of regret.

"Oh, Niko," she repeated as her husband simply held her tight.

#

"Fun, ain't it?" Mother Black said to Sally and Clara as they watched the reunion through the witch's scrying ball. "She's comin' back ta him," the old witch croaked. "Gonna be fun. Great, god-blessed fun, eh?"

"They're happy," Sally groaned in surprise. "How's that gonna be fun?"

"They're not happy at all, " Clara said with a cruel grin.

"But she's lovin' him again. That's what he wants."

"Think so?" Mother Black answered through her cold, toothless smile. "Is she lovin' him really? Or is she jes scared en confused?"

"Holly doesn't know what she wants," said Clara.

"But Niko wants 'er," Sally added. "He kin win er back."

"Ah, chil, ya don't know men at all, do ya?" Mother Black said.

"That WAS what he wanted," Clara added. "WAS. But now he's as confused as she is. Look!"

Clara swept her hand across the ball, and the image shifted. The three witches were now looking at Holly through

Niko's eyes, but it wasn't just the point of view that had shifted, it was the girl herself.

As he continued to kiss and caress his beautiful wife, her image changed to that of Jeannie Morrison... and then back again to his lost little girl, and then back yet again to his new creative partner, perhaps his new love.

"Think 'er gonna be happy?" Mother Black cackled. "Now at 'er both so God-blessed mixed up?"

"Excellent... excellent," said Clara, and she clapped her hands in wicked glee. And then she turned and looked into the shadows. "I think there's someone here who deserves a real debt of gratitude." Clara said as she gestured to the fourth witch in the room.

"Very clever, Jeannie," Clara said. "Excellent work."

Standing far behind Mother Black and Clara, looking over their shoulders, seeing and hearing all that was happening, Jeannie Morrison didn't seem proud of her work at all. She watched the scene nervously. Yes, she acknowledged Clara Goriki's compliments with a simple grateful nod, but the truth was that the greatest struggle was not going on in Niko's mind or Holly's. It was between this newly formed Jeannie Morrison, formerly Rosie Osborn, and Marla...the witch within her.

Chapter 37
Caged

The dead ballerina witch, Marla Morrison, never looked more beautiful. Her hair swirled wildly about her face. Her eyes were bright with a look of defiance, eyebrows arched, jaw set. Her shoulders were bare!

The neckline of her black witch's gown plunged deep between her breasts. The luxurious velvet that was gathered tightly about her waist opened again in front to reveal those arresting ballerina's legs.

Behind Marla were the Carpathian Mountains, set against a threatening Polish sky.

A raven circled ominously in the distance.

Niko recognized the style of the painting at once: romantic, Byronic. It portrayed Marla as the heroine of some great epoch. And, in her mind, he had no doubt that was how she'd always pictured herself.

The large portrait dominated the witch room, and Niko shuddered as he stepped up to it. It was 8:30 in the morning, and he was alone when suddenly...

"Screeeeee!"

The scream of a big, black cat almost stopped his heart. The creature scurried past him and took its place in the corner beside the teakettle, which Niko was surprised to see bubbling away. The aroma was spicy and familiar and reminded him of that first day in this very room when Marla had worked her magic on him for the first time. She had turned an angry young man into what many people said was a creative genius.

"Quiet, CatMan!" Niko whispered to Vaughn's pet. The creature curled up beside the bubbling kettle, closed his eyes, and waited.

Niko looked around the room and saw that Jeannie's storyboard sketches for Rapunzel covered every wall. The drawings were very much in the style of Rosie Osborn. The characters' eyes were so deep and intelligent, you could almost see into their souls.

Jeannie's drawings departed dramatically from Niko's. They hearkened back to the original, more gruesome Grimm's Fairy Tales in which the witch was victorious.

Niko stepped closer to the drawings. Without any apparent knowledge of his grandmother, Jeannie had fashioned Mother Gothel, Rapunzel's nemesis, into the exact likeness of Babcia.

How could she have done that? Niko wondered and felt a slight chill shudder through him. Then he heard someone coming, very softly, as though she were trying to sneak up on him.

The door suddenly slammed.

"Drat!" called a soft voice. In spite of its sweetness, he jumped. It was Jeannie. She'd hauled a large, metal cage into the room. Niko remembered it well.

"I don't think I'm ready to crawl into that thing again," he blurted out before he had even greeted his partner.

She smiled. "Let's just keep it here for good luck, okay?" Her smile was warm and comforting as though they'd been close friends for a very long time. How could he disagree?

"I started the tea a few minutes ago," Jeannie continued. "It's Marla's brew. Hope you like it."

"Laced with marijuana?" Niko asked.

"Oh, no," she answered as she set the cage down right next to the table... in the very spot where Marla had placed it years before. "I can't work when my head's full of that stuff."

"I can't, either." Niko walked to the kettle, poured a big mug of tea, and handed it to Jeannie.

"Thanks," she answered. "Lugging that thing over here has left me a little breathless."

She took a deep swallow. "Mmmmm."

"I was just looking at your storyboards," he said. "Have you had a chance to look at mine?"

"Oh, I did," she answered. "They're great. I have them here in a stack. It's just that I think the original story is so much more exciting, don't you? It's so much more..."

"Spooky?" Niko suggested. "Do you think the MikleyToon folks will go for it?"

"They should if they like a good story," Jeannie responded. She pulled Niko's drawings up from the table and held them under her own for comparison.

"We pretty much agree on the opening," she said. "A poor woodsman and his wife live next door to the walled castle of a great witch.

"Here's the wife who longs to have a child, and here," she pointed to the next drawing. "She's pregnant. The husband doesn't know it, but she is, and she craves rampion. You changed it to a rutabaga. Why'd you do that?"

Niko laughed.

"Guess I never heard of rampion."

"But Rapunzel is another word for rampion. And even if you don't know what rampion is, it sounds a lot more romantic than rutabaga."

She giggled.

Niko smiled. "Guess you have a point," he said, stepping toward Jeannie. Even in her simple, tan, workday cotton blouse and skirt, she was gorgeous.

"Here's the witch confronting the woodsman after he's climbed over the wall to steal the rampion for his wife. They bargain. In exchange for his life, the woodsman consents to give their child to the witch after it's born.

"Now this is where we actually disagree. You have the witch luring him into her home with an offer of tea and cookies, apologizing for not being a good neighbor and then casting a spell on him. Frankly, that's no fun at all.

"My witch is a monster," she continued. "She does it all with cold terror. She threatens to scratch the woodsman's eyes out, kill his wife, and eat their baby. Now that's scary."

Jeannie turned toward Niko. Her eyes were bright with creative energy.

"The Mikley people will never go for it, though."

"I don't care," she said. "Let's do something new, Niko. The witch is the key to the whole story. Look at my drawings. Here she descends into the woodsman's home in all her horrible beauty. Horror can be beautiful, don't you think?"

What Niko thought was that Jeannie was beautiful, and her creative energy made her even more so. It gave her a little of the wild appearance of her sister who seemed to be looking down approvingly from the huge portrait.

"The witch captures the baby, Rapunzel, and imprisons her in a tower," Jeannie continued as she pointed to her next story sketch. "A dark, evil tower, deep in the mountains..."

"I put it in the forest," Niko interrupted feeling just a little defensive for the first time. "I had a foresty tower growing up out of the trees."

"There's no drama there. Look at my tower. It's in the heart of the mountains, gray granite, black lichen growing all over it. It's hideous, foreboding. No door, only one window. How did she get in there?"

"You tell me."

Jeannie grabbed her next drawing from the wall and pushed it toward his face.

"The witch forces Rapunzel onto a mountain ledge. Then she waves her magic wand, and the walls of the tower thrust themselves up out of the bedrock. They grow up around the little girl! Rapunzel is trapped. And as the tower rises, it carries her up with it, high into the air until she ends up in the very top room of the thing with only a single, little window for light."

Niko looked back and forth between the sweet face of Jeannie Morrison and the dynamic but horrifying drawings she had created.

"You're amazing," he said at last as he stepped closer to her.

The young woman cast her eyes downward and shrugged modestly. And then creative excitement grabbed her again.

"This is where you got it right," she said with a grin. "The song, the beautiful song: Rapunzel begins to learn it as a little girl, and the witch teaches it to her, teaches her how to play the guitar to accompany herself. The witch sits there in the afternoons listening, and the little girl is happy. It's a moment of tenderness between a sweet young child and a frightening old woman. How did you think of that?"

Niko realized that Jeannie had pinned up all his drawings of that part of the story. Their drawing styles were dramatically different. His were simpler, nowhere near as insightful, he felt, but somehow they fit together well. Now, it was his turn to shrug modestly.

"The Mikley people will love it," Jeannie said, "Because it's never been done like that before. Great work! Got any more great ideas?"

Niko was caught off guard and stared at her blankly for a moment.

"Come on, more!" Jeannie challenged.

Niko shrugged.

"Okay, then," she added in utter exuberance. "Into the cage!"

His expression was one of absolute shock. So much so that it stopped Jeannie cold. The two stared at each other for a long moment before Jeannie regained her enthusiasm.

"Come on, we need creativity. Take off your clothes and get into the cage."

"I – I can't."

"But I read about it," Jeannie said. "Here." She pulled out a set of handwritten pages, carefully transcribed in an artistic hand (Marla's?) The title said it all: *The Ballerina and the Cage*.

Niko read the title in utter shock. It was a chapter from the book: *Grimm's Fairy Tales*, the additive book that was now in his daughter's possession. Marla had shown the newly forming chapter to him when she'd asked him to step into the cage, just as Hansel had done in the story they'd been writing at the time. And when Niko had entered the cage naked, he found new confidence and skill, had shed all inhibitions and concerns, and discovered a wealth of creative energy.

"I'm not going to do it," Niko said, but Jeannie could see that he was already wavering.

"Of course, you are," she responded with a smirk. "Don't mind me. I'll look away or something."

"Or something," he added.

But she didn't look away, and he didn't either. He locked on Jeannie's eyes, and she returned his stare defiantly.

He unbuttoned his cuffs and collar, slipped out of his tie, and stepped out of his trousers, shoes, socks, and shorts. Jeannie was delighted. She made no pretense of looking away at all. She took in his entire body, which was scrawny after his long hospital stay.

"Now into the cage," she commanded, and Niko obeyed at once. He crept into it on all fours, knelt on the soft-carpeted floor and felt safe and secure just as he had when Marla had insisted that he do so. And, just as then, something remarkable happened, something that surprised Jeannie and the witch within her.

"Oh, my God! I can SEE that tower," Niko shouted. "I know where it is!"

"What do you mean?" she asked.

"I can see the actual, damn tower."

"It's real… it exists?"

"Yes. And we have to go there and see what it tells us about the story."

Jeannie paused for a moment. This wasn't what she had expected at all. And then...

"What a brilliant idea!" she screamed deliriously. "You're right! We do have to go there. It'll help us finish the story. But who knows where it is?"

"I do," Niko answered. "Somehow, I just know."

He struggled to pull himself from the cage and stood looking at her. His body was quivering with the shock of his insight. Suddenly, she put her hand to her mouth and burst out laughing. He laughed, too, stumbling toward her and hugging her. Then he backed away and stared at her.

"Where is the tower, Niko?" Jeannie asked at last.

Niko simply murmured one word, the name of a place that sent shudders through the girl's entire multi-souled being. It was certainly the last place on earth Marla or Mother Black would ever want to go. Clara Goriki, on the other hand, would feel very much at home there even though it was the stronghold of Babcia Czarownica.

"The Mountains of Poland!"

Interlude Five

"Are they coming here?" asked Matryoshka. "Are they coming to Poland?"

As the warming fire died, she slid her robe up over her shoulders and pulled it around herself to keep out the growing chill just as many of the other witches had also done.

The warlock now looked out over a coven that was almost completely clothed once again, though not all of them. Chantel took no notice of the cold and continued to expose her slightly goose pimply flesh to the elements. So did Morgan Cummings even though her sister, Megan, was once again wrapped tightly in her black woolen gown.

"Indeed, they are coming," said the warlock. "And we have to get ready for them. We have an important role to play in this epoch story… and believe me, it won't be easy."

"Babcia will join us, then?" asked Megan.

"I've already told you that the great witch won't come," Wicktor answered. "There are so many other things she has to attend to. I'll tell you about them all in just a moment. But it really doesn't matter whether Babcia comes or not, does it?"

"She has allies here in the woods, doesn't she?" Chantel asked, as her eyes grew wide and darted out into a forest that almost seemed to be closing in around the circle and its dwindling firelight.

"They are more than her allies, Chantel," Wicktor answered. "The great witch has a relationship with these creatures that goes back for centuries…. in fact, they feel as though they are family."

The warlock turned and walked back to the fire. He began pitching heavy logs into it, and soon half a dozen of his coven were assisting him, carrying wood from near the goat pens to the edge of the fire where he tossed them almost magically

174

into a perfect arrangement for burning. Then he raised his hand again gesturing for the young women to go back to their seats.

"Quickly, quickly," he urged, and with a sharp flash of his fingertips, he brought the fire to wild flames once again.

Heat rushed up into the amphitheater forcing more than one young witch to remove her robe immediately.

"That's much better," said the warlock when the girls had settled into attentive silence once more. He could still hear them breathing heavily from the hard work of stoking the fire.

"Listen, young witches," he began. "And I will tell you about the greatest dangers we are facing, and how they came to be."

The twelve-year-old child witch, Michalina Czarownica, also known as Michalina the Witch, walked from her ancestral home on the edge of the dark forest, walked from the grave of her father so freshly dug by her own hands, walked beside the great, gray wolf who had been her companion since her father had died.

She walked deep into the forest, past the witches' coven where she must now make her home, past the wild witches' Sabbath whose spectacular fire lit the nighttime sky. She walked into the deepest, most forbidden part of the forest.

She trudged blindly along, tears blurring her eyes, her body convulsing with sobs, tiny feet stumbling over leaves and roots and hollows on the forest floor until she tripped and collapsed into a heap. She lay there then. She was someday to be a great, powerful witch, but at that moment, she was only a child.

The wolf nudged her. She turned away. Michalina swiped at him when he did it again, and the wolf stepped back. Then he simply lay beside her, lowered his chin onto his paws, and whimpered in unison with the little girl's sobs. The wind picked up and rain began to fall as though in sympathy with little Michalina Czarownica, the child witch.

175

She was soon drenched to the bone and shivered in the growing cold. Now the great wolf took action, clasping her sodden clothes in his sharp teeth and pulling her to her feet. He growled when she tried to fight him off this time, and soon the little girl took her first shaky steps moving slowly and stumbling along beside the wolf.

The creature led her up into the hills along the farthest reaches of the forest, deep into the great mountains where an ancient ruin stood stark against the sky. The ruins were once the outer courtyard of a great, high tower, much of which still stood jagged and forbidding. It was built before the time of the Tartars, perhaps. A thousand years before! And in its base, the wolves now made their home.

On the way to the tower, the little girl tripped and caught herself, fell forward, regained her footing, and kept pace with the wolf who led her patiently until they came to the protection of the ruins.

Michalina threw herself on the ground then. She lay there shivering and sobbing, but slowly the other wolves gathered around her. One licked her face, another curled up beside her, and then another as well, giving the warmth of their bodies to Michalina until she slept.

In the days that followed, the little girl's sadness seemed to grow. She would not stand, would not eat, only slept and sobbed and, sometimes in the depths of the night, she would sing softly to herself, sad songs her father had taught her. And then she would lose herself again in fitful slumber, hoping to find her father in her dreams, but somehow not finding him there at all.

At last, on the fourth day of her mourning, when the child-witch was so weak she could hardly stand, the mother wolf came to her and, driving away her own hungry brood, she gave young Michalina her milk. And Michalina suckled at the she-wolf, drank heartily, and from that milk she gained the strength to stand, to walk out of the den into the sun-drenched forest, to return eventually to her Coven.

But she would never again be the same little girl, would she? She had suffered sorrow upon sorrow, which lingered though she lived for hundreds of years. And, though she was only with the wolves for a few short days, they had changed her in a way that would last all her lifetime and more. She was one of them now, a wolf as well as a little girl...

A wolf as well as a witch.

Chapter 38
Principal Hunter

Principal Hunter stood to greet Joy Madonie as she entered his office. She was such a beautiful little girl, he thought, so much like her mother with big green eyes, choirgirl hair, and a little figure that was already perfect.

"I have something for you," Joy said. "It's from my mom."

She reached into her book bag, pulled out a sealed envelope, and handed it to the school principal. Hunter took the envelope and then gestured to the chair in front of his desk. Joy took a seat.

"Go ahead," she said with a cheery smile. "Open it."

Hunter sat down behind his desk and opened the envelope. There was a note from Holly and a set of pictures, sexy pictures, Harry Rodgers pictures, the early more innocent scenes of Holly in her bikini by the swimming pool. She had intended to give them to Niko when Harry had taken them so many years ago.

Hunter shuffled through the pictures quickly and blushed. He was getting an erection. He didn't want to, especially when he was in the same room with Holly's little daughter. But hell, those pictures! He looked up at Joy. She was dangling her legs off the end of the chair and swinging them back and forth while she looked out the window. He turned back to the note. It was written in Holly's unmistakable hand.

"John - I'm very sorry for the harsh words I said to you last night. Believe me, I understand and appreciate how good you've been to me, and I want you to know that I will wait for you as long as I have to. So, let's try and make up, please? I can't stand having you angry with me.

"I'll be at the Girl Scout camp at Crystal Lake this evening. There's a beautiful cabin up there, away from the scout area. It's a perfect place for us to spend a little time, talk, and have some fun.

"Joy and two of her friends need a ride up to the campground. If you bring them after school, it will give us a perfect excuse to get away for a few hours. Please come. These pictures are only a hint of what I have in store for you.

Love you – Holly"

Hunter felt excitement crackling through his whole body. He looked at little Joy again. She was still staring out the window, oblivious to him.

"Would you like me to drive you to the camp-out?" he asked the little girl.

"That'd be great, Mr. Hunter," Joy answered.

"Tell you what," he continued, "Why don't you and your friends meet me at my car after school? Tell them to make sure they have their permission slips and all their camping equipment. No one goes unless I have an okay from their mothers. Make sure they know that."

"I will, Mr. Hunter," Joy answered. And with that, she jumped down from her chair and ran from the room to tell her friends.

What a smart kid, Hunter thought as he watched her leave. Just as smart and sweet as her mother.

He walked to the door and locked it behind the little girl. Then he went to the window and closed the Venetian blinds tightly so that no light or prying eyes could intrude. He pressed the intercom.

"No more calls," he told the receptionist.

"Yes, sir," she answered.

John Hunter opened the envelope he'd received from Holly. He took out the sexy pictures again, and this time he spread them out across his desk.

He was sweating now, and his hands were shaking.

He struggled to undo his belt and lowered his pants to his ankles.

"All right, Mrs. Madonie," he moaned softly leaning over the desk to take a closer look at those pictures.

"Please come, you say?

"Don't mind if I do!"

Chapter 39
Gingerbread Houses

Twisted branches seemed to claw at the windows of John Hunter's Ford Crown Victoria as it struggled up the deeply rutted gravel road that led to the upper cabin at Crystal Lake. Perhaps the branches were trying to unlatch the door and catch hold of him, Hunter thought for a crazy moment, pull him out from behind the steering wheel, drag him into the marshes that stood along the sides of the road, plunge him down among the gnarled roots and hold him under till he drowned.

Christ, what's happening to my mind? He wondered.

He had dropped Joy and her friends at the main camping area and received direction from some of the senior girls. The drive was quick and cheerful for about the first five minutes. Then suddenly, things began to turn very dark.

It was all about Holly wasn't it, he decided. She was complicating his life, but what could he do about it? He wanted her with him, always. He had realized it in the dark calm of his office. And it wasn't the pictures that made him decide that he wanted Holly with him forever. It was the understanding that somehow with the return of her husband and the things she had said, he could lose her.

Sure, Hunter loved banging Holly every damn afternoon, no doubt about that. Chances are that could end when the thrill of illicit sex wore off. But hell, he suddenly saw their love as something more romantic, the kind of love he'd pictured as a young Lit major at San Jose State. It reminded him of *Wuthering Heights*, a Cathy and Heathcliff kind of love in which Niko, a poor slob like Edgar Linton, stood on the sidelines knowing he could never have what they'd found.

"This can't be the way," Hunter muttered out loud as he drove further. "Can't be the way at all."

181

But it had to be.

He was exhausted from an entire afternoon of driving around town searching for a gift for Holly, one that would say everything that he hadn't been able to say over the last few desperate weeks, one that would undo all the mistakes he'd made in those useless conversations they'd had. He'd searched everywhere, and just as he'd been about to give up, he'd found the perfect answer: a simple silver ring! Not an engagement ring, certainly not a wedding band, just a plain ring with those most important words engraved inside: "Marry me, Holly."

Hunter had found an engraver who'd done the work on the spot, but it was expensive and had cost him a bundle out of his savings, his and Susan's. That bitch would go nuts if she knew what he'd done. But he had to, had to get the ring, return in time to pick up the little girls, and drive up to Crystal Lake. And now it was time to be with Holly, HIS Holly. He'd tease her a little and give her the ring in the most romantic way possible. Then it would be time for his big reward.

Hunter played the whole scene through in his head, losing himself in it for a moment. He saw himself on his knees before Holly, holding the ring in front of her, telling her how special their love was, beyond all rational thought. He'd tell her how he'd finally realized that he was desperate to have her all to himself. Holly would be delighted; her eyes would sparkle, and then it would be her turn to reward him in one of those magical ways that she knew so well.

Hunter was wondering just which magical way it would be when the road betrayed him.

It sucked his tires into its deep, muddy ruts, and suddenly the rear wheels were spinning wildly and getting him nowhere. He was trapped.

He floored it, and the car surged forward with a terrible whir. Then the tires stopped moving over the slimy surface. He slammed the car into reverse and floored it again, dropped back into the same rut and then, as he shifted, the car jumped forward once more, this time careening sideways in the mud.

"Shit!" Hunter spat.

He tossed the gearshift into reverse, let the car settle and then slammed it back into drive and floored it one more time. The wheels spun wildly. He let up quickly and floored it again, and this time the tires grabbed and propelled the car forward up and over the ruts. Rocks pounded against the bottom of the car as he climbed out of the slag.

"Christ, don't tear out the gas tank," he cursed out loud.

As though in response, the car quickly lifted up out of the mire and onto a smooth gravel road that was level. The trees in front of him finally opened up, and he got his first glimpse of a little, redwood cabin far ahead in the clearing.

"That's better," he said with a sigh.

As though to tease him, the road took a sudden dip, and the trees closed tightly around the cabin once again. Hunter slipped into a world of shadows with more trees and more darkness. Then his car pulled up over a rise in the road, and glaring sunlight flashed between the trees and across the hood of the car. It blinded him for an instant. And there it was again: the cabin. No! It was a little house up ahead, a gingerbread house!

"This can't be right," Hunter said out loud. It had to be the crazy light playing tricks on him or a distortion through the tinted windshield because, when he looked again, the building was nothing more than a rustic redwood cabin, like those in every other state park in California.

That's better, he thought, Holly in a rustic cabin, Holly in her tight little scout leader's skirt and blouse. How long would it take to get her out of it and into bed? What new treats would she be able to think up with that little silver ring on her finger, the one with the engraved proposal?

Low, afternoon sunlight flashed in his eyes, and the transformation occurred once more. There it was, a house made of nothing but frosting and spicy sweet gingerbread. A chimney puffed out warm, inviting smoke, complete with twisty black sparks that danced above it, sparks that were echoed in the squiggly shapes in the gingerbread paint that decorated the house.

Funny, thought Hunter, those shapes looked like witches.

#

A large gray cat scurried across the road and into the door of the cabin, and suddenly she was there, standing at the window: a fabulous woman. Hunter had never seen her before. She was young, wearing nothing but a short red cape. Prettier than Holly, he thought for a moment, if that were possible.

She stood at the window watching him pull up onto the dry ground in front of the cabin, slamming the door to his Crown Victoria, and then stomping his way up to the little cabin, which suddenly was one hundred percent redwood again with no trace of gingerbread.

Hunter shook his head. "Damn crazy place," he said out loud, and then he tromped across the porch and up to the door. Through the window, he caught another glimpse of the girl in the red cape. She had Polish snow-white hair and sparkling deep blue eyes. She danced through the room and then ducked back into the depths of the house.

"Holly," he called. "Is that you?" But he knew it wasn't. Maybe it was a friend of hers, someone to join us in a threesome. Was Holly into that kind of thing? It would be all right, he thought. This girl could be a witness to his proposal, and then they could share an incredibly hot ménage-a-trois.

He threw open the door and watched the girl in red peer around a corner and duck back into the darkness.

He was a good four steps into the house when he noticed the smell. What was it? Not Holly's perfume, which was seductive enough, but this smell was overpowering.

He drew in a deep breath, and felt it tingle through his entire body before it coalesced between his legs. The girl giggled in the other room. He rushed toward the sound and into the room, but she was gone. The scent was there, though. And it was hungry.

The little room was decorated modestly with a bed, nightstand and a small Tiffany lamp that sent a kaleidoscope of colors across the walls. Very simple, very inviting. At the far end of the room a closet door stood slightly ajar.

Hunter moved toward the door and opened it finding not hangers and clothes, but another full bedroom and across it yet another door.

The girl stepped into the far doorway, lolled there for a minute toying with the edges of her cape, eyes downcast innocently as if there could be any innocence in the presence of that hungry smell. It seemed to be calling for him, and Hunter was ready to answer if he could only catch her.

But she was already padding off on bare feet. Hunter rushed through the doorway only to see her duck into the back of the distant room.

He noticed that he was sweating, and the air was growing thicker with that hungry smell. It seemed to catch in his throat for a moment, seemed to want to strangle him.

Hunter raced into the far room and spotted yet another doorway, this time leading to a downward staircase. Now the girl came running up the stairs until she was almost face to face with him. Her smile was inviting. He grabbed for her, got the edge of that red cape, and pulled it from her. She turned and looked over her naked shoulder at him. She batted her eyes, smiled, and rushed down the stairs and out of sight.

Hunter moved deliberately down the stairs. He undid his collar button, pulled off his tie, and ripped the whole damn shirt right off.

He reached the bottom of the stairs and looked around. He was in a basement room decorated with wallpaper that seemed to have the same squiggly designs he'd seen coming out of the chimney.

The smell came back now too, and it grew stronger. It was stifling and musky. What was it?

He was certainly not a man given to fear or superstition. But at that moment, he was feeling more than a little frightened. He looked up the stairway. The doorway seemed far away and getting farther.

The girl giggled again. That was all Hunter needed. He turned just in time to see those pretty feet slide under the curtain of a big four-poster bed that sat at the far end of this largest and final room. He stepped carefully across the hardwood floor, making his way to the edge of the curtain, half-hypnotized now by the dancing images of the witches in the wall-paper and the overpowering scent of the woman's lust. He could hear the girl giggling behind that curtain. She was ready for him.

Hunter grabbed the edge of the curtain and yanked it back abruptly.

There she lay, across the bed looking like some perfect Goya nude, reclining with her hands behind her head... naked, upturned breasts rich and full, heaving with desire... long legs crossed toward him, revealing wispy curls in that magic place where they came together. Her lips pulled into a lustful smile; her eyes were filled with longing, her nostrils wide. She reached a pretty hand toward his head, caressed his cheek and pulled him toward her. He felt her lips touch his and then her hand pulled back.

It raked down the side of his face in a gruesome caress that dragged with it the skin and hair and ear from the whole right side of his face. It popped his eyeball from its socket and tugged it downward until it hung by a slim tendon, swinging freely from the oozing mass of flesh.

Hunter pulled back and looked with his one remaining eye at the woman who was no longer a woman but an enormous wolf, a wolf who was a grandmother, a grandmother who was a witch.

He froze at the sight of the great pointed ears, the huge saucer eyes, the teeth, the claws of a monster bundled into bed as though it were some kind of grandmother. (Granny, what sharp teeth you have!)

Was he really looking at a wolf?

Insanely, Hunter wasn't sure. Even as he saw the wolf chomp down on half his face, spurting his own blood back at him, slobbering up his eye and skin and hair and flesh before gulping them down with evil relish.

He reached out still hoping to caress the beautiful girl in the red cape. What he got instead were deep guttural words that sounded as though they came from the devil himself.

"All the better to eat you with, my dear!"

Slowly, the wolf opened its huge jaws and let its great tongue loll out between its teeth. It sniffed the air, breathed in the sweet scent of its victim, just as Hunter had done.

He staggered. Was it possible now to escape? Could he crawl under the bed, find a place to hide? Could he curl up into a ball, cover his bloody head, and save himself?

But the smell was calling to him, wasn't it? The scent of a woman in heat. And so, like the fool he was, he stepped closer to the wolf. The hypnotism of that witch-dancing wallpaper, the scent of lust held him there, freezing him for the monster that now pulled its massive body up above the covers and stood on all fours leering at him hungrily from the bed. The wolf reared up, pausing for a moment to take in the half-face of its victim and then it lunged forward, burying its great jaws into the delicious heart and liver and stomach of John Patrick Hunter.

From on top of the bed, the beast mauled the school principal. It grabbed what was left of his head in its jaws and bounded forward, yanking the lifeless body back into the center of the room. There, it settled in for the afternoon to feast on the bloody remains...

Of Holly Madonie's lover.

Chapter 40
Holly Finds the Body

John Hunter's clothes had been torn from him and thrust into a bloody heap in a distant corner of the little redwood cabin where he had been murdered. Yes, that was where it had happened, not in some labyrinthine cottage made of gingerbread and reeking of the smell of witch-woman sex.

Holly now approached the blood-soaked pile of rags. Her eyes were wild with shock, and she trembled all over. She pawed through the pockets looking for some sign that this was indeed her lover, though her heart told her it must be. She found Hunter's wallet. Inside the blood-smeared leather was what she'd been looking for: an incriminating picture of the two of them together. She snatched up the photo and stuffed it into her pocket and rifled through the other bloody clothing not knowing what she was looking for. That's when she discovered the simple silver ring.

For some reason, she turned the ring and noticed the words engraved inside. And now she knew that John had wanted to marry her and wanted them be together always.

Holly fell to the floor, wailing. She pulled her hands above her head and crushed them into her hair. She curled up like a newborn baby and poured her soul into a tumult of endless sobs.

That's when her little daughter came up to her, pried the ring from her trembling fingers, and stuffed it into her own pocket. She had led her mother to the door of the cabin, telling her that Hunter wanted to meet her there. Now she took her mother by the arms, pulled her to her feet, and nearly dragged her out of the door before the forest service and police had a chance to arrive.

Chapter 41
The Mikley Meeting

At the same time that Holly discovered the deadly revenge Babcia had exacted on John Hunter, Niko was facing a crisis of his own.

What was happening?

That's what Mary Beetle wanted to know. She was the MikleyToons executive who had worked so damn hard to set up this meeting. The whole deal had been her idea from the beginning. She had brought the Mikley-VVA relationship along so carefully and nursed it through those desperate days when Niko was near death. Now, she'd managed to get the top five men in MikleyToons over to VVA for this presentation.

So, what the hell was going wrong?

Jeannie Morrison was doing her part. She had virtually turned into her sister, Marla, not the hideous undead witch who inhabited her body, of course, but the lithe, exciting ballerina who had captivated so many executives in story presentations in the past.

She danced through the story of Rapunzel, eyes sparkling, becoming in one moment the beautiful girl from the fairy tale and in the next a humorous caricature of the old witch who had imprisoned her.

It was her idea that Niko play the young prince and tell his part of the story, gesturing to the storyboards, acting the part, and portraying a perfect Prince Charming.

Chuck Vaughn looked on proudly, like a father watching his children perform in their best school play. He was starry-eyed.

So why weren't the Mikley people captivated?

Well, to be fair about it, some of them were. Don Kimball for one, the renowned animation director sat chuckling through the entire presentation. He couldn't take his eyes off of the flirtatious Jeannie. He moved with her, tapping his foot along with her songs, and nodding his head in response to her questions as though she were speaking only to him.

Tom Mikley, the young nephew of the late Win Mikley who had founded the MikleyToons Empire forty years earlier, also understood Jeannie's presentation. He laughed out loud at many of her clever little jokes and looked concerned when the witch threatened the father and the prince. He and Don even applauded when Jeannie spoke the obligatory final words.

"And they all lived happily ever after."

Vaughn and Mary Beetle loved the presentation as well. But the Mikley men sitting on the other side of the table did not.

Bob Story, head writer at the MikleyToon Studios, might have been tuned in to Jeannie for the first few minutes, but as he saw her intent, to depict the old Rapunzel story where the witch wins, he became tenser. In the end, he sat there, sullen, arms crossed over his chest, a bitter snarl fixed on his face.

Bill Sanderson, Head of Production, was just as grim. As the presentation neared its climax, he took out a folder and began reading it as if to make certain that everyone knew he couldn't care less about the TV show or about acquiring the company that was pitching it.

That left Terry Worthy, President of MikleyToons, Win Mikley's son-in-law and former football star. Many people said that he was more of a studio caretaker than anything else.

"Win surrounded himself with used car salesmen and yes-men when he was alive," Don Kimball once remarked, and now someone was going to pay the price for that failure of executive recruitment. Most likely it would be Charles Martin Vaughn.

Perhaps Vaughn and Niko and VVA and even MikleyToons would have paid the price, but no one had counted on the fact that the presentation was being run by a woman who was at least one half undead-witch. And she knew exactly how to handle the situation.

"Our audiences expect more from us than this," Bob Story said. "They want happy endings."

"Win wouldn't like it," Sanderson added.

Those words were almost always the kiss of death when spoken by a studio executive even though it was clear to Don Kimball, at least, that Sanderson couldn't imagine what Win Mikley would like if his life depended on it. It didn't matter, though, because the witch within Jeannie Morrison took that opportunity to do something very simple, yet absolutely decisive.

She pressed a very clear memory into the minds of the Mikley team. In that memory, all the MikleyToon executives present including Terry Worthy were sitting in one of the old sweatbox viewing rooms at the studio. Win was alive then, and he had turned to Don Kimball and said,

"Someday, just to be different, we need to try one where the witch wins. Now that would be a hell of a story."

All right, so Jeannie/Marla colored those words a little. It didn't matter because it stopped the criticism and gave Terry Worthy an opportunity to respond.

He began by giving the Devils their due:

"I think Bob Story and Bill Sanderson are right," he said. "Win wouldn't like the ending as it stands now. But I think the story is splendid. The ending just needs a little work. Win always wanted to try one where the witch came out on top in the end, remember?"

Of course, they did.

"Just needs a little work," Mary Beetle agreed. So did Don Kimball.

"We're still working on the ending," Jeannie answered. "In fact, we're hoping to go to the site of the tower that inspired Rapunzel's story."

"There really is a tower?" Vaughn asked.

"It's in Poland." Niko answered.

"Better get over there, then," Worthy responded. "Find us an ending that will satisfy everyone here."

Vaughn, who might have resisted the cost of a trip to Eastern Europe, a flight to a Communist country no less, now responded gladly. "Niko and Jeannie will go over there and be back with a new ending for you in a couple of weeks."

Sanderson grimaced. The whole conversation was giving him a headache.

"I like it," Worthy said. And then he stood indicating that, in his mind at least, the meeting was over.

"What about the studio buy-out?" Mary Beetle called while everyone rose to leave.

"Keep working on it," Worthy instructed. "Move it along. I'd like to take one more look at this Rapunzel thing before we settle. But if these guys can find an original ending that will satisfy this committee, then they're worth every penny Vaughn wants for his operation." Then he eyed Vaughn and added, "The production arm of your group is invaluable too, of course."

"Of course," Vaughn answered with a smile. He turned to Niko and Jeannie, "You're on your way to Poland, kids."

"Yes!" Niko answered, and he grabbed Jeannie and gave her a great big kiss on the lips.

Right there in front of everyone!

Chapter 42
Joy Comes Home

Niko was downtown celebrating his victory with Chuck and the gang when Holly needed him most – nothing had changed, had it? But Joy had been there for Holly. The little girl was with her mother when one of the other parents drove her home. She helped Holly undress for a shower and, a little later, helped her crawl into bed.

Who was the Mommy and who was the child? Someone might have asked until they saw Joy sitting on her bed later that evening, quivering in grief with tears streaming down her face.

Emmy hopped up onto the bed and came to her. Joy pushed the cat away.

"You helped her, Emmy. You helped Babcia kill Principal Hunter."

Emmy gave a soft meow and insistently made her way back to the little girl who soon took her in her arms, buried her face in the cat's soft fur and began sobbing.

It was hours later after Joy had cried her eyes out and could hardly keep them open that Babcia appeared in the mirror above the dresser.

"It need be done," she said softly to Joy.

"But not like that!" Joy shouted back in anguish. "I was part of it. My Mommy knows it, too."

"Is all right, Kochanie," Babcia murmured. "Is almost done now."

"You mean there's more?" Joy shouted as she picked up her shoe and threw it at the mirror. It bounced off harmlessly. Apparently, one of the benefits of being a possessed mirror was that it was unbreakable.

"I won't help you anymore!" Joy shouted.

"Is good," Babcia murmured. "Cat will serve."

"I won't let you use Emmy to destroy people, either!" This time the little girl shouted even louder.

"Cat will serve," Babcia said firmly. "And will be like you sometimes."

"She'll look like me, act like me?"

"Yah, Kochanie," Babcia answered.

Joy grimaced and shuddered all over. Then she let out a wail and spun back onto the bed, slipping under the covers, and pulling Emmy in with her.

"Sometimes I hate you, Great Grandma," she whimpered.

"Must be done," Babcia repeated. "WILL be done!"

In her bedroom down the hall, Holly lay fast asleep. She had taken four of the Valium the doctors had prescribed to help Niko with his recovery. She slept through all of Joy's shouting, Niko's late night return from work, and even his rising the next morning.

He thought he was doing Holly a favor when he helped little Joy get dressed and packed her off to school. Joy was sullen and didn't say a word, as though all this was as much Niko's fault as his grandmother's. And so he passed through that evening and the entire day without ever learning that his greatest enemy, Holly's lover...

John Hunter had been destroyed.

Chapter 43
Father Tim

Obscene pictures of Holly Madonie, some with her lover John Hunter, and others with a different man, a younger, rugged-looking hippie! Father Tim couldn't put them down. And there was a note, too, from Holly. In it she pleaded with the priest to hear her confession, but not in the church, not even in his office in the hospital. Holly had asked the priest to meet her in Griffith Park in a little gingerbread playhouse that had been set up at the end of a long deserted road.

Father Tim thought he knew Griffith Park very well. It was a huge sprawling hunk of wilderness someone had managed to preserve in the middle of Los Angeles. There were many attractions tucked in around the edges, that was true, maybe too many to keep track of. But most of the park was still wilderness, and Tim had never heard of the gingerbread playhouse before.

Joy, of course, had been insistent when she delivered the note to the priest. Her father had been taking her there for as long as she could remember, she said. It was wonderful.

Father Tim also asked little Joy if she'd seen the pictures her mother had sent. He certainly hoped not. Joy was just as insistent that Holly would not allow her to see the pictures. They were just for Father Tim, and she was a good little girl and would never disobey her mother.

The priest had only recently been released from the hospital. He had not had the magical intervention that had restored Niko's health so quickly. But in his recovery, Tim had thought a great deal about Holly, about how innocent she was, and yet how she had been led into evil again and again by her own animal desires.

Fascinating!

Tim realized his vocation was to save beautiful souls such as hers. They deserved his attention.

He was in a relatively healthy frame of mind when those tempting pictures were delivered to him. The question, of course, was what to do about them? Answer Holly's request surely, go to her and hear her confession (in vivid detail), and then steer the beautiful young woman onto the path of righteousness and help her find the goodness within herself. Yes, that was critical, but what about the pictures themselves?

Father Tim knew why they'd been sent to him; they offered proof of Holly's infidelities. He must destroy them, of course. But before he did that, he thought...

Perhaps he should spend a little time with them.

Chapter 44
Holly Finds the Book

Holly Madonie could not stop screaming: loud, high, electric screeches that drained every ounce of air from her body and left her feeling as though she would strangle to death before she could grab her next desperate breath of air.

The tips of three of her fingers were cut deeply spilling their blood out over her daughter's prettiest sweaters and drenching them with a deep crimson that she knew could never be removed. But that wasn't the cause of her frantic cries. It was the hideous object that had caused the bleeding that sent her into hysterics.

It was the mask of Babcia, the mask that supposedly was cast from the very face of Niko's wicked witch grandmother when she was a hideous crone living in Poland.

The mask had seemingly bitten her when she'd reached deep into the bottom drawer of Joy's little Winnie the Pooh dresser.

Yes, Holly was searching, looking for some indication of Joy's relationship with Babcia, a relationship she'd never fully understood. But that evil mask, a mask that Holly knew only too well, was only the first piece of evidence that she found in Joy's room.

As Holly sacrificed Joy's prettiest light blue angora sweater by tying one sleeve tightly around her fingers to stop the bleeding, out of the corner of her eye she spotted another object buried at the far, almost hidden, end of Joy's bookcase. It was a large, thick book, a book that she knew almost nothing about.

Holly grasped the book, pulled it out from behind five works by Dr. Seuss, and set it onto her lap: *Grimm's Fairy Tales* illustrated by Arthur Rackham. She began flipping through the pages, past the frightening picture of Little Red Riding Hood's meeting with the wolf. She'd never know that a living, breathing version of the same hideous sight was the last thing her lover had seen before his death.

Holly's terror, which hadn't abated since she'd seen the bloody corpse of John Hunter only the day before, now raced to fever heights as she encountered a story called *The Unborn Sacrifice*. That horrific tale featured an illustration showing a very pregnant woman who looked exactly like Holly being dragged into a witches' Sabbath where dozens of witches of every shape and age were about to tear her baby from her and throw it into a boiling caldron.

Holly's heart nearly stopped as she read the final sentence that described how Babcia herself had entered the ceremony "to save the wife of her beloved grandson."

Yes, those were the exact words in the book, as though the only reason Holly had any right to be saved at all was because Niko's grandmother loved HIM.

Holly's hysteria was now racing out of control. A heavy sweat burst out all over her body. Her rapid, uneven breathing and the deep murmured conversation she seemed to be having with herself (repeating over and over again, - "Oh, no, oh God, no,") now grew louder and louder as she turned to the next chapter entitled *The Ballerina and the Cage*. That explained a lot, didn't it? Then there was a tale called *Witch Girl* that gave Holly the specific answer she was looking for and yet so desperately feared. She gazed around the room in terror. She was so totally alone.

Even though it was mid-day, ominous shadows appeared to be moving toward her. Could she go on? She had to. And so she turned to the very last tale in the book. It was not yet complete. And yet it featured a brilliant, new illustration done in the same style as the others. This was a drawing of a terrible tower set high in the mountains, a tower that was dark and foreboding surrounded as it was by sharp spikes of granite that thrust up wickedly on all sides. There was only one window at the very highest point of the tower, too far above the ground for anyone to fall from and survive. The tale was called *The Tower of Death* and under the illustration was this caption:

"Deep in the mountains, the evil tower waited for the artist and his daughter."

Chapter 45
Holly and Father Tim

Holly's response to extreme stress in her life had always been a return to religion, and now she made her way down the long antiseptic hallways of St. Joseph's Hospital toward the office of Father Tim. When she arrived at the door she uttered a deep, desperate sigh. The door was closed.

"Father Tim," she called weakly, but there was no answer. She knocked softly, then more loudly. Nothing. Tears began to form in her eyes.

"Ohhh, Tim, please be here," she sighed.

As a last hopeful act, she tried the door handle and felt a great sense of relief when it turned easily, letting her into his office.

There was no one in the room, but in her desperation, she dared to walk inside, right up to the priest's desk, and there...

She couldn't believe her eyes.

Scattered across the desk were photographs of a young woman, her eyes closed in insatiable passion.

Wait! Holly thought for a moment. She recognized the men in the pictures: Billy Bright! John Hunter! Worse than that, behind that contorted smile of ecstasy, beneath those eyes closed in glowing lust, was Holly herself. These pictures were of her making love, horrible incriminating pictures on the desk of a priest.

"My God!" she screamed out loud just as Father Tim entered the room.

The priest had only the slightest hint of embarrassment in his eyes.

"Where... how did you get these?" she demanded.

Father Tim (amazingly) was taken aback.

"I got them from you," he replied with a look of surprise.

"I've never seen them before in my life."

"But, what about the letter?" Father Tim asked. "That letter you sent me with these pictures?"

He reached under the pictures and pulled out a one-page letter and handed it to Holly. In an instant, she recognized her own handwriting.

"My God, Father!"

Now the priest was embarrassed. He began gathering up the pictures and shuffling them into the manila envelope in which they'd arrived.

"How did you get these?" she asked. She was trembling all over.

"Joy brought them."

"Joy!" Holly's eyes blazed with fury.

"I've been tricked, haven't I?"

"Joy is a witch," Holly responded and she snatched the envelope from him.

"Literally!" Tim added.

"What do you mean?"

"She's literally a witch possessed by the spirit of her dead grandmother and forced to do evil to hurt you and anyone who looks at you in, in...."

"Lust?" Holly asked and shivered with fright. Her eyes burned Father Tim with a look of accusation, anguish, flattery and flirtation. How could a single look convey all those emotions? And yet her eyes said all that and more.

"Holly," Father Tim began. "My child."

"Don't give me that shit," Holly fumed. "How did you know about Joy?"

"Niko told me."

"He told you, and he didn't bother to tell me?"

"He loves you. He wanted to spare you."

"Spare me? This is how he spares me?"

And then Holly wilted right there in front of the priest.

"What are we going to do, Father?" she whispered as she collapsed into a chair.

"I could call in an exorcist," the priest answered. He almost felt proud that his profession was able to offer some kind of solution. "We could drive this demon out of her!"

Holly just shook her head. She feared the harm that such a terrible procedure would inflict. And besides:

"You don't know this witch," she whispered. "She's a monster, a savage ancient beast. She's already killed a half dozen people she thought were threatening our marriage. She even tried to kill me."

Father Tim shook his head. "Does that make her any match for the power of Christ?"

Holly lowered her eyes. She didn't know. She thought back to those times when she had any sense that her prayers had been answered, and it didn't seem to rival the hideous evil that had been heaped upon her in the name of Babcia.

"You need proof then, don't you?" Father Tim asked as he began wringing his hands. "I owe that to you. I've sinned against you and God, and I need to do penance."

"Tim," Holly whispered. But the priest's face was suddenly turning from a look of desperation to one of excitement.

"Yes!" he exclaimed as though possessed himself. "And the way to do penance is to challenge the witch with the power of Our Lord."

Tim reached across and took Holly's hand. The young woman was so much a creature of lust that she still felt a tingle of passion in his touch. An electric tingle of sexuality raced through Tim's body as well, and he quickly pulled his hand from her. He stared at her almost accusingly, and she turned her eyes away.

"How will you do it?" she asked at last. "How will you challenge Babcia?"

Father Tim looked at the beautiful, young woman who had come down to his office with such an extreme sense of terror, yet somehow, almost automatically, she'd made herself beautiful for him, dressing in an attractive skirt and blouse with an open collar that was almost revealing. The small crucifix around her neck was meant just for him. What kind of witchcraft flowed through the channels of HER mind? Tim wondered. Whatever it was, it made him want to be her hero, her champion, and he could use the power of Christ to do it.

"How will you challenge Babcia, Father?" Holly repeated, but now there was a little thrill in her voice. She was calling on her champion and using all the powers of her sexuality to do it.

"Simple," answered the priest with a careless smile. "I'll do exactly what she's asking me to do.

"I'll meet her at the gingerbread house in Griffith Park."

Chapter 46
Gingerbread

Holly read the directions to the gingerbread house... directions written in her own handwriting, but not by her, directions to a place she was sure did not exist.

Soon enough, though, just as the gingerbread house had appeared and begun playing tricks on John Hunter as it led him to his death, so, too, this house now appeared and began playing peek-a-boo between the trees of Griffith Park, luring the young woman and the priest to perhaps the very same fate.

Holly, of course, could not believe her eyes. There were no rides or booths of any kind in this part of the park. She had been here hundreds of times. But somehow, there it was.

Holly knew Babcia had spared her for Niko's sake... saved her from death again and again. As long as she stayed with Father Tim, she reasoned, the priest would be safe, too. But this was not what Tim wanted. How could he prove the power of his God, and his manhood if he could not confront the witch in direct and terrible combat?

He wanted to look directly into the demon eyes of Babcia just as he'd done only recently when he'd seen the face of Clara Goriki when she' tried to murder Niko in the hospital.

That image came flashing back to Tim as he drove his small, black Chevrolet Nova through Griffith Park. He shuddered at the memory and drove on, seeing the structure appear to transform in the sunlight from a gingerbread house to an abandoned maintenance shack and then into a bright, new children's playhouse again built of gingerbread and trimmed with white and pink frosting.

Strange squiggly shapes were set into the frosting. They were also reflected in the sparks that came twisting up in the smoke that billowed from the chimney. They were the shapes of witches dancing, singing, casting spells, flying on brooms.

Holly saw all of them, and there was something very familiar about it. She'd seen the exact same building before in a drawing. It was the design that Niko had created for the animated TV special Hansel and Gretel. And she also knew that he had based his drawings on pictures that Babcia had made for him when he was a little boy.

Father Tim steered the car off the road and pulled it up in front of that sweet confection of a building. He stepped out of the car on the side away from it and walked around and up onto the sweetly colored porch. He peered through the window and caught a glimpse of a beautiful, young woman standing just inside. She wore a red cape that covered most of her body, but as she moved away from the window, it became clear that she was wearing little else.

"Tim, wait!" Holly called from the car. She ran up next to him and took his hand.

"Don't go in there unless I'm with you."

A look of great frustration crossed Tim's face, but still, he walked with Holly to the front door and pushed it open. As he did, he caught another glimpse of the beautiful, young woman in the red cape who suddenly ducked behind the doorway of a distant room. But when he and Holly stepped into the cabin together, he saw something far more real and surprising. Little Joy Madonie was sitting on the floor, playing jacks, tossing the ball up into the air, scooping up the jacks and then catching the ball on the bounce.

"She wasn't invited," Joy said pointing to her mother. And then she turned to Holly.

"Mommy," she called. "I hope you realize that you've just ruined everything." And then another face flashed across the little girl's. It was the face from the evil mask that had terrified Holly when she'd found it in Joy's drawer.

Holly's response was harsh and immediate.
She began screaming hysterically.

Chapter 47
Niko Learns

"Holly! Guess what happened?" Niko called as he raced from room to room in their little home. "Hey...Where the hell are you?"

The young man was almost giddy knowing that they were on the verge of becoming millionaires.

"Holly, the presentation was a success! Mikley wants to buy our company! All we have to do is...."

But she was nowhere in sight. Niko was about to start his second search through the house and then out into the back yard, when there was a hard pounding on the front door. He turned, went quickly to the door and opened it.

It was Father Tim, looking very concerned. Niko's little girl was standing beside the priest. Her expression was almost happy in spite of the words she knew Tim was about to speak.

"I heard you calling Holly," Tim began.

"Do you know where she is?"

The priest nodded. "May I come in?"

"Sure," Niko said as he pushed the door wide open.

"I took her to St. Joseph's Hospital," Father Tim said softly. "I'm afraid she's had a bit of a breakdown."

"What? What kind of a breakdown?"

"Just a little nervous exhaustion. She'll be okay."

Niko stared at the priest uncertainly, and then led him through the entryway and into the living room. He gestured for the priest to sit down on the large sofa. As he did, Father Tim couldn't help but notice a row of framed pictures lined up on the mantel over the fireplace. There was a snapshot of Holly and Niko as teenagers standing at a high school fair. Holly held a little plush elephant that they must have won on the wheel of fortune. Other photos showed them at Leland

University with two attractive classmates (Billy Bright and Nancy Swallow). And there was Holly beaming as she held one of Chuck Vaughn's Oscars as she stood between Niko and Vaughn at the VVA studios.

Niko took a seat on the couch beside the priest. He had turned pale in an instant.

"Don't worry, Daddy," Joy said as she stepped in front of the priest and took her father by the hand. "I'll take care of you." Then she smiled, "In a minute that is. Excuse me." And she ran upstairs to her room.

"I have such great news for Holly," Niko said. "MikleyToons is gonna buy VVA. We'll be rich."

"I'm sure Holly will be very happy," Father Tim answered. "But right now her condition and Joy's..."

"Joy's?"

"We need to talk about your daughter, too," Tim whispered. He glanced over his shoulder and saw her coming back down the stairs. She had Emmy draped over her shoulder.

"We need to talk in private," Tim added before Joy could reach them. "Just you and I."

"When?" Niko asked eyeing Joy just as Tim had done.

"Early tomorrow," he answered. "That would be a good time to see Holly, too."

"I need to see her now," Niko said standing until he noticed that the priest hadn't moved and so he sat back down.

"She's heavily sedated," Tim said. "She'll be better able to recognize you and talk to you in the morning."

"What happened?" Niko asked.

"We can talk about it tomorrow."

"John Hunter had something to do with it, didn't he?" Niko demanded.

"John Hunter is dead. Killed yesterday near Crystal Lake."

Niko's face twisted in disbelief. He pulled his hand to his head and ran it across his brow.

"My God!" he said finally. "Is it possible?" Two feelings collided in his mind and left him speechless: relief that John Hunter was no more, (was it really possible?) and concern for Holly, after all, she still loved him.

"It's true," whispered the priest.

"I've been working so hard. Hardly know anything that's been going on outside the studio. I didn't know. How did he die?"

"There hasn't been any official word yet," Tim responded. "They're still investigating. But, according to one report, he was killed by a wolf."

Niko froze.

"SHE did it!" he said suddenly. "Holly knows it and Joy...."

The two men turned toward the little girl who returned their gaze with a cold insolence.

"Let's talk about all this tomorrow," Tim repeated and added. "I'm afraid there's more."

"But you say Holly's all right?"

Father Tim patted Niko on the shoulder and nodded. "She is. You can see for yourself tomorrow. I'd better go."

Niko led the priest slowly to the door and gave him a quick goodbye.

When Niko returned to the living room, Joy was looking at him with the most penetrating stare.

"I don't like that man, Daddy," she said.

"He's a priest. Why wouldn't you like him?"

"He wants mommy."

Niko shook his head and sighed heavily.

"It's nothing new," he said. "Most men do."

"He can't have her."

"No," Niko agreed. "He can't."

"I hope Babcia doesn't have to kill him too," she said. And then she burst into tears.

"Too?" Niko mumbled.

Joy didn't respond. Instead, she ran up to her room sobbing, leaving Niko alone with the calm, frightening presence of Emmy, the cat.

Chapter 48
Leaving the Cat

"You can't leave that beast in this hospital," Sister Alexia yelled at Niko.

The young man spun around, and the cage holding Emmy almost knocked the elderly nun to the floor. Inside the cage, the cat was raging, and that certainly didn't help. She spat and sputtered like a beast possessed, which, of course, is exactly what she was.

"Listen," Niko responded to the nun. "This cat is very important to my wife. She wants her here. It'll help her recovery."

"Not a chance, dear boy."

"I'll take care of this, Sister," Father Tim said as he walked into the hospital room.

And just like that, the excited old woman melted the way any good nun would in the presence of a young, handsome, dedicated man of the cloth, and she left the room immediately.

"I'll take care of Emmy," Father Tim offered, and Niko looked at him with grateful eyes: grateful and pitying at the same time. He realized that Father Tim had no idea of the deadly deal he was making.

Niko had spent the last half hour at Holly's bedside. She was still heavily sedated and bleary-eyed, agreeing to almost everything he suggested, looking angelic as always and feeling that only he could save her from the evils that were spinning all around her.

Taking Joy far away was something Holly hadn't counted on. But maybe that was for the best, too. Having Joy disappear for a few weeks seemed like an excellent idea to her, especially if it meant that Babcia would be gone as well.

Of course, Holly was not privy to the knowledge that Babcia could move freely between the bodies of the little girl and the cat. She was unaware that Niko and Joy (and Babcia, for that matter) had agreed to leave Emmy at the hospital where Babcia could keep an eye on Father Tim and his less than priestly desires.

The priest may have welcomed it, though. He might have seen the witch as yet another fascinating, though terrifying, subject. But he didn't know about Babcia and Emmy, and so he was unaware who was listening when he leaned forward to tell Niko that his daughter was possessed.

"Keep an eye on her while you're away," Tim began. "And when you return, I can arrange for an exorcism if you and your wife will agree to it."

"If I were you, I'd forget about Joy and just look after Holly," Niko answered.

Tim nodded.

"The only thing is, Father," Niko said softly...

Father Tim moved closer to hear him.

"If you come on to my wife in any way..."

"Come on to her?"

"Try to seduce her...."

"You can't be serious."

"Deadly serious. If you try to seduce my wife, you'll die. Believe me. And it will be horrible."

Father Tim tried to laugh, as though Niko meant his words as a joke. But the laughter trailed off into a hollow cough. He was well aware of what had happened to John Hunter. And Niko wasn't laughing at all.

"Well, as they say in Poland, 'Vaya con Dios.'" Father Tim tried to joke.

Niko smiled and nodded as the priest took the cage holding the cat and carried it down the hall and into his office, closing the door behind him.

"What happened?" Holly called weakly to Niko from her bed.

"Just saying our good-byes."

He walked back to his wife and kissed her again.

Holly looked up at her husband. "Where will you be going?"

"A little town in Poland called Zakopane. Shouldn't be gone more than two weeks."

"And who'll be with you?"

"Just some people from work and Joy, of course."

Holly nodded in acceptance.

"Will I see Joy before you leave?"

"She really wants to see you, but I'm afraid there isn't time."

Holly nodded slowly. She was so heavily sedated that she couldn't really think clearly, and yet there was one final question she had to ask. She raised herself onto her elbows, turned to her husband and whispered:

"This doesn't have anything to do with a tower, does it?"

Niko looked at his wife in astonishment.

And then he lied.

Interlude Six

The warlock pointed to the very top of the high tower... at Matryoshka who now stood at the little window looking down.

"You do trust my magic to save you, am I right?" He called up to her.

"I believe," the girl answered, though her smile betrayed a considerable amount of anxiety.

"Jump then, will you?"

Matryoshka looked down at the warlock who, though he looked small from such a great height, was still a commanding presence. Even the positions of his young witches, fanned out as they were around him, still leaning toward him with rapt attention, showed their awe of his power.

"Jump!" Wicktor called.

And she did.

The girl soared up above the edge of the window and then plunged straight downward with a long, desperate cry:

"Wicktorrrrrrr!"

Those beautiful, handpicked witches let out a collective gasp. Some of them screamed in those long seconds as Matryoshka fell.

The warlock spun and thrust his hand at her, almost as though he were throwing a baseball. And she came to an abrupt stop in mid-air just inches above the ground.

The members of Wicktor's coven sighed in relief and launched into a round of applause as the hairy monster strode proudly up to Matryoshka like some great magician. He smiled at his girls and gestured to Matryoshka who hung in the air now as though she were lying on a sofa. She smiled comfortably at the crowd and waved.

The warlock bent down and ran his hand beneath her to show that there was nothing that supported her. Then he took her in his arms and, like some gallant ballet dancer, lifted her up and set her gracefully on her feet.

Silently, the Cummings twins and three of the other witches had set up a feast on the far side of the great marble circle. There were tables full of grapes and bread and cheeses and wine, entire stuffed chickens and lamb, salads, fruit, and pudding and pastries galore... all provided by an anonymous supporter from a nearby community who perhaps owed Wicktor some devilish debt.

The rest of the girls walked over to the food now, some of them moving slowly, chatting among themselves about the marvels they had just seen, others looking quite ravenous after so many hours listening to the warlock's tale without a bite to eat. They seated themselves and began. Many of them were still completely naked, still basking in the warm glow of the great fire. Other teenage witches wore only the silver cords from the black satin robes around their waists. Some even sat on their robes as they gobbled up all the goodness that Megan Cummings and her cohorts had served.

The warlock sat at the head of the table with a huge chicken leg in his hand. He'd already taken a bite out of it, and his face was covered with grease as he chewed open-mouthed, smiling at his brood.

"Eat heartily," he called. "For the story becomes much darker from here on."

"As if it hasn't been dark enough," Chantel said. She was on the master's left, Matryoshka on his right.

"Ah, but it gets darker still, girls. So if any of you are squeamish, unwilling to hear, and want to give up witchcraft, please leave now."

The women eyed each other nervously then began chatting and eating again.

"We're anxious to hear more of Babcia's adventures in America," said Megan Cummings, and the others nodded in agreement.

"Yes, and Niko and Joy's adventures in Poland, for they are coming here when our story continues," said the warlock.

"More than that," and here his eyes began to sparkle. "There's the added treat I mentioned. You will soon meet them and join in a witchy celebration with one of them, and perhaps even play a role in the final outcome of this adventure."

The girls gushed and giggled.

"You mean this story is not yet complete then?" Megan asked.

"Hardly," answered the warlock with a smile.

There were more ooohhhhs and aaahhhs.

"So, why don't you continue then... bring us up to date?" Megan asked.

"Right here and now while we eat," her twin insisted.

"If it pleases you, it pleases us," said Chantel. And again all the girls nodded in agreement.

"Alright, but we'll have to go back in time first to pick up a bit more of the old crone Babcia and her murderous revenge on those who executed her husband and child. One thing you'll learn is that she hasn't changed much over the centuries."

Most of the girls had stopped eating at this point. Many of them leaned forward in eager anticipation.

Wicktor eyed them. Then, he wiped his hands on his napkin, took a quick swig of wine, and continued his story.

Babcia Michalina Czarownica moved farther and farther into the forest. She was now an ancient hag, a creature accustomed to living alone, never speaking to another human being for years on end.

So much had been taken from her. When she was but a sixteen-year-old girl, witch-hunters murdered her husband and baby son right before her eyes.

She remembered it all very well, how she'd watched as the hunters invaded her home, castrated and butchered her husband, snatched her infant son from her and began recklessly tossing him back and forth across the room letting him fall hard onto the floor over and over again.

Then, at last, when they were about to skewer the infant by driving a stake right through him from head to foot and roasting him over the open fire (as was only appropriate for witches and their children), Michalina felt the blood of the wolves coursing through her veins and felt fangs and talons growing from her.

From that moment on, the witch-hunters were no match for the hunted. Little sixteen-year-old Michalina became a monstrous she-wolf then and there, and destroyed every one of the witch-hunters. Of course, it was too late; her child was already dead. Still, terrible vengeance would be exacted upon her coven because of Babcia's deeds.

The leader of Michalina's coven sent her away, deep into the forest where no one could find her. And while the witches performed rituals to ask the goddess to protect their coven from further witch hunts, who should happen upon them but the very Wynofski brothers who had murdered Michalina's father.

How young Michalina wished she could have been with the coven as they fell upon the evil brothers, scratched their eyes out, and tore them to shreds. But, in the end, this act of vengeance only begot more vengeance, only added to the horror that would follow when an entire brigade of the Polish Army descended upon the little village that was home to the coven and annihilated its occupants.

All but the oldest of the witches were raped before they were forced to join their sisters to be burned at the stake. And any man who sought to save a young woman, if only for himself, was likewise burned as a witch. Soon the smell of the burning village and burning flesh filled the nighttime skies until at last, it reached young Michalina living alone in the woods.

The girl knew at once what was happening and that her coven was no more. And yet she could save herself and live to carry on their work and their worship of the goddess. And so, that is what she did. She moved still deeper into the most forbidden part of the wood. And centuries passed.

It was two hundred years later when Michalina, no longer a beautiful girl but now a terrible hag, twisted with age and hatred, found a way to seek revenge on the witch-hunters who had killed everyone she loved. She found the very site where the wolves had taken her the night her father had died. It was a great stone tower built perhaps by some ancient people who had lived in the area. Babcia did not know or care. What she did know was that it had a vast, open courtyard before it and that the tower itself rose high into the skies where only a single window offered entry.

The wolves, her brothers and sisters, had long ago moved on, but the place had been taken over by a huge flock of ravens. Great, black birds strutted proudly around the courtyard or soared up into the tower window. Babcia settled in among them, fed them her food, made friends with them. And soon the ravens called to her, invited her to ascend to the high window with them. And so she did.

Babcia allowed herself to be carried by the largest of them. The huge, black birds sunk their claws into her tattered old clothes and lifted her up and through the high window of the tower, into a wide and beautiful room where a great soft bed waited for her, a room with chests full of jewelry and beautiful clothes. There were thick, oriental carpets, enormous mirrors, and hundreds of books on many subjects including The Craft.

Babcia realized that the place must have once been the home of another powerful witch, perhaps a very vain witch, but one who had left a warm and comfortable spot for her, nonetheless.

And so she made the tower her home. And the ravens came and brought her food and other necessities. And if Babcia ever wanted to go out into the world, they would carry her down from the tower and accompany her on her rounds, bringing her back to the tower at last to that wonderful bed, which was, perhaps, as great a pleasure as any witch could ever have in her lifetime.

Babcia could have been very happy there, it seems. She might have been, but revenge had become the goal of her old age, and a terrible goal it was, unworthy of her darkest magic, and yet, in the end, the beneficiary of it all.

She poured through the books in the tower and found the Spell of Becoming. She giggled like a schoolgirl as she prepared the potion that would turn her, once again, into young Michalina. It worked wonderfully... for short periods of time. Babcia also perfected a sweet and magical lullaby that she would sing every afternoon sending its melody out across the deep forest, luring anyone who heard it to come to the tower and see the beautiful maiden who lived there.

Many brave young men did venture there, saw Michalina the maiden and called to her. Captivated by her beauty, they wondered how they could climb the tower's heights to save the girl for an evil witch must have imprisoned her. In fact, now and again a traveler would gaze up into the tower for a chance to see Michalina and instead would catch a glimpse of a horrible, old hag tottering around as though she were very much at home.

All was in readiness, Babcia thought. All she had to do was be patient and wait. Soon enough, the first male descendant of those cursed witch-hunters would make his way to the foot of her tower. Then others would follow.

And she would have her revenge.

Part Three
Rapunzel's Tower

Chapter 49
The Plane Ride

Jeannie Morrison strode carefully into the first-class section of the plane and took her seat across the aisle from Niko Madonie. Joy sat at the window beside him. The little girl was now entirely herself without the witching presence of Babcia. And so she was unable to recognize Marla Morrison within the sweet façade of her sister. And that was just as well, because, on this day at least, Marla's vengeful presence was laying low and old Rosie Osborn was in control of Jeannie.

"Is this your little girl?" Jeannie asked with a sweet smile.

"Yes," Niko answered. "Joy, this is my writing partner, Jeannie Morrison."

Joy smiled happily at the young woman. It was going to be a very pleasant flight.

Certainly, Jeannie was "pretty as a picture." Those were Mother Black's exact words when she saw the young woman dress in a most attractive outfit: a rather tight cashmere sweater and a plaid skirt that was a little long for the era but still able to invite glances at Jeannie's shapely legs. She had pulled her hair up and a mound of tousled blond curls sat atop her pretty head. Jeannie wore a gold necklace with a very nondescript symbol on it, no reference to The Craft, certainly. Still, the way it rested in the center of that sweater was bewitching enough.

Inside the attractive frame of Jeannie Morrison, Marla cursed. Babcia's absence meant that she couldn't finish this ugly business at the tower. Oh, how she wanted it to be over. But perhaps it was safer this way. Marla, Clara Goriki, and Mother Black understood that the tower was a place Babcia knew well. She may even have friends there that could help her. Better to wait for a safer place for their confrontation. But in the meantime, what was Babcia up to? And what would become of Holly and her holy boyfriend in Niko's absence? Certainly, it would be something that could bring great pain to Niko Madonie and could fit right in with her plans, Marla hoped.

#

"I'm surprised you didn't bring your wife along," Jeannie said to Niko as the plane neared its cruising altitude. Joy was now asleep in her seat against the window.

"Holly's had a rough few weeks," Niko answered. "We thought it would be better if she took the time and rested. One of her co-workers just died."

"Oh, I'm sorry," Jeannie said. "Was it someone I knew, someone our age?"

"I don't think you could have known him," Niko answered. "It was John Hunter, the principal at the school where Holly worked. He was only 43."

"An accident?" Jeannie asked. A sense of concern seemed to grip her whole body and made Niko want to tell her everything.

"He was killed by a wolf," Niko answered. "Torn to pieces. Holly saw the body just after it was discovered... gruesome sight. She was really shaken."

"I would have had a complete breakdown," Jeannie said.

"Well, actually, she is suffering from nervous exhaustion," Niko admitted.

"But she's in good hands now, right?"

"Yes, I spoke to her doctor and the priest at the hospital, her advisor. She started consulting him when I... I..."

Almost killed myself! Niko hadn't thought of it in months.

Jeannie Morrison touched his arm gently. Her eyes spoke only of compassion and understanding. She was feeling a love for him that must have dawned during those long sessions when she was Rosie Osborn, the ugly, old woman neither liked nor spoken to by anyone except Niko. He had been kind to her then, and now she had become this beautiful vessel for the goodness of Rosie's love.

"It's all right," she whispered as she drew closer to him. "You don't have to worry. Holly will be fine. You can take your mind off of her and think about us."

"Us?"

"Sure, think of how much we'll enjoy creating a fantastic new ending to our story, exploring the spooky old place we're going to visit. It'll be great fun."

Jeannie kissed him on the cheek. Here was something to live for.

But deep within Jeannie Morrison, the wicked soul of Marla was not relaxed. She was doing everything she could to hold her anger because she could read the feelings of the girl whose body hosted hers. She could feel the love that was spreading through her, and she knew that there was a very dangerous component being born in Jeannie: the desire to protect Niko, to save him from the vengeance she knew Clara Goriki and Mother Black had in store for him.

Far below them, in her little bungalow in old Hollywood, the hundred-and-fifty-year-old Missouri backwoods witch gave an audible groan. She and Clara were watching the entire incident through her scrying ball, and they could read Jeannie's feelings.

"Dat gal ain't wit da program," Mother Black mumbled to Clara. "She wants ta bollix up our 'r whole plan an save dis boy. Maybe even 'is kid."

Clara's expression moved from worry to a sudden look of serenity.

"You know, I've been missing my old home in the Polish Mountains," she said. "Perhaps it's time I went back there and kept an even closer watch on our little Jeannie... make sure she fulfills the promise she made to us."

Mother Black nodded. "Otherwise, the girl's askin' ta die, by Lucifer!"

"That she is," Clara added. "And I can make that happen too, if necessary."

Chapter 50
Babcia Remembers

Babcia contemplated the fate of her next victim: Father Tim. This wasn't just about saving Niko's whore of a wife from her own indecent desires. This was about revenge: against the Catholic Church and the forces that had taken her child from her so long ago. And then there would be more revenge against the descendants of those evil brothers who had killed her father and had so much to do with the destruction of her village.

Why had she waited so long to exact it, five hundred years? Well, she'd had a great measure of revenge at Rapunzel's Tower, hadn't she? Babcia had destroyed so many of the young men who came calling on Michalina (Rapunzel), the beautiful reincarnation of her younger self.

She saw them in her mind's eye now as they ascended the face of the tower: strong, young, overflowing with lust, climbing the long braids of hair that Babcia herself had fashioned.

They came answering the siren song of Rapunzel, climbing higher and higher, driven by such desire that they often bounded over the window ledge and into the tower only to come face to face with Babcia herself. She charged madly at each of them with flailing ancient arms and long, vicious talons. Her look was one of pure bloodthirsty vengeance. A wild, piercing, banshee scream roared from her twisted cavern of a mouth so thick with the stench of open coffins and decaying corpses.

Most of the young men turned then and threw themselves from the tower. But not all! Some fought to save the maiden they believed to be imprisoned by the witch. For those fools, Babcia had an even more horrible fate. She would scurry away from each youth and they, with swords drawn, would follow her into a chamber where the beauteous Michalina would stand, shivering in fear.

Every one of the young men would then sheath his sword and approach the maiden to kiss, comfort her, and gaze upon her beauty. And that's when it would happen!

The soft lips of Michalina would part and slowly reveal those rotting witch's teeth. Her back would arch, her skin would wither until it hung from her like a shroud. Her arms would grow bony, twisted, and ancient. Her lustrous hair would turn to gray, mangled, spider-web straw, and, worst of all, her nails would grow into claws that would quickly slash at the eyes of the terrified hero. Within seconds, Babcia would scratch his eyes out, perhaps devouring those succulent orbs in the process, letting him witness the destruction of one before she took his sight completely as she snatched out the other and gobbled it up.

Then she'd lead the blind, trembling youth back to the window. By that point, not one of the heroic young men would have the strength or will to fight back. So Babcia would simply push him from the high tower herself and the youth would fall willingly, often silently to his deaths.

All but one of the young men, that is, and that one, nearly mad from the experience, lived on after the fall. He went wandering into the forest searching, he thought, for his lost Rapunzel, coming after weeks upon some huntsmen who took him back to their village.

He told his story, and the tale of Rapunzel was born. It was sanitized, of course, simplified. In only a few of the oldest books, such as *Grimm's Fairy Tales*, was the tale told in any way that resembled the truth. The witch had won!

Now Babcia, in the body of Emmy the cat, settled herself in the priest's bedroom. She drew in her claws and purred. She wondered if she could make her new persona as seductive and appealing as she had made Michalina in the tower so long ago. Could Emmy seduce others the way Michalina had seduced those young men? She knew that, in a way, the cat could. It would be fun.

In the meantime, Babcia considered the fact that she had chosen to stay behind and protect Holly from her own lustful desires, using them as a tool to exact her revenge on Father Tim.

Why wasn't she in Poland defending Niko against the evil witch who accompanied him to her homeland? The answer was simple: opportunity. Revenge here and now against this all too self-sanctified figure from a church that had caused her so much suffering. This was the thing to do. And besides, Babcia knew that, at the tower, THEY would be there. And THEY would protect Niko and Joy.

There was only one problem for the witch at this point. As usual, she told herself she was too good, too loving, and too generous. She had made a promise to Niko's little daughter, a promise she regretted almost as much as the one not to harm Holly. But it was, like all her promises,

One she intended to keep.

Chapter 51
Poland

Niko and his party were whisked from the Krakow airport into a moldy little bus that took them through twisting old city streets, an invisible nighttime countryside, and finally to a small hotel in the little village of Zakopane.

They slept like infants that first night, except for Jeannie, who was at least fifty percent the personification of Marla Morrison, a witch who never slept. She kept careful watch through the night and, in spite of her witchery, she felt relief when the sun began to brighten the sky in this remote and unfamiliar place.

At approximately 7 AM Polish time, Jeannie slid out of her bed and found her way into the bath. Sun was blazing through the little slit of a window, and it warmed her as she showered and washed her hair.

The shower itself was quite clean and proper. The fixtures sparkled, but the crazy communist shampoo was gray. Jeannie rubbed it into her hair anyway. It felt strong and good. She dried herself on towels that were clean even if they were faded and rather worn.

Jeannie slipped into some fresh jeans, a red T-shirt and a heavy, natural wool sweater. To complete the outfit, she donned a pair of designer tennis shoes that she'd brought with her from the U.S.A. Then she dashed to the front door of the little hotel.

And what a world she found.

The village of Zakopane had been the home of Niko's grandmother before it was given that name, and it immediately presented Jeannie with a complex vision of communist Poland in the 1970s.

It was a prosperous little resort bustling with tourists from Krakow and Warsaw and the most distant reaches of the Communist Empire. The tourists seemed to want to appear American. And even though none of them could match Jeannie's high style, they tried with their own imitation jeans and T-shirts and American-looking ski-jackets. Jeannie was starting to feel quite comfortable until she felt a very firm hand grasp her arm.

She turned to see a towering Polish police officer staring down at her. He wore a huge Russian fur hat and a thick woolen coat even though the brisk mountain air was already warming and making such apparel unnecessary.

"Czy ty mowisz po polsku?" he asked. And, although Jeannie had a sense of what he wanted, all she could think to say was, "American?"

"Tak," the police officer responded rather gruffly and added, "Please then to show me your papers?"

Jeannie fumbled through her pockets desperately and was rather unnerved when two more officers came to join their comrade.

"Blondie," one of them said with a smile that was far friendlier than the expression on the face of the first officer.

"Movie star," the third officer added.

Jeannie blushed.

"Well, I'm hardly a movie star," she said softly. "But I do work in the movie business." And just then she found the little wallet with her papers in it. She pulled out the passport and visa that had been created with one of the simplest pieces of witchcraft Mother Black had ever worked. She gave it to the officer along with a letter of introduction from VVA. It had a picture of CatMan Due printed across the top of it.

"CatMan," the Polish officer grunted with a sudden grin. "Am big fan of such comic cartoons."

"I am, too," Jeannie added. She was pleased to see how totally smitten all three of the police officers were: staring, smiling, and even awkwardly trying to flirt with her.

"Enjoy Zakopane," the officer said as he folded the papers and handed them back to her. Then he gave her a quick salute.

"I'll try," she answered as she returned the gesture and turned away from them.

"Is very beautiful girl," she heard one officer say to the others in English. "And CatMan too," another responded. Then they all began to laugh heartily. Jeannie giggled as well. "Beautiful girl," they had said. She liked that very much.

She soon came to the end of the little street that fronted the hotel and turned down the broad main avenue of Zakopane. And it was there that she stopped dead in her tracks.

Suddenly, the dark, brooding Carpathian Mountains loomed above her. They seemed far more mystical than any mountains she could ever imagine. They glowered down from almost on top of the town, giving a chill to the air, and to the souls who lived there. And then the sun burst through, casting diamonds across the snowy peaks and bringing a shimmer to the dark forests that marched up to the very edge of the village.

Marla awoke within Jeannie Morrison at that moment and listened. The mountains seemed to be speaking directly to her, calling to her witch-nature, offering stories of wolves, warlocks, vampires and all the other mysteries they had held for centuries. Marla soaked up the evil magic of the locale until her dark soul was full of it. She had been here before. As a ballet student, she'd wandered into this village and decided to take up the study of witchcraft with Clara Goriki, the pupil of Babcia Czarownica who now was surely the great witch's worst enemy. It was at that time that Marla began to develop the suicidal idea that she could somehow capture the powers of Babcia and use them to her own ends. How foolish, she thought in retrospect, how very, very foolish.

Suddenly, an old man was cheerily dancing a marionette right up to Jeannie, away and then back up to her again. The marionette was dressed like a harlequin.

"Kup te piekna marionetke?" he called to her. Jeannie shook her head.

"I'm sorry," she said sweetly. "But I definitely can't afford it. And I hate clowns anyway."

"But is from darkest forest," the man said in barely discernible English. "Will protect from witches!"

There was a moment of confusion inside Jeannie's soul. Protection! She smiled sweetly. "I really don't need it," she replied with a somewhat worried look and moved up the street where other merchants began descending upon her from all sides.

Jeannie turned to get away from the throng and ran into a young couple. They were so wrapped up in each other's company that they didn't see her coming. And so, all three took a tumble. Jeannie jumped up and hurried to help the young couple to their feet.

The girl dusted herself off. She wore a white blouse and a black vest embroidered with bright, colorful flowers. Her skirt was a gay, floral print. Jeannie looked around and saw many other locals dressed in much the same fashion, as though the brightness of the colors were meant to stand in sharp contrast to the harshness of the communists and the forbidding shadow of the mountains.

The young man was even slower to get to his feet.

"I'm so sorry; I hope I didn't hurt you, comrade," Jeannie said. The young man clearly did not like the use of the word and reached for his walking stick as if to raise it against her. The stick was taller than he was, carved with leaves and flowers and topped with the face of a bearded nobleman who could very well have been his own grandfather.

"Please don't be angry with me," Jeannie pleaded. As the young man started to raise the stick, the young woman grabbed it and held it.

"American," she said to him.

He studied Jeannie's face for a long minute. "Uncle Sam," he said with a sneer and spat on the ground in front of her. Jeannie didn't know what to do, so she just nodded.

"Nixon!" he said next, "Bah!"

Jeannie reached into her wallet and pulled out the little Polish/English dictionary that Vaughn had provided for each of them. She scanned it quickly for any word to describe the president. She said the first one she found.

"Potwor!" she said quickly and nervously.

"Nixon?" the youth repeated.

"Potwor!" Jeannie said again.

"Nixon jest potwor?" the young man asked.

Not exactly sure what he meant, Jeannie nodded anyway, and the youth began to laugh.

"I think so, don't you," Jeannie said smiling hopefully.

The young man dropped his stick and ran to Jeannie and embraced her. His companion smiled, too, though she would have liked it better if Jeannie hadn't been so drop-dead gorgeous. Finally, she went to the young man and pulled him away from Jeannie. Then she smiled and bowed to Jeannie while she led her friend away. He was still laughing and repeating the phrase, "Amerykanka powiedziala, 'Nixon jest potworem!'"

"Nixon's a monster!" Jeannie said to herself. "Guess just about everyone agrees with that."

She walked on for a few more minutes and suddenly spotted their little hotel. She had somehow walked in a complete circle. The building was small, made entirely of finished wood, with flower boxes and shutters painted in bright colors. It seemed very inviting. She skipped for a few girlish steps and then lit out into a run. As she did, she felt youthful energy exploding through her body, surging into her muscles and blood. She was running effortlessly. It was wonderful!

Inside Jeannie's body, Marla recognized this new twist in her host's outlook. Ancient, bent-over Rosie Osborn was experiencing youth, strength, and beauty in ways she hadn't in decades. It must have felt like a dream come true.

How could Marla use these new feelings to offset the love for Niko that was growing in Jeannie's heart? It did present an interesting opportunity, she thought.

Marla was so taken with the idea that, as Jeannie ran back to the hotel, Marla forced a frightening witch's cackle from the lips of the beautiful young woman. It seemed a strange, terrible sound to emerge from her. So much so, that a man who was marching down the street toward his place of business turned and looked at her with suspicion but not complete surprise. These were, after all, the Carpathian Mountains that extended from Poland deep into the region known as Transylvania.

Little did that man, that Pan – Mister – Michalowski, (Matryoshka's father) know how greatly that laugh would come to haunt him or how deeply he would become involved with Jeannie Morrison, Niko Madonie, and their dangerous and deadly adventure.

Meanwhile, thousands of miles away, two pairs of ancient eyes looked at Jeannie Morrison through the scrying ball. Mother Black had so distrusted the Spell of Becoming that she had stayed away from it for a hundred and fifty years, even though she knew that she could use it to make herself as young and beautiful as any of her charges.

"I think it might do you some good, old mother," said Clara Goriki. "You could be as lovely as Jeannie ever hoped to be."

Mother Black looked up at the ancient Polish witch. Clara was as hideous as they come, with the scar and that dead white eye, straw hair, and crippled body. She had decided to take on the appearance of the crone and keep it.

"Ah jes don' know," answered Mother Black. "What about yerself, Clara."

"No, sir. I prefer ugly," said Clara. "Suits my frame of mind. But you, old mother, you could be gorgeous."

"But there's always so dang much pride, selfishness, an destruction that comes along wi at spell, gal."

"Hell, selfishness and destruction are standard parts of witchery," answered Clara. "It sort of makes us who we are."

"It's the pride at worries me. It kin, you know, shrivel up an old gal's soul... shut down all her reason."

"Temptin', though, isn't it?" Clara asked the old, black woman who had already waddled over to the mirror on the far wall and posed just for a moment, batting her eyes and lifting her flabby breasts, as though she were some old tart on the streets of Memphis.

"Temptin'," Mother Black repeated, and she smiled a broad, toothless smile that might soon be...

Very much improved.

Chapter 52
The Maui Shirt

Holly awoke from a drug-induced sleep to a swirl of scary colors: horribly bright fuchsias, glaring purples, painful reds, and yellows. Amid the swirl, there was black too, and suddenly, added to it all, the wicked face of Babcia. All these elements swam toward the young woman closing in on her, and she screamed.

"Dear God, save me!"

And then there was a voice, a kind, comforting voice that assured her that everything was all right. She gripped the sides of the hospital bed desperately, her heart still pounding and little by little, the images of the real world began to take shape in front of her.

"It's all right, Holly," the voice said again, and slowly she recognized Father Tim. As the world shifted back into focus, she could see that all those unsettling colors were in his shirt. It looked like he was wearing a nightmare.

"What's that shirt?" she asked and he laughed. So did that strange apparition behind him. It was dressed all in black. But the face that Holly thought at first was Babcia turned out to be Sister Alexia.

"It's my golf shirt," Tim answered. "One of my parishioners brought it back from Maui. I'll admit it's a little loud, but it never made anyone scream before."

Holly felt dizzy. The drugs that had been calming her had also brought weakness and nausea.

"I'm sorry," she said at last. "It's just that I didn't expect it."

Father Tim knelt beside her and brushed the hair from her face. "It's going to be all right. Isn't it, Sister?"

"Oh yes," Sister Alexia answered. "God will protect you."

"That's exactly right," Tim added. "And, Holly, you said the perfect prayer: 'God save me.'"

Holly's look was a little skeptical.

"He will you know," Tim assured her.

Holly smiled. "Thank you, Father."

"Keep thinking of Christ, the protector. None of the witchery in the world can match His power."

"I know, Father. I know," Holly said. "It's just that sometimes I get so scared." And she began sobbing softly. Father Tim sat beside her on the bed and stroked her hair.

Sister Alexia walked around the priest and up to the terrified young woman.

"You'll be all right, Mrs. Madonie."

"Will you stay here with me, Father?" Holly managed to choke out the words through her sobs.

"Father's going to play a few rounds of Golf and then he'll be back," Sister Alexia said. "Right, Father?"

Tim nodded. But Holly grasped his hand.

"Don't go."

"I'll keep an eye on you, Mrs. Madonie," the nun said. "I'll be here all day. In the meantime, is there anything you want, anything at all?"

"Don't wear those clothes when you come back," Holly begged the priest.

"I promise," Tim answered with a chuckle.

"And can I please wear something other than this horrible hospital gown?" Holly asked. "I brought some nightgowns of my own; they're very simple, but wearing one would make me feel so much better."

"Let me check with the doctor," Sister Alexia answered. "Usually it's against the rules, but in this special case...."

"Thanks," Holly whispered to both of them. And Tim took the opportunity to move toward the door.

"Have a good game, Father," she called.

"If my shirt is as devastating to the Monsignor as it's been to you," he answered, "I'll win easily." And with that, he left the two women together.

"Isn't he a wonderful man?" the nun asked.

"Oh yes," Holly answered through adoring eyes. Sister Alexia caught a bit of their glow and worried for a second about the desire she'd witnessed. But she shrugged it off. Tim was a devoted priest, one well beyond the temptations of the flesh; Sister Alexia was sure of it.

Holly, of course, knew better.

Chapter 53
Promises

Emmy, the cat, curled up on Father Tim's bed and reflected on the day's activities. Within her soul, Babcia still regretted the promises she had made, that stupid set of promises that little Joy had wheedled out of her.

The night before Joy had left, before she'd completely entrusted the soul of her Great Grandmother to the body of a cat, she sat on her little bed, cradling the cat in her arms, and stared bitterly at the apparition of Babcia that had once again materialized in the mirror over her dresser.

"I hated Principal Hunter, too," Joy said in words that were punctuated by bitter sobs. "I hated what he did to my mom and dad, but I didn't want him turned into a bundle of gooey, bloody guts! Uugghh!"

"Is all right, Moje dziecko," Babcia responded in that raspy voice of hers.

"No, it's not all right," Joy snapped back. "And I'm not your jenko!"

"Must protect mother."

"From what?" Joy sobbed. "The only thing she needs protection from is YOU! You're driving her crazy."

A Polish expression that could roughly be interpreted as 'out of the mouths of babes' flitted through the mind of the ancient witch. Was that a possibility? Babcia didn't think so.

"Promise me you won't hurt my mommy," Joy pleaded through her tears.

Babcia looked at the little girl, a child she loved with an intensity that she'd only felt for her little son and then for her grandson, Niko.

"Is promise," Babcia answered.

"Promise me that you won't mutilate anyone."

Babcia flinched, but Joy's look was insistent.

"Is promise," the witch repeated.

Joy's look was searing through the witch with a strength that seemed almost impossible for such a little girl.

"Promise me that you won't KILL anyone."

That was a tough one, not at all what Babcia wanted to agree to, and yet...

"Yes," she whispered to the little girl.

"Really?"

"Yes, Moja Droga," Babcia murmured and smiled as kindly as she could. Joy returned her smile until another thought occurred to her, and her expression changed to one of distrust.

"Promise me that you won't harm my mom in any way." And then Joy shouted the last three words again. "IN ANY WAY."

"Shhhh," Babcia whispered. "No wake papa."

"IN ANY WAY!"

"Is promise."

Joy rubbed her runny nose on her sleeve and sniffled. She dried her eyes on the tail of her shirt.

"Thank you, Great Grandma," she said with a smile. "I believe you."

"Is promises."

Joy released the cat, and Emmy dropped to the floor and scurried away. Joy slid under her covers and turned toward the wall. Within minutes she was asleep.

Babcia did not sleep, of course. Instead, she moved into the body of the cat. It was time to go out and prowl. Still, there had been the beginning of an idea in that conversation somewhere amidst all those awful promises.

#

Now, days later, Emmy and Babcia sat merged as one being in Father Tim's room meditating on the promises and the conversation, regretting them at first and then remembering an idea that Babcia had dismissed far too quickly, an idea about how to achieve her revenge.

There were, after all, things far worse than death, Babcia mused.

Madness, for one!

She wouldn't harm Holly in any way, she would honor that promise, but Father Tim....

She'd said she wouldn't mutilate or kill him. Okay, still... Madness –

What an attractive alternative.

Chapter 54
The Shop and the Map

Rosie Osborn, trapped with the evil Marla in the lovely young body of Jeannie Morrison, had a sense of foreboding as she tripped along the bustling main street of Zakopane. The village, with its dark spiritual undercurrent and mountains that sang of witches and wolves, did little to reassure her of her safety. Marla may have liked it, but Rosie did not.

Niko was beside her, though. That was good. Joy was on his far side holding his hand and skipping along. The little girl seemed perfectly happy and at ease with her surroundings. Occasionally, she'd stop and ask one of the street vendors about a toy or a little blouse or some trinket in perfect Polish. How did she know the language?

The trio passed the small post-office and a general store without the long lines of people waiting to buy supplies. Even under the weight of communism, things were not like that in Zakopane.

Still, Niko and Jeannie could sense the strict controls placed on expenditures by the communists. They probably included the rationing of food and even medications.

The police station seemed to be the dourest sight in the town, a huge, dark, stone building whose walls might have been two feet thick on every side. But, as though to mock its authority, a little curio shop stood just beside it, its walls painted an uncharacteristically bright yellow and the shutters a brilliant orange.

"Let's duck in here," Niko suggested. Jeannie and Joy were happy to agree.

#

A bell tinkled as they stepped across the threshold and into the shop. Its song was in perfect harmony with the brightest features of the world outside and a perfect welcome to a display of crafts and toys, the likes of which Niko had never seen.

Along one wall, dozens of pisanki were on show. They were Easter eggs, each one with its own unique, hand-painted design. A few steps further along the same table, they found little straw figurines of animals including goats, lambs, and pigs.

"Gotta get one, Daddy," Joy called out. "Mommy will love it."

She held up a carefully crafted figure of a ram bound together with bright orange ribbons. Its face, the ends of straw that had been neatly woven into ram horns, blustered out at them.

"Can I buy it for her?" Jeannie asked.

"Better wait," Niko responded. "We'll be here for a while, and she may see something she likes even better."

And there was so much to choose from: wooden toys, teapots, candleholders, sugar bowls, mugs, coffee cups, and plates. Each was decorated in colors and patterns that were uniquely Polish, bright and happy and yet somehow completely in harmony with the deep spirit of the forests and the mountains and the mysteries that swirled through them.

Along the opposite wall was a vast display of nesting dolls, each doll in the set a smaller version of the previous one, each fitting neatly inside the other as many as ten at a time. The dolls often represented cute, young girls with Polish white-blonde hair and flowers all around them. But there were also chubby, old women wearing babushkas on their heads. Each large figure was duplicated in smaller and smaller sizes, and merely unscrewing them around the middle would open any one of them.

Jeannie played with the most perfect looking set, a pretty blonde doll whose rosette lips and sparkling eyes looked almost like hers. She unscrewed the figure, and inside she found a slightly smaller version of the same doll. She unscrewed that one too, and another smaller but still perfect figure emerged.

Jeannie opened that tiny doll and caught her breath when a dark and ugly little shape suddenly fell from the doll. The witch within her!

And then, to Jeannie's horror, the miniature, witchy figure began to squirm on the counter, turning sideways upon itself and writhing like some hideous worm. Smelling of some pungent, ancient chemical compound, it melted into a dank, oily puddle, and seeped into the wood.

Jeannie would have screamed, but Niko did it for her. The young woman turned, and her eyes grew even wider. At the very back of the room, an entire wall was filled with dozens of ornate masks in as many different horrible expressions, and each was a replica of Babcia's face!

Jeannie felt Marla cowering inside of her at the sight of the creature who had murdered her only a few years before. Jeannie moved carefully toward the display, puzzled at the expressions on the faces of Joy and her father.

Joy's look was most amazing, not one of horror at all, but almost one of adoration. (Thank you, Great Grandma.) Niko's look was also surprising. He had clearly come to grips with this monster, his twisted protector he called her.

"Dzien dobry." A rather pleasant voice said hello from the other side of the display. Jeannie looked up to see a nattily dressed man in his late 60s stepping forward to greet them.

"Czy Pan mowi po angielsku?" Joy asked confidently.

"Speaking English a little," said the man. "But not so well as you speak Polish. Where you learn such perfect talk?"

"From her," Joy responded pointing directly to the only mask of Babcia that could in any way have been considered friendly.

"Don't think so, Moje dziecko," the man said. "She is famous witch, Babcia Michalina Czarownica, born eight hundred years before."

"She's my great grandma," Joy answered, "And I love her."

"Must be very special little girl," the man said. "To love witch born so long ago."

"She's my great grandmother," Joy repeated.

"And she was MY grandmother," Niko added with a smile. "And I was very afraid of her."

The older man grew silent. He peered at Niko suspiciously, and then his expression changed to one of absolute disbelief.

"Grandson of Babcia," he said in utter amazement, and he suddenly rushed behind the counter and pulled out an enormous leather-bound book. He opened it and flipped through pages of handwritten text reading quickly. Then he looked up.

"So you are..."

"Niko..." the young man answered.

"Madonie," the older man finished. "Son of fine American physician, Louis Madonie who fought heroically in great world war."

Niko nodded.

"You knew witch," he realized becoming even more excited and stepping around to the front of the counter to shake Niko's hand.

"Is great honor for humble shop, and for village of Zakopane, and even all of Poland."

Niko didn't know quite how to respond, so he bowed.

"My name Michalowski," the shopkeeper said. "Now, your profession is..."

"Writer," Niko added.

"Of televisions about witches: Hansel, Gretel, Snow White, Rose Red, we hear of them in village. We hear you work on another witch story. Is true?"

"It is," responded Joy.

"May I guess?" Michalowski asked.

Niko nodded his approval.

"Snow White?"

"There's already been quite a few of those," answered Niko. "Win Mikley's was probably the best."

"Is so," the shopkeeper affirmed. "Could it be..."

"Rapunzel." A soft voice came from the opposite side of the store. Everyone turned and looked at Jeannie Morrison as she walked very slowly toward the counter.

"Rapunzel," responded Michalowski, doing his best to hold in a sudden sense of alarm. "Not good choice to do that one."

"Why?" Jeannie's eyes darted around the shop fearfully as though she already knew the answer and was very much afraid of it.

"Because," the shopkeeper answered, "Rapunzel is Babcia, witch and maiden. Both is her. You know terrible story. Still haunts village and people here.

Besides," he added, now turning to Niko, "In spite of you, I not do it!" And he stomped his foot in finality.

"Do what?"

"Show you, won't give you."

"We don't know what you are talking about, Mr. Michalowski."

"You do," the shopkeeper insisted.

"But we don't need it, anyway," Joy added.

"What are you all talking about?" Jeannie asked.

"He means the map," Joy said with a hard accusing stare at the shopkeeper. "Don't you?"

"Of course," he answered. "I have map to tower. Grandfather found tower, drew map, but is evil. And would be even more evil with capitalistic exploitation."

Niko shook his head. "We just want to tell a story about it."

"Sure," Michalowski responded. "Make TV show, tell world. You not think will bring tourists to sacred spot?"

"Sacred?" Jeannie asked.

"Sacred evil," Michalowski answered. "There is such thing you know."

"To nie ma znaczenia," Joy answered in perfect Polish and repeated the entire sentence again in English for the benefit of her father and Jeannie. "It doesn't matter. We have our own map right here." And with that, she pulled a crisp, new piece of paper from her pocket, unfolded it, and placed it on top of the counter.

Michalowski gasped and turned back to the big, leather-bound notebook. Without uttering a word, he flipped through several pages and pulled out a similar map drawn in a different hand. And then he pulled out another sheet of paper; this one ancient and yellow with a dark scrawl in faded black ink perhaps centuries old.

"Is map grandfather drew," Michalowski said, gesturing to the illustration. And then his eyes grew wide with wonder, "And this terrible yellow page with scary black ink is only known anything in hand of Babcia Czarownica."

He laid the two sheets beside the map Joy had produced. His perspiration dripped like blood on the pages because the ancient yellow map was very much the same as the one Joy had. But even more alarming, was the shape of the characters and letters on the map. They were remarkably like the scribbles that Babcia had made centuries before.

"Who drew map?" Michalowski demanded. "Drawn by witch herself?"

"I drew it," Joy answered with an unnerving giggle.

"And where you copy from?" he asked.
"My own mind, Pan Michalowski."

Chapter 55
Carefulla Pry

Mother Black's scrying ball was like a modern day TV set. She and Clara could watch the horror story that was beginning to unfold in Poland and then wave a hand over the ball and tune in to the rodeo that was going on in Chuck Vaughn's office.

Chuck had become so infatuated with Sally Fukes that he was allowing more and more of her Cowgirl Show to find its way into his work. She'd convinced him to create an animated character based on her favorite lifestyle, and Chuck had bought into it lock, stock and both "double D" barrels. To promote what he thought was a great new creative direction for the studio, he'd also purchased an enormous mechanical bull that he installed in the Witch Room. Except, of course, it wasn't called the Witch Room anymore. It was now dedicated to his newest creation: Midnight Cowgirl.

This morning Sally had brought in several of her sexiest rodeo outfits, including boots, hats, vests, fringed mini-skirts and all. She would put one on, climb onto the bull, and assume a series of sexy poses while Chuck sketched away like a madman.

"Wonder what he'd think if he saw her real self?" Mother Black asked Clara Goriki as they looked on.

"She's over three hundred pounds now," Clara said. "I'm surprised she doesn't just snap that mechanical bull in half." Clara laughed heartily. But Mother Black did not.

"Ah'm not likin' any a this," the old backwoods witch said. "Marla's hidin' out in at hot little bod a Jeannie Morrison and letting the spirit a Rosy Osborn pretty much take control a the whole sit-y-a-tion. Meanwhile, Sally's forgettin' the whole mission as she strutted her stuff fer this handsome, older gentleman."

"The gentleman is certainly not good looking," said Clara. "He's short, round, and can't stop chewing gum."

"But he's so god blessed creative," Mother Black responded.

It was a talent Mother Black admired and one she thought she possessed as well. Certainly, her spells were plenty creative; just look at what she'd done for Sally. Hell, there was no doubt why Vaughn was nuts about her. Mother Black had made Sally into someone so "dad blasted" delicious that he couldn't resist.

"I think you could give yourself a little taste of that Spell of Becoming," Clara tempted Mother Black.

"Best be careful a' pride," the backcountry witch answered as she padded around her bungalow now. Only, when she said it with that Tennessee twang, it sounded more like: "carefulla pry."

Pride went before a fall; pride was the one sin that both Father Tim and Mother Black agreed upon. Pride, in fact, may just have been the root of all evil.

"Carefulla pry," Mother Black said again as she stoked the fire under her big black caldron and watched the slimy ooze surge toward a boil.

"Looks to me like you've already decided to give it a try, old Mother," Clara said with a smile.

"Carefulla pry, bitch," Mother Black said to her own image as she passed in front of the fish tank with its all-knowing reflective surface. She snatched a piranha from the tank and flung it headlong across the room and into the pot.

"Yee-hawh!" she snarled. "Ah's made everyone beau'ful, 'cept mahself."

Clara pulled back the moldy old couch and reached down to grab a great green toad that had been hiding under it for months. "Gotcha," she said as she pulled it up before her withered, toothless old face and looked into its yellow eyes for just a moment. Who was more ugly, the toad or the witches? she wondered.

"Sorry, but ah needs ya, boy," Mother Black squealed and snatched the toad from Clara, kissed it, and took a hook shot that sent the creature spinning far across the room before it banked off the far wall and plopping into the boiling brew.

Clara's eyes narrowed as she watched the old backwoods witch give in to a temptation she'd managed to avoid for over a hundred years. For all their camaraderie, it certainly seemed that Clara was goading Mother Black into an act that would eventually destroy her when Clara no longer needed her help.

Mother Black was on autopilot though. She was going to work the Spell of Becoming on herself, and nothing and no one could stop her, not any thoughtful words from Clara, not even her own dark misgivings. She intended to enjoy some of the joys of youth and beauty that she'd given so freely to her protégées.

There was only one problem, wasn't there? She realized as she went about her business.

"Ya know what da Spell of Becoming does ta witches, dontcha?" She asked Clara who had just snatched up a foot long centipede and pinched it between her long, curled fingernails. Green goo spilled from the bug as it writhed and wriggled in pain, all hundred legs fluttering in agony.

Clara blew some nasty breath at the centipede and then just flipped it carelessly into the pot.

"Yes, I know what the Spell of Becoming does to witches," Clara answered. "But it doesn't always work that way. Sometimes it's benign, just serves the witches wonderfully then leaves them alone."

"Never heard a that happenin'," Mother Black answered. "Far's I know there's always hell ta pay."

"Not always, trust me," said Clara.

"Carefulla pry, girl!" Mother Black repeated. "Tha's what I thinks. But what the hell… maybe you's right...

"But probably not."

Chapter 56
Cat Assisted Strip Tease

"I've brought you a friend," Father Tim said, and he held up Emmy, the cat.

Holly, still on drugs and a little bleary-eyed, tried to focus on the cat's sweet face.

There was no denying that Emmy was cute and continued to be cute even when Babcia's hideous presence descended into her soul. Babcia, it turns out, did cute very well.

Michalina, in her own sensuous way, had also been cute in her teasing movements that could drive almost any man to succumb to her witchcraft. Holly had the same trait, actually. She could be very cute when she wanted to be. And now, propped up in bed wearing a white nightie that was not at all hospital regulation, she looked more than cute.

The cat swatted at Holly's nose, and the young woman laughed. Father Tim smiled and tried to ignore the perky tips of Holly's nipples as they pushed up against the soft cotton of her gown.

"Niko left Emmy to help with your recovery," Tim said as he gently set the cat at the end of the bed. Emmy walked carefully up to Holly and gave her a friendly lick on the cheek. Holly smiled.

"How are you feeling today?" Tim asked.

Her expression darkened.

"Still kinda haunted."

"Don't think about that stuff. Those thoughts are like temptations. Fight 'em off." Tim made a few quick boxing moves as he said the words.

"Is that how YOU handle temptation, Father? Or don't you have to worry about things like that."

"I'm just like everyone else."

253

"Oh?" Holly said feeling a little more awake and warming up to the topic. "Then tell me, Father. What's your biggest temptation?"

Babcia listened attentively. She, as the cat, that is, had curled up beside Holly and was purring as the young woman stroked her fur. Babcia's plan was crystallizing. She would gain revenge on this ludicrous priest by driving him out of his mind. And Holly's beauty could be a primary ingredient in that effort.

"My biggest temptation," Tim said with a smirk, "is chocolate cream pie."

"Yucchhh," Holly responded with a giggle.

Emmy purred. This was going well: discovering lust she could use to great advantage, especially when it was mixed in with.... Well, she knew where it was all going. Tim would get there soon enough. He wouldn't present any real threat to Niko's marriage, though; she'd see to that.

Emmy purred louder still.

"I usually just give in to temptation," Holly said with a smile. It was a joke, but Tim didn't take it that way. Those nipples wanted desperately to be caressed, he thought. Now there was a temptation, and he was having a very hard time fighting it off.

He thrust his hand into his pocket and began to fumble with his rosary.

Hail, Mary, full of grace.

"How'd you sleep?" he said at last.

"Very well. No nightmares for a change."

"And have you started to think about God as your protector against witchcraft?"

Emmy winced. She actually dug her claws into the bedding, not quite far enough to reach Holly, and that was good.

"I'm trying not to think about witchcraft at all."

"That's probably for the best until we both get a little distance from what's happened."

Emmy decided it was time to force things a little. So, she tried to crawl under the covers with Holly. The action pushed the soft, white sheets down revealing the soft curve of the girl's waistline and more of those inviting breasts.

"Emmy!" Holly called in embarrassment. Tim swallowed hard as the young woman adjusted the sheets and pulled the cat up in front of her face.

"Whose side are you on?" she asked Emmy with a smile.

One line from Tim's prayer seemed to be stuck in his head, repeating over and over again: "full of grace, full of grace, full of grace!"

"Let me take the cat," he said at last. Emmy dove back under the covers, and this time pushed them down to Holly's knees. Her nightie stopped at mid-thigh. Tim's eyes almost jumped out of his head. The cat began to purr, and Holly giggled.

"I'm sorry I wore such a skimpy outfit. I never thought that Emmy would be trying to put me on display like this."

Yes. Holly was displaying herself for him, Tim thought, inviting him in. Tim suddenly wanted her more than he had ever wanted anything in his life.

"Guess Emmy knows how beautiful you are," he whispered at last.

"Am I beautiful?"

"Oh, yes."

Holly smiled the way she always did when she felt a man falling under her power. It was a great feeling. She loved it.

Emmy purred and scrunched down deeper into the bed, pushing the sheet down still further.

Suddenly, Tim couldn't stand it any longer. He reached for the cat, grabbed her by the scruff of the neck, and tried to lift her from the bed. Emmy grabbed for Holly's nightie with her claws, and as Tim pulled the cat up, she pulled Holly's nightie up with her, way up above her waist and breasts. Tim's eyes took in Holly's shapely thighs, her soft white cotton panties with little hearts embroidered on them, even her navel, and then the fullness of her breasts and those maddening nipples.

Tim had seen pictures of Holly naked, had even seen pictures of her having sex with other men, but this wasn't a picture; this was a living, breathing woman right in front of him.

Holly screamed in embarrassment and pulled the nightie down and the bed covers all the way up to her chin.

Father Tim's heart was pounding, and his eyes were wild. He looked at the cat to see a terrible, red glow searing from its eyes.

He dropped the cat in horror, and the creature immediately bounded back onto the bed and crawled up next to Holly. The young woman cuddled up to Emmy pressing the cat to her breasts and petting her.

"Are you all right, Father?"

Tim flinched, and his color passed beyond red to a deep scarlet. His lips moved, but nothing came from them. Emmy began purring again. Somehow she was once again nothing more than a cat.

"I've got to go," he said.

"But come back soon, okay?" Holly called. "I need you."

"Tomorrow."

Holly sat up in bed and lifted Emmy to him. Tim recoiled for a moment and then saw that Emmy was indeed very much a cat and nothing more. And so he took her.

"Are you going to bring Emmy with you when you return?"

"Do you want me to?"

"Oh, yes," Holly answered. "She keeps my mind off other things. Drives those nasty images away."

Tim nodded as he made his way toward the door. Different kinds of images were implanted in his mind now: Holly's beautiful body revealed in more ways than he could ever hope for and that red glow searing into him from the eyes of the cat. That was an image that would haunt him in an entirely different way.

Madness was a beautiful form of revenge, Babcia realized then, and in Tim's case, the ingredients were already there. All it would take now would be a few long, desperate nights and the combined witchery of a cat...

And a very beautiful woman.

Chapter 57
Michalowski and the Map

Jeannie had returned to the little curio shop in Zakopane. She'd come by herself to talk to the shopkeeper about the Babcia masks that hung on the wall.

"Is great mistake, you know," he began. "Rapunzel tower is place of death. Not kind of place pretty thing like you is seeking out."

"I can take care of myself," Jeannie answered.

"Against what?" Michalowski asked as he pulled his great leather-bound notebook from behind the counter once again.

"Against anything," she responded with a firmness she did not seem to believe. "I've got my friends to protect me. Niko will take care of me and his little girl."

"Yes," Michalowski answered. "But there are others in your party, no?"

"No," she said. "Just the three of us. We work for Chuck Vaughn in Hollywood."

The shopkeeper's expression shifted toward a smile. "I know," he said. "This CatMan Due, this saxophone cat, I like him."

"Mr. Vaughn also created Hansel and Gretel and Snow White and Rose Red."

"Yes, we discussed," said Michalowski. He now walked around in front of the counter and began to straighten the masks that hung on the opposite wall.

"I heard," he continued. "From woman is a very good friend of mine and also student of Babcia that second of those programs, Rose Red, I think, not as good as first."

Marla, conceited artist that she was, still very much present deep inside Jeannie, delighted in this observation, so much so that she almost forgot for a moment that she was surrounded by images of her murderer. She loved remembering how she and Niko had created the storyline for Hansel and Gretel together. Though Vaughn had refused to use her brutal ending, the bulk of the story was still very much collaboration. Snow White and Rose Red, on the other hand, was all Niko. Obviously, it lacked a witch's touch. And it must have shown.

Marla manipulated Jeannie over to the shopkeeper. She flashed her eyes at the old man. "What else can you tell us about the tower?" she asked.

"Wolves no longer there," the shopkeeper replied doing his best to be positive.

"Oh, thank God!" Jeannie sighed.

"But, of course, THEY still there."

"They?"

Michalowski began to explain, but at that very moment, Niko and Joy came rushing through the door.

"There are guest rooms now," Niko said as soon as he reached them. "Rapunzel's tower is a hotel?"

"Not exactly," answered Michalowski. "Is more very exclusive lodge, is hard to get to, is requiring special permissions to use and more than a map to find. Who told you?"

"A lady in the village," Joy answered. "She said that for five thousand American dollars she would tell us..."

"How to get into place," Michalowski said. "And I suppose she volunteers me as guide?"

"In fact, she did."

Joy was staring at the man accusingly as though she were disappointed in her countryman.

"Well, what you expect?" he said to her. "Communism is robbing us of everything. Only chance survival is to sell what we have, and most rare thing in Zakopane is knowledge of tower.

"Once grandfather learned witch gone, he created entrance at base. Of course, THEY try stop him, but..."

"Never mind all that," Niko interrupted. "The question is: will you guide us?"

Michalowski looked at the party that confronted him, a great artist and storyteller, grandson of the most powerful witch in the world, a potent little girl who somehow spoke perfect Polish, and a magnificent young woman whose eyes could not hide a deep inner conflict.

"Who are you?" he suddenly asked Jeannie.

"Why, Jeannie," she answered. "Jeannie Morrison."

"Morrison... Morrison," the shopkeeper repeated rolling his eyes. "Might have known." He shook his head and sighed. Then he staggered back behind the counter.

"I show you," he said at last and once again flipped through the pages of his notebook until he came to a single, large page that folded out.

"Look this."

Niko, Jeannie, and little Joy, up on tip toes, gathered around the countertop and peered at the image folded out from the book. It was a table that showed seven family trees.

"Families," the shopkeeper said, "of men who killed Babcia Michalina's father, husband, and little boy."

He took his pencil and traced over the lines showing how many of the families had died off after two hundred years.

"Were massacred one by one," he said, "in very tower you wish to visit."

He looked back at them and especially into Jeannie's soft but terror-stricken eyes. Then he moved his pencil to the center of the table and pointed to the single bloodline that had continued.

"This is line Wynofski," he said. "Descendants left Poland, traveled, married, and escaped Babcia revenge. Became part of finest families in Europe and America."

The shopkeeper's pencil traced the line down through generations of Poles through intermarriage into Italy, to the Mortellaro family, then over into Spain, to France, to Ireland, and at last to Great Britain and the line of Morrison.

"You are descendant of family Babcia vowed to destroy," he whispered to the terrified girl. "And you asking me to lead you to spot where Babcia killed so many."

"But she's not there now," Joy said.

"How do you know, little girl?" Michalowski asked. "Can you imagine how powerful is she? She can travel anywhere on earth."

"Not now, she can't," Joy answered. "She's a cat, and she's got other business.

Make him take us there, daddy," she insisted.

"How much will you charge to be our guide?" Niko asked.

"Now price is ten thousand U.S. dollars," the man responded.

"Let's make it fifteen," Niko said with a smile. "Just to be sure you're comfortable, okay?"

"Will never be comfortable at tower," Michalowski answered.

"We have to leave tomorrow," Niko added.

Michalowski thought for a moment seeming to weigh the choice between danger and poverty as so many Poles before him had done. And in the end, he chose danger.

"Will do," he responded. And then he turned back to Jeannie whose eyes were fixed on the most evil looking of all the Babcia masks. She caught his movement toward her and looked at him with her passionate, blue eyes.

"Too bad for you, beautiful lady," the shopkeeper said at last. "Miss MORRISON! I am so sorry."

Inside the young woman, Marla was raging with fear and anger because of all that the shopkeeper had said, but also because she could read the mind of the woman she possessed.

Jeannie was trying desperately to formulate a plan to rid herself of Marla Morrison now, to save herself.

The undead witch was certain of it.

Chapter 58
Madness Part 1

Emmy bounded across the bed at midnight right over Father Tim as he slept. The action woke the man, and he sat bolt upright in bed.

His dreams had not been gentle. He constantly found himself running down hallways in ancient seminaries, opening doors he'd never seen before, and time and again encountering floor-to-ceiling mirrors just inside the doorway. The mirrors all bore his reflection at first, and then the images would suddenly shift into the horrific shape of Babcia.

Each time it occurred, Tim awoke gasping for air, his heart pounding wildly, wondering if a man as young as he could be frightened to death in his sleep. But then he'd drift off again, and the dream would recur as though it had never been interrupted.

Tim was sweating so profusely this time that his hand slipped when he tried to switch on the little lamp at his bedside. Finally, he got it on. Across the room, he saw the cat staring at him. He sighed with some relief and then jumped back against the headboard. The cat cast a shadow, not of an animal but of Babcia, a witch's shadow that appeared to be reaching out for him.

Tim threw the lamp at the cat. Its cord caught in the wall socket, and it fell just short of hitting her. Emmy cast a disdainful glance at Father Tim and walked slowly out of reach. The lampshade had hit the floor, but the light bulb didn't break. Instead, it continued to illuminate the room, now throwing strange, twisted shadows up onto the walls and ceiling.

"Tim?" came a soft voice from beyond the bedroom door. "What's happening?" It was Holly.

How could she have heard the crash of a lamp in a room that was so far from hers?

"Come in," Tim answered almost desperately, and Holly made her way into the twisted illumination. The lamp, now shining up from the floor, lit her face from below making her look almost ghoulish.

Holly picked up the lamp and brought it to the priest. "Are you all right?" she asked.

"I had a nightmare," he responded with half a smile, "And then your cat scared me."

Holly walked over to Emmy and lifted her.

"Why can't you two get along?" she asked as she stared into the cat's face. Emmy licked her and purred.

Tim pulled himself out from under the covers and turned to sit on the edge of his bed. He was wearing a white T-shirt and a pair of navy boxer shorts. Holly wore that same too-sexy gown that she'd worn the last time he'd visited her.

"Maybe you shouldn't be here, Holly."

She responded with a naughty smile. "But I want you to..."

"Holly!" Tim called certain of what she was about to say.

"Touch me," she finished and took his hand. "Right here."

Her eyes were almost hypnotic as she brought his hand inside the fold of her gown and pressed it between her legs. She parted them and guided his hand upward.

"Holly," he whispered when he saw her close her eyes and shiver with pleasure. He closed his eyes as well and listened while she began to moan softly.

She worked his hand harder and harder against herself until Tim felt moisture trickling over his fingers.

"Holly!" he called when she began to tremble with passion. He suddenly jerked his hand away, and as he did, Holly vanished without a trace except for the wetness all over his hands.

"Oh, Holly," Tim whispered as he pulled off his sweaty shirt and dried his hands on it.

It was all a dream, he suddenly realized. He hadn't thrown the lamp, the shadow of the witch hadn't been on the wall, and Holly hadn't even been there that night.

The cat stared back at Tim from across the room. Above her, the image of the witch reappeared. Tim felt a sudden terror take hold of him.

He turned off the light, slid back under the covers, and lay there awake, still looking at the silhouette of the cat and the witch-shadow that wouldn't go away...

Even in the darkness.

Chapter 59
Marla Vs. Jeannie

Jeannie Morrison carried a bowl of porridge and a mug of Polish coffee back to her table in the breakfast nook at the Zakopane hotel. When she arrived, she found little Joy Madonie sitting there drawing pictures in a small sketchbook.

"Daddy's asleep," Joy said with a smile. "Want to eat with me?"

"I'd like that," Jeannie replied as she juggled her breakfast onto the table. "Can I get you something? After all, a great artist shouldn't have to worry about food."

"Just a little porridge and milk, please," Joy answered and turned her attention back to her pad.

Jeannie went to the sideboard, gathered the requested breakfast items and returned.

"Whatchya drawin'?"

"Jadwiga," Joy answered and turned the book to show Jeannie a sketch of a Polish girl of about 13.

"Not bad," Jeannie said. "She's all dressed up."

"For her wedding," Joy responded.

"A little young to be getting married, isn't she?"

"She was 13," Joy answered. "And she was the king of Poland at the time."

"A girl king?"

"The nobles didn't want any big wars about who was supposed to be king. So when she was ready, instead of making her queen, they just made her the king instead."

"Practical and simple."

Jeannie delicately dipped her spoon into the porridge.

"Is this a picture of her on her wedding day?" she asked.

"Yes. Jadwiga married Jagiello, the King of Lithuania, and together they ruled wonderfully until she died in childbirth."

"Awwwwh," Jeannie said with a pout. "And when was that, exactly?"

"1399," Joy answered. "And even though she was 27 when she died, Jadwiga is still considered one of the greatest rulers Poland has ever had."

The little girl pushed the sketchbook over to Jeannie. "Why don't you draw her?"

Jeannie took the sketchbook and turned to an open page.

"Okay, I'll draw. You eat."

"Deal!"

So while Joy took the big silver spoon and dug into the porridge, Jeannie did her own sketch of Jadwiga.

"She was a real person, you know," Joy said as soon as she'd gulped down her first few mouthfuls of porridge.

"I can tell by the way you describe her," Jeannie answered. She held the pages of the sketchbook so that she could flip back and forth between Joy's drawing and her own. Little by little, she was redrawing Joy's picture. She kept many of the cute features the little girl had created: the style of the dress, the overall proportions, even some of the childlike mistakes that gave the drawing its charm. But she also made the drawing her own, or more specifically Rosie's, because the old woman's masterful skill was guiding Jeannie's hand filling the drawing with a brightness that she stole right off the face of her little companion.

"You like my daddy a lot, don't you?"

"Of course, I do. I love working with him. He's excellent at telling stories."

"And at drawing."

"Yes, that too,"

"Would you like to marry him?"

"What kind of a question is that?" Jeannie smiled and frowned at the same time and suddenly she began to change her sketch of the little girl. There was something in Joy's eyes that she'd missed. What was it? More than sweetness, there was a directness that Rosie now sought to bring into the eyes of the person she drew.

"He loves Mommy," Joy continued. "And we're protecting her."

"Protecting Mommy? You and Daddy?"

"Me and my Great Grandma," Joy said off-handedly.

"How do you do that?" Jeannie felt suddenly elated because, yes... in her drawing, she'd captured that look – the direct, commanding, insistent look that was so much a part of Joy.

"Great Grandma does it mostly," Joy responded. "She's a witch, you know."

"Yes, I know," Jeannie answered feeling a sudden shudder. "We saw her masks yesterday, remember?"

"Did you know that she kills people especially if they try to come between my mom and dad?"

Jeannie didn't know whether to be amused or terrified and felt a little of both.

"I would never want to come between your mom and dad," Jeannie said carefully. "Or be killed by your great grandmother either."

She smiled and turned back to her drawing, but as she did so, she began to tremble.

Inside Jeannie's body, Marla's gruesome spirit was convulsing with anger and hatred. She knew Babcia firsthand, of course: Babcia had murdered her.

No less an artist than Rosie Osborn, Marla now began to take over the drawing. She forced Jeannie's hand and pushed it to darken the expression on the portrait. She added age lines and wrinkles to the face and moved the pencil to Jadwiga's mouth and began to destroy her teeth. Jeannie held the pencil more firmly and fought with Marla. She flipped the pencil over and tried to erase the age lines that Marla had added. She gripped the pencil with both hands and then fought with Marla over it until the pencil broke in two. Now her hand reached down and grabbed at the page, crumpling it. Then the other hand rose and began tearing it apart.

Joy looked on in shock.

Suddenly Jeannie jumped to her feet, dropped the sketchbook, and ran from the room. She raced down the hallway and ducked into the tiny lavatory that was at the very end of the hall. She slammed the door, locked it, bent over the sink and stared into it for a very long moment.

"No more, you bitch!" she fumed. "No more!"

She was screaming at herself and through herself, at Marla. But the creature that rose up from the sink and into the mirror in front of Jeannie, the hideous undead countenance of Marla Morrison, was smiling.

"Listen good," hissed Marla. "You can have this guy, you know. Fuck him till you're overflowing. He can be your little toy for the whole rest of this trip if you want. And I won't say a word about it. I won't bother you in the least. In fact, I'll probably enjoy it as much as you do.

"You can get away with it, you know," Marla continued, "because as gruesome as his bitch-witch Grandmother is, she's not here. That little girl is her vessel but she's empty now. Babcia is somewhere else. So you CAN have Niko with no strings attached."

"But I don't want him. I don't want him hurt anymore," Jeannie sobbed.

"Well, I'm going to hurt him plenty, you know," Marla hissed. "There's no way you can stop me. So you might as well have your fun while you can."

"I love him. I don't want to see him suffer," Jeannie cried.

"Well, he is going to suffer and die no matter what you do, so why not fuck him first. Hell, get pregnant, have his kid, I don't care!"

Suddenly Marla fell silent. What had she just said?

Jeannie raised her eyes and looked into the mirror at the decaying witch who was supposed to be her sister.

Jeannie had heard her words, too. It made her wonder.
What had she just said?

Chapter 60
Madness Part 2

"What a strange object," Holly said as she unwrapped the little package she'd just received from Niko.

"It's some kind of crystal wind chime," she added and shook it. A little chill ran through her as she heard its gentle sound. The chime had been set in a minor key that seemed rather ominous.

"Very Polish," said Sister Alexia, who had taught her share of "Polaks" (as she called them) in her early years in Chicago.

"Let me hang it here for you," the nun said and hooked it over the end of the window shade. As she did, she gasped. For the little mirror that was the centerpiece of the chime reflected the ghastly figure of Father Tim as he entered the room. He looked pale, thin, and terrified.

"Sweet Jesus, Father," she said. "What's happened to you?"

"Nothing," the priest murmured. "But I do need to have a moment alone with Holly." And he gave the old nun a wave of his hand to shoo her away.

"By all means, Father," the nun answered and walked from the room closing the door just as Emmy managed to scoot through it.

The cat jumped up on Holly's bed and padded up to her. Holly pulled Emmy onto her lap and began petting her.

"What can you tell me about Babcia?" Tim asked urgently.

"I thought you knew everything."

"Niko told me that she's tried to destroy anyone she thinks will threaten your marriage."

"Yes," Holly answered trying to fight off the sudden memory of John Hunter's mutilated body.

"And she thinks I am a threat to your marriage, too, I guess."

"She must," Holly replied remembering the incident in Griffith Park. But she also agreed because the priest had changed so much in the last few days. There was a look of constant terror about him. He flinched at the smallest things. And at that very moment, Emmy began to purr, and even that seemed to make him jump.

"Holly, this cat, is she...?"

Holly looked down at Emmy who had closed her eyes and seemed so peaceful.

"What, Tim?"

"Is it possible that somehow Babcia's managed to... to... live inside the cat?"

Holly's mind flashed back to a terrible dream she'd had just after Niko had shot himself. She could hear Joy's voice commanding Babcia to 'be the cat' and the thought made Holly push Emmy away from her. The cat just let out a questioning meow and moved slowly to the foot of the bed where she curled up again and gave a cold, secretive squint to both of them.

Holly sighed as she pulled herself from the bed and walked to the priest.

"I don't know."

"They're still letting you wear your own night clothes," Tim murmured.

"They're more comfortable."

More seductive, Tim thought, but he didn't say it.

"Tim, what's happening to you?"

"If I didn't know better," he answered. "I'd think that Babcia was working on me, giving me horrible nightmares."

At that moment, the little Polish wind chime caught a brief draft from the cracked window. It sang out its melancholy chorus, and Tim looked at it. The tiny mirror that formed its center twisted from side to side, and with every twist, he caught a glimpse of Holly's bed. And in one flash, the image he saw was the innocent form of Emmy, but in the next, there was Babcia herself glowering at him, then Emmy, then Babcia once more staring at him with those deadly eyes.

"I'll make you pay, priest," she seemed to growl. "For your sins and the sins of your church."

The words were there, weren't they? Tim could hear them. He was certain of it.

He looked at Holly and realized she had heard nothing. Her look of concern was only for him. She saw the terror in his eyes, moved toward the priest, and pulled him to her.

Father Tim buried his face in Holly's breasts, losing himself in them, loving the sin of their softness, loving the sin of being with her, of desiring her and wondering if even his forgiving God could save...

Such an evil man as he.

Chapter 61
Wolf in the Woods

Despite her terrifying encounter with Marla, despite the gloom that filled her, Jeannie Morrison took long, healthy strides up the steep mountain trail, setting the pace for the others who followed. It was almost as though she were running away, running into the mountains, running from a witch she'd never be able to escape.

Still, she could not have looked more athletic or more beautiful. She wore a heavy, white, cable-knit sweater, khaki shorts, high socks, enormous hiking boots, and a tragic look in her eyes.

Niko was close behind her, dressed in similar socks, boots, and shorts, but with a dark red sweatshirt emblazoned with the Polish eagle. He held Joy's hand, and the little girl, who might have been the fittest of them all, actually skipped along in her snow pants and ski jacket.

Michalowski followed the trio huffing and puffing but taking solace from his knowledge that the trail would soon level off.

Behind Michalowski came a new member of the crew: Feliks, an eleven-year-old Polish boy from Zakopane. He was half pushing, half pulling Osiol, a stubborn and angry old mule that was burdened down with all their provisions.

Occasionally, Osiol would stop dead in his tracks, let out an angry bray, and refuse to go any further no matter how Feliks tugged.

"Glupi Zwierzak!" Feliks cursed in a Polish phrase that only Joy and Michalowski could understand. The old man just shook his head and laughed, but the little girl skipped back to the boy, gathered some nettles from alongside the trail, and held them invitingly in front of Osiol, which caused the stubborn creature to move again.

"We take trail to camp at four thousand feet," Michalowski informed Niko as they trudged up the sharp incline. "Spending first night there."

#

Two hours later the hike had not gotten any less arduous, but they were all doing well. Even Jeannie couldn't help but smile at the bright green meadows that appeared now and then or the tiny stream that was now flowing gently beside them. It was singing to them, she felt, trying hard to cheer her up.

The full trees that had shielded the little party from the sun earlier in the hike had given way to small-leafed bushes and wide stretches of exposed granite. Now only an occasional poplar or willow rose up from beside the stream to offer a brief respite from the boiling sun.

Beyond it all, the gray granite cliffs of the Carpathian Mountains stood like a jagged wall. They glistened here and there with fingers of snow that seemed to be reaching for the little party, threatening to grab them and drag them up into a secret world full of even greater witchcraft and magic.

"Tower is at snow," Michalowski told Niko and pointed to the longest of the snowfields.

"Very far away," Niko commented.

"But view is magnificent, no?"

Niko nodded. "But it's gotten so damn hot."

"And will be for long while."

"So, I guess it's time to strip down, "Niko said and he pulled off his Polish sweatshirt to reveal the Leland University T-shirt underneath. Joy smiled at him and yanked off her snow pants and ski jacket to show off her new lederhosen, a gift from Jeannie in Zakopane and a reminder of the time when this area of Poland was part of the vast Hapsburg Empire.

Peeking out from under the leather straps of the lederhosen, CatMan Due sang out from her T-shirt: *Give a Friend a Hug!*

Jeannie too, pulled off her sweater to reveal a much cooler cotton blouse. Her expression bore only the trace of a smile at best. She brought the sweater over to Feliks who folded it together with the other discarded clothing and strapped them all on the back of poor Osiol who became even more ornery because of them. Feliks, fortunately, had learned Joy's trick of luring the stubborn beast along with nettles, and that helped greatly.

"Wish Mommy was here to see all this," Joy said to her father when they began walking again.

"She'd love it," he replied with a look of sadness.

Almost in harmony with Niko's change in mood, the mountain trail took a sudden dip down out of the bright sunlight and back into the woods.

Trees, heavily laden with moss and lichen, crowded in around them. Boulders seemed to grow out of the little stream, reducing it to no more than a trickle. But far ahead, Jeannie could hear a heavy rushing of water that suggested that the stream must flow into a powerful river.

The floor of the trail was now matted with fir needles and moss and the skeletons of leaves that seemed as though they had been there for decades.

Impossible. Leaves rot away every year, Jeannie thought, but still, these leaves looked as ancient as the rocks themselves.

At this point, the sun disappeared completely as heavy tree branches curled in around the little party. Perhaps to snatch them up, Jeannie thought again as she marched forward. Her nervous energy was taking her farther and farther ahead of her companions. And now, as she hiked up over another little rise, she could see a powerful river rushing in from her left, welcoming the little stream to a wild world of swirling rapids.

The roar of the water was suddenly deafening. Spray splashed over Jeannie, drenching her shirt, her shorts, and her hair. She watched gooseflesh rise on her arms, and she was sorry that she'd given up her warm sweater so quickly.

She turned to see that Niko and Joy were now quite far behind her, and Osiol and those warm clothes were farther back still. She might have turned and gone back for her sweater except that at that very moment she was gripped with a fear so powerful she never could have imagined it. Rosie Osborn, at least, had never experienced anything like it. What was it?

Marla had spotted something across the bank – that was it – something that made her blood run cold, something that consumed her with an unimaginable fear.

Jeannie felt herself breaking into a run, away from Niko, away from the rest of the party along the trail but deeper and deeper into the woods. She was running beside the river now, gasping desperately for breath, feeling her entire body drenched in the powerful spray that was thrown off by the surging rapids beside her.

She pounded along the trail, tromped through nettles, skeletal leaves, and large sharp rocks sticking up from the trail that twisted her feet and ankles and made her stumble again and again. She splashed through a rivulet that cut across the trail. And, in its reflective surface, she saw the most horrifying sight she would ever see in her life: Marla. This was not the hideous, angry Marla whose evil often twisted Jeannie's face into some hateful thing that she could not bear to look at. Nor was it the monstrous undead Marla with maggoty flesh and spider filled eye sockets. This was so much worse than any of that. This was a Marla whose look of terror transformed her into the personification of fear and horror herself, a Marla whose mouth was shaped into an endless scream, whose entire face was drawn back in wide-eyed terror.

Suddenly, the roar of the river was shouting a prayer as though it were Marla herself calling out through the rage of the rapids: "Save me, save me. Oh Goddess, save me!"

"From what?" Jeannie cried aloud, and then, suddenly she knew.

There, across the river, charging along a trail that paralleled the one she was on, was an enormous black wolf, a monster, its hair bristling with rage, its lips drawn back in hunger. It growled wickedly at her. Was it more than a wolf? Could it be Babcia's emissary? Marla was sure of it.

The wolf charged along the trail. Now, images began flashing through Jeannie's mind, images of the last moments that Marla had spent alive. There in her secret room where she had prepared an altar to sacrifice Holly Madonie and her unborn child to the hate and lust of Babcia Czarownicka, Babcia the greatest of all witches. Marla had hoped to gain Babcia's near-infinite power from the sacrifice. But it hadn't worked out that way, had it?

Jeannie tripped in the deep mud of the soggy trail. She scrambled to her feet as the wolf howled at her from across the river. Then, driven by Marla's fear, she surged down a steep embankment, pulling away from the river, plunging into the blackness of the forest. The trees hung thick with witch lichen that seemed to become the image of Marla's terrified face at that most unbearable moment of her life, when Babcia had transformed herself into that great wolf and reared up above her hissing, growling, teeth gnashing, monster jaws drooling, eyes raging, the breath of the dead blasting into Marla's face, the deadly wolf/witch teeth parting (all the better to eat you with my dear)!

Jeannie found herself now charging out of the hollow woods, climbing a rise to see how the two paths (hers and that of the wolf) drew closer and closer together. Could the wolf jump the river there? Could it catch Jeannie and tear her to pieces as it had Marla?

Images of tearing flesh, Marla's flesh, HER FLESH, flashed through Jeannie's mind. She felt the slice of wolf/witch claws as they screamed across Marla's stomach opening her, tearing out her insides, then those huge jaws seizing her guts and devouring them.

Jeannie plunged ahead.

Up over the rise, she was running stride for stride with the wolf now, and her only hope was to beat the horrid creature, wasn't it? Yes, charge out ahead of the wolf, OUTRUN A WILD WOLF.

And suddenly, Jeannie felt a growing sense of youth and power: her muscles tightened, her heart grew stronger, her speed increased, and her breath came in great welcoming gulps of energy. Yes, she could feel sexuality, too. Marla was intensifying the Spell of Becoming and releasing it again into Jeannie. The spell was flowing freely through her now, giving her the power to ascend a steep, broad hill and fly past trees.

She charged up out of the hollow. The river had dropped far below into a ravine that appeared to be growing narrower as she ran. The wolf was there, too, on the other side of the ravine snarling as it ran, almost cursing at her, almost calling to her that it would soon catch her and tear her apart.

Jeannie felt the Spell of Becoming grow stronger still. She began to out-distance the wolf, but she knew in her heart she could never outrun the beast, not in the end. If the ravine continued to narrow, as it seemed to be doing, the wolf would soon find a spot where it could leap across. Then it would have Jeannie, Rosie, and Marla - that horrible trinity - three persons in one poor, sorry, young woman.

"Save me, Goddess!" Even Jeannie was shouting it now as she began to make out an enormous boulder up ahead of her. Whatever lay on the other side of that boulder was the answer to her prayer: a widening of the ravine (please, Goddess) or a narrowing that would bring the wolf and a swift but terrible death. She raced for the boulder with all her might. The wolf was almost right beside her now, its wicked spittle flying everywhere.

Jeannie reached the boulder and scrambled around it. The sun blazed down on her, and the river's roar became a wild shriek and then...

A rockslide!

A recent rockslide filled the valley in front of her. It was vast, as though the whole side of the mountain had tumbled in. Giant boulders, twenty and thirty feet high, rose up all around her. They sealed off the wolf's trail forming an impenetrable wall that offered the beast no passage whatsoever. The creature dropped back, growled viciously, and then it threw its head back and howled, a horrid blood-churning howl that ignited Marla's fear and released yet another strong dose of Becoming into the eager, young body of Jeannie Morrison.

She now clambered frantically across the boulders, showing a skill and agility that would put the best-schooled rock climber to shame. She stopped and turned to see the wolf raising its head and howling yet again, and then she climbed on reaching the other side of the trail and leaving the wolf so very far behind.

Within minutes, Niko and Joy were at the edge of the rockslide too, as though they had seen Jeannie's frantic pace and had done their best to keep up with her. Soon, Joy was scampering across the boulders, moving far more quickly than a little girl should have dared. She rushed into Jeannie's waiting arms, held onto her tightly, and kissed her. Jeannie broke into tears.

The little girl pulled Jeannie to her and consoled her as a mother would her child.

"Did you see that horrible wolf?" Jeannie sobbed.

"I saw her," Joy answered. "I thought she was beautiful."

"Maybe so," Jeannie answered. "But she was after me. I think she wanted to kill me."

"But why?"

Jeannie just shook her head and broke down into tears.

"I have to start taking better care of you," Joy said with all the seriousness of an eight-year-old.

Jeannie looked up gratefully, smiled and then pulled the little girl to her and hugged her tightly again.

By this time Niko had reached them. He stopped a short distance from them, took in the sight and smiled at this vision of his daughter and Jeannie together, almost a family.

Marla, still cowering in fear, had thoughts like these as well. She hated Joy, of course, and Niko and Holly and Jeannie, too, for that matter, but seeing the expression on Niko's face reminded her of the idea she'd had when she and Jeannie had confronted each other in that little lavatory in Zakopane.

It was time to talk things over with Clara Goriki, Marla decided. After all, what if Jeannie could seduce Niko? What if she could become pregnant with his child?

Would Jeannie be willing to do it? At first, Marla didn't think she would. But then she had another realization. Their little dash through the woods had reminded Marla that Rosie was, after all, an alcoholic and an addict. And Jeannie was suddenly displaying all the signs of addiction, wasn't she?

Marla smiled inside the sad, trembling body of her sister. How wonderful, she thought.

Jeannie was becoming addicted to the Spell of Becoming.

Chapter 62
Becoming

"Damn shame," Mother Black mumbled as she brushed back her long, snakelike hair and turned to the mirror. There she was: old, rumpled and toothless, dark sickly eyes, nonexistent ass, hollow chest, no boobs at all.

"Gwoin' change all dat," she said and suddenly broke into a loud, cackling laugh. She and Clara had been whipping up her new concoction for days. It was the Spell of Becoming – Mother Black's Becoming. She had watched Sally's daily adventures with Chuck Vaughn and had grown more and more jealous. So, why not create a new vision of herself... today!

"Too bad doh," she sighed. She knew where it was all headed. Sally was her favorite disciple, almost like a daughter to her, someone she loved. But once the Spell of Becoming renewed her body, they would be mortal enemies. Sally probably wouldn't know it at first. But she'd find out soon enough. And she almost certainly would not survive.

"Double curses," snarled Mother Black out of the mirror's reflection. "Guess it can't be helped, though. Ah wants that man, that Vaughn boy, want 'im fer mahself. Taken 'im away from Sal won't be hard, nope."

"I don't think it's any problem at all," Clara answered. "Sally is so close to the edge of grotesque that I'm not sure the Spell of Becoming will contain her much longer."

Midway through this discussion, Mother Black's scrying ball began to glow. It was almost like a silent telephone ring that told the old women that another witch was trying to contact them. It had to be Marla.

They hobbled over to the ball and Mother Black swiped her hand over it very quickly. Leering up at her was the face of Jeannie, but a Jeannie now under the complete control of

Marla Morrison. Her eyes were black, hollow pits, her hair a messy tangle, her skin bone white, and her mouth a brutal crimson gash.

The face grinned ghoulishly up at Mother Black and her mentor Clara Goriki, and then she screeched.

"I have it, Witch Bitches!" she called trembling with excitement.

"What do you have?" Clara responded.

"It's so simple!"

"Will ya talk straight, gal? Whatchya talkin' bout?"

Marla's evil grin broadened.

"Jeannie seduces Niko!"

"Easy enough," said Clara. "If ya let Rosie be herself. There's no way he'll sleep with a likes of you!"

Marla nodded in enthusiastic agreement. "Yes, you know, but that's okay because then... Jeannie fucks Niko. Jeannie gets pregnant. Jeannie has Niko's baby. His daughter is Babcia's great granddaughter!"

Mother Black reflected on this for a moment and then let out a loud whoop and began to do a little dance around her scrying ball. "Yeah, yeah," she burbled.

"What can the old witch do to us then?" Marla asked.

"We'll be relations," Mother Black cackled. "We'll have 'er! We'll have 'er power, too."

"And we'll have Niko if we still want him," Marla cried. "Why, I could inhabit that new child. I could become Niko's new daughter!"

"Or I could ring the life out of the brat, Joy, cause Babcia so much suffering she'd be down on her knees begging me for forgiveness."

"Oh yes. Oh yes," Mother Black cackled and clapped her hands. "Ah likes it, chil'! Oh, yo is one bright, bright gal."

"We should do it right, of course," Marla continued, calming just a bit.

"Of course, we should," Clara answered. "A complete Black Sabbath with all the trimmings!"

"You betcha," Mother Black called as she danced back into the darkness of the room and up to the boiling pot that was churning, hissing, and popping.

"Would you like to preside?" Marla asked gleefully.

"It will take some planning," Clara said thoughtfully. Suddenly there was a loud, happy shriek, and Mother Black cackled. Then silence again.

"Where are you, Mother?" Marla called.

"Right here!" came the response. A sleek, handsome, young, black woman approached the scrying ball. Her skin was chocolate, her hair soft and lustrous, her lips full, her backside epoch, her breasts young and inviting. And her eyes, her eyes were pure, glorious BLACK!

"Mother?" Marla asked in trembling tones.

"Mah name's Dinah Dee, gal," came the response. "An you best respect me!"

Marla was dumbfounded. "The Spell of Becoming?"

"Course! An' ain't I jes so, so damn becomin'?"

"Better do something about that accent, though." Clara said.

"A course, a course, soon enough, bitch. But first, lis'n up!" And her voice and her diction began to improve.

"There's a warlock in Poland," Dinah continued. "The leader of a coven of the cutest Polish witches you've ever seen. You may not be into the woman-woman thing, but I tell you, girly-girl, they are hot."

"I'll contact him," Clara said. "Maybe I'll even show up for the big event."

Marla nodded happily.

"And how about you, Mother? Don't you want to be here, too?"

"Ah do, sugar," the new and improved Mother Black responded.

"But I've gotta get me a man." Her glorious black eyes were glowing. "And his name is Charles Martin Vaughn."

"Meanwhile, I'll track down that warlock," Clara said with a cruel grin. "His name is Wicktor an' he'll initiate our pretty bitch into his coven...

"Good and proper."

Chapter 63
Wolf in the Woods Part Two

Rosie Osborn stared up from the dark, muddy puddle. She was as ugly as ever: no chin, all wrinkles, body bent and twisted. Jeannie shuddered as she considered this reflection of her former self.

Marla approved. She enjoyed reminding Jeannie of what she had been and how awful it had felt. She liked to have Rosie feeling that she (Marla) had done wonders for her. Maybe she would cooperate a little more when she did.

"Whatcha lookin' at?" asked someone from behind Jeannie. It was that pesky, little know-it-all, Joy Madonie.

"Triple curses!" Marla snarled from within Jeannie's body. There was no doubt in her mind that some of her darkest magic had to be saved for this precocious, little bitch.

The reflection of Rosie's twisted finger moved into the puddle stirring the water before Joy could have a chance to see the hideous image.

"Just checking my face, honey, that's all," said Jeannie. "What's up?"

"It's story time," Joy answered. "I've come to get you so that you can hear my story."

"Is that really the way it's supposed to work?" Jeannie asked doing her best to tease Joy in spite of the sadness she was feeling. "Little girls tell stories while the grown-ups listen?"

"Why not?" Joy responded. "I've got a good scary one, and I know you'll like it. So come on."

"Tell you what," Jeannie answered. "I really feel more like taking a nice, long walk. I need to think, and you can tell me your story another time. Is that okay?"

"Aw," Joy said sadly but then brightened almost at once. "Okay. I like to tell it, so sure. But be careful on your walk."

"I will, honey. I promise."

Jeannie watched Joy head off toward the huge bonfire that Michalowski and Feliks had built at the center of their campsite.

Then she knelt and looked back into the puddle. What she saw this time made her gasp. It wasn't the wrecked old face of Rosie Osborn at all. It wasn't even her own face or that of Marla. It was a new Jeannie appearing more radiant and beautiful than she ever had before. She was brighter now somehow, glowing. And that glow filled Jeannie physically. It shot across her whole body, tingling through her blood, filling her with energy, youth, and sexuality.

"What's happening to me?" she whispered.

"I've called up the spell again," Marla called from within her. "I thought you might like a little bigger dose of Becoming."

"Oh, I would," Jeannie answered enthusiastically.

"This is just a taste," Marla continued. "You'll feel even better after tonight."

Jeannie breathed in deeply, "I never thought it could be this good."

"There are so many degrees," Marla cooed seductively. "We want you to be beautiful for Niko, you know. We want you to make love to him and have his child. Niko deserves it."

Jeannie thought about that idea for a long moment. She fought off the screams from Rosie's conscience that were calling, "no, no, no!"

"He might like that!" she affirmed at last as though hypnotized by the new energy that was flowing through her. And then another idea suddenly occurred to her, a very un-Rosie-like idea.

"I'm more beautiful than Holly ever was, aren't I?"

287

"Yes, you are. And when Holly grows old and ugly, you will still be youthful and lovely... forever."

"I can have his child?"

"We want you to."

"You won't hurt Niko?"

"Not if you don't want that."

Jeannie's eyes sparkled. She tingled all over. What a fabulous feeling. She stood and turned to the woods.

And suddenly she screamed!

The great, black wolf was right there, leering at her, standing no more than ten feet away. It peeled back its lips to reveal deadly, yellow teeth, and it growled with a deep guttural roar that sent chills into the heart of Marla's black soul. Was it Babcia's emissary?

Jeannie turned.

An even larger wolf stood at the beginning of another pathway into the woods, and it was growling... Jeannie turned again looking both ways. The two wolves were advancing on her, seemingly trying to drive her back to the campfire.

"Run!" Marla screamed, and Jeannie flung herself into the woods between the two wolves.

There was no path there, just wild brambles, and yet she charged right into them. The wolves gave chase, howling wickedly.

Jeannie drove herself through the underbrush and between the huge trees that stood like black sentinels all across the forest floor. Guardians! But for whom?

Jeannie cut onto a path that led deeper into the woods and ran in that direction, but five more wolves blocked her way.

"Noooo!" she screamed and plunged back into the dense underbrush. She was running away from the campground and deeper into the woods on no path at all. That vibrant, sexy energy that she'd begun to feel moments earlier was still with her. Blood was coursing through her veins, thrilling her. If she had stopped to think for only a moment, she might have realized that she was running away from the safety of her companions and their campsite. But she didn't think of that. Perhaps Marla wouldn't let her.

The wolves were hot after her now dodging between the trees that Jeannie skirted like Goddess Diana, surefooted and swift. She came to yet another trail. More wolves! This time they were to her left, so she ran to the right. They gave chase, howling wildly, growling like deadly thunder, baring their fangs, gaining on her, lunging for her legs and heels to catch her and tear her apart.

Marla was nearly hysterical now. Ten wolves were chasing her. She took control of Jeannie's body, driving her, cursing wickedly as the wolves continued to gain on her. They split up and ran alongside her. She slipped and fell! And they lunged for her. One bit her shoulder and tore at her flesh. Another dropped back, preparing to pounce when suddenly...

A monstrous man dropped down beside her. He had a handsome face and a body covered with thick, black hair and rippling with huge muscles. He grabbed the first wolf and flung it back at the others. Then he flashed his hand, and fire shot from his fingertips. He swung his arm in an arch and flames shot out, creating a wall of fire all around them. Through the flames, Jeannie could see the wolves snarling at them: fangs bared, jaws chattering, claws digging at the ground, thunderous growls rumbling from their lungs. One lunged into the flames but then dropped back.

The man let out a great bellow that shook the forest as he turned and looked at Jeannie with a hungry grin. Then he swooped her up into his arms.

"Welcome to our Sabbath!" he cried and carried her through the flames and away from the wolves...

Toward a great clearing in the forest.

Chapter 64
The Initiation

"The time is NOW, my young witches," the warlock called. "At last... it is the moment we have all been waiting for. I've led you away from the tower and down the mountain for this. And he stepped behind a huge stone circle and brought Jeannie Morrison out before them.

Heading down the mountain had taken far less time than ascending, and the warlock (still storytelling as he came) had led his troop to this sacrificial site where they would celebrate the black mass of Jeannie Morrison's consecration.

In the few moments that he had been gone saving Jeannie from the wolves, his girls had uncovered an ancient, marble altar that stood just to the right of a deep, stone fire pit.

Joyously, the young witches added cured hardwood to the pit in front of the altar. With all their giggling and gossiping, the warlock wondered if they knew the solemn and bloody ritual they would soon share. Perhaps not, but they would learn soon enough.

All was in readiness when he flashed his hand at the fire pit, and the hardwood exploded into flames. The warlock bellowed out a great laugh because he could see that the act both terrified and thrilled Jeannie.

Beside the altar, a small pen held a trio of baby lambs. Local witches had loved and cared for the animals all their lives, and the warlock's appearance only drew their curiosity as they trundled toward him without any sense of fear.

Wicktor carried Jeannie to the pen and set her gently down beside it. She looked up and smiled.

She knelt and reached for the smallest of the lambs, pulling it close to her.

"Feeling better?" the warlock asked with a seductive smile.

"I think so," Jeannie answered as she cuddled the little lamb against her breast. The innocent creature seemed calm and relaxed, and it made the girl feel better as well.

"You're safe here," Wicktor whispered.

Jeannie did not really want to trust her unknown savior, though he was very handsome. In fact, he looked like a more dangerous version of the enchanting lovers she had read about in romance novels.

"Is this your favorite?" asked the warlock gesturing toward the lamb. She looked into the eyes of the little creature.

"Oh yes," she said with a smile and held the little animal closer still.

"Good," said the warlock and turned toward his crew.

"Come, girls! Bring the ingredients and pour them into our caldron. Let's boil up a brew good enough to call forth Old Nick himself."

He took the large, wooden staff he'd carried on his hike and slammed it into the boiling caldron that hung suspended above the fire pit. The staff hissed like a snake as it touched the liquid.

"Ingredients, more ingredients!" demanded the warlock, and his teenage witches came running with armloads of bottles and jars each containing some awful element.

"Grab that little, wiggly one," he called.

Chantel reached into a jar, chased a black, slimy thing around the rim for a moment and let out a yelp when the creature bit her on her fingertip. She snatched it out and tossed it into the caldron.

"Snakes! Come dig them out for me," called Wicktor.

Matryoshka knelt beside a bucket seething with vipers. They glistened as they writhed and tangled.

She reached into the roiling mass, gritted her teeth, and pulled out a handful of the squirming monsters. One huge serpent reared its head above her and was about to strike when a hand suddenly caught it in mid-air.

Clara Goriki snatched up the squirming viper and threw it headlong into the boiling brew. Then she grabbed all of the others from Matryoshka and tossed them in as well.

Matryoshka smiled gratefully.

"Back to your work," the warlock told the girl, and he fetched her a good kick right on her witch's bottom.

She smiled and whispered, "Thank you, Pan Wicktor."

"Welcome, Mistress," the warlock said to Clara. "You made it just in time."

The old witch gave Wicktor a toothless smile and nodded. "Wouldn't miss it for the world," she said and moved slowly up to Jeannie.

"Well now," she said assaying the beautiful young woman who knelt beside the pen clutching the little lamb. "You seem to be in good health, Miss Morrison."

"I am. Yes I am. Thank you."

"And I see you've made a friend."

Jeannie felt a sudden chill, more perhaps from the over solicitous tone with which Clara had asked the question.

"It's just a lamb," she said releasing the little creature and shooing it back into the pen. Then she stood to greet the witch who had played so big a part in the most horrific and magical of night of her life... the ceremony of her BECOMING when the body and soul of Rosie had blended with the spirit of Marla to create Jeannie Morrison.

As she watched the teenage witches scurry about the clearing preparing the ingredients for the brew and noticed the look of intense interest that the warlock and the witch were showing her, she knew that this was to be some kind of initiation.

"Bring the little one," the warlock called and pointed to the pen. He smiled at Jeannie, who couldn't help but return the smile nervously. Wicktor was just so very handsome, though she could also see that his smile was somehow frighteningly wicked.

"Why must I bring him?" she asked.

"For the sacrifice, girl," Clara answered in the voice of the devil himself. "To consecrate your pledge."

Jeannie looked from the witch to the warlock and froze for a moment.

"Bring the damn lamb, Jeannie," Clara called. "Or we'll sacrifice you instead!"

Jeannie swallowed hard and stepped cautiously over to the pen where the lambs were standing. They seemed to sense the danger in the witches' conversation.

Jeannie reached for the oldest of the trio.

"Not that one," said the warlock. "We need the one you love the most."

She sighed. And then she felt Marla's spirit taking over her hands and reaching for the littlest lamb. Jeannie struggled with the witch within her, yet couldn't win. In no more than a few seconds, she had (unwillingly) pulled the little creature from its pen and carried it to the altar.

Clara now stepped around behind Jeannie and grabbed her by the wrists. Together they brought the lamb to the center of the altar and held it there. The frightened little animal let out a mournful bleat and turned toward Jeannie with a pleading look in its eyes. The young woman began to sob.

"Do we have to?"

"Afraid so," Clara hissed. "There's a price to pay for your youth and beauty after all."

And with that, Clara offered Jeannie a huge, butcher knife.

"Slit it open," she commanded.

Jeannie reached for the knife, barely able to hold it in her hands. As she did, Clara reached down and held the lamb's back and front feet together so that the little creature lay on its side.

"Please, no," Jeannie pleaded.

"Do you want youth, beauty, and to be Niko's lover, or not?" Clara asked with a cruel smile.

Jeannie closed her eyes, flushing the tears from them. "Yessss," she whispered. And Clara took her wrist and directed the knife to the lamb. Jeannie opened her eyes long enough to see that, with one swift stroke and a massive spurt of blood, she and the old witch together had slit the little creature from top to bottom and quickly ended its life.

"At last," said the warlock. "You're a real witch." And he took a handful of lamb's blood and smeared it across Jeannie's face.

Matryoshka and the other youthful witches cheered as they gathered around Jeannie. They pulled the lamb from the altar and lifted the beautiful, young girl onto it. Jeannie was somehow smiling now as they tore off her clothing and began to smear blood all over her body.

"Yessss," she sighed again as she felt the witches' hands swarm over every inch of her, caressing her face, her breasts, her shoulders, her arms, and all of her most hungry places.

"We're going to make you Niko's witch-lover," Clara shouted.

"Yessss!" Jeannie answered and felt the Spell of Becoming surging through her once again.

Then the young witches stepped back, and Clara shrieked with wanton glee as the warlock brought his enormous body above the naked, blood-drenched form of Jeannie Morrison.

"And now, the consummation!" Wicktor roared...

And he fell upon her.

Chapter 65
Joy's Tale

What had been magically long and horrifying hours for Jeannie, had been only a few minutes for her companions. And now, while Niko, Michalowski, and Feliks stoked the fire and began to talk about going into the woods to look for her, she almost danced back into their camp.

Her steps were light, and her lips turned into a wistful smile. Her complexion seemed warmer and more radiant than ever, in spite of the cold that now began to spread mercilessly through the woods.

"We heard the howl of wolves," Feliks said.

"Starting to worry," added Michalowski.

"Don't be silly," answered the young woman. "I mean, I heard the howls, and they did frighten me for a moment, but then I decided to head back as fast as I could. I did get a little bit lost and tripped or something. I don't know what happened exactly, I may have blacked out for a moment or two, but then I turned and... well, there was your fire blazing only a few yards from where I stood. It probably drove the wolves away, too. So now here I am, and everything's fine."

"You look fantastic," said Niko as he came up to Jeannie and gave her a quick embrace. Then he held her at arm's length to study her. He cocked his head and smiled. "The truth is, you look more radiant than ever."

"Silly," said Jeannie sweetly. She was surely still high on the latest dose of the Spell of Becoming and the bloody but somehow restorative initiation at the hands of Wicktor and Clara. Oh, the witches had carefully blotted it from her mind before they bathed her in witches brew and brought her sleeping body back to the edge of the camp.

"It's the firelight," Jeannie whispered. "That's what's giving me a glow. It's just very flattering. That's all."

"If you say so, beautiful," Niko added with a smile and took Jeannie by the arm to lead her up to the roaring campfire. "You're back safe and sound. Still, you'd better warm yourself."

"And I haven't started my story yet," added Joy. "You can hear the whole thing. Plus, I taught everyone how to make a special treat called s'mores. Would you like one?"

Jeannie did feel a bit hungry, wasn't sure why, but still she smiled and nodded. The little girl passed her a plate filled with a concoction made from graham crackers, marshmallows, and chocolate all melted together over the fire.

Jeannie took a bite.

"Mmmmm. These are delicious," she said at once.

"Wash it down with a little cocoa," Niko added as he passed her his mug. Jeannie took it, smiled at him, and sipped.

\#

The warlock, Clara, Matryoshka, and all of the teenage witches watched the party gathered around the campfire from a safe distance.

"As you see, the story I've been telling you has caught up to the present," whispered Wicktor. "So, let us go back to the tower and prepare for the arrival of Babcia's grandson and his band."

And so they did, and yet as they began their trek back to Rapunzel's tower, they still heard much of the story that little Joy told to her companions.

\#

"Okay... Once upon a time," Joy began while Niko, Jeannie, Pan Michalowski, and young Feliks looked on.

She told the complex tale in the simple words of a little girl, enhancing it somewhat with vocabulary she had learned from her great-grandmother. Still, how could she do it full justice, a little eight-year-old, when, in reality, the very adult tale went like this:

Hundreds of years ago, there was a young man from the village of Zakopane, and his name was Jan.

Jan wanted to be an artist and, though his hand was steady and his eye was good, every painting he made just seemed to be missing something.

He studied under the best teacher in the village, Wadislaw Wynofski, who was convinced that the boy's problem was his impatience. Jan didn't look at things carefully enough. He wanted to finish his paintings too quickly, and so he missed the all-important details that somehow held the truth about the person or object he was painting.

"Look carefully," Wadislaw would remind him. "Be a keen observer." But in spite of his teacher's efforts, Jan could not produce a single piece of art that seemed to have any truth to it. His paintings of apples, pears, and other fruit were uninteresting. His landscapes were flat and boring. His portraits had no soul. And so, after years of effort and failure, Jan came to the old man pleading for an answer.

"Go for long walks in the woods," Wadislaw told him. "Study everything you see, but look closer! Pay attention! Find the truth in things!"

And Jan tried. But as keenly as he looked, he could find nothing that excited or interested him, nothing that drew him in enough to reveal its truth. And so his paintings were just as bad as ever, and eventually he painted less and less.

Now Jan's long walks were even sadder as he wandered deeper and deeper into the woods, growing more melancholy with each visit.

"One last trip," Wadislaw encouraged. *"Just one more. Go as far into the woods as you dare to go, look as hard as you dare to look. Don't come back until you find something with a soul."*

And so Jan set off again this time carrying Wadislaw's own pack, complete with a warm sweater and some provisions for the longer journey. He traveled into the mountains for days until at last, he came to the snowline of the high Carpathians. There, legends told that an enormous tower imprisoned a beautiful, young maiden. You could hear her song, the legend said, and if you followed it, you would come to the tower itself and to her.

He hadn't thought of this old legend since he was a little boy, and he wasn't much in the mood to think about it now. Yet, he did seem to hear something, didn't he? At first, it appeared to be nothing more than the rustling of the red and yellow leaves that had fallen during late autumn and were now being shuffled around by the breeze. Or maybe it was the birds as they flitted through the treetops, their songs combining into something that was new and wonderful.

Yet, the more he listened, the more he realized that there was something very human about the sound and something very lonely as well. He concentrated. It was a song that was almost heartbreaking.

"Come and save me," it seemed to say. *And, though Jan had been very much preoccupied with his own failures, he couldn't get over the melancholy beauty of the song or the sweetness of the voice singing it. And so he followed the song and let it lead him higher and higher into the mountains until the terrain became barren and the wind became harsh. It bit at his hands and face and made his entire body tremble with the cold.*

Jan opened the pack old Wadislaw had given him and took out the wool sweater. It bore the crest of the Wynofski family.

He donned it and continued on following the song higher and higher into the mountains. And soon the wind wailed, snow swirled all around him, and his fingers seemed to be turning to ice. Yet he continued, because the song was always there, always calling to him with its sweetness and its sorrow.

Eventually, Jan was able to make out the ramparts of the legendary tower, which seemed to soar even higher than the mountains themselves. The song grew louder, and now he could tell more about the singer. She was a young girl, perhaps as young as sixteen. Her voice became clearer, and he realized that she was singing to him alone.

He was stumbling now, legs shivering in the snowy cold, hands trembling, lips and eyes and nose nearly frozen at the elevation. Still, as he entered the courtyard of the tower, at what was now almost midnight, he was warmed by the light from a window that looked out from the very top of the tower. Jan hobbled, nearly crawling around the outside of the place looking for entry, finding none, and wondering how the maiden, or anyone for that matter, could ever enter.

It was then that the maiden came to the window and smiled at him, a smile that seemed to light up all the night. She was so fair, with long, white-blonde hair that was braided and fell over her shoulder and out of sight. Her eyes sparkled with the deepest blue. It was magical how he could know that from so far away, and yet he did.

"My lady," Jon called out in sudden inspiration,

"Let down your hair

"So I may climb

"Without a stair."

The girl giggled at the silly rhyme and then lifted a large coil of braids to the window ledge and pushed it forward. Her braids fell, unfurling the entire height of the tower. She waved to Jan and pulled her pretty head to the side of the window to slip the ribbon braided into her hair onto a huge hook that held it in place without straining her.

Upon seeing that the girl could accommodate his weight, Jan began climbing the braids; hand over hand, legs outstretched behind him, swinging wildly back and forth, he rushed to get to the window and the beautiful young woman awaiting him. As he climbed, he could picture himself bounding over the sill and wrapping his arms around her at once, delighting in hungry kisses from someone who must be as lonely and frustrated as he.

But as soon as he reached the window, swung up onto the ledge, and dove into the room, the beautiful young woman was nowhere to be seen. Instead, shuffling out of the shadows came the stooped figure, twisted claws, and hideous face of Babcia Czarownica, the witch.

"Wynofski," she hissed moving slowly toward him, backing him up to the very edge of the window. "Your clothing says you are of family Wynofski."

Jan was terrified and speechless, and yet there was something about this creature that caught his eye. He studied her for a long and desperate moment. What was it? Something about her face, not that hideous old toothless mouth, of course, not that horrible witch's hooked nose. Not the straw hair or those deep hollow eyes.

The witch shuffled toward him raising her claw of a hand to slash at his face and take his eyes out. But then she stopped. His reaction was strange. It wasn't the fear she'd seen in the eyes of the hundreds of Wynofski descendants she had already murdered. This was different.

"You're the maiden," Jan suddenly gasped.

The witch cocked her head, gazed at him for a moment, and then moved on toward him raising her claw-like hands once more.

"No," he called. "You're in there, beautiful girl. I can see you. How can I save you?"

The witch let out a loud cackle.

"Save yourself, boy, if you can."

But the boy was stubborn. All his efforts to learn to see, to observe, had suddenly come to him in a moment of brilliance so that he saw the beauty in the girl's eyes buried deep in the soul of that murderous, old hag. And then something more amazing happened: he began to see the witch's beauty, too.

"You're beautiful," he said stepping toward her. The witch growled, but he didn't care. He reached for her gnarled old hands and pulled her closer to him.

"I must paint you," he cried. "Now!"

But, of course, there was no paint, no canvass, no inks, pencils, or paper in the tower. He looked around the room frantically for a medium to capture this amazing face. At last, he spotted something. There was clay in a pot in the corner of the room, beside a rack of bottles that contained all manner of evil-looking, wiggly things. He went to it and picked up the clay, He smelled it, tasted it, and rubbed it between his fingers. He lifted the pot toward the old witch and pointed from the clay to her face and back again.

Babcia smiled and nodded. She moved away from the window and toward Jan, the artist who would soon make clay masks of that withered old face and, in the process...

Gain both of them immortality.

Chapter 66
The Beginnings of Madness

Timmy Brennan was once again in the tent with teenage witch, Marla Morrison. Except that this was nineteen-year-old Marla, and Timmy was still very young.

That big table was there just as he remembered it, and Marla was sitting behind it, naked down to the waist, her breasts much more full and inviting now, he realized.

She smiled wickedly at him. She was creating a little, wax poppet, one she would use to fondle and tickle Timmy once she had taken hairs she'd pulled from his head and pushed them deep into the wax.

Timmy remembered it all.

Marla molded the stuff, shaped the figure of the little boy. She pulled and kneaded the wax until the poppet was the shape of an adult man. Timmy was breathless as he felt himself growing... maturing. He was a twenty-year-old now, in his first year at St. Martin's Seminary, the year of the wildest fantasies about Marla.

The wind whipped up and buffeted the tent. The tent posts rattled and the roof billowed as though it might tear the flimsy little structure right out of the ground. Suddenly, the flap blasted open and in stepped Holly Madonie carrying Emmy.

Holly wore a bright yellow raincoat and high, matching galoshes. She approached Marla as though she were in a trance. The witch stealthily took a knife from the table, moved to Holly and quickly sliced off a snippet of her hair. Then she grabbed a fistful of fur from the cat and yanked it out as well. The cat hardly stirred, and Holly didn't even blink. She merely turned and moved (zombie-like) toward Tim. Her eyes suddenly flashed with recognition and she smiled at Tim while she looked him up and down.

"Oh, I see," Holly said with a little smirk, putting her fingers over her lips demurely. "Little Timmy's all grown up."

She batted her eyes and moved past Tim to the far side of the tent where she let the cat fall from her arms.

Emmy curled up comfortably and began to purr in a low, seductive way, one that added to the mood that Tim felt growing in the tent.

Holly turned to Marla. The teen witch had poured out a huge blob of melon/flesh-colored wax from a beaker that had been bubbling over a little burner on the table. The witch fashioned a lifelike poppet from the wax, a perfect little figure of Holly Madonie. Marla pressed Holly's hair into the poppet and began stroking it. She caressed the poppet's cheek, and Holly let out a sigh as she reached up and touched the side of her face just as Marla had done. Then Marla slid her fingers skillfully down the poppet.

Holly shuddered with the feeling and immediately reached for the top of her raincoat and ripped it open. She was stark naked underneath, and she tossed the coat carelessly behind her.

Tim was wide-eyed at the sight and that's when he saw Marla set Holly's poppet aside and move back to his. She lifted it and began stroking it. He closed his eyes and his body went mad with pleasure.

Madness: it begins in dreams.

He opened his eyes expecting to see Marla sitting back enjoying the view. But instead, Marla was working feverishly on another poppet... of the CAT.

She finished the poppet of Emmy, and then grabbed a long pin and thrust it right through the poppet of Holly Madonie.

The young woman recoiled. She staggered backward as a huge wound opened in her chest, and blood began gushing from it.

"My God!" Holly cried as she realized what was happening. Another pin shot through her crosswise, and she gripped the bloody wound and fell beside the cat.

Marla now began stabbing pins into the poppet of Emmy, picking at the figure, throwing off chunks of its flesh, and the same bloody mutilation was happening to Emmy herself.

The cat screeched, writhed in agony, and then moved on Marla. The teenage witch could see the wildness in the cat's eyes. She jabbed at the poppet, again and again, hoping to slow it, kill it, but now the stabbing seemed to have no effect at all.

Marla turned to run, but the cat pounced.

Emmy flew at the witch, dug her claws into the girl's chest, and buried her fangs (yes, fangs) into her neck. Marla fell to the floor trying to push the cat away, but Emmy only dug her claws in deeper.

Timmy jumped to his feet then. He grabbed the cat, which turned and raked its claws across his chest and down below his waist. The pain was beyond belief. Tim dropped the cat and fell back. Marla scuttled backward too, away from the cat that was now transforming into the horrible, hulking figure of Babcia.

Looking like death itself, the black-robed great witch reached out her withered hand, grabbed the poppet of Emmy, and scooped out the wad of cat hair that Marla had embedded into it. Then she leaned forward and snatched a handful of Marla's raven locks and pressed it into the wax.

"No!" Marla gasped at the realization of what Babcia was about to do. The ancient Polish fingers worked magically, and in seconds she had formed the wax into a poppet of Marla.

Babcia pulled it up before her deadly eyes and studied it. Then she smashed the poppets of Holly and Marla together twisting them into a single form.

She stuffed the new poppet into the beaker that was still sitting above the burner on Marla's worktable. Holly and Marla let out terrible cries of pain as the wax melted inside the beaker, and, just like the melting wax, their bodies began to flow into each other. They were becoming liquefied: shoulders, bellies, legs melting together, forming first a young woman with all the perfections of both, and then a molten stream of liquid that was now spilling toward Timmy. And all the while, the air was filled with the high-pitched death cries of Marla and Holly.

Tim tried to stand and pull away, but he could not. He looked at Babcia. She was holding another poppet: the one Marla had made of HIM. She was stuffing his poppet into the beaker too, where the wax from the figures of Holly and Marla still boiled and bubbled.

And now the molten creature, the deadly flow of the two women combined (eyeballs, fingertips, painted lips, a fleshy stream that still bellowed with cries of death) reached Timmy's feet.

It burned up his legs and onto his hips; it gurgled up onto his chest. And it was rising.

Tim felt a pain searing onto his face, charring his lips, destroying his nose and fuming up toward his eyes. He could feel the heat; he could feel himself melting. His eyeballs liquefied. He was losing his sight completely, but through those melting eyes, he could still make out the figure of Babcia laughing at him from across the tent, across the face of this maddening dream.

"Is madness," she laughed. At least, that's what Timmy thought he heard. His ears were nearly gone by then, melting along with his eyes as his hair burst into flames.

"Madness," the horrid witch repeated to the liquefying boy.

"It all begins in dreams."

305

Chapter 67
Snow Play

Joy scampered up the face of an enormous boulder.

"I see it!" she called. "I see it!" And soon Niko, Jeannie, and the others saw it, too: Rapunzel's Tower, jutting straight up out of a vast field of snow-bound boulders, which grew sharper and more vicious the closer they came to the huge monolith.

After three days of hiking, innumerable s'mores, and countless scary stories, they were well beyond the tree line of the Carpathians wearing the warmest clothes they'd brought with them.

Osiol let out an eager bray and perked up his ears. He was ready to charge on down through the boulders, find the nice, soft manger that must be hiding at the base of the tower, eat an extra portion of oats for all his good work, and lay down to pleasant donkey dreams. Now that all the heavy winter clothes were off his back, he felt as though he had the strength of ten full-grown horses, maybe twenty.

"Is farther than looks," Michalowski warned. "But if we make great effort, can get there by darkness."

"Well, let's go then," Jeannie called with the boundless energy she had purchased so dearly. In spite of the heavy Russian wool coat and furry Cossack hat she wore, she raced past the rest of the group and out across the field of boulders, negotiating the narrow trail with surprising skill. Niko was right behind her, running to catch up with her, scooping up a handful of snow from one of the boulders and flinging it at her. The loose snow bounced off the middle of her back. She turned and grabbed her own handful of the white stuff and tossed it at him in a powdery cloud. Niko couldn't dodge it, and the snow blew onto his face, down his neck, and into the collar of his parka.

"Gotcha!" Jeannie called as she grabbed him, spun him into the snow, and then fell right on top of him.

Niko felt the warmth of Jeannie's face against his. And suddenly she was kissing him. Niko resisted and tried to fight her off, but she seemed so very strong (witch strong).

There, buried in the deep snow so close to the base of Babcia's Tower, Jeannie ravaged Niko with kisses that were so hungry, so full of longing that he didn't know how to respond. He felt her whole body pressing against his, her hips grinding into him, wanting so much more.

"Daddy, where are you?" Joy yelled. She was struggling toward them. The snow was almost up to her waist. She didn't see them at all and was unaware of the inviting look that Jeannie now burned into Niko's eyes.

"Why not take me?" she whispered to him with a sexy smirk. "Why not!"

Then Joy tripped at the edge of the deep indentation that Niko and Jeannie had made in the snow and fell right in on top of them. The little girl pushed Jeannie back down onto Niko. The young woman buried her face beside Niko's ear and took a sexy, little nip.

"Let's get outta here," Joy called as she sat up and rolled off Jeannie.

"And get off my Daddy," she added. "We don't want to suffocate him."

"Of course not," Jeannie answered pulling back from Niko and struggling to her feet. She stood beside him and offered her hand yanking him to his feet, her eyes still bright with desire.

Niko stared at the radiant, young woman for a long moment. He read the longing in her eyes.

"We need to cool you down," he called suddenly and picked up a huge, armful of snow and dumped it right on top of her. Joy looked on and giggled.

Jeannie shook off the snow and turned to Joy. "Let's get him!"

They both grabbed armloads of snow and flung them back at Niko. Then they dove at him, knocking him onto his back, and continued to heap on piles of the white stuff until he couldn't be seen at all.

"Enough!" Niko called as he fought his way out from under the freezing powder.

"You got the best parka, Daddy," Joy teased. "Snow can't bother you."

"But it just might bother YOU," he answered as he dove at his daughter's feet, pulled them out from under her, and dumped her into an enormous drift.

"Don't be so rough with her," Jeannie cautioned.

"It's okay," Joy called. "I can take it." She stood, shook off the snow, and went barreling into Jeannie, pushing her into a deep snow bank. The young woman was buried up to her shoulders, Russian coat, Cossack hat and all, but her expression was almost as sparkly as the snow itself.

Niko realized at that moment that this was the image of Jeannie he would hold in his heart forever, seeing her bright, laughing eyes, her golden hair pulled back and tucked up under that silly hat, her sweet, full lips that had just kissed him so eagerly. Jeannie's cheeks were flushed bright red by the cold winter wind. Her playful giggle echoed the happiness of his little girl. He saw so much love in her eyes as always, but now there was something more: that sense of desire to take him, to make him hers, to own him. He had that feeling, too for a moment, almost felt that same longing himself. But he also knew that he would never let it happen. And it was that decision that would almost certainly doom the beautiful Jeannie Morrison in less than two short days.

"No more time to play," Michalowski shouted suddenly. "Tower is long way off.

"Night is coming."

Chapter 68
Witchy Preparations

Far ahead of Niko and his band, Wicktor, Clara, Matryoshka, Chantel, Megan, and all the other young witches were already at the tower. They were already preparing for Niko's arrival and the obscene sacrament that Clara was planning.

Megan Cummings and four of the other girls wielded pitchforks, rakes, and shovels as they dug out the ground floor entrance that had been added centuries after Babcia had lived there and Rapunzel's tale had been born. Mounds of debris and countless winter snows had buried it.

Meanwhile, Metroishka and several other members of the coven were setting right the stables, pouring steaming kettles of water over the moldy old troths, sweeping up the decaying straw, flushing out the dung from the corners of the stalls, and adding fresh cold water and new hay that they'd brought with them.

Chantel had an entire crew of young witches clean up the dusty old guest rooms, refreshing the comfortable beds that had become part of the tower after the locals had found it and turned it into an exclusive lodge.

Clara Goriki used all of her magic to prepare a delightful meal for the wealthy Americans who now made their way across the vast field of ice and boulders and toward the tower. She took care to see that certain ingredients were added to Niko and Jeannie's dishes so that they would see each other through hungry eyes and find each other irresistible.

Morgan Cummings and other members of the coven washed the ornate dishes and crystal glasses that were dark from disuse and neglect and used them to set the massive oak table in the great banquet hall where the evening's grand feasting would take place.

At last, the chores were done, and Clara's scrying ball told her that the guests were still two hours away. And so there was time for a steaming plunge in the boiling springs that ran near the very edge of the tower.

Young witches, nowhere near as afraid of water as some legends say, stripped joyously naked and then dove, cannonballed, plunged, or jumped right into the roiling streams. Clara shamelessly tossed aside her housecoat and floated her bulky old body into the river. And soon even the hairy warlock pulled off his cloak and joined them.

"So tell us, Pan Wicktor," Matryoshka asked as they were resting by the fire after their exuberant swim. "What is the most recent history of this tower? After so many years hiding in legends, how has it been turned into...." She looked around for the right word and then finally settled on, "A hotel?"

The warlock laughed. "Babcia would strangle you if she heard you say that. Let me tell you all a little of the history, so you will understand. Some amazing things have happened here even in the last hundred years.

"In the early 1920s, your Grandfather Waclaw Michalowski discovered the place and brought news of its existence to several wealthy Polish landowners who were business associates of his. They made the terrible journey to the tower and were immediately intoxicated by its rugged beauty, its wide-open courtyard and, of course, by the magnificent room at the very top of it. They spent large sums of money to turn the whole place into their own personal hunting lodge for expeditions in search of bear and wild boar.

"They blasted an entryway into the ground floor of the tower, then built up the stables and fashioned a well-equipped kitchen as well as cozy bedrooms with efficient fireplaces. Soon a spiral staircase led from one room to the next, culminating in the very topmost room... Rapunzel's Room, they called it.

"Adolph Hitler was said to have spent part of one night in that very room, but something happened there, something that terrified that evil and superstitious man. And before it had even reached midnight, the Fuhrer fled the room commanding that it be walled off from the rest of the lodge so that its dark magic could be imprisoned forever.

"Under the callous reign of the communists, the tower has been largely ignored, and so it has become a secret destination for anyone who is able to bribe the local residents for a guide who would lead them to it. Of course, most of the place has been neglected for decades, and that is why you and I and the other witches have had to work so hard to prepare for the arrival of your father and the Americans he brings with him.

"They may be laughing, singing, and telling jokes now, but nonetheless, when they arrive they will be very tired and looking forward to a hearty supper and the cozy rooms that Michalowski has promised them...

"...No matter how much dark magic they fear finding here."

Chapter 69
Tim's Transformation

Holly was going home! As she stood at the foot of her hospital bed putting on her new "duds" as she called them, she felt hopeful and happy. The clothes were helping, too. Doctor Doren, her lead physician and psychiatrist, had instructed Sister Alexia to take her down to the local Macy's and try not to be too judgmental as Holly purchased a whole new outfit to remind herself that she was now a new young woman. The choices were still dictated by the same old Holly, of course. And so she purchased a clingy, navy blue sweater, extremely tight-fitting jeans, and a pair of underthings in the sheer, see-through fabric she'd been reading about in all the women's magazines ("If you really want your man to pay attention").

Holly was nowhere as new as her doctors wanted to believe.

In any event, Sister Alexia had taken her from Macy's to the beauty parlor and asked for the latest style, which was a shag haircut that worked perfectly with Holly's thick, naturally curly hair.

She felt absolutely ravishing now as she squeezed into the tight sweater, and saw that the tips of her nipples pushed sexy, little nubs into the fabric. There was only one question, then. Which man was available to tease with this new look? The obvious answer was very dangerous, wasn't it? Father Tim.

Okay, so he was a priest, and it would be especially naughty to try and see if she could get a rise out of him, but then it was all in good fun, she told herself. No harm there, and besides, Tim had been acting so spooky lately. He needed a good shot of testosterone to snap him out of it.

Minutes later, Holly knocked happily at Father Tim's office door and eagerly responded to his call to come in. She slid through the doorway and right up to Tim's desk. The man looked young again, quite cheery, happier and more at ease than he had seemed to be in weeks.

"Wow," was Tim's one-word reaction to Holly's new duds.

"Do you like the look?" she asked turning this way and that.

He nodded. He was looking directly at her breasts in a rather unholy manner, and then his eyes rose to her smiling face.

"What are you up to?" she asked.

"Just studying about witches and witchcraft," he answered. "The topics are fascinating, don't you think?"

Holly was a little taken aback by the question. She forgot all about her sexy new outfit and his immediate response to it and began to look more closely at the man and what he was doing.

Father Tim was wearing his cassock, the long black gown that priests put on for religious services. He almost never wore it, she thought, and yet he had it on as though he needed to feel the full power of his priesthood.

His eyes were sparkling, though; his smile was healthy. But all across his desk were stacks and stacks of thick books about witches and witchcraft. There were Catholic prayer books scattered among them, too, some very old. The oldest of all the books looked as if it might have been written in the Middle Ages. It was open to a page that was illuminated with hand-drawn letters and ornate illustrations of witches in every act imaginable, including some that were quite obscene.

Holly recognized the language in the book from her years of Catholic high school; it was Latin. Tim had draped a rosary across the open pages as though he were using it to protect himself from the contents.

"Witches preserved the ancient herbal cures that women passed on from generation to generation for centuries," he said enthusiastically.

"They stood as a beacon for women's rights and safety in a world that was totally dominated by men.

"They perfected brews and potions that had genuinely curative properties."

Holly shrugged in agreement. This whole thing seemed very weird.

"Too bad," Tim added in sudden anger, "that they repudiated our Lord and Savior!" And with those words he jumped to his feet like some itinerant preacher and slammed the book shut to punctuate his sentence.

Holly stumbled backward. "I guess so," was all she could manage to say.

"Don't you realize what's going on here?" Tim asked, "Babcia and those like her are servants of the devil. They are trying to take over our minds and souls."

"Okay," she answered and tried to pull even farther away from the priest whose eyes were now blazing with evangelical madness.

"We have to drive them out. We have to exorcise them... from you, from me, from your daughter, your husband, even your cat!"

Holly had lost all her self-confidence and sense of well-being. She felt as though she were being swept up once again into madness that didn't seem any more holy because it was coming from a priest.

"Holly, I have to drive the witches from my mind," he ranted. "From my evil dreams and from you."

"From me?" she gasped. She was circling away from the priest trying to get closer to the door and eventual escape. But just then Tim turned from her and marched back to his desk. He slammed himself into his chair, flipped open the ancient Latin book, pulled the rosary from it, and began thumbing

315

through the pages. He found what he was looking for and opened the book fully.

"Holly," he continued. "You bewitched me the first time I saw you."

She cast her eyes down modestly. It was a compliment, she hoped.

"I've been going through these books trying to find out what's been happening to us. And it's all here. Look at this!" He opened the book and held it up for her to read. She stepped toward him and peered at the book. It was in Latin... no way.

"Dementia somnium initium facere," Tim read and turned to her with his eyes blazing. "Madness. It all begins in dreams!

"I know that's what's happening. Babcia is trying to drive me mad through nightmares! She's trying to take control of me, turn me into a..."

Tim's words trailed off. He cocked his head distractedly.

"What were you thinking when you put on that outfit this morning and before that when you bought it, what were you thinking?"

"That you might like it."

"And that it might turn me on?"

"I guess so."

"Were you thinking that I might spend my nights dreaming about making love to you?"

Holly shook her head. "Of course not."

"But that's what you planned... at least subconsciously. There's a name for what you are, Holly."

She could think of a dozen dirty names that he could call her but didn't say them.

"You're a temptress sent to seduce me, some kind of demon."

"That's crazy. Demons don't exist."

"Don't they? Witches do, we know that. And you do like to tempt men, don't you?"

"Maybe I do. So what?"

Tim fell back into his chair, crossed his arms, and smiled triumphantly at her. He had gotten her evil confession and now he no longer needed to be the grand inquisitor.

Then he seemed somehow to age in an instant. His body appeared to twist and hunch over before her very eyes. His cassock looked more and more like the tattered robes of an old woman. His face became gaunt, his lips quivered, his eyes grew dark and hollow as though they were no more than empty sockets.

Tim grabbed at the corner of the desk, his hands scraping over the surface like twisted claws, unable to catch hold of it as he hobbled toward Holly.

She whimpered and stepped back, but he wasn't after her. He dragged himself past her to the door. Then he opened it and turned to the terrified young woman.

"Best be going, dearie," he said.

Holly lowered her eyes and moved cautiously through the doorway giving Tim as wide a gate as possible.

The door slammed shut as soon as she was through it.

"Demon!" she heard him cackling madly from behind the door.

"Temptress! Succubus!"

Chapter 70
Dinah Dee

Sally Fukes wasn't feeling quite herself this morning. For one thing, she had felt a little sick to her stomach all the previous day, and that had prompted her to pass up her usual night at the Room at the Top with Chuck Vaughn. Those nights were always so great, she remembered. All that eating and not a single ounce of it added to her waistline. It was the spell, of course, the one that kept her thin no matter how much she ate.

But she'd come home without downing the usual five pounds of chicken wings and mini burgers, and then she'd dared, just because she was feeling a little woozy, to look at her reflection in Mother Black's fish tank. She was shocked at the grotesque image there. Sally Fukes, appearing as a slim one hundred ten pound gal, was really four hundred and fifty pounds, a veritable mound of blubber whose legs and arms hardly existed at all; her neck certainly didn't.

She had run to find Mother Black and tell her about it, and that was the other unsettling thing; she couldn't find Mother Black. The old woman was out for the night. It said so in a note that was much too neatly printed to be written by the real Mother Black. Instead of the barely discernable squiggles that the old witch usually penned, this hand was neat and precise. Sally didn't know what to think, and so she just went to bed, hoping for better things in the morning.

The morning had dawned gray and soggy as it often does in Los Angeles in the springtime just the way she liked it, actually, but she still felt out of sorts.

Sally put on her most festive clothes, the powder blue satin cowgirl mini skirt with the white go-go boots and the white cotton halter that tied in front with a big (easy-to-loosen) bow.

She looked more like a cheerleader than a cowgirl when she strolled into the Midnight Cowgirl room at VVA. Vaughn was at the conference table. He looked up and smiled broadly at her, not at all aware of the mood she was in.

"Have I got good news for you, gal," Vaughn chomped through his gum when he saw her. A great steaming cup of coffee was sitting in front of him, Sally noticed. Getting coffee for the boss was HER job.

"Where'd ya git thayt?" Sally asked plopping herself down in a chair across from the master.

"It's part of the good news I got for ya, Sal," Vaughn answered.

Just then the door opened, and a fabulous, young, sleek, black woman made her way into the room. She was dressed in a short, tight, lace dress: all black. It came to mid-thigh and revealed the kind of perfect legs that Mister Vaughn was famous for hiring. She wore a string of pearls around her long neck, and high, black, patent leather heels. She was carrying a pot of coffee, and a huge plate of glazed donuts.

"Sal, I'd like you to meet Miss, uh..."

"Dinah," the vision in black prompted.

"Yes," Vaughn continued. "Miss Dinah..."

"Dee," the vision added as she smiled at Sally.

"Miss Dinah Dee, our new receptionist."

Dinah put the plate of donuts down right in front of Sally. The cowgirl immediately grabbed one and chomped off half of it in one bite.

"Coffee?" Dinah asked raising the pot.

"Muuffff huhhhh," Sally answered with a nod.

Dinah grabbed a cup from across the table, bending low in front of the old man, drawing his eyes down the front of her dress. She caught the stare, looked back at him and smiled. Vaughn winked at her.

"But, ah'm the receptionist," Sally stammered. She didn't like any of this.

"That's the good news, Sal," Vaughn responded. "You're no receptionist anymore. I'm making you the president of Midnight Cowgirl Enterprises!"

Sally hesitated and looked at the old man and the new girl. Then she looked over at CatMan Due, Vaughn's big black cat who snoozed in the corner.

"Sounds good," she answered. "But what's it mean?"

"It means that you'll be in charge of the product. We'll hold Midnight Cowgirl back from MikleyToons. It's not their kind of thing, anyway. You can run the show, and once I get the Mikley deal in place, I'll take over, and you and I will have our own little company together."

"Wheeee!" Sally cheered though she still didn't quite get it. She liked some of the words he'd used, though, especially "our own company" and "you can run the show." But she didn't like this new presence, this Dinah Dee, this black woman. Not that she had anything against black women, after all, Mother Black....

Sally stopped cold. She watched the new girl batting her eyes at old Mister Vaughn (HER Mister Vaughn). Mother Black had often commented on how much she liked him, hadn't she? And she sure knew how to work the Spell of Becoming. Hell, if she wanted to, she could make herself as young and beautiful as....

"Have another donut or two," Dinah said to Sal, pushing the plate closer to her.

Sally smiled carelessly and shrugged, shaking those troublesome thoughts from her head and digging in.

"Ah, what the hell," she burbled and crammed an entire French cruller into her mouth.

"Have one more," Dinah added immediately.

Chapter 71
Preparations and Doubts

"I think he's absolutely dreamy," said Matryoshka as she ran a brush through Jeannie Morrison's beautiful, blonde hair.

"I just don't want to hurt him," Jeannie responded softly. She was having second thoughts about it all, sobbing a little as she sat on a straight-backed chair in the middle of her room, the largest bedroom in the tower. Niko and Joy had insisted that she deserved it.

The warlock stood at the back of the room watching the preparations, and now he stepped forward.

"You understand," he said, as Matryoshka dabbed at the eye makeup that kept running with Jeannie's tears. "That if you have Niko's child, Babcia will be the child's grandmother. You and Marla will be his mother, and Babcia will dare not act against your child or you or your family. Clara will have gained control over Babcia without needing to battle her. Oh, she can make life miserable for the great witch, but Babcia won't be able to resist her. You can prevent a war of witches that could destroy us all."

"But it's so wrong," Jeannie whispered almost to herself.

"I thought we had this all settled," said the warlock. "I heard you scream a resounding 'yes' as I fucked you at your initiation."

"I did," Jeannie answered still sobbing. "But now, I don't know. I can feel what Marla's thinking. I know she says Niko will be safe, but I sense her hatred, and I don't believe her."

Clara Goriki stepped out of the shadows then and moved in front of the girl. She looked deep into Jeannie's eyes and spoke directly through them to the witch within her.

"Marla, can't you take control of this simpleton?"

321

Jeannie's face suddenly twisted into an ugly sneer, her eyebrows arched, her whole body stiffened as the persona of Marla took control of her being.

"I'd love to," Marla growled. "But I can't."

Clara shook her head in disgust. "If Niko saw Jeannie looking the way she does when you show yourself, Marla, he'd never want to touch you. Even this horny warlock wants to keep his distance."

"Oh, I don't know about that," said the warlock. He moved toward Jeannie and touched her watching her melt back into the sweetness that emanated from the soul of Rosie Osborn. He knelt in front of her and whispered, "We need your innocence, Kochanie. Come, help us."

Jeannie turned her head away from him.

"See what I mean," said Clara and moved purposefully to the bedside table to pick up an ancient mirror with a hand-carved wooden frame and handle. The glass was cracked, and still, she brought it back to Jeannie, turned it toward the girl and forced her to consider the haggard, hideous countenance of the old Rosie Osborn staring back at her in the broken reflection.

"Would you like to go back to being that again?" Clara shrieked. "Do you think Niko would care about you if you looked like that?"

Jeannie shuddered as she looked at her former image, and yet she smiled slightly and murmured, "Niko did care for me when I looked like that. That's the problem."

"Okay, okay. No more discussion," Clara said and laid the mirror aside. "But tell me then, Ms. Morrison, how does this make you feel?" She placed her palm gently on Jeannie's cheek and whispered the word "Becoming."

Suddenly, the electricity of the Spell of Becoming stormed across Jeannie's face and sizzled through her entire body.

"Feel it!" Clara cried.

"Oh, my God!"

Jeannie thrilled to this latest jolt of pure unadulterated youth.

"This is what you'll get when you help us!" Clara cackled. "If you turn against us you become the hag or something even worse than that. But if you are with us, the joy of youth and beauty can be yours forever."

Jeannie closed her eyes and smiled in ecstasy as the spell cycled through her over and over again.

Now Wicktor eased Clara aside and took both of Jeannie's hands. "You will help us, won't you Jeannie? You will remain young and beautiful. You will become Niko's lover, and you will have his child... for all of us."

The Spell of Becoming still crackled through the girl. Though Marla had retreated, Jeannie still reveled in it.

"Yes," she answered softly.

"Louder," the warlock commanded as he withdrew his hands.

And Jeannie shouted her confirmation through the room, "YES! YES! YES!"

"Finally," Matryoshka said grabbing a towel and rubbing it harshly over Jeannie's face removing all of the runny makeup so that she could start over again.

"Think about how hot it's going to be to have him inside you," Matryoshka whispered. "Think about having his baby."

"I'll be his wife," Jeannie answered warming to the idea again.

"That's right," said Clara Goriki. But then she turned and grimaced at the warlock in a way that contradicted her words.

The young witch finished redoing Jeannie's makeup while Wicktor ran the brush through her hair yet again. Next, they undid the straps and hooks of Jeannie's undergarments and removed them. They powdered and perfumed her entire body, and just for fun, the warlock grabbed the tip of one nipple and gave it a good tweak.

"You're about to fuck the boy of your dreams," he said. "Enjoy it."

Jeannie giggled as her nipples stood up proudly, suggesting that any doubts she had talked about earlier were far behind her now that this latest jolt of Becoming was coursing through her.

Matryoshka reached into the large wardrobe that stood at the very back of the room and brought out a nearly transparent, white lace peignoir. Jeannie held out her arms and let Matryoshka slip the beautiful garment over her shoulders. There was soft, white silk stitched along the collar and pink rosebuds embroidered across the front. The material gathered in a most flattering way.

"Mmmmm," Jeannie sighed and her eyes began to sparkle.

"Now you're starting to feel it," Clara said as she hung a silver pentastar around Jeannie's neck.

The warlock knelt before the girl and helped slide two clear glass slippers over her pretty feet.

"Feeling like a princess?" he asked.

"I am."

"Then sit back, and we'll show you some real magic."

Jeannie settled herself on the huge bed that stood in the very center of the room, and as she did, Clara Goriki began lighting the circle of candles she'd placed around the room.

She lit incense of myrrh and lavender and breathed deeply as the sweet aroma spread. This was the setting for a true handfasting. Jeannie was going to marry Niko in a witch's ceremony, and the fact that he was already married didn't matter in the least.

The ancient evil witch, the warlock, and the youthful Matryoshka stepped to the door then and looked back at the vision they had created: a gorgeous young woman in a nearly transparent robe whose breath came faster and faster with her growing desire. She sat at the edge of an enormous bed piled high with plump down pillows and topped with a down comforter. A circle of candles surrounded the entire scene.

"Feel it, girl," Matryoshka cheered.

"You look delectable, Kochanie," the warlock added.

Clara, the ancient witch, said nothing and didn't even look at the girl, perhaps knowing that if she did, Jeannie would get a greater sense of the consequences of her actions and begin to doubt her decision all over again.

The three ducked out the door, and no more than a minute later, there was a knock. It was Niko calling out,

"Jeannie, I got your note."

"Is there something I can do for you?"

Chapter 72
Handfasting

The vision that greeted Niko was beyond his wildest imaginings: the youthful body of Jeannie Morrison, bright-eyed and eager, pushing up from the toes of her high heel glass slippers, curvaceous legs visible through her nearly transparent gown, rising into an unmistakable mound of lovely curls.

Her beautiful hands were beside her, pushing her body toward him so that her breasts fell forward invitingly. The little rosebud embroidery that swept around her in an empire waist pressed her tight pink nipples high, making them stand out proudly through her gossamer gown, offering them up to Niko.

Jeannie's smile was willing and her eyes sparkled with hope.

"Please come to me," she whispered so softly that he stepped forward immediately.

"Closer," she sighed, and she stood moving toward him, holding out her arms and inviting his embrace.

Niko stepped within the candle circle, reaching for Jeannie and, taking her to him, feeling her luscious kisses, opening his lips and inviting her in. And she came.

She led him to the bed, pushed him back, making him sit while she slid her hands over his chest and down onto his thighs. Whatever reservations the young man may have had as he'd stepped through that doorway, whatever pledges of fidelity he may have made, began to peel away as Jeannie lifted a chalice of May wine from the table near the bed... from beside a silver dagger she would soon use to mingle their blood in the witch's ceremony.

"Drink," she whispered and handed the chalice to him. "To our love."

Niko stared into those bright, willing, seductive eyes, and sipped from the cup. As he did, Jeannie reached up to the silk collar of her peignoir and pulled it down below her breasts, letting them jump brazenly out toward him, inviting him to taste.

She placed her hand on his cheek and drew him down toward her rock hard nipples. He sucked one deep into his mouth. The May wine, still fresh on his lips, made it tingle, and she sighed with passion.

She slid her hand up his thighs to an immense hardness that was more than she could believe. She reached for it while he continued to cover her breasts with wine-soaked kisses.

"You're delicious," he whispered, somehow forming a wall in his mind that shut out all thoughts of Holly and Joy and everything they meant to him.

Jeannie giggled. She felt Becoming shooting all through her, filling her with lust, but also with a feeling of absolute perfection. She was so proud of what she had become, so sure she was perfect for Niko and so much better than Holly, that she had to ask it. She had to ask that one prideful question (Carefulla pride), the one question that Marla would never have allowed her to ask, but one that Rosie, for entirely different reasons, demanded.

"And am I?" Jeannie whispered. "Am I as delicious as Holly?"

"What?"

"Am I as delicious as Holly?" she repeated and her soft inviting eyes searched Niko's for reassurance.

He suddenly pulled back and stared at her. Jeannie had asked about his wife? His lost little girl!

She recognized the expression that now filled his eyes, recognized her mistake, recognized her sin of pride, recognized Marla's hate and Rosie's purpose. But it was too late. Her words ended their lovemaking for the night, ended her handfasting, and soon would end her life.

They were the very last words that Niko would ever hear her speak.

Jeannie's eyes pleaded with him to stay, to marry her, to give her a child that very night. But he would not. Instead he stood, walked slowly and purposefully to the door, and opened it.

"What was I thinking?" he murmured turning back to Jeannie for just a moment.

And then he was gone.

Chapter 73
The Shower Scene

Jeannie sat in the darkness sobbing. She shook her head, kicked her high heels off her feet and halfway across the room. She reached behind her and unfastened the silver pendant from around her neck.

"Oh, no," she whispered to herself. Would Niko ever speak to her again? And what revenge would the witches have for her?

"Oh, no," she repeated aloud.

But did it even matter?

She stood, let her peignoir fall to the floor, stepped out of it, and moved to the bathroom. The powder that covered her body, that had made her feel so sexy only seconds ago, felt suddenly sticky and uncomfortable.

"Oh, Niko," she sobbed as she moved to the old freestanding bathtub and turned on the faucet. She held her wrist under the flow of water until she knew that it was warm. Just right, she thought with a sudden smile.

Could she have done the right thing?

Had Rosie somehow coaxed her into asking about Niko's wife to remind him of his marriage, to save him from Clara's plot? Jeannie wasn't sure of any of this, of course, but she felt good about it... at least for the moment.

She flipped the lever that directed the water through the showerhead. Then, grabbing the side of the tub, she stepped daintily over the edge and into the warm spray. She pulled the shower curtain halfway closed behind her.

The water soaked into her hair and drizzled over her lashes and eyes. She tasted its sweetness. The spray was purifying, clearing the lust from her mind, the evil from her heart. She was suddenly grateful that they had not consummated their love. She would find him and tell him so, she thought.

She reached behind her to pull the shower curtain closed and looked up.

Glowering at her from the large mirror that hung across from the tub, was the ghost-image of Marla still inhabiting the gorgeous, naked body of Jeannie, still young and beautiful, but the expression on her face was bloodthirsty.

Marla had retrieved the silver dagger from the nightstand and held it in her hand. And now it was in Jeannie's hand as well. Together they raised the dagger above Jeannie's head and sent it plunging into her chest, into those soft, beautiful breasts that only a moment before Niko had kissed with such passion.

Jeannie screamed as Marla shrieked with glee, and the face in the mirror shifted back and forth from innocent victim to wanton murderess. Jeannie's own hand, controlled by Marla, jerked the dagger out of her chest, pulled it high into the air, and plunged it into the young woman's body again and again and again. It hacked away at her arms, her shoulders, her thighs, her belly, sending great spurts of blood splattering across the shower curtain and the walls, slashing wildly as two souls in one body struggled for supremacy, screaming louder and louder. And, as they did, blood poured down Jeannie's arms and legs and swirled into the drain.

She clutched at the shower curtain to maintain her balance, but she was too weak. She tottered back and forth, then tore the curtain completely from the rod as she crashed to the floor of the tub. Her face slammed hard onto the porcelain, crushing her lips, her cheeks, and her nose against the cold, white surface. Her bloody hand released the curtain, and her arm fell helplessly behind her, twisting into a grotesque, unnatural shape in the process. Her eyes stared off into nothingness.

Jeannie lay dead, eyes wide open, lips parted almost in a kiss. Her life's blood pumped from her body and flowed down the drain. Her sweetness and the sweetness that was Rosie Osborn were gone forever.

Yet, only moments later, the bloodstained body began to stir and the eyes flashed open. The figure of Jeannie Morrison rose slowly to her feet. She could see herself in the mirror. Her wounds were healing quickly, and the color was returning to her cheeks. She was smiling again, but not a sweet smile this time. It was wicked. Her eyes did not sparkle with eager innocence. Instead they were cold and calculating. Jeannie Morrison was no longer alive.

But within her body, Marla was reborn.

Chapter 74
Rapunzel's Room

Joy pestered Michalowski until he agreed to show her the secret stairway that led to the very top room in Rapunzel's Tower.

They carried lanterns as they ascended the long, dingy steps with none of the bright illumination, colorful wallpaper, or soft carpeting that adorned the tower's main corridor. Here the walls were broken lath and plaster and open beams.

Occasionally, they'd hear a rat scurry off in front of them as it ducked away from the approaching light.

The floor was bare wood, covered with a thick layer of dust and rodent droppings. Every corner reached out for them with sticky spider web tendrils, and sometimes an enormous black widow would spy out from the shadows, not the least bit interested in retreating from the brightness.

"Gross!" Joy screamed when her hand brushed over a large ball at the edge of one step. Michalowski raised his lantern and looked at it closely. The ball was made entirely of spider webs, and inside the ball, the old shopkeeper was able to make out the body of a large dead rat, entombed, captured, and preserved as food for the next generation of spiders.

Michalowski felt his dinner welling up into his throat and had to swallow hard again and again to keep it under control.

"Don't look at it!" Joy called. She was far braver than Michalowski could ever be.

Bits of stone and gravel littered the landing at the very top of the stairs. A dusty canvas tarp hung across the passage blocking further progress. Michalowski pulled it back to reveal a rough gray wall built of plaster and brick. It looked as though it had been created in a desperate hurry, as in fact, it had. The

Nazis had built it to contain that "unspeakable evil" that had horrified Adolph Hitler the night he'd slept in this topmost room of Rapunzel's Tower.

Recently, a new generation had worked to breach the wall so that now there was a narrow opening through which Joy and Michalowski could pass. Joy scampered through it into the darkness. Michalowski hunched over and eased himself through the opening. He tore the seat of his pants and gave himself a nasty scrape in the process.

Joy and Michalowski lifted their lanterns then and turned as Rapunzel's room opened before them.

There was a humming in the air, a low sizzle that was barely audible and yet quite distinct. Somehow it made perfect sense that, by itself, it kept away all the vermin in the tower and the dust, too leaving the room immaculate and bright.

Michalowski approached an old Tiffany lamp standing on a bookshelf along the very far wall and flipped the switch. After a moment, the bulb popped on illuminating a room full of heavy wood furniture. In Joy's eyes, it all seemed very comfortable.

A quilt lay over the bed with simple white squares bordered in Polish red. At the centers of each square, symbols of the craft were embroidered into the fabric. The bed had a sturdy pine headboard and beside it stood a small nightstand made of the same material. The nightstand was covered with a hand-knitted doily. Centered on that was a great crystal ball. Michalowski reached to lift it, but it wouldn't budge though it did not seem to be attached to the nightstand in any way.

Across from the bed, a dresser offered three wide drawers and a small cupboard. A bookcase filled most of the far wall. It was crammed with ancient books, many featuring signs of The Craft on their ragged spines. They all looked worn and well-studied. Michalowski inspected the books while Joy opened the cupboard.

Pushed deep into the back was a parcel, something wrapped very tightly in red and black cloth. Joy pulled the package from the back of the cupboard and unwrapped it. The cloth itself was a Nazi flag, and there were two items wrapped within it: a thick book and a wand. She eyed the book for only a moment. It was covered in very worn, cordovan leather, and there was no writing on the cover at all.

She immediately turned to the wand, clutched it, and jumped to her feet. As she moved it, the wand let out a zinging sound quite in tune with the low buzz that filled the room. It was as though the wand itself were causing the hum.

Joy waved the wand as she'd seen many witches and fairies do in MikleyToon movies, and suddenly a beautiful, young woman stood before her. She wore a simple, peasant dress from long ago.

"Rapunzel?" Joy asked.

"Michalina," the woman answered with a nod, and as Joy stared into her eyes, she recognized the image of her grandmother. Joy dropped the wand and ran toward the woman with her arms outstretched. But before she could reach her, the woman vanished.

Suddenly, there was another loud zing, and a small grey-black blob appeared in the center of the floor right in front of her. It smelled of raw sewage and strange poisonous chemicals. And then it began to move.

The blob seemed to consist of tar and mud mixed with slime from the sewers. Its amorphous shape stretched and squeezed, and within it, arms and legs appeared to be moving amid the mass, expanding it wider and reaching for the little girl with fearful claws.

The figure within the blob hunched over for a moment and then rose up. As the ooze dripped from it, a skeletal face appeared with death-socket eyes and an enormous gaping mouth. It reared higher and lifted its arms far above Joy, spreading its talons wide as though to descend upon her and snatch her back into the deadly ooze.

The creature let out a tortured wail and then suddenly split in two. Now there were two such monsters, still joined in the sticky, smelly ooze, still shuffling toward her with undead faces that peered out from the slime.

Joy turned frantically to see Michalowski holding the wand. He was frozen in fear.

"Do something!" she screeched. But the old man couldn't move a muscle.

Joy rushed to him, snatched the wand, and spun toward the blob. It had split again and now consisted of four undead creatures reaching for her from out of the slime.

"Back, you stupid beast!" Joy ordered.

She waved the wand quickly, and the creatures disappeared without a trace.

"What did you do?" she shouted frantically at the old man. "What did you ask to see?"

"What scared Hitler," Michalowski murmured sinking onto the bed. "Wanted to see things he saw in room, what made him close off the tower."

"Hitler's nightmare?" Joy asked accusingly. She shook her head in exasperation. "Grownups can be so DUMB!"

Michalowski nodded as though in complete agreement. He gathered himself, walked to the window, and looked out. He grimaced for just a moment as he imagined all the young suitors who had fallen to their deaths from this high place.

The little girl gathered Babcia's book of spells and her wand and wrapped them back up in the Nazi flag. Then she stuffed the whole package deep into the cupboard.

"No more of this," she said and closed the door.

"But look here," Michalowski called from the window. Joy came over and stood beside him, peering out into the moonlit night. "There," he said pointing to an area just under the base of the highest mountain peak.

335

"It looks like a lake," Joy said, "a black lake."

Whatever it was shimmered in the moonlight, but it was an odd shimmer, not at all like the movement of waves in the breeze. This movement could start at any point on the surface and almost ruffled, turning the black surface into uneven shades of silver. It might fan out like droplets in a puddle, but just as likely start at one place and then be echoed far across the surface where another ruffling motion would begin. And there was a sound to it, too, a sharp rumble that might be the fierce struggle of the wind within the trees or a series of angry cries.

"Burr," Michalowski shivered and pulled back from the window. He shook his jowly face as though he were trying to shake the vision from his head.

"Not liking that," he said. "Not at all." But then he looked down at the little girl, and she was staring at the same mysterious sight...

And she was smiling in deep fascination.

Chapter 75
Sally's Banquet

Sally Fukes was as happy as a pig in shit (her words). Not only had she received an invitation to a candlelit dinner with her boss, but Chuck Vaughn had asked her to wear her favorite outfit, the sexy denim thing that had brought the boys a runnin' down at the watering holes in Pomona.

"Yee-ha!" called Sally as she slipped on her cowgirl boots and headed out the door. A stretch limo was waiting for her.

"Miss Fukes?" the driver asked. "President of Midnight Cowgirl Enterprises?"

Sally nodded happily.

"Right this way, Ma'am."

Inside, the limo featured spacious leather seating, a full bar, and a snack counter. The counter was loaded with treats: canapés, hors d'oeuvres, candy bars, cookies, cakes and pastries of every kind. Sally grabbed a bowl full of fried chicken wings and a glass of champagne and settled in for the ride.

#

Chuck Vaughn had asked the chef at the Sheraton Universal to prepare a complete Texas barbecue, and the man had done just that: baby back ribs, potato salad, baked beans, Texas toast, coleslaw, pork sausage, mashed potatoes with thick brown gravy, applesauce, and broiled chicken. Sally was bug-eyed when she found her way into Vaughn's suite and saw the spread.

"Chuck, it's the most beautiful thang ah've ever seen in mah life!" she cooed. "Kin we skip the pleasantries and get right ta the food?"

"It's all yours, doll," Vaughn said with a smile. "Though an appreciative little smooch would be nice."

"Ah'll do more an that," she said as she sidled up to Vaughn and gave him a long, passionate kiss. Then she grabbed him by his backside and pulled him to her so that she could grind her hips into him just a little.

"Plenty more where that came from," she added. "But first, less eat!"

Sally made her way to the head of the table and took her seat. Vaughn followed like a hungry puppy, and it wasn't the meal that was tempting him.

"Shall we start our personal Bar-B-Que?" the room service waiter suggested as he pulled a large plate from the cart and set it in front of her. "Hollywood's version, better than you'd get at the LBJ ranch."

He ladled a mountain of mashed potatoes onto Sally's plate, added a slab of ribs, some baked beans, some pork sausage, and then dumped a sea of gravy over all of it.

"Beer preference?" he asked.

"Coors?" she cooed.

"Oh, we have imported, too, if you like?"

"Nope, need mah Rocky Mountain High." And she grabbed the huge mug of beer before the waiter had even finished drawing it.

Sally had all she could do to wait for Vaughn to be served, and when he was, she immediately slammed her soupspoon into the mound of mashed potatoes and gulped down a large mouthful.

"Sally, control yourself," Vaughn said.

"Not now," she replied. "And not later either when we're bumpin' bods in the bedroom." Then she stuffed half a pork sausage into her drooling face and munched on it heartily.

Vaughn looked toward the server with more amusement than disgust.

"I see the young lady likes our food," the server said. "Shall I set out all the rest of the portions?"

"Ya mean there's more?" Sally burbled through the sausage grease.

"That won't be necessary," Vaughn interrupted.

"Nah," she added. "Jes leave it all here, an ah'l serve mahself when I'm good an ready."

The waiter rolled his eyes and nodded, then turned to Vaughn. "Will that be all, sir?"

"Yes, thank you."

The great animator was trying not to watch Sally as she guzzled down spoonful after spoonful of baked beans. The server bowed, headed for the door, and let himself out.

Chuck sighed. His celebration with Sally was suddenly taking on aspects of a carnival crazy house. She was starting to shift her shape as though he were looking at her in one of those wavy mirrors. If he could steer her away from the food and get her mind back on sex, he hoped things might still work out.

Unfortunately, the chicken that the waiter served wasn't about to cooperate. As soon as she took her first bite, a little bone snapped from its ribcage and lodged in her throat. This sent the girl into a wild orgy of gagging and coughing.

Sally's image twisted again as though she were in that crazy house mirror. She choked, wheezed, grabbed her throat, and began stumbling around the room.

Vaughn ran to the cowgirl and clapped her hard on the back, but that did little more than slam the girl forward and onto the floor. She began rolling around, turning beet red, grasping at her throat. Her eyes flowed with tears and bugged out from her head. Her gravy-laden mouth smeared over the carpet, leaving ugly smudges as she rolled.

"Let me get someone," Vaughn squealed as he ran to the door and raced out into the hallway, and who should somehow be standing right outside, but Dinah Dee.

"It's Sally," he called. "She's... she's..."

"Ah know what she is, sugar," Dinah responded. "She's a fat pig."

Vaughn blustered his disapproval.

"Stay outside here in the hall, hon," Dinah instructed. "I'll take care a her." And with that, she entered the suite where Sally lay on the floor twisting this way and that, still clutching her throat, though she had now turned bright red and was nearly unconscious. Whatever ounce of energy was left in the woman went into a welcoming smile that beamed weakly, yet hopefully at Dinah. It was hopeful, at least, until she heard the spell Dinah was reciting. She recognized the words. She recognized the spell: UNBECOMING.

Dinah was Mother Black, and she was turning Sally back into her former self, but now that former-self weighed five hundred pounds.

Sally tried to rise up on one elephantine arm and waved the other frantically at her mentor. She shook her head and coughed out pleading phrases. But Dinah's eyes were fixed, her expression frozen. And then zap! Sally lost the support of her arms as her entire body shifted back into a shape that resembled a beached whale.

"Ah think ahm gonna explode," Sally called when the pressure inside her body became too great. And, with the sickening sound of an overloaded sack of manure that was suddenly ripped from end to end, she blew up, blasting guts, entrails, half-eaten Hollywood-style Texas Bar-B-Que, and all manner of ugliness across the room.

"Damn," Dinah called as a slab of blubber flew by her and thunked against the wall. It smeared its way down the ornate wallpaper, leaving a wide trail of blood behind it. Dinah ducked for cover and somehow managed to avoid the worst: the chunks of flesh and globs of internal organs that sprayed wildly around her.

Dinah's image then shifted, too, back to the hideous old crone that was Mother Black.

340

The old woman shook her head.

This new generation of witches, she thought. It was all about greed, wasn't it? Imagine trying to take her man away from her or was it the other way around? No matter. Sally was no more. And now Dinah would have her day.

She contemplated the mess. Then she shrugged, and with a wave of her hand, she made the room spotless instantly. All that was left of her former pupil was a little puddle of heavy grease that had congealed near the far end of the dining room table.

Next, Mother Black breathed a single word and once again she was Dinah Dee, the beautiful African-American witch. She shook herself a little, hiked up that tight little black lace dress, mussed her hair to make herself slightly disheveled, and walked slowly from the room and into the anxious presence of the world's greatest animator.

"She needs help, sugar," Dinah cooed to Vaughn. "But I've made her as comfortable as possible. Then I called the front desk and St. Joseph's Hospital. There's an ambulance already on its way."

Vaughn started to move toward the door. This was certainly not the way he had intended to celebrate his Cowgirl's promotion.

"Don't disturb her now," she murmured. "She needs to be alone. Just come on with me. I'll make it all right for ya."

Vaughn lowered his head...

And followed the witch obediently.

Chapter 76
Submission

Father Tim rifled through the book of spells until he came to the right page, and then he ran a twisted finger down the list until he reached the appropriate spell: The Spell of Submission.

The priest cackled as he pulled the required ingredients from the little rack of bottles in the corner of his desk. Then he poured them into a large beaker that sat over the exposed flame of a Bunsen burner.

His eyes looked tired, his face wrinkled and unshaven. Still, there was an evil smile on his lips, and he never stopped mumbling: "Now the willow, now the lamb's blood," and on and on.

Tim's black cassock hung open as though it were more the robe of a witch than a priest. He was not wearing his Roman collar but merely a sleeveless undershirt and a pair of boxer shorts. Their loose fit suggested just how thin and wasted his body had become.

"A lively newt," he mumbled as he picked one up by the tail, watched it wriggle desperately, and dropped it into the brew.

"Need that, don't we, Emmy?" he asked.

Across the room, Holly's cat purred her approval. The witch-shadow of Babcia flickered wickedly behind her. They were only lit by the glow from the burner, which gave Tim's face a ghoulish look.

"A little cup and straighten up," he mumbled while a smile curled the corners of his mouth, and his eyes flashed in excitement.

"A little cup and straighten up."

He gathered the books on his desk and organized them into a clumsy pile. The book of spells was topmost as though its very sight would inspire him.

He pulled his cassock around him and buttoned it, slipped his bare feet into his shoes, and pulled on his Roman collar. At least he would have the appearance of piety, he thought.

A little cup and straighten up!

Tim poured the contents of the beaker into a teacup, flipped on his small desk lamp, doused the Bunsen burner, and shuffled it and all the other spell-casting paraphernalia under his desk. An enormous black tarantula in a half-gallon jar scrambled wildly around as it was transported into the shadows with the rest.

"The time, the time," he warned himself. "Gotta fill the cup and straighten up." He placed the cup full of his potion on a small saucer in the middle of his desk and filled a matching cup with tea placing it beside the first.

"A little cup, and straighten up," he sang to Emmy and shooed her into the far corner of the room so that her witch shadow was minimized.

He gave the room one last look to make sure that all was in readiness. Then he touched his hand to his face and felt the stubble there.

Tim ducked back into his bathroom for just a minute so he could run an electric razor over it.

"All done," he announced to the cat a few minutes later as he hobbled back into his office. Emmy purred her approval and, at that very moment, he heard Holly's familiar, hesitant knock on the door. Tim adjusted his cassock and then opened the door.

Mrs. Madonie had chosen to look her most modest on this occasion. Her skirt was plain brown wool and fell unfashionably far below her knees. She wore flat, sensible shoes with white bobby sox. Her blouse was starched and white and not at all revealing. Over the blouse, she wore a tan cardigan sweater, and around her neck, she'd hung a very large Miraculous Medal.

It was the medal that gave Tim a start. He hadn't expected to come face to face with such a specific remnant of his professed religion. It shook him so much that he trembled visibly for a long moment before he said a word to Holly.

"Should I come in?" she asked.

"Oh, yes, of course," he answered, and he moved behind his desk before gesturing for Holly to take the seat in front of him.

"How have you been, Tim?" she asked as soon as she was settled.

"Studying hard," the priest answered with a nervous nod.

"Witchcraft?"

Tim nodded.

"Do your superiors approve?"

He coughed and began to run his hand back and forth over his forehead. That damn medal was most distracting. It reminded him of his mother who had been a devout believer in the powers of the Virgin Mary.

Let's see if its powers protect against The Spell of Submission, he thought to himself.

"I came for my cat," Holly said. "I mean, I know she likes it here and everything, but I need her, too. I'm alone in that big house and it's a little frightening. So, if you don't mind...."

"Of course," Tim answered and lifted his cup to his lips taking a long sip of tea. His hand was still trembling, and the cup clanked loudly against the saucer as he set it down. That damn medal!

"She's happy here," he continued. "But if you need her...."

"Thanks," Holly answered, and she brushed her hair back from her neck. It was the first gesture that was in any way inviting, Tim thought, but it couldn't distract him from the glow of that damn medal.

Of course, how wise of Holly to wear it for protection, he realized. The image of the Blessed Virgin was even more arresting to a good Catholic than the crucifix itself, and it ran in direct contradiction to Tim's intentions in preparing The Spell of Submission. Still, he had to have her this night. He knew it. He had to cast the spell. It would work. Every book he'd read told him so.

"Tea," Tim suggested.

Holly reached across the desk with the medal dangling directly in front of the priest. From across the room, Emmy watched stoically.

"So, any plans?" Holly asked as she took the teacup and set it on her knees without drinking it.

"I need a rest," he answered with a heavy sigh.

"You've been through so much."

"Yes. I'm planning a trip to Rome."

"Sounds great."

Tim was doing his best to turn his attention from the medal to Holly's beautiful eyes. They were her one mistake. She'd put on eye makeup, hadn't she, making her eyelashes long and sexy especially for him.

"I was hoping you'd come with me," he admitted nervously.

Holly, who was raising the cup to her lips, was so shocked at the idea that she immediately lowered it again, spilling just a little back into the saucer as she did. "How could I?"

"I checked," Tim said. "The hospital would consider it part of your treatment; they'd make sure that your insurance covered it all."

"I see," she answered suspiciously. She let one hand reach for the medal and began squeezing it with those perfect, long fingers of hers. Her nails were polished with a pink gloss... another mistake.

You want this as much as I do, don't you? Tim thought. Of course, he didn't mention it to Holly. What he said instead was:

"There are experts within the Vatican who can help you and give you advice about dealing with your husband's grandmother and your little girl."

Holly just shook her head.

"I think Niko and I will be able to do very well without any of that."

She was still fumbling with that medal, drawing Tim's eyes back to it and reminding him of his own devotion. His inner voice reminded him in that one critical moment to believe in his own goodness, to start accepting it, and building on it. And how was he doing that? By trying to enslave this beautiful, young woman even as she wore that sacred medal.

What was he thinking?

Holly dropped the medal, reached for the teacup again, and raised it to her lips.

"No!" he called suddenly and lunged at her from across the desk. He grabbed the cup, pulled it to his own lips, and gulped down the entire contents himself.

Emmy stood, arched her back, and screeched.

Tim fell back for a moment. He began to shake violently. He turned and staggered toward Holly, raising his trembling hands to reach out for her. All the color had drained from his face, and his skin had begun to turn a cold, pasty white while beads of sweat glistened across his forehead. He was shivering.

"Holly," he cackled. "In the name of Babcia!" And then he fell to the floor, his body now convulsing wildly.

"In the name of Babcia?" she cried. "What does that mean?"

She turned from the thrashing body of the priest to the evil presence of the cat that seemed ready to pounce upon the young man.

"YOU!" Holly screamed at Emmy.

The cat bounded from the corner, leaped onto the windowsill and raced out into the night.

"Tim," Holly whispered as she knelt beside the priest. He was gasping for breath, his body still in spasms.

"What were you thinking?"

Tim's eyes turned wild. For a moment he seemed to gather all his energy so that he could raise himself on one elbow. He clutched at her with twisted hands and croaked, "You... I...

"FASCINATION!"

Chapter 77
Holly's Horror

Holly pulled back from the madman. She scrambled to her feet and raced from the priest's office and into the antiseptic glare of the hospital corridor.

"Doctor!" she yelled. "Doctor! Help!"

Around the corner, a young intern came running with a nurse right behind him.

"In there!" Holly called, as she pointed into Tim's office. The intern did not hesitate. He rushed past her and into the room where he fell to his knees beside the wretched, trembling priest.

Holly was shaking all over. She stopped for a moment to catch her breath and, unbelievably, spotted Emmy through the window. The cat was just outside the hospital door. Holly walked as quickly as she could, doing her best not to break into a run, but then she did, chasing down the last few yards of the glittering corridor and out into the night.

The wind grabbed her and spun her around as soon as she stepped from the building. It buffeted her, caught her hair and threw it wildly across her face. Holly grabbed her hair and held it while she looked up and down the broad street beyond the hospital. And there was Emmy again, darting away from her, across the hospital entryway and out into traffic. Holly chased after her.

"Come back here, cat! Damn you! Damn witch-cat!"

Emmy bounded across toward the island in the middle of the highway. Holly stumbled along after her, grabbing at her to try and scoop her up. Once on the island, she reached again for the cat, but Emmy bounded away again...

Right into the path of an oncoming truck.

The driver didn't swerve, didn't brake, didn't slow down, just crunched right over the cat, hardly feeling the bump at all. And then he motored on.

Holly moved slowly toward the cat.

"Emmy?" she whispered as she looked down at the broken body.

Suddenly the spirit of Babcia reared up out of the beast. It spun high into the air glowering down at Holly for a moment and then cackling wickedly.

"FREE!" the monster screeched. And then she swung into the night wind and was gone.

Lightning abruptly sliced open the sky and poured a tidal wave of rain down onto Holly.

She stood there looking at her dead cat, looking at the street that was first a glistening mirror of her own frightened image and then a river that flooded the gutters and poured across the highway.

Without thinking, Holly gathered up the bloody, rain-soaked body of Emmy and carried it back to her car.

She dropped it on the floor of the passenger side and trudged around to the driver's door. She was soaked through to the bone. Her hair was drenched, and even after she got into the car and closed the door, her hair continued to send rivulets over her forehead and into her eyes, spreading mascara down her cheeks toward her tragic lips.

Holly's hands were bloody from the broken body of the cat. She raised them onto the steering wheel, held it for a moment and wiped the rain from her eyes, smearing her mascara, even more and, streaking her cheeks with blood. Then she sighed, started the engine, and drove home.

#

The rain attacked Holly as she lugged Emmy's body from the car. In spite of the violent downpour, she paused on her way up the steps and peered into the narrow window beside the front door.

Illuminated by the porch light, her reflection was almost scary: stringy hair, a rain-drenched cardigan, mascara hollowing her eyes and smearing down her face, and hands and fingers caked with blood from the cat.

Was there something else? Holly wondered. For a terrifying moment, she feared some ghost-witch would suddenly spin her around and claw her to death.

But there was nothing.

She struggled to get her key into the lock, pushed the door open, and dropped the dead cat onto the little throw rug to the right of the entryway.

At the end of the dark hallway, a mirror image showed her the same scraggly creature she'd seen in the window. She looked closer. Babcia!

Would the witch be back to claim some terrible revenge?

No! It was just Holly's own ghastly face.

The frightened young woman pulled her feet out of those sensible shoes, stripped off her sweater, skirt, and blouse, and dropped them into a stinking, wooly puddle beside the dead cat. Then she trudged up the winding stairway to the bathroom.

She turned on the bathroom light from outside the door and stepped in. The mirror on the back of the door was a perfect place for the evil presence of Babcia to reveal herself.

Holly forced herself to look.

But it was only her own sad, silly face: runny mascara, stringy hair and all. Her bra and panties felt like they were pasted to her body. She peeled them off clumsily, almost falling over in the process. She threw them at the hamper, and they spilled onto the floor making a soggy puddle of their own.

That sense of foreboding was still there.

Holly turned to the shower. She was shivering now, teeth chattering, shoulders shaking, skin pimpled-up with goose bumps, her breasts all puckered, nipples twisted hard and tight. Nothing about her was attractive in any way, she thought.

It was what she deserved.

She stepped into the tub, pulled the shower curtain closed, adjusted the temperature of the water, and flipped the knob up so water would come out of the showerhead. She stepped back until the cold water in the pipe was spent. Finally, she stepped into the cleansing warmth of the water letting it wash over her. She shampooed her hair, rinsed, and repeated. She was beginning to relax. And then, she heard a strange, bell-like tone from far away.

Every muscle in her body tightened. That terror was there again.

Where was the bell tone coming from?

Holly turned toward the shower curtain and saw a huge, black shape arched just beyond it. She fell back against the far wall, and stared. Her breath came faster. Her chest tightened, and she gasped for breath.

"Calm," she murmured as she grabbed at the showerhead.

She turned the water on super-hot and then quickly directed the stream of scalding water out of the tub and into the darkness beyond the curtain.

The water blasted across the room and onto the little bathrobe that hung on a hanger beside the sink.

"Owwww!" Holly screamed as she turned the showerhead back into the tub, and the scalding water burned her feet. She danced painfully while she twisted the faucet back to cold, and then frigid water flowed down on her, making her shiver all the more. She fumbled with the knob, making the water too cold and then too hot again and again and again. She danced in pain from the flow until she was finally able to adjust the temperature, getting it just right so that she could stand there

351

and soak in its warmth for a long, sweet, wonderful moment. And then she stepped from the tub.

That tinkling sound came again. Was it Babcia calling to her? Inviting her to some deadly confrontation over Tim or Niko?

Holly turned toward the mirror on the closed bathroom door and jumped at the sight of her own reflection. She almost slipped and fell down hard on the sodden floor but caught the edge of the shower and steadied herself.

The deep puddle of scalding water on the bathroom floor had cooled and was almost comfortable. It lapped at the sides of her feet as she moved toward the sink.

"Mistaking my bathrobe for a witch," she mumbled to herself sarcastically.

She reached across the bathroom sink, pulled out her old metal hair dryer, and plugged it in. She was about to switch it on when that tinkling sound came once more.

Holly felt a shiver flash up her spine.

"Babcia?" she called out loud, and even that act unnerved her. She waited a long time. The silence lingered. No more bells, no more tinkling sounds, no more Babcia. Still, the horrible dread was there. Why? What for?

Would she die this night?

She reached for the hair dryer again, stepping forward as she did so, feeling the water sloshing up around her feet. She felt a little shock as she touched the dryer's metal handle, and it made her jump back anxiously.

The bell rang softly again.

Holly suddenly realized that she was in danger. But not from Babcia!

The metal hairdryer was in her hand, plugged solidly into the wall socket while her feet were planted in nearly an inch of water on the bathroom floor.

Had she almost electrocuted herself?

The bell rang again. Holly shuddered all over. Then she unplugged the hair dryer, stepped out of the puddle, dried her feet, and carried the deadly device with her into the bedroom.

She was naked as she walked into the darkness. She grabbed a little nightshirt that was lying at the end of the bed and slipped it on. Then she punched the light switch hard, and the overhead light came on with startling brilliance that made her jump once again.

Her bright, almost antiseptic reflection appeared in the bedroom mirror.

Good old Holly, now much warmer, no longer shivering. Hair a little wet but no longer tangled and sodden.

Still, the silence in the room was profound.

"Babcia?"

There was a rustling behind her. She slowly turned and saw the bedroom window drapes flapping in the breeze.

Just above it, those little Polish wind chimes sang to her, not in that ominous minor chord that she'd heard in the hospital but now with a much sweeter tone, one that was cheerful and consoling.

Holly padded over to the chimes and looked up at them. The little mirror that hung in the middle of the chimes twisted this way and that. Was Babcia there? The mirror showed nothing but Holly's own tired face, which now finally broke into a smile.

"Silly," she said to herself and walked back to the bedroom mirror. She grabbed a brush and turned on the hair dryer. As the warm air roared over her head and neck, she thought about Niko.

How had those chimes sounded to him when he'd bought them? She wondered. She could picture him buying them with little Joy at his side deciding just which tone would suit her.

How sweet he was, she thought. How she missed him. Tears welled in her eyes as she finished drying her hair. God, how she wanted her husband!

She went back to the door and flipped off the glaring overhead light, buttoned her nightshirt leaving the hair dryer where it was and the bathroom floor flooded. She left her wet clothes in the hallway and the broken body of Emmy just inside the front door.

To hell with all of it, she thought.

She crawled under the covers.

She lay there thinking of Niko wanting him with her desperately. And then she began to fantasize about his return, about kissing him again, about their first night together, and what she would wear.

It would be a soft, white peignoir, she decided, nearly transparent with silk stitched across the neck and down the front and little rosebuds embroidered around an empire waist.

She slid her hand inside her shirt. She felt sexy and wonderful after such a long, terrible day.

She continued her fantasy. Soon she was asleep, a long dreamless sleep that ended only with the bright sunlight of mid-morning. She smiled. The little chimes rang a cheery welcome. And Babcia was nowhere to be found. That thought made Holly feel wonderful.

But had she reflected on the last few moments of that previous evening, she might have considered the terror that had gripped her from an entirely different perspective. Yes, Babcia was gone, but so was her very protective spirit. Were those Polish chimes warning Holly about the danger she was facing? Of course not! It was just pure, blind luck that saved her from electrocution. Luck: a very poor substitute for the protection of an all-powerful witch.

Still, no wonder that deep in her subconscious...

Holly had been so afraid.

Chapter 78
Michalowski Brags

Jeannie Morrison strode into the breakfast nook. She wore a pretty peasant blouse, hiking boots, and short shorts that showed off her ballerina legs. She didn't look at all like someone who had stabbed herself to death the night before.

Michalowski was already sitting in the tower's small breakfast area. Across from him, Feliks was wolfing down an enormous bowl of Polish oatmeal topped with heavy cream and brown sugar. The coffee was steaming and Michalowski poured himself another dark cup getting ready to add his own generous portion of heavy cream and brown sugar to it as well.

"Guten morgen, freulein," he said to Jeannie.

Now that Rosie Osborn had been destroyed, Marla was in charge of the girl. And she made sure that Jeannie looked as radiant as ever. She had done her golden, blonde hair in pigtails that made her look like a sexy German beer maid. Michalowski immediately liked the look.

"Guten morgen, mein herr," she answered.

Marla was doing her best to preserve the sweet tone that Rosie had brought to Jeannie. "Anything new happening?" she asked.

Michalowski grinned. He just needed to brag a little.

"Great discovery in room of Rapunzel," he said.

"Oh..." Jeannie responded demurely.

"Joy and I uncover it."

"And what did you find?" she asked as she poured her own cup of dark Polish coffee and leaned back against the sideboard so that she could take full advantage of the hypnotic power of those legs of hers.

"A crystal ball, for one thing," he said. "Heavy, could not lift off table. Seemed very magical."

"Interesting, you know," she answered. "And what else did you find up there?"

"Joy found amazing thing," Michalowski continued. "Was in old cupboard: big book, Babcia's book, and also found a... a..."

"A wand?" she asked unable to contain her enthusiasm. "Babcia's wand and book of spells. My God, what could top that?"

"Even more amazing thing," he went on.

Jeannie and Feliks both looked at him with fascination.

"Was big black lake. Could see from tower window."

"A lake?" she repeated as she sat down across from the old shopkeeper.

"I think was lake. Not sure. But had ripples."

"Circles with a silver sheen?" Jeannie asked excitedly. "Were they echoed at some other part of the lake?"

"Exactly like that."

"It couldn't be a lake, Pan Michalowski," Feliks commented. "At this altitude and temperature, water would freeze."

"Not look *exactly* like lake. Could be field... of black wheat, maybe."

"You know, Pan Michalowski," Jeannie said. "I'd like to go up to the top of the tower and take a look at all those wonders."

Her eyes sparkled, and she smiled at the old man. He smiled back. Feliks almost broke out laughing, but he was too polite a boy to do anything so disrespectful.

"Would like to show you," Michalowski said.

"Would you like to come?" Jeannie asked Feliks.

"Can't," he answered as he stood and put on his cap. "But maybe Joy and Niko."

"Joy's already seen it, you know," said the evil Jeannie. "I'd like to have *my* chance as soon as possible. Right after breakfast, Pan Michalowski?"

"Would be great there with you."
"You know it, handsome."

Chapter 79
Role Playing Innocence

Niko and Joy were out hiking in the mountains, looking for the black lake that Joy kept insisting she'd seen from the tower window. She scrambled up onto any ridge or pile of rocks that looked as though it might offer a view of the countryside. It didn't matter, though. The lake, or whatever it was, must have been too far off for her to find, and in the end, she and her father turned back and headed to the tower with a growing sense of mystery and confusion.

#

Jeannie, now completely under the control of Marla, stood before the full-length mirror in her room practicing subtle expressions and ways of saying things that would capture and hold the love of Niko Madonie. Of course, she had to undo the damage Jeannie had done in reminding Niko of his wife and child.

"I know you'll be seeing Holly very soon," the evil Jeannie said with an innocent flutter of her eyelids. "And we only have this short time together to make some... some...."

"Magic," Clara Goriki prompted from behind her. "We only have this short time together to make some magic."

The old witch was doing her best to coach the girl, though at this point, she had little hope of succeeding. Rosie had made Jeannie just too damn sweet for Marla's tastes, and this new Marla-driven version of the girl doubted that she could be very seductive with a man she wanted to murder.

"Role play with me," the warlock said. (Yes, he was there too.) "I'll be Niko. I'll respond to you the way that he would."

Jeannie turned to the warlock and smiled. This kind of practice might be fun.

"We may be leaving Poland very soon," she said with an innocent smile. "Once we get back to Hollywood, it will be all business again..."

"Let's try a different angle," Wicktor suggested.

"Tell me, Jeannie, how did you feel last night when Niko walked out on you?"

"Furious," Marla growled from inside Jeannie's body."

"You're being too honest, girl," Clara said. "Be more seductive."

"How do you think, Jeannie and Rosie felt last night?" asked the warlock. "Talk to Niko about that."

She looked at the floor for a moment almost as if she were praying for guidance. And then she turned to the warlock. Her eyes were so gentle. All the hatred of the previous night and day was gone.

"You know, you really broke my heart last night, Niko," she said to Wicktor.

The warlock looked at her in surprise. Then he smiled and role-played Niko's response. "I'm sorry, but when you mentioned Holly..."

"I know, but she's so perfect, so beautiful, so faithful," Jeannie answered.

Wicktor turned to Clara with a smile, and she smiled back. "It might work," the witch whispered. "Go with it."

"And I've sworn," the warlock continued. "To always be faithful to her."

"I understand completely," Jeannie said. "You're not as weak as she is."

"Weak?"

"Come now. You know she cheated on you."

"But that's all behind us now," the warlock improvised.

"I'm glad to hear that. Then you can be happy again."

Clara turned to the warlock and smiled approvingly.

"Only don't you think you're entitled to maybe one very minor indiscretion?" Jeannie added.

The warlock said nothing.

"I can be a very good girl you know. I can work beside you when we get back to Hollywood and keep a secret that's ... personal."

The warlock was entranced.

Jeannie now began to walk slowly around the warlock sometimes moving closer to him, and playing with her fingers in apparent nervousness, glancing at him occasionally.

"We have so little time together now, Niko. I just want you to know that if you come back to my room tonight, you'll find the door unlocked. And you'll find me...."

Suddenly, Wicktor swept Jeannie up off her feet and raced with her to the bed.

"Stop it, stop it," she cried pounding on his chest in joyous rebellion. And so the warlock set her back on her feet, hugged her, and applauded. Clara Goriki joined in.

"By George, she's got it," he said. "You can be Jeannie when you want to, Marla. You have to be patient and clever. But after all, Niko's only a man."

"A very good man, I suppose," she said biting her lip. "But I can get him."

"Yes, you can," Clara responded. "If you're careful."

"And if not," Jeannie said returning once again to the leering, evil persona of Marla. "We just kill that bitch daughter of his. Get rid of Joy. Throw her from the tower window. It'll serve her right."

"It's nowhere near as effective as seducing Niko and having his child, though," Clara said.

"Okay then, how about this?" Marla countered. "Up in Rapunzel's Room, there's a book and a wand: Babcia's book of spells and her magic wand. They're there for the taking."

Clara's fists suddenly tightened. Her ugly mouth closed into a hard line. She moved in front of the girl and glared at her. Clara's mind reeled at the possibilities. Revenge was her ultimate goal, and there were oh so many ways to achieve it if she had Babcia's wand and her book of spells.

"Those things will allow us to steal her power," Clara hissed. "We can turn her spells against her and reduce her, that simpering granddaughter of hers, and that stupid Niko and his slutty wife into so much road kill."

"I like it," the warlock answered. "Of course there'll be a war."

"Oh yes, indeed," Clara answered. "A war of witches with every witch living and dead rising up and taking sides. It could be apocalyptic!" She clapped her hands at the idea.

"Many will side with Babcia, of course," the warlock said.

"Ah, but if I have her spell book and her wand, they'll know it and more than a few will side with me."

The warlock now began to pace the floor with his hands behind his back. "We will all be in great danger."

"Nothing tried, nothing taken," cackled the witch.

"But what do I have to gain from this approach?" Wicktor asked. "Life is good as it is."

"An army of witches would be in love with you," Marla said suddenly. At that moment, the shell of Jeannie's body did nothing to mask the powerful image she projected."

"In other words...." the warlock coaxed.

"You'll be a ROCKSTAR!" Marla answered. And as she spoke, she glanced back into the mirror and caught this haughtier version of Jeannie that she was becoming: less humble, less uncertain, a true woman of the world, a real WITCH.

"Seduction is far safer," the warlock said.

"So we try that first," said Clara. "If that doesn't work, we take the wand, we kill the little girl, and we prepare for all-out war."

Outside, the world was getting darker. The moon would be up soon ready to guide Clara and her cohorts to mischief and revenge.

Marla felt exhilarated. Why not? She was now in full possession of a beautiful body and her mind was strong, logical, and really none the worse for wear.

She giggled as Clara cackled, and then all three of them broke into loud, wicked laughter that was clearly full of evil hatred...

And murderous ambition.

Chapter 80
Struggle and Seduction

"What are you doing?" Niko called as he stepped through the narrow passageway into Rapunzel's room.

Jeannie jumped at the sound of his voice. She had wanted to be alone, but now she stepped in front of the little valise that she'd brought with her and blocked his view of it.

She forced her eyes to soften at once giving them the love Jeannie had always shown Niko. It was Rosie's love.

"You scared me, you know," she said with the semblance of a grin.

"Sorry."

She gave him a gentle kiss on the lips and whispered, "I'll leave my door open for you tonight. Come see me."

Niko stared into those deep blue eyes. Then he turned from her to the ancient cobblestone floor, the very floor that Babcia had trod, the floor that had seen her transform into the image of Michalina, the floor that had witnessed so much death and horror and betrayal.

"I can't," he sighed.

She lifted his face to hers. Her eyes were as soft and loving as ever. "I know you can," she said firmly and smiled sweetly at him. "You've been through so much, Niko. I think you're entitled to a little personal happiness."

He stared back at Jeannie, considering the full meaning of what she was suggesting.

"I can be a very good girl you know," she added. "I can work beside you and keep a secret that's very… private."

Again he said nothing, just stood very close to her. She kissed him softly again. "Please," she whispered.

Another long silence… finally:

"No," was all he answered.

"But we could spend so many nights of wonderful love together before you head back home, and even then I'll be by your side."

"I'm sorry," Niko said, and his look was a mixture of apology and regret.

"But you deserve real love from someone who adores you, not a wife who's been sleeping around, who even now is falling in love with that evil priest."

"Tim?"

"They're lovers," Marla lied. "Come to my bed tonight."

Again Niko was silent. Jeannie could see the war going on inside of him until finally he answered "No" again. But that one word was final and was enough.

Jeannie's eyes turned in that instant from the warmth of love to dark pools of rage.

"Go ahead then, fool. Save yourself for that slut wife of yours... if a whore is what you really want."

Niko stepped back as though he had been slapped. Jeannie's whole being seemed to change at that moment, a transformation made entirely of pure anger. And then another voice cried out.

"She's not the same person, Daddy. Can't you see that? She's not really Jeannie!"

Niko spun around.

It was Joy who came rushing into the room not stopping to look at either of them.

The little girl's eyes were fixed on the valise. She dove at it and almost knocked Jeannie over in the process, sending the valise flying up into the air and falling to the floor with a harsh bounce that sent its contents spilling out everywhere. Out came the Nazi flag, Babcia's book of spells, and her wand.

The girl and the witch looked at each other for a desperate moment. Then both of them dove for the wand each grasping it at the same instant.

"Let go!" Joy yelled.

"Not on your life, bitch-kid," Jeannie answered and pulled on the wand so hard that she spun the little girl up into the air and smashed her into the side of the bed. Joy nearly broke in two before she was forced to let go of the wand and fell to the floor. It flew out of Jeannie's hands, too and spun through the air right into the waiting hands of Clara Goriki.

"Destruction time!" the ancient witch sang out. She swooped the wand around, and suddenly, the dark, oozy puddle of Hitler's Nightmare began forming in front of Niko.

Joy got to her feet, flew at the witch, and grasped the wand. She jerked it out of Clara's hands, but now Jeannie was there to snatch it, spin the little girl onto the bed, and jump on her.

Niko tried to rush at them and grab his daughter or tackle Jeannie. But suddenly that blob was moving toward him, oozing, moaning, reaching for him with claw-like hands, a hideous undead face appearing through openings in the slime, calling to him, cursing him, walling him off from the struggle.

"Let go, you little bitch!" Jeannie foamed as she pushed Joy backward and tried a series of jerking motions intended to snap the wand from Joy's hands. It didn't work. The girl's grasp was stronger than ever.

"YOU let go, you monster!" Joy screamed back at Jeannie. She was sobbing now. Her eyes were red with tears and her nose was running. Her mouth was half open as she gasped for breath and drooled in bitter anger.

"Hell, I will!" Jeannie called. It was the undead voice of Marla Morrison whose monster soul was rising fully through Jeannie's beautiful body. It hollowed her cheeks and deadened her eyes. It drew tight the sinews of her arms and legs, caved in her chest, arched her back, and turned her into the ghoul she really was. From that moment on, not only Jeannie's soul, but also her body was that of dead Marla.

Niko lunged for her, but the blob was there, blocking his way, moaning its sorry call, slapping out muddy tendrils of slime that mixed the stench of hell with the stink of the gutters.

Marla spun the little girl toward the open window. Joy still would not let go of the wand even though she felt herself flying toward the opening.

"Let her go!" Niko shouted.

The slime monster lifted a death cry that seemed very much an echo of his words. The thing was splitting now: two, four, eight of them, all advancing on Niko, reaching for him with talons that grasped out from the slime... with bony fingers twitching at the end of skeletal arms. Death-mask mouths gibbered hungrily for him. Rotting teeth ground in anticipation of his flesh.

At the same moment, Marla spun Joy through the open window. The little girl was suddenly hanging outside the tower with only her grasp on the wand to keep her from falling to her death.

"Let go of it!" Joy called even though she knew that if Marla were to do so, she would surely die.

It didn't matter. Marla would not give up the prize. Instead, she pressed the wand down against the windowsill, onto Joy's hands, crushing the little girl's fingers to make her release her grasp.

Niko caught a glimpse of the struggle through the drooling slime that moved toward him, and now he threw himself into the monsters. He buried his face in the sewage fighting off the deadly claws that reached for him and raked over his body. He struck out at the hideous death masks that chattered at him in the ooze and tore away from the deadly teeth that tried to bury themselves deep into his flesh.

Somehow he pulled through the oozing blobs of filth dragging them with him as he came closer to the window, stretching out his fingers to snatch that wretched undead witch and save his daughter. But just as he reached Marla, Joy swung out into mid-air, jerked at the witch, and pulled her almost entirely out of the window. Marla kicked back at Niko, slamming both of her hiking boots hard against his face, knocking him backward deep into the slime where he looked up to see those deadly, hollow-eyed faces with their chattering teeth closing in on him once again.

"Die, you damn bitch-kid!" Marla screamed as she hung onto the edge of the windowsill by nothing more than the toes of her boots.

"Then you die with me!" Joy shouted back through all the tears and snot and spit. And with that, the little girl swung her legs up under the windowsill, planted her feet against the side of the tower and yanked back on Marla with all her might. The witch's boots dislodged, and with horrid desperate cries, the two fell away from the window as they plunged toward the rocks below.

At that moment, with monster talons and chattering teeth ready to feed upon his eyes and face, Hitler's Nightmare vanished instantly and left Niko sprawled across the floor of Rapunzel's Tower in a state of total exhaustion and deadly despair.

His little girl was gone.

So too was Clara Goriki and Babcia's book of spells.

Chapter 81
THEY

An excruciating, bone-chilling SCREEEE made Feliks think that someone had placed million megawatt speakers all across the Carpathians and suddenly cranked them up to full volume blasting feedback and distortion across the midnight sky!

The sound also struck Niko the moment his little daughter fell from the tower window.

He slammed his hands over his ears and rushed to the opening only to see a thick, undulating blackness swirling past it.

The cyclone of black drove downward, a rolling horror that filled the window and reminded him of once standing too close to a huge, black dragon as it snaked its way through San Francisco at the Chinese New Year's Parade.

THEY had come!

Soon, amid the terrible din, he could make out beaks and claws and wings and feathers swirling in the black, while it formed a tightening circle, pulling away from the window and, pile-driving directly into the ground, into the dank, rocky spot were Marla (Jeannie) Morrison's witch-body had struck the granite ledge.

A murder of crows and ravens, millions of them screeching with all their might, THEY twisted into a true death spiral that drove the witch deeper and deeper into the earth, perhaps to its very molten core.

The deafening cries continued as some birds pulled up from the suicidal cyclone. They peeled away and drifted back to the spot where their shimmering bodies had once appeared to form a great, black lake. Soon, more and more of them pulled away. The screeee diminished until it was only a series of isolated caws.

Niko pulled his hands from his ears gasping for breath as though he'd been part of the astounding death dive. Shaking all over, he clutched the window ledge and looked at the black feathers that had been stripped from the birds as they'd been buffeted against the tower. The feathers were now stuck in the bricks and caked to the outer wall with the birds' own blood. Below him, Niko could see the lower part of the tower looking as though it had grown its own horrible coat of black. He peered down even further to the courtyard in front of the tower to what appeared to be a massive black-crested chasm, a well hole that surely must have been drilled thousands of feet into the earth.

Niko gasped, as he awoke to a crushing reality... Joy was down there at the very bottom of it all.

He dropped to his knees. "Oh, dear God!" he called in a voice that sounded almost like the ravens as they'd plunged to their kamikaze deaths.

"Joy!"

He knew of no way to stop the shuddering, suffocating sobs that were escaping from him now, almost choking him. They seemed to be sucking the air right out of his lungs, leaving him without the strength or the will to inhale.

"Daddy?" a soft voice whispered from behind him.

Niko turned, took his first full breath of air in nearly a minute, and saw little Joy standing there.

"THEY saved me, Daddy," she called. "They swooped me up and brought me to the door all safe and sound."

The little girl tried to laugh, but it came out as a tragic sob, and then she was crying aloud from her ordeal. She stretched out her arms and ran to him with tears streaming down her face. She threw her arms around him and hugged him desperately.

"Oh, Daddy. I don't want to be here anymore, not anymore!"

Niko held her tightly, and the two sobbed together in exhaustion and relief. Finally, he pulled back to look at her. She was crying, yes, but she was also untouched as though the ravens in their rescue hadn't treated her with the animal savagery they had visited upon Marla. They had shown great gentleness to his daughter.

Niko smiled, and Joy drew in a long sniffle and smiled back. Then she wrapped her arms around him and began crying all over again.

#

A loud tromping came up the stairs leading to the tower. It was Michalowski. He forced his body through the entryway and looked down at father and daughter still holding each other tearfully. He didn't even ask what they were crying about. He was smiling, and he looked absolutely radiant.

"You see that?" he called. "Ravens twisting into ground?"

Niko stood and nodded. Joy got to her feet, too, but kept her arms wrapped around her father.

"Never heard of such a thing! Never could imagine it! Amazing!"

Niko stared at the old shopkeeper for a long moment. He smiled at the old man too tired to share in his enthusiasm. Then he took his little daughter by the hand and led her to the stairway.

"He's right, Daddy," Joy said with a sigh. "It was amazing. Too bad I was in the middle of it all."

And then she heaved a big sigh and smiled very slyly.

"But you know, it might be a way to end your Rapunzel story, Daddy, with the ravens flying in that circle."

"Think so?"

"Betcha Mr. Vaughn would like it."

"I guess he would," Niko answered. "After all, he sent us here to get an idea for an ending." Then he lifted his little girl in his arms and carried her down the stairs.

"Jeannie would like it, too," Joy continued. "You know, not the Jeannie who tried to kill me, not that wicked Jeannie, not her."

"No," was all he could think to say.

"The good Jeannie, the one who loved us. She would like it."

Niko didn't say anything, just hugged his little girl tighter.

"Daddy, I want to go home," Joy whispered suddenly. Her tears were back, and they were filling her eyes, and soaking into his shirt.

"Me, too," Niko answered with a sob of his own.

"Me, too."

Chapter 82
Happy Returns

Walt Gliskowski slapped another coat of yellow paint on the corner of the little house in Toluca Lake. Then he turned to the woman who had hired him.

"All done, pretty lady," he said with a grin. "You'll never know those cracks were ever there. A good coat of sealer, three coats of primer on top, then two coats of the best exterior latex on top of that. You'll never see 'em again, even if you live here another fifty years."

The pretty lady was beaming. It made Walt love his job. Just setting off a smile like that from a sweet, young Southern California housewife; what could be better?

"Thanks, so much," she answered. "And you'll send the bill directly to me, won't you?"

"Sure will, Mrs. Madonie," Gliskowski answered. "But why not let the old man pay for it? You couldn't have caused this. It was just nature takin' its course. Homes always settle. Cracks appear no matter how well-built the place is."

"I know," Holly answered. "But my husband has been away so long, I wanted to make everything perfect for him."

Gliskowski had his own pretty lady waiting for him only a few blocks away where the wealthy homes of Toluca Lake suddenly gave way to the rather pedestrian residences of Burbank. He gathered up his brushes and carted them back to his truck. Like any master handyman, he hadn't gotten a drop of paint on him or the sidewalk or the ground around the house. He was that meticulous.

Holly watched Gliskowski for a moment, then sighed and checked her watch. Not long now, Niko and Joy would be back, and their lives could become what they were supposed to be before all this madness had started, a madness that seemed to have suddenly cured itself when the old witch, Babcia, had disappeared from her life.

Forever, she hoped and prayed. Forever!

As she turned toward the front of their home, she saw the mailman heading up the walkway. He carried a big bag of letters over his shoulder and was smiling at her.

Who wouldn't smile? Holly was beaming, and her golden choirgirl hair glistened in the California sun. The mailman walked right up to her and put the mail into her hand.

"Niko coming home today?" he asked.

She smiled a big "yes." She felt like jumping up and down in anticipation.

"Yep," the mailman said. "When they're away this long, it's like falling in love all over again."

"Hope so."

"I know so," the mailman answered. "Good luck."

"Thanks." Holly waved while the mailman headed back up the walk. She looked down at the mail he had placed in her hands: the Burbank Pennysaver, the gas bill, and a letter from the rectory at St. Joseph's Hospital.

She opened that last item nervously. "Tim," she whispered, but the letter wasn't from Tim. It was from Father Rodriguez, the pastor of the rectory and St. Finbar's Church. She scanned it quickly picking out a few words here and there:

Tim... recuperating... gone to Rome...

Psychiatric care... evaluation... exorcism... on Tim!

Tim was being evaluated to see if it was necessary to perform an exorcism.

Holly studied the letter for a long moment and sighed. He'd been bound and determined to have an exorcism performed on someone. And now it looked like he might just end up having the devils driven out of him.

Holly felt so sorry for the poor man. His troubles were so much a result of her own sinfulness. She felt a sob catch in her throat, and as she did, she looked up to see Niko and Joy stepping from a sparkly Yellow Cab.

"Mommy! Mommy!" Joy called and ran toward her mother with open arms.

Holly grabbed the little girl off the ground and hugged her tighter than she ever thought she could. Now her sobs were suddenly transformed into tears of joy.

"Mommy," the little girl cried. "It was all so terrible. We missed you so much."

By then Niko had joined them, wrapping his arms around both of them instantly. He kissed Holly on the lips, the eyes, the tear-stained cheeks.

"I missed you," she sobbed not daring to put the little girl down, not daring to pull away from Niko for even a single moment.

"And we missed you, Mommy, and we're not going anywhere without you ever again. Right, Daddy?"

"Right," Niko answered and moved to start kissing his wife all over again.

"You seem pretty hungry for something," she said with a little grin.

"For everything."

"Well, we can start with food. Want something to eat?"

"Anything that doesn't involve pork or cabbage."

"Or pirogues," Joy added.

"How about something American like southern fried chicken?" Holly's smile glowed.

"Perfect!"

"Where's Emmy, Mommy?" Joy asked as the trio made their way to the house still unable to untangle themselves from each other.

"I'm afraid there's some bad news there," Holly sighed.

Joy turned and looked into her mother's eyes.

"I'm sorry," Holly responded. "Emmy got hit by a car. She's..."

Joy's eyes widened and Holly knew exactly what she was asking.

"Your special friend seems to be all right, though," she answered. "I don't know where she is. She certainly wreaked havoc while you were gone, but I know she's all right."

Niko took Holly's hand and squeezed it. Then his young wife looked at him and smiled the kind of confident smile he hadn't seen in her eyes in over a year.

"Come inside, and I'll tell you the whole story," she said and led her little family into their home and a newer, happier life.

She was certain of it.

#

At that very moment on the 7th floor of the Sunset and Vine Tower Building, in the space formerly known as the Witch Room, Dinah Dee was proving to Charles Martin Vaughn that she deserved to be the new President of Midnight Cowgirl, Inc. She sashayed into the place wearing Sally's own cowgirl duds complete with fringed satin mini-skirt, cowgirl hat, halter-top, and high-heel boots.

"Wanna see me ride that bull, sugar?" she cooed.

Vaughn grinned. "You applying for the position of Midnight Cowgirl?"

"Sho' nuff," she answered with a sexy smirk.

"An African American cowgirl?"

"Ever hear a' the Buffalo Soldiers, boy?"

Vaughn nodded.

"How 'bout the Buffalo Cowgirls?"

"Guess the job's yours."

"Only thing," Dinah added as she sidled up to him. "I expect some fringe benefits, you know, allowances for special religious observances and the like."

"Like what?"

"Oh, I don't know, Mr. Vaughn. Maybe Halloween."

"Why don't we step into my office, Miss Dee, and we'll do a little negotiating."

"Sounds like a plan," she answered and followed the great animator into the darkness where she immediately melted into his arms.

#

As the night grew colder, the spirit of Babcia rode the winds across Southern California. She was far away now in a desolate part of East LA. As she moved silently through the night, she suddenly heard a heavy, heartbreaking thud, the kind of thud a dead body makes when it falls from quite high. And then the body of a young woman rolled out from under an over-crossing and onto the sidewalk beside the deserted street.

She wore ragged jeans and a red T-shirt that surely didn't offer much protection on this frigid California night.

At first, the young woman appeared to be dead, but then she drew in the slightest breath. She was drugged, pumped up with heroin, trying to commit suicide, probably. But somehow, maybe with the luck of the damned, she'd rolled out from under the over-crossing, down the embankment, and fallen onto the sidewalk. She might survive the night depending on who came across her unconscious body as it lay on the walk.

The spirit of the ancient crone considered the young woman. Could she be a new host for Babcia's deadly presence? Did the witch want to be imprisoned again? Of course not, but there was something about having a host, a body to inhabit. There was so much more you could do (and so much less at the same time).

A little slip of newspaper peeked out of the girl's back pocket.

"What this?" Babcia cackled as her ghostly fingers drew out the paper. It was a section of the LA Times want ads. And circled in the middle of the page was this entry:

Wanted:

Live-in cook and cleaning person

Apply Holly Madonie, Toluca Lake CA.

The spirit of Babcia hovered undecided in the air above the young woman. The witch was still considering the possibilities, (a new way to be near her grandson and his daughter, and his oh so sinful wife). But at that moment, at the very end of the sidewalk, footsteps signaled the arrival of two men dressed in dark blue: two police officers. They'd save the girl's life, wouldn't they?

What to do? What a decision!

"Fascynujace," Babcia cackled to herself in Polish (fascinating), and she thought for just a moment of Father Tim when she said it. The poor, mad priest would have agreed with her use of his favorite word. The word that had really been his undoing, hadn't it?

But perhaps there was unfinished business to attend to first. After all, she could return and inhabit the body of this girl any time she wanted to if Holly hired her. She could rejoin Niko's household just like that, but first things first.

And why not?

Chapter 83
Final Initiation

It was midnight, and the young witches were back at Rapunzel's Tower. They had erected a new altar and decorated it for the final step of their initiation into the warlock's coven. Layer upon layer of thick mattresses were piled high on the hard stone surface with satin sheets overlaying all. They had scattered plump pillows everywhere and had run ribbons of Polish red and white and even ribbons of black around the edges.

At last the warlock himself strode out in front of the frothy concoction of a bed with a horny look it was impossible to hide. The girls lined up in a single row. They still wore their black woolen robes. Some had seductive smiles while others were rather nervous at the prospects of what was to come. A few of them, including Morgan Cummings, had dropped their robes from their shoulders hoping that their excited breasts might encourage the warlock to choose her first.

Matryoshka Michalowski bit her lip in eager anticipation, and that had been the deciding factor. She'd regained some of her earlier baby-fat in their days with Niko and Jeannie at the tower, and it had rounded her face and figure making her less perfect but far more desirable to the eyes of the warlock. And so he selected her and reached for the knot in her belt, undid it, opened her robe and pulled it gently from her shoulders letting it drop to the ground.

Like some courtly lord leading his lady onto the dance floor at a grand cotillion, Wicktor, the warlock, led Matryoshka forward toward the altar that was now a bed. He put his hands gently on her hips and lifted her up onto the satin sheet and the layers of mattresses.

The rest of the coven looked on eagerly... giggling and sighing, each anxious to have her moment with the beast. The wind picked up, and the goats and horses stirred in their pens. The fire blazed while the warlock crawled up onto the bed with his Matryoshka.

But, while all this was happening, a dark figure moved slowly out of the forest and down the center row of the small amphitheater. She was ancient, hunched-over, dressed in tattered black rags, and carrying a long staff that was taller by far than she. A pair of wolves flanked her. They hissed and snarled at the young witches as they moved past them. Yet the wicked girls were so caught up in the anticipation of this last step in their initiation that they hardly seemed to notice this monstrous apparition until she'd trudged all the way down the stairs and stood directly in front of Matryoshka and the warlock as they kissed obscenely.

The new arrival let out a wail and raised her staff. Lightning sparked and crackled all around them. Thunder rumbled behind the vast forests causing the warlock to stop. He quickly pushed aside his partner and slid backward away from the visitor who was surely the greatest and most powerful witch who had ever lived: Babcia herself.

She swung her staff, and the fire went out.

All was blackness then except for the glow of her staff, which provided an eerie green light that cast the warlock in a terrible, hopeless pall that only added to the horror that filled his eyes.

"Your eminence," he whispered with his best effort at a welcoming smile.

"Silence!" Babcia hissed. "Traitor! Agent of my enemy!"

She drew closer to him now pointing at him with her staff. "Friend of Mother Black! Friend of Marla! Friend of hideous, old Clara Goriki!"

Wicktor tried to scuttle away from the witch, but she reached out and touched him with her staff freezing him in place.

"Where is that wicked Polish witch?" she demanded. "Where is Clara?"

"I don't know, I swear," the warlock, immovable as he was, was barely able to say.

"And who do you swear by?"

"The Goddess, of course," said the warlock. It was the best answer he could think of.

"Where is Clara? Where is my book of spells?"

"Honest, Grandmother…." But the great witch waved him to silence.

"She wants a war then," Babcia said thoughtfully. "But is incapable of such a thing."

"I don't know…" the warlock began as a curious smile played on his lips.

At that instant, Babcia thrust a gnarled finger at the warlock with a force that swept him into the air and sent him hurdling through the highest window of Rapunzel's tower.

"STAY!" she called and waved her staff across the face of the tower making the lower doors disappear and the tiny openings that offered light into the bedrooms wall up once again. Heavy steel bars slammed across the upper window trapping the warlock in the top of the tower, perhaps forever.

"Clara will save me," he called down. "You'll see."

The great witch shook her head sadly. "Afraid we will see," she sighed. "Very much afraid."

Now Babcia turned to Matryoshka.

"Shoo," she called with a flick of her hand. "Go home to Papa. Be good girl. Witch no more."

The novice witch jumped to her feet and raced off into the night carrying her black robe with her and running on bare feet through the thorny undergrowth, heading home to Pan

Michalowski and the twenty-seven glowering masks of the great witch in his gift shop.

Babcia turned back to the steps of the amphitheater then, but the rest of the coven had already fled. The place was empty except for the wolves that now came slowly down the steps and clustered around her. She tipped her head toward the fire, and it roared into flame as she sat down beside it to take in its warmth.

With wild welcoming screes, ravens swooped down from the sky and formed an outer circle around the ancient crone. Some dared to hop up onto her lap, and she petted them. Wolves curled at her feet. Others came and licked her hands. She smiled at them all and spoke to them in words of friendship. She sat there peacefully, and as she did, oh so slowly, she began to transform once again into the beautiful, innocent shape of Michalina, the young maid who so many centuries before had left her home in the middle of the night... when she was only a small child...

And had been taken by witches.

THE END

Summary

TAKEN BY WITCHES

It's just after the end of World War II, in the city of Rochester, New York.

"Bob-cha," as little Niko Madonie calls her, is obsessed with protecting her grandson, Niko, from the evils she sees in this new world. He reminds her very much of her own infant son who was murdered by witch-hunters 800 years earlier. The old woman terrifies the little boy with her broken speech, her hideous face and her brutality. He actually sees her chopping off the head of a great, noisy, neighborhood dog one night. And on the very next night, his parents insist that he spend the whole evening with her.

"Niko, come play me," Babcia calls in her broken English, but Niko refuses, and he runs and hides in the closet. While he's hiding, he hears his grandmother making frightening animal noises. She's turning into a wolf, he thinks, and he's right. She must be a witch, he concludes, and he's right again.

Babcia dies, but Niko eventually realizes that she's still with him, now hiding in his bedroom closet while she watches him grow up.

She steps openly into Niko's life when he's 18 years old and is falling in love with a beautiful and flirtatious young woman named Holly Blue. Babcia tries to interrupt their first torrid make out session at the neighborhood drive-in movie, and she haunts the girl ever after.

But Holly marries Niko anyway.

The two go off to Leland University where Niko does graduate work in art and film production. It's the 1960s, and along with the Vietnam War and the peace movement, there's an interest in free love that attracts a sexy young couple named Nancy Swallow and Billy Bright to Niko and his wife. Nancy and Billy plot to add Niko and Holly to their circle of swinging lovers, a circle that Babcia finds infuriating.

Niko discovers a set of witch masks in one of Leland's art classrooms. Each is a perfect likeness of his grandmother, and each has her name etched on its back. He's horrified, and when he has to shoot a film in the same room, he asks that the masks be taken away. Somehow, images of the masks find their way into his film anyway, but they are so dramatic and effective that they make the film an enormous success.

Nancy Swallow finds Niko more and more attractive. Her open advances make Holly jealous, and Holly suggests that she and Niko take a getaway trip to the mountains. On that trip Babcia, who still feels Holly is a threat to Niko's happiness, suddenly appears in the back seat of the car and urges Niko to drive off a cliff, jump from the vehicle at the last minute, and send Holly to her death.

Niko refuses, screaming, "SHE'S MINE!"

Still, the car goes into a spin and surges toward the cliff. At the last minute, it collides with a huge camper coming up the other side of the road. The couple is saved.

Nancy is not so lucky.

Babcia stalks her on the jogging trails at Leland. The old witch turns into a wolf and destroys the girl. Niko and Holly hear about Nancy's death on a television news report while they're still in the mountains and, in a moment of hysteria, Niko cries out to Holly, "SHE did it! And she wants to kill you, too!"

Niko's film is so successful that it lands him a job at the prestigious animation studio, Vaughn Visual Arts (VVA). There, Chuck Vaughn is working on an animated version of *Hansel and Gretel*. Chuck can see that Niko understands witches, and he wants the young man to help write the show. Niko's co-writer will be neurotic, ex-ballerina Marla Morrison.

Meanwhile, at home, Holly fears that her husband is losing his mind. His constant references to his dead grandmother frighten her. That evening she receives a package for Niko, sent as a nasty joke from Billy Bright. It's the Mask of Babcia, one of the very masks that appeared in Niko's film. When Niko sees the mask, he's terrified. That night he has a terrible nightmare in which Babcia once again tries to murder Holly.

In a meeting at VVA the next morning, Niko learns that Marla, his neurotic co-writer, is also a practicing witch. In fact, she studied in Poland with a woman who was a disciple of Babcia. That disciple, Clara Goriki, knew Babcia and hated her, because they lived in the same village and Babcia, even then an old woman, transformed herself into a beautiful young maiden and married the man that Clara loved with all her heart. Clara has still not recovered from the loss and has inlisted Marla to help her gain revenge.

Marla teases Niko about his fear of his grandmother. She also tells him that Holly has become pregnant. But Marla does not mention Clara or her plans for revenge. Instead, she tells Niko that she has been channeling Babcia, and when she murmurs, "Niko, come play me," the young man becomes terrified and runs from the meeting.

Under Chuck's instruction Marla catches up with Niko and takes him home. There, Holly confirms that she and Niko will have a child. During the visit, Marla obtains a lock of Holly's hair.

Marla knows that Babcia hates Holly and decides that she can gain greater success in Hollywood and greater revenge for her patron, Clara, by ingratiating herself to Babcia and drawing on her power. To do this, she plans to murder Holly.

Marla uses the snippet of Holly's hair to make a wax figure of Niko's wife. Through this "poppet," she's able to arouse Holly's sexual desire. This makes Holly especially vulnerable when Billy Bright comes to town looking for work. Billy convinces Holly to help him get a job at VVA, and then while she is under the control of Marla's poppet, he seduces her. Unbeknownst to Billy or Holly, the apartment manager, Harry Rodgers, takes obscene photos of Holly's infidelity, which he uses to feed his own sadistic fantasies.

Marla works her magic on Niko as well. During one amazing *Hansel and Gretel* story session, Marla convinces Niko to strip naked and get into a cage the way Hansel did in the fairytale. Inside the cage, Niko suddenly feels protected from all the evil forces around him. He becomes very creative and grows in self-confidence. So much so, that he, Marla, and Chuck Vaughn are soon struggling as equals over the creative elements of *Hansel and Gretel*.

Marla hires Billy Bright as her assistant. She then initiates him into her witches' coven with the help of Chuck's chubby receptionist and wannabe witch, Sally Fukes. Sally's knowledge of witchcraft comes not from Europe but from Africa. She learned her skills in the back woods of Tennessee from a 150-year-old woman named Mother Black.

It is months later, and Chuck, Niko, and Marla are still having creative struggles over *Hansel and Gretel*. Marla thinks the witch should win in the end and convert Gretel to The Craft. Chuck thinks the idea is ludicrous and prefers Niko's teenage rock and roll version of the story. Chuck decides to take Niko to New York to present his concept to the network executives. Marla is insulted and angered that Chuck rejected her approach.

While Niko is away, a very pregnant Holly feels that Babcia is haunting her. During a terrible lightning storm, she sees the mask of Babcia suddenly appear in the living room. The witch herself seems to be standing just outside. In terror, Holly calls Billy and runs to him. But Billy is working with Marla now. And the young witch is finally ready to destroy

Holly. She plans to tear Holly's unborn baby from her and sacrifice them both. Holly is trapped in a little bedroom in Billy's house when she hears the horrific plans. She also hears Billy suddenly change his mind and try to defend her... only to be bludgeoned to death by Marla's magic.

In New York, the presentation is a great success, but Niko finds sketches for an alternate ending to *Hansel and Gretel* that Marla submitted to Chuck. The sketches show a Witches' Sabbath in which a pregnant mother who looks just like Holly is used in a human sacrifice. Niko realizes that that is exactly what Marla plans, and he rushes to catch the next plane back to Hollywood. He arrives just before midnight.

Desperately trying to escape from the room where she's held captive, Holly hears Marla summon the spirit of Babcia to join in the sacrifice. But Babcia will not go against Niko's love for Holly ("SHE'S MINE!") and, in the end, the old crone turns on Marla becoming a wolf and clawing her to death.

Babcia then enters the room where Holly is held captive. She approaches Holly, points to the baby within Holly's womb, and cackles that familiar phrase, "She's mine!" Then she vanishes. But in truth, Babcia has decided to take over the soul of Holly's baby.

Niko arrives in Hollywood and goes first to his little apartment where he runs into Harry Rodgers. Harry shows Niko the obscene photos of Holly's infidelity with Billy Bright. Niko determines that Holly must be with Billy and rushes to Billy's home at the last moment, sees the carnage, and rescues Holly just as Marla's magic spins out of control and burns down the entire house.

Six years later, Niko reflects on the great success he has enjoyed since that terrible night. He has been made Creative Director of the studio and has produced another huge animated hit, *Snow White and Rose Red*.

Holly can't remember anything of that night except that her life has become almost frighteningly easier since then.

Niko goes to visit Joy, his little girl. She has an unusual copy of *Grimm's Fairy Tales* that explains the present and predicts the future. Niko has seen the book before, and it has always been a harbinger of evil.

Joy asks her father to read a new story to her. It's called "Witch Girl" and is about a witch who loves her grandson so much that she takes over the soul of his daughter and moves into her very body just to be near him. Then, very much in the voice of Babcia, Joy whispers, "Niko, come play me."

Niko is astounded, but he also realizes that Babcia can protect him and even aid his success. He finally accepts his fate and relishes the love of his grandmother that now flows to him through his daughter.

This entire story is told to Pan Michalowski, an old Gift Store owner in the ski village of Zakopane, Poland.

A few years earlier, Michalowski had sent a warlock named Wicktor to America to collect and buy up all of the Babcia masks because they were originally made in his village. Wicktor retrieves all but one of the masks, which is still in the possession of Niko's little daughter. Of course, Babcia now possesses the girl's soul.

Listening as Wicktor tells the story to Michalowski is the shopkeeper's seventeen-year-old daughter, Matryoshka, an attractive girl that Wicktor hopes to lure into his witchy coven. After the story is told, the girl becomes so intrigued with the warlock that, against her father's wishes, she agrees to attend a witch's Sabbath as soon as she turns eighteen.

And so our new story now begins.

About the Author

Nick Iuppa began his career as an apprentice writer with famed Bugs Bunny/Road Runner animator Chuck Jones and children's author Dr. Seuss. He later became a staff writer for the Wonderful World of Disney. *As VP Creative Director for Paramount Pictures, Nick did experimental work in interactive television and story-based simulations. He is the author of* seven novels, Management by Guilt *(Fawcett Books 1984—a Fortune Book Club selection) and eight technical books on interactive media. He lives in Northern California with his wife, Ginny. For more about Nick, visit www.nickiuppawrites.com.*